Catrin Collier was born and brought up in Pontypridd. She lives in Swansea with her husband, three cats and whichever of her children choose to visit. Her latest novel in Orion paperback is *Finders & Keepers*, and her latest novel in hardback, *Tiger Bay Blues*, is also available from Orion. Visit her website at www.catrincollier.co.uk.

By Catrin Collier

HISTORICAL

Hearts of Gold
One Blue Moon
A Silver Lining
All That Glitters
Such Sweet Sorrow
Past Remembering
Broken Rainbows
Spoils of War
Swansea Girls
Swansea Summer
Homecoming
Beggars & Choosers
Winners & Losers
Sinners & Shadows
Finders & Keepers
Tiger Bay Blues

CRIME (as Katherine John)

Without Trace
Midnight Murders
Murder of a Dead Man
By Any Other Name

MODERN FICTION (as Caro French)

The Farcreek Trilogy

A Silver Lining

CATRIN COLLIER

An Orion paperback

First published in Great Britain in 1994
by Century
First published in paperback in Great Britain in 2001
by Arrow Books
This paperback edition published in 2006
by Orion Books Ltd,
Orion House, 5 Upper St Martin's Lane,
London WC2H 9EA

1 3 5 7 9 10 8 6 4 2

A CIP catalogue record for this book is available
from the British Library.

ISBN-13 978-0-7528-7746-4
ISBN-10 0-7528-7746-1

Printed and bound in Great Britain by
Mackays of Chatham plc, Chatham, Kent

The Orion Publishing Group's policy is to use papers that
are natural, renewable and recyclable products and
made from wood grown in sustainable forests. The logging
and manufacturing processes are expected to conform to
the environmental regulations of the country of origin.

www.orionbooks.co.uk

For all the refugees who came to the valleys in search of a new life, especially my mother, Gerda Jones, née Salewski.

Chapter One

OIL LAMPS GLOWED, a straggling line of beacons wavering in the damp wind that whistled and tore through the sodden canvas that tented the market stalls. The cobbled gangway between the trestles that lined Market Square was far too narrow to accommodate the swell of late-night shoppers who spilled continuously into the area from both sides of the town. And not only the town: the lilting speech of those who lived in the multi-stranded valleys above Pontypridd could be heard mingling with the sharper, more commercial accents of the traders and the softer intonations of the townsfolk who were attempting to push their way through the jammed throng.

The air, even beneath the canvas shroud, was thick, heavy with moisture; the atmosphere rich with the eye-stinging pungency of paraffin oil, the sour odour of unwashed clothes, and the reek of seasonal nips of whisky and brandy wafting on the tides of the traders' breath as they called their wares.

'Last chance for a bargain before Father Christmas comes down the chimney to burn his bum on hot ashes tonight, love. Come on, two a penny. You won't find cheaper anywhere.' A tall, thin man with a pockmarked face, shabby clothes and military bearing held up a pair of unevenly hemmed, coarsely woven handkerchiefs.

'Not today, thanks.' Alma Moore tucked her auburn curls beneath her home-knitted tam without relinquishing her hold on the cloth purse that contained her wages from both the tailor's shop where she worked mornings, and the café where she waitressed most nights and weekends. Once she'd secured her hair she thrust her purse deep into her pocket, burying it securely beneath her hand.

Nearly all the money she carried was earmarked for necessities – rent, coal, and paying something off the 'tab' on their endless bill in the corner shop. She knew if she spent the remainder on Christmas cheer for her mother and herself, there'd be nothing left for coals or food at the end of the week. But then – she gripped her purse so tightly that the edges of the coins cut into the palm of her hand – it *was* Christmas. And if she couldn't treat her mother to a little luxury at Christmas, what did she have to look forward to?

Using her shoulder as a wedge, she nudged and jostled through the dense crowd until she reached an alleyway fringed by an overspill of stalls that led off Market Square. Two minutes later she was outside the old Town Hall that housed the indoor second-hand clothes market. She forged ahead towards Horton's stall.

'Come for your mam's coat?' Seventeen-year-old Eddie Powell, resplendent in an almost new blue serge suit which had been knocked down to him in two days' work in lieu of wages, smiled at her. It was a smile she didn't return. She couldn't forget that it had been Eddie's sixteen-year-old sister Maud who'd captured the heart – and hand – of Ronnie Ronconi, her ex-employer and ex-boyfriend of more than four years.

'The coat, and—' she pulled her purse from her pocket – 'I was hoping you'd have a good woollen scarf to go with it. Real wool, mind. None of your cotton or rayon mixes.'

'We've sets of matching gloves and scarves. All brand spanking new,' Eddie suggested eagerly, scenting a sale in the air. 'Boss bought them in as specials for Christmas. So many customers came asking he looked around for a supplier. We don't get many second-hand accessories.' He was proud of the 'trade' word he'd heard Wilf Horton mention and had never used himself before now. He picked up a woollen bundle from the top of an enormous, roughly crafted pine chest behind him. 'Just feel the quality in this. Go on, feel.' He thrust the grey cloth into Alma's blue face. 'It's the best machine knit you'll find anywhere,' he continued, still imitating his boss's sales patter. 'A lot smoother than anything that comes off your mam's needles, and pure wool. Soft wool,' he said persuasively. 'Not the scratchy kind that brings you up in red bumps.'

Alma reached out with chilled fingers and tentatively rubbed the cloth.

'That's a real crache scarf, just like the nobs on the Common wear.' Eddie leaned over the counter and she jumped back warily as his mouth hovered close to hers. 'You won't find finer than that, not even in there.' He pointed down the lane where the gleaming electric lights of the Co-op Arcade cast strange elongated patterns over the shiny black surfaces of the pavements behind the stalls. 'Or even at Gwilym Evans',' he added recklessly, conjuring images of the silver and gold tinsel-bedecked windows of the most exclusive and expensive shop Pontypridd had to offer. 'Go on, take it. Try it. Wrap it around your neck. Think what that will do for your mam on a cold winter's night,' he concluded on a hard-sale note, his mind fixed on the shilling bonus Mr Horton had promised him if the takings outside of what had been 'put by' on penny a week cards, topped fifteen pounds that day.

Alma didn't need the sales pitch. She was already envisaging her mother wrapped snugly in the scarf and their old patched quilt, sitting next to the kitchen stove which was blasting out heat in imagination as it was never allowed to do in the cold reality of frugal coal rations. Her mother deserved warm clothes. Particularly on the four days a week she economised by not setting a match to the stove.

'There's gloves and hat to match. All the same quality.' He rubbed his frozen hands together and danced a jig. Centre doorway might be a good spot from a trade point of view, but it played hell with his circulation.

Alma extricated a glove from the bundle Eddie pushed towards her. She pulled the woollen fingers, stretching them, looking for dropped stitches, signs of unfinished seams or loose knitting. There were none. Then she picked up the second glove.

'This one is bigger than the other.' She held up the offending garment. 'And the wool is different. It's coarser, greasier.'

'Then try these.' Eddie reached behind him and withdrew a pair of gloves from another bundle.

'They're two right gloves.' Costly experience had taught Alma every trick the market boys with their second-quality wares had to offer.

'How about this set, then?' Undeterred, Eddie opened the chest and produced a new pack from its depths. Hat, scarf and gloves were stitched together with huge tacking stitches in thick brown twine. Alma carefully loosened the threads and went through each piece. She put the hat and gloves to one side but held up the scarf.

'Dropped stitch in this.'

'Then swap it with the other one.' Eddie's patience was wearing thin; he'd just caught sight of his boss eyeing him suspiciously from the other side of the stall in a way he wouldn't have if Alma had been old, or ugly.

'Colour's not the same.'

'Tell you what.' Eddie glanced over his shoulder to make sure no one was listening. 'I'll knock it down to you at a special price.'

'What kind of special price?'

'For you, two bob the lot. Hat, scarf and gloves.'

'Two bob!' Alma tossed the bundle aside in disgust. 'It's not worth that. Besides . . .' she dangled the promise of extra trade. 'It wouldn't leave me enough to pick up the coat I've put by, or buy the jumper my mam needs.'

'You've come for your coat, Alma?' Wilf pushed Eddie out of his way. 'Mrs Edwards needs seeing to, boy,' he ordered brusquely. 'She's after a suit for her son, and she wants you to try the jacket to check the size.'

4

'Right away, Mr Horton.' Eddie wasn't sorry to leave Alma. She might be a looker, but she was nineteen; far too old for him, and boy, was she fussy! No wonder Ronnie had taken off for Italy with Maud.

'You looking for something beside your coat, Alma?' Wilf lifted the tips of his fingers to his wrinkled, red-veined face, and blew on them.

'I'd like to buy my mother a scarf, gloves, and if I've enough money left over, a jumper, Mr Horton.'

'Right, let's see what I can do for you.' He bent beneath the counter and rummaged among the boxes under the trestles.

'I'd like the jumper to be the same quality as this, please.' Alma held up the only perfect scarf Eddie had shown her.

'You know what to look for. This suit you?' He held up a mass of purple, green and red wool. 'Colours ran in the dye batch, but they didn't affect the quality. It's lamb's-wool like the scarf. I'll be with you now Edith!' he shouted to a woman who was pushing a man's shirt under his nose.

'I want it for a present, Mr Horton,' Alma retorted icily.

'That's what I thought. It's warm and your mam wouldn't know the difference,' he said bluntly, too pre-occupied with the buying potential of the customers pressing around his stall to concern himself with Alma's sensitivity.

'My mother might be blind, Mr Horton, but that doesn't mean I'd allow her to walk around looking like something the cat dragged in.'

'Suit yourself. That one I can do for one and six. Perfect like this—' he tossed an emerald green pullover at her – 'I can't do for less than five bob, and then I'd be robbing myself. Got your card for the coat?' Wilf turned his back on Alma and took the shirt from Edith. 'A shilling to you love, and seeing as how it's Christmas I'll throw in a hanky for free. How's that for a bargain?'

'I'll take it, Wilf.' The woman opened her purse as Wilf

5

threw the shirt and handkerchief at Eddie to be wrapped in newspaper.

Mesmerised, Alma stared at the jumper. It was such a deep, beautiful green. A jumper like that could make even the old black serge skirt she was wearing look good. She brushed her hand lightly against the surface; it was softer than any wool she'd ever touched. But five shillings! Reluctantly she dropped the jumper on to the counter, and picked up the one that looked as if it had been attacked by a colour-blind artist. Wilf Horton was right: the colouring hadn't affected the quality. She pulled her card out of her pocket and looked at it. Not that she needed to. She knew exactly how much she owed.

'Coat was ten bob, less . . .' Wilf took Alma's card and peered short-sightedly at the numbers scrawled on it. 'Fifteen weeks at sixpence a week. That leaves half a crown Alma. What do you want to do about the jumper?'

Alma heard the clock on St Catherine's strike the half-hour. Tina Ronconi was covering a double station of tables in the café, but Tina wouldn't be able to do that for long. Christmas Eve was always busy, and she still had to buy the other things on her list. She clutched the scarf and fingered the multicoloured pullover.

'How much for everything?' She comforted herself with the thought that it cost nothing to ask.

'This pullover, the scarf, hat and gloves?'

'The lot.'

'You broken a set there?' Wilf looked suspiciously at the garments she was holding.

'The gloves that went with this scarf were odd.'

'Call it five bob with what you owe on the coat.'

'I don't want charity,' Alma snapped, pride stinging.

Wilf sighed. You just couldn't win with some people. It was open knowledge in the town that Alma Moore and her mother had lived hand to mouth since Ronnie Ronconi had left Pontypridd for Italy. Alma couldn't even afford bargain prices, but she wasn't past holding up business to haggle, and now, when he was offering her

6

goods at a loss just to get rid of her, she wouldn't take them.

'That's my price, take it or leave it.'

'She'll take it. And the green jumper.'

Alma whirled round to see Bobby Thomas, who collected her rent, holding a ten-bob note high in his hand. Hot, rum-laden breath wafted into her face as she nodded briefly before turning back to Wilf. Anxious to avoid a scene she pulled out her purse. 'I'll take everything except the green jumper, Mr Horton,' she said hastily, fear of Bobby and the propositions he'd put to her every rent day since Ronnie had left making her reckless. She dug into her purse and produced a couple of two-shilling pieces, and four joeys.

'Eddie, wrap for the lady!' Wilf ordered.

'And the green jumper.'

Wilf looked from Bobby to Alma, wondering if Alma had found herself a new fancy man. If so, the few people who bothered to talk to her now would soon stop. Bobby Thomas had a wife born and bred in East Street, who was five months gone in the family way.

'Thank you Mr Horton. Hope your wife likes the jumper, Bobby,' Alma said loudly for Wilf Horton's benefit as she walked away from the stall. She pretended not to hear Bobby calling out, asking her to wait. The last thing she needed was to get involved in a conversation with a drunk on the market. With Ronnie gone from Pontypridd people were saying enough about her as it was.

Trying to concentrate on the task in hand, Alma fought her way from the clothes to the butcher's market. Her mother had scraped together the ingredients for a cake weeks ago, but they hadn't been able to run to what was needed for a pudding. There was no way she could afford a chicken, and now that Ronnie had left she wouldn't be getting one as a Christmas bonus as she had done in previous years. Christmas! Her mother was looking forward to it because it was the only day of the year Alma didn't have to work, but what was the point in celebrating when they couldn't even afford to buy themselves a decent Christmas dinner? Clutching the carrier bag Eddie had given her in one hand, and fingering her lighter, slimmer purse with the other, she pictured the coins in her mind's eye. Sixpence for a tree. That had to be bought no matter what, and sweets to hang among the old paper decorations, made and carefully treasured from year to year. It didn't matter that her mother couldn't see the tree, she would be able to smell it. She wondered how many boiled sweets she would get from Mrs Walker's stall for sixpence. Then there was fruit. Two of those bright paper-wrapped oranges, two apples and some nuts: that would be at least another fourpence. She was already into next week's rent money, and that was without meat.

'Bag of ends for fourpence! Come on Missus, just what you need for Boxing Day when your old man is growling with his belly stretched by Christmas dinner.' William Powell, Maud Powell's cousin – Alma felt surrounded by Powells, she couldn't seem to get away from them no matter which way she turned – was standing on a box behind Charlie the Russian's butcher's stall.

'How about it, Alma?' he shouted. 'Bag of ends for fourpence?'

'What's in it?' she demanded sceptically.

William balanced the bag precariously on his outstretched palm and peered theatrically inside. 'Now what do I see?' he mused in a loud voice as he gathered a hushed crowd around the stall. 'I see two neck of lamb chops . . .' he looked up and beamed at a plump, toothless old woman who'd pushed her way to the front, 'a pair of sweetbreads. Just what you need to get yourself going, eh, Mrs Jones?' he winked impudently, a dark curl falling low over his forehead.

'Come home with me and I'll show you what I need to get myself going, Willie Powell!' she chuckled throatily.

'Willie! Willie! I'm not sure you know me well enough to call me Willie . . .'

The phrase was one she'd used often enough herself during deliveries.

'Midwives! They always make the worst patients. Wouldn't you agree, Doctor John?'

Andrew smiled vaguely, too preoccupied with Bethan's pain to follow Lettie's conversation.

'I'm only half a trained midwife,' Bethan corrected, gasping as another pain gathered inside her.

'And it looks as though you're going to be too busy for a while to see to the other half. Doctor John?' Lettie looked enquiringly at Andrew. 'Do you intend to deliver your baby yourself?'

'No. Doctor Floyd's coming in,' Andrew replied quickly, deferring to his immediate superior.

'Then it's time I called him. You'll be all right for five minutes?' she asked Bethan.

'Ten if you can't reach him.' Bethan continued to smiled with clenched teeth.

'I'll reach him.' Lettie marched out of the room, closing the door behind her.

'Are you really coping?' Andrew grasped Bethan's hand as he sat on the bed beside her.

'You're the doctor. You tell me.' Her smile deteriorated into a grimace as yet another pain sliced through her abdomen. Sharper and more intense, it made her feel as though she were being torn in two. 'I never minded this happening to anyone else,' she joked feebly.

'Neither did I.' He enclosed her hand within both of his. 'If you want me I'll be just outside the door.'

'Coward!'

'Absolutely.' He squeezed her hand mutely. The door opened and the nurse returned.

'Doctor Floyd's coming, and you,' she glared at Andrew, 'can get off that bed when you like. I shouldn't need to remind you, of all people, of the rules.' Andrew rose quickly.

Lettie studied Bethan for a moment. 'Doctor John, if

you're not here in a medical capacity, I think it's time you left.'

'Midwives are the same the world over,' he complained. 'Bossy.'

Bethan wasn't fooled by his mild protest. She read the relief in his eyes as he walked to the door.

'See you later, Mrs John,' he whispered as he disappeared into the corridor.

'Husbands! When the going gets rough they cut and run, even doctors,' Lettie Harvey said in a voice loud enough to carry outside. 'Now look at what I've brought you. A nice smart hospital-issue gown, the absolute latest in maternity wear.'

Bethan struggled to sit up but another pain prevented her. The nurse pressed her gently back on to the bed. Laying her hand firmly against Bethan's abdomen she pulled out her watch and timed the contraction. 'Nice and regular now, Mrs John, it won't be much longer.'

'Thank you,' Bethan murmured, drifting helplessly as the pain ebbed. The bare light bulb wavered overhead. The atmosphere was tainted by a strong smell of disinfectant and rubber from the sheeting she was lying on. She stared blankly at the ceiling. It was meshed with a myriad hairline cracks. She traced their origins, following them backwards and forwards, her mind meandering through black and crimson tunnels of pain as a dense cloud floated towards her. It drifted slowly, gradually sinking over her. Soft, warm, it obliterated everything from view.

'Mrs John! Bethan! Bethan . . .'

'What's the problem?' Andrew's voice, rough with concern, penetrated her consciousness. A face loomed overhead, bushy eyebrows and curling grey hair above a white mask.

'You'll soon be all right, Mrs John. We're just taking you to somewhere more comfortable.'

She tried to say she was quite comfortable where she

was, but her mouth was dry and her lips refused to open when she tried to speak. A damp-stained ceiling flowed rapidly overhead. She saw Andrew, wide-eyed, white-faced, his back pressed against the tiled wall of the corridor. A different room flooded around her, bright with lights and the silver glint of chrome. Again the pungent nauseating odour of rubber assailed her nostrils and she plunged downwards, swinging backwards and forwards . . . backwards and forwards . . . backwards and forwards . . . clinging for dear life to a thin, stretched, bouncing, strand of rubber.

Fear clawed at her throat as she realised that her tenuous grip on the elastic frond was all that kept her from falling into the black abyss that lapped at her feet. The rubber band lengthened . . . snapped . . . and she hurtled helplessly downwards.

'Bethan, can you hear me?'

She struggled to open her eyes. A mask pressed over her face, white gauze tented over a metal frame. She could smell iron as well as chloroform. Chloroform! Sweet, overpoweringly soporific chloroform – Andrew had been using chloroform the first time she'd seen him, when she'd been asked to assist him in that dingy, delivery room off the maternity ward in the Graig Hospital.

A pain pierced the numbing effect of the anaesthetic, shattering the sides of the abyss into a million crimson fragments.

'Andrew,' she moaned.

'I'm here, darling. Right here.'

'No!' she screamed as loudly as she could. 'No!' She thrashed her arms wildly as agonising pain after pain pierced her body. It was worse than anything she'd ever experienced – she knew only that she wanted it to end, whatever the price. She should never have allowed Andrew to make love to her. He had made her pregnant and then left her – alone. No, not alone. Not entirely alone. She'd turned to her hidden comfort: the bottle of brandy she'd secreted behind the drawer in her dressing table away from her mother and sister's prying eyes. At first she'd believed that brandy could make anything go away but then she'd learned that it couldn't help with the things that mattered, only the unimportant things, like blotting out the here and now.

It hadn't taken away the baby – or brought Andrew back when she'd needed him most, but he'd come later . . .

'Andrew!' she screamed again into the black void only to hear her cry fall unanswered, on deaf unhearing ears.

'We're going to have to use forceps.'

'There's something seriously wrong, isn't there?' Andrew's voice, sharp, anguished, echoed outside the darkness that had closed around her again.

'There's nothing wrong. Nothing at all, darling. How could there be when you came back for me. I left Pontypridd. Went to London with you.'

She spoke but he didn't hear. Warm, opiate-seasoned tides washed over her, filtering out the pain. She wanted to think of something pleasant. Not the time Andrew had left her. A day when she had been happy. Her wedding! Here, in London, away from family and friends – no, not all her friends. Laura and Trevor had stood behind them, happy honeymooners, married for almost two weeks. She'd worn the indigo dress and dark green coat Andrew had insisted on buying her although it had taken almost every penny of his spare money.

'I do.' Andrew looking at her, love etched in his deep brown eyes. 'That's it, Mrs John. You're not going to get away from me now. Not ever again.'

His lips warm, moist, closing over her own as he carried her over the doorstep of the beautiful, modern flat he'd rented.

Her protest. 'We have to save . . .'

'For a rainy day? It'll never get any wetter than it is

now. Another year or two and we'll be rolling in it. I'll be a senior doctor, and you'll be a mother.'

Her Aunt Megan had said the same thing. 'The rainy day is now.'

But it hadn't been. Not for Megan. The rain had turned into a cloudburst the day the police took her Aunt Megan away for handling stolen goods. Megan who had meant so much to her – the only woman apart from her dead grandmother who'd been kind to her when she was small – was serving ten years' hard labour.

'Mrs John? Mrs John? Bethan? Come on now. Wake up, it's time to wake up.'

There was a baby crying. She could hear its wail: weak, resentful.

'Mrs John? Bethan?'

Andrew's voice, harsh and bitter. 'Take it away before she sees it.'

'It!' Her baby? She made an effort, swam upwards towards the light. Fought to open her eyes. They hurt so. Every part of her hurt. She felt as though she'd been trampled on by an army of miners wearing hobnailed boots.

'My baby?'

Andrew looked at her. Doctor Floyd stood next to him. Both had pulled down their masks, and both were wearing gowns.

'You're doing fine, Mrs John. We'll just make you comfortable, then you can sleep.' Lettie bustled around the bed.

'My baby?'

Andrew turned away. Doctor Floyd was kinder.

'He has a few problems, Mrs John. Nothing for you to worry about. I've sent for a paediatrician. Don't concern yourself. All that can be done for him will be. You have to concentrate on yourself. Get well and strong for your husband.'

She couldn't see Andrew's face. His back was still

turned to her and he was looking out through the door. The wail grew fainter. She closed her eyes. Don't concern yourself? With her own baby?

It was all her fault. When Andrew had left her she'd tried to murder the poor mite even before it was born. But the drunken fall down the stone steps of the Graig Hospital hadn't worked, nor had the brandy and boiling foot-bath. Not mercifully quickly they hadn't.

Chapter Two

IT WAS WARM in the tailor's shop despite the frost that iced the window panes. Warm, with the oppressive heat that only a paraffin stove in an ill-ventilated room emits. Mary Morris nudged her neighbour and they both looked across the large central cutting table littered with cloth scraps, pins, chalk and wooden measuring poles, to where Alma Moore sat crouched over a treadle sewing machine.

Alma's light auburn curls fell forward, covering most of her face, but what little skin could be seen was deathly pale. Her lips were as bloodless as her cheeks, and every minute or two her hands slipped beneath the bed of the sewing machine and the trouser leg she was stitching to clutch her abdomen.

'What did I tell you?' Mary whispered knowingly to Freda. 'She's in the family way. No doubt about it.'

'Something wrong, Mary?' Mostyn Goldman, the tailor who owned the shop, glanced up from the corner nearest to the stove where he was shaping felt pads on a dummy's shoulders, a skilled task he never entrusted to any employee.

'Nothing, Mr Goldman. Nothing at all,' Mary answered innocently with a snide smile on her face, and a sly peep at Freda.

Alma had noticed the two women watching her and exchanging glances. Unnaturally high colour flooded into her cheeks as she rose hastily from her chair and dashed out of the workshop.

'What's up with her?' Mostyn enquired sternly. The first rule on the list pinned above the door was that no one could leave the shop without asking his permission. It was a rule none of the women had dared flout before.

'Up with her?' Freda who was younger, sillier, and plainer than Mary, giggled archly.

'If there is anything wrong with Alma she hasn't told us about it, Mr Goldman,' Mary chipped in, giving Freda a warning look.

'Well, get on with your work,' he ordered curtly. 'Don't turn every little thing into an excuse to down tools and gossip!' He glared at George, his young nephew and apprentice, as well as the two women. Mary and Freda bent their heads and carried on diligently with their buttonholing while George tailor-tacked a paper pattern on to a bed of cloth. Mostyn laid down his shears, stretched his cramped fingers, and walked over to the window. The tailor's shop was long and narrow with two windows, both small, set either end of the room. One overlooked Taff Street, hardly bustling, although most of the shops were open in the hope of attracting some Boxing Day trade; the other framed a dingy, high-walled, concreted back yard. Mostyn walked to the window that gave a view of the yard. He stared at the ragged planked door of the ty bach, the 'little house' that held the WC, watching for Alma to emerge. Despite the cold, beads of perspiration blossomed on her forehead, and her hand shook as she latched the door. He turned his back on the glass and glared at his workforce.

'I'll be in the stockroom if anyone wants me.' Mostyn Goldman never allowed customers into the tailor's shop itself, so all fitting was done in a cubicle that fronted the storeroom where he kept his bales of cloth. The communal stock and fitting-room door was barely four feet away from the shop, and well within earshot.

He walked on to the landing, but instead of opening the fitting-room door, he tiptoed lightly down the bare wooden stairs along the stone-flagged passageway that ran the length of the building, and into the yard where Alma was washing under the outside tap. She had screwed her handkerchief into a ball and was rubbing it over her forehead.

'Sorry, Mr Goldman,' she said contritely as soon as she saw him. 'It's just that I felt so awful. I had to—'

'What's the matter with you?' He peered suspiciously into her face.

'It must be something I ate,' she replied, clinging to the tap for support. 'Yesterday. You know what Christmas is like. Too much rich food,' she began, remembering the ridiculously large bundle of meat Charlie had handed her in exchange for her fourpence. There had been two thick pork, not lamb, chops in the bag, as well as half a pound of sausages and a slice of liver. If her mother hadn't been so excited at the prospect of cooking real meat for once instead of tripe and scraps, she would have kept them and thrown them back in Charlie's face. Living hand to mouth had made her overly sensitive to anything that smacked of charity.

Mostyn Goldman eyed Alma's slender figure critically. He was past fifty, a grandfather with a wife who'd long since run to fat, but he could still remember the times when his wife, pale and trembling, had run to the ty bach as a result of eating too much rich food. He had three strapping sons to show for her upsets, but they had all been born safely within wedlock, unlike any brat Alma Moore would carry. And the last thing he was prepared to risk was a scandal that might affect his depression-depleted business with the upright chapel and church-going citizens of Pontypridd's elite, or 'crache', as they were known in the town.

'You'd better go home,' he ordered abruptly realising that he'd been staring at her.

'There's no need, Mr Goldman,' Alma protested, thinking of her outstanding tab in the corner shop.

'You can't work the way you are. I won't run the risk of anyone vomiting in the workroom with all that expensive cloth lying about. Besides . . .' he looked pointedly at her cold, clammy hands, '. . . you'll more than likely stain any cloth you work on with your sweat.'

'Then I'll come in same time tomorrow, Mr Goldman,'

she broke in as a ghastly suspicion formed in her mind. 'I'm sure I'll be right as rain after a lie down,' she added as convincingly as she could. She hesitated as she counted off the chimes on the church clock. It was only ten o'clock. Mostyn Goldman wouldn't pay her for four hours' work when she had barely completed two.

'I've been meaning to talk to you for some time.' Mostyn stepped back out of the yard into the marginally less freezing air in the passage. Averting his eyes he evinced a sudden interest in a block of peeling plaster on the wall. 'What with the slump, the crache patronising the big tailors in Cardiff who can afford to undercut small operatives like me because they buy their cloth in bulk, and even the town's businessmen making a good suit last two years instead of one, trade's not been what it was.'

'But the depression can't last for ever Mr Goldman?' A chill rivulet of fear ran down Alma's spine. Losing her credit in the corner shop would be devastating; losing a vital chunk of her weekly wage, catastrophic.

'Business doesn't warrant our present level of staffing,' he proclaimed pompously. 'I've been meaning to lay someone off, and it makes sense to lay off the part-timer.' He thrust his hand into his trouser pocket. 'When business picks up, I'll let you know.'

'Mr Goldman?' She searched her mind feverishly for something to make him change his mind, but no phrases came. 'Please, Mr Goldman,' she repeated lamely.

'Here. That's a full week's wage.' He grasped her fingers and dropped two half crowns into her palm. 'I know you've only done two and a half days with it being Christmas, but we'll call the extra a bonus, shall we?' He smiled without meeting her panic-stricken gaze.

'Mr Goldman?'

'Take care of yourself, Alma. You haven't left anything upstairs, have you?'

'No, but Mr Goldman . . .'

'In that case there's no need for you to come up again.'

'You'll let me know?'

'Know?' he repeated blankly, pausing for a moment with one foot on the bottom stair.

'When the work picks up?'

'Of course.'

His heavy tread thundered overhead as she reached for her threadbare navy blue mac, thrust her arms into the sleeves and fumbled in the pocket for her comb. She rarely carried any money to work, there was no need when she lived only ten minutes' walk away. But she had money now. She opened her hand and stared at the half-crowns. She could pay off the grocer's bill, but then what would she do for rent next week? It would be a struggle to make ends meet on the seven shillings she earned in Ronconi's working Saturdays, Sundays, and five nights. The Ronconis were opening a new café soon and she had been promised a full-time job there, but would it come soon enough to keep her and her mother out of debt, and more important still, out of the workhouse?

Damn Mostyn Goldman and his cold-blooded talk of staffing levels! Fury coursed fiercely through her as she walked towards the front door for the last time. She slammed it behind her, her mouth acrid with the taste of unshed tears. The gossips were busy shredding her reputation, she'd lost her job, and she couldn't even see a way to fight back.

The nagging ache in her stomach getting stronger and more unbearable with each passing minute, she stumbled along the icy pavement. The sound of tapping fingers on glass rattled above her. She looked up. Freda and Mary were watching her from the window. She longed to wipe the smug expression off both their faces. They had never liked her. A horrible suspicion crossed her mind. Had they said something about her to Mr Goldman? Mary had been trying to get her niece a job in the sweatshop for years and Mr Goldman's reasoning about the effects of the depression didn't hold water when she remembered that orders fell off every year around Christmas time. Mary wiggled her fingers and Alma saw red. Resorting to sheer childishness she stuck her tongue out. Mary and Freda finally withdrew from the window, and she walked away, dragging one foot in front of the other, the unremitting pain making her dizzy and faint. Gathering the remains of her strength she headed towards the grey concrete and red-brick YMCA building intending to cut up the side-street alongside it on to Gelliwastad Road, and through the network of alleyways and terraces behind it to Morgan Street.

A horde of boys dressed in rugby strip and boots donated by the town's chamber of trade thundered down the stone steps of the building, charged across the road and around the corner past the old bridge, heading for the park gates. Of course! Boxing Day rugby match! She rested for a moment, allowing them to pass. William Powell waved to her as he ran alongside his cousin Eddie. William thickset, heavier than Eddie, but both of them tall and good-looking, with black hair and brown eyes; and behind them sixteen-year-old Angelo Ronconi, swarthy with flashing dark eyes, curly hair, and olive skin that instantly, and painfully, reminded her of his brother, Ronnie.

The overcast sky, the frosted grey pavement, the ring of boot studs on concrete as the boys dashed past in their white strip swirled around her. She made a conscious effort and took a deep breath. Her lungs craved oxygen but there wasn't any in the air. Only pain – thick red pain.

'Are you all right, Miss Moore?'

She focused on the startlingly white blond hair and deep blue eyes of Charlie.

'Quite well, thank you,' she answered stiffly, swaying on her feet.

'You don't look well to me.' He caught her elbow in the palm of his hand.

'Don't you dare touch me!' The stream of boys slowed their pace. Some were staring but suddenly she didn't give a toss about them – or anyone. Everyone in the town thought the worst of her, so what did it matter how she behaved?

'I was only trying to help,' he complained mildly.

'I've seen how you try to help,' she countered acidly. 'When I buy fourpennyworth of meat from a butcher I expect just that. Not a charity handout that's more than any normal family can eat in a month of Sundays.'

'But Miss Moore . . .'

She didn't wait to hear what the 'but' was. Wrenching her elbow out of his supporting hold she strode round the corner and up the hill. Sustained by anger she managed to ignore her pain until she turned into a small grimy street hemmed in on both sides by narrow terraced cottages. Morgan Street – home. An inviting image of her bed hovered tantalisingly in her mind. At that moment all she wanted was to lie down and close her eyes against the world, but even as the desire formulated itself her fingers closed around the unaccustomed weight of the two half-crowns in her pocket. There was something she had to do first, before she lost, or was tempted to spend, her unaccustomed riches.

She halted outside the first stone house in the terrace. Inside, a table had been pushed close to the sooty window of the front parlour. Dusty packets of tea, dried peas, sugar, and four small pyramids of tins were displayed against a background of deep blue sugar paper. Two of the tins contained luxurious corned beef, the others held the more everyday tomatoes, beans and sardines. At the very front, within easy view of even the smallest child, lay a large open cardboard box jammed with wooden twigs of liquorice chews, farthing 'dabs', halfpenny everlasting strips, toffee and coconut scrapings, and sherbet screws.

Pushing open the warped wooden door she walked over the uneven flags of the passage and turned into the front-room shop that was dominated by a rough, waist-high counter. There was room enough – just – to stand in front of it and study the goods ranged on the shelves behind.

'Don't normally see you in here at this time of day, Alma.' Edna Hopkins wrapped a wafer-thin slice of cheese she had just cut for Lilian Bartlett, the only other customer in the shop.

'Come to settle our tab, Mrs Hopkins.' Alma looked round for something to lean against. There was nothing but the wall behind the door.

'Well that's welcome news.' Edna lifted a child's red-covered exercise book from the deep wooden tray that served as a till. 'I wish all our customers were as prompt.' She gave Mrs Bartlett a sideways glance.

'Three and six, I think.' Alma took the two half-crowns from her pocket and pushed them over the counter.

'Come into a fortune, Alma?' Lilian Bartlett joked as Mrs Hopkins pencilled a large cross over the page and extracted the change from her box.

'Hardly,' Alma closed her eyes for a moment as another pain gripped her abdomen.

'You look peaky, love. Are you all right?'

'No. I think I've eaten something.'

'Always the same at Christmas,' Edna interrupted as she replaced the red book. 'Stuff ourselves silly with things we can't afford the rest of the year only to suffer for it for days afterwards.'

'That's it,' Alma agreed as she pocketed her money. 'And thank your Iorwerth for me will you please, Mrs Hopkins. It was good of him to carry my tree and parcels back from the market.'

'Think nothing of it, love. He's always looking for an excuse to flex those muscles of his. Especially in front of Madge.'

'She seems a nice girl.' Alma bit her lip to stop herself from crying out.

'That she is. He's done well for himself there.'

'Nice to see someone happy.' There was an unmistakable edge to Alma's voice: she wondered if Mrs Hopkins would have made her as welcome if she'd been the one Iorwerth had brought home.

Lilian nodded knowingly as Alma made her way unsteadily out of the shop. 'She *is* looking peaky. Did you know about that one and Ronnie Ronconi? . . .' her penetrating voice followed Alma to her own house, but by then she was too ill to care what was being said.

She turned the knob, taking care not to kick the rotten panel on the bottom of her door. It needed replacing, but the last time she had tackled Bobby Thomas about it he had told her in no uncertain terms that the rot was due to her neglect, and all tenants had a responsibility to keep their houses in good decorative order, which meant painting them at least once every two years. The price paint was, he might as well have suggested her financing the redecoration of the Town Hall.

Keeping her coat on, she walked down the bare, cheerless passage. Pushing aside the curtain that hung in place of a door, she went into the kitchen. If there was any residue of Christmas warmth, she couldn't feel it. The room was cold and uninviting. Her mother had economised again by not lighting the kitchen stove. The table had been cleared of their breakfast things, and a clean cloth laid; the floor swept, and the rag rug shaken. It had probably cost her mother a few knocks and all morning to complete the simple tasks, but she knew it was useless to remonstrate. Her mother would only deliver her standard martyred reply: 'If you stop me doing what little I can, I may as well lie down in my box now. At least then I'll no longer be a burden to you.'

Her mother's chair, the only chair in the house that boasted a cushion, was cold. She opened the door to the washhouse and called out, 'Mam!' There was no point in looking in the tiny parlour. The three-piece and piano her mother had bought with her father's first year's wages had long since been sold to pay pressing bills. She went into the back yard and opened the door to the ty bach. Another griping pain came and she fell in front of the thunderbox. She retched, but there was nothing left in her stomach except bitter green bile. As she lay on the stone floor she heard her mother's voice echoing over next door's wall. She should have known. Betty Lane made a point of asking her mother over on days when their chimney failed to smoke. There was always an excuse – her mother was needed to unravel old sweaters for wool so that larger striped ones could be re-knitted for Betty's eight growing children, or to tell stories to keep the little ones amused while Betty coped with the family wash or the baking. Alma was grateful because it meant her mother could sit in the warm, but that didn't stop the imitation of charity from hurting.

She returned to the house and walked up the stairs to her bedroom. The temperature was no warmer than outside. Condensation on the window had dripped into icicles that hung like stalactites from the sash. The water in the jug on the rickety chair she used as a washstand had frozen, and even the bowl she washed in was fringed with hard, beaded droplets.

Her entire wardrobe of waistcoat and skirt, second white blouse and 'best' summer sprigged cotton dress hung from bent wire hangers hooked on to the curtain rail behind the old chintz curtains her mother had bought years ago from Wilf Horton.

She laid her coat over the patchwork quilt that her mother had stitched eight years ago. It was the last thing she had made before losing her sight, and Alma thought of it as a patchwork of her life. In the centre were the thin cotton pastel squares of her baby dresses, stitched double thickness for extra strength. Around them were six large pieces of rich red velvet, all that remained of the only party dress she could remember, which her mother had made from her own 'best' pre-marriage dance dress. Then came circles of navy cut from her school gymslips interspersed with the white of old sheets and blouses, and the green and gold striped silk lining from the only suit her father had ever owned. He had been killed in a pit accident when she was three years old, but the suit hadn't been unpicked until four years ago; her mother couldn't bring herself to take the shears to it before then. Alma had asked her to, time and again, because she had wanted to remodel the cloth into a skirt and waistcoat, the same skirt and waistcoat that now hung from her curtain rail.

Next to her bed was a wooden orange crate she'd begged from the market and covered with a tablecloth the Ronconis had discarded because it had one too many cigarette burns. She had darned the burns and used the cloth to conceal her underclothes and jumpers. Two pictures were pinned to the faded blue paper that covered the walls. One was of her and Ronnie. The photograph had been taken in the café by Bruno the cook just before he had left Wales for Italy. The other had been cut from an illustrated magazine: a highly coloured portrait of an idyllic rural summer scene complete with lurid yellow sun, improbably blue sky, white-tipped mountain peaks and greener grass on the lower slopes of the hills than she had ever seen on the slag heaps of Wales. She had cut it out before Maud Powell had come between her and Ronnie, because she had associated the scene with Italy – the land of Ronnie's birth.

She stretched out her hand intending to tear down both pictures, but another pain came. Aching at first, it soon honed itself into a sharp, agonising point. Without bothering to undress she crawled into bed, leaving the quilt and coat on top of the blanket. She closed her eyes and tried to conjure images of a blissful world where young girls were allowed to have stomach cramps without everyone assuming they were pregnant. And where Ronnie waited for her just over the horizon with open arms, a smile on his face and no Maud Powell at his side. But no matter how she concentrated she failed to picture him. His features blurred into indistinct shadows, replaced by the grinning, lecherous face of Bobby Thomas.

Boxing Day found Charlie Raschenko confused and disorientated. It was a Wednesday, a market day only marginally less important than Saturday, yet it would have been ridiculous for him to have opened up his stall because most of his customers had bought enough meat on Christmas Eve to see them through to the following

Friday; and those who hadn't, wouldn't have any money left from Christmas to spend anyway.

He'd whiled away the morning hunched in his overcoat watching his fellow lodger William play rugby in the park, and trying to stem his irritation with Alma Moore for creating a scene outside the YMCA. He usually succeeded in containing his emotions, priding himself on never feeling very much of anything. Anger, irritation, displeasure, or happiness – especially happiness, because that sooner or later gave rise to memories. Bitter experience had taught him that they inevitably led to pain. No, it was better to live life as it came. One day at a time.

Still trying to forget Alma's outburst he'd returned to Graig Avenue with William and Eddie Powell for a midday dinner of Christmas leftover 'fry-up'. Afterwards he tried to spend the holiday the way he usually spent Sundays; and as he never attended chapel – much to his landlady's disgust – that meant passing the hours playing chess and reading.

But this Boxing Day was different to a Sunday, when everything in the town except the Italian cafés was closed. Before the dishes were cleared from the table, William and Eddie disappeared to a special showing of *Song of Freedom* featuring Paul Robeson, in the White Palace. And Diana Powell, William's sister, wasn't around; she was working at her job in the sweet shop in High Street. It would have been madness for her boss to have closed it with all the Christmas pennies burning holes in small children's pockets.

Charlie's only consolation was that his landlord Evan Powell, who 'called' the streets on a rag and bone cart, was at a loose end too. It was his landlady, Elizabeth Powell's habit to sit in the icy front parlour reading the Bible after she had cleared and washed the Sunday dishes, and she took advantage of the extra holiday to do the same. As soon as she left the warm back kitchen, Charlie went into the downstairs 'front' room he lodged in and returned with a long, flattish wooden box, crudely varnished with alternating dark and light squares. Lifting the catch he opened it out on the table and removed the chess pieces carefully, handling them as though they were delicate, precious objects, not roughly carved chunks of stained wood. He set up the board on the side of the table closest to the stove, and Evan joined him.

An hour and one game later, Evan had smoked half the pipe tobacco his son and nephew had bought him for Christmas, and shared all of the chocolate that Diana had given him with Charlie. The room was warm from the kitchen stove, and fragrant with the smell of pine logs and the chicken soup Elizabeth was simmering from the carcass of their Christmas dinner. Both men were content and pleasantly drowsy when their peace was shattered by a knock that echoed down the passage from the front door. The knock in itself was bizarre, as all the Powells' friends and neighbours simply walked into the house. Evan opened the kitchen door and shouted irritably down the passage, but not soon enough. Elizabeth had put aside her Bible with a martyred sigh and opened the door.

'Doctor Lewis?' She successfully concealed her surprise. Trevor Lewis, the young local doctor, had been a friend of their eldest daughter, Bethan before she had left Pontypridd for London.

'Is Mr Powell home, Mrs Powell?'

She inclined her head. 'In the kitchen.'

'I wonder if I might have a word with both of you?'

'Yes of course. Come in.' Elizabeth stood aside to allow him to enter the house. She was curious to know the reason for his visit, but not curious enough to ask.

'Dr Lewis. Nice to see you,' Evan extended his hand hospitably. 'Would you like some tea?'

'Nothing, thank you, I've just had my dinner.'

'Shouldn't we sit in the parlour, Evan?' Elizabeth reprimanded.

'It's freezing in there.' Evan opened the door to the back kitchen. Charlie had already packed away his chess set.

'Please Charlie, don't leave on my account,' Trevor said politely.

Charlie merely smiled before he left. Elizabeth walked in. She'd combed her short straight hair and pulled the creases from her skirt.

Trevor turned to face them. Thin, tall, and despite the efforts of his wife Laura, always slightly unkempt, he usually managed to look cheerful. Today was different. His cheeks seemed unnaturally hollow, his spirit crushed by the news he was carrying. 'Mrs Powell, I think you should sit down.' He looked into their faces. He couldn't keep them in suspense any longer. 'Andrew telephoned and asked me to come here. Bethan's baby was born early yesterday morning. A boy.' He took a deep breath. 'I'm sorry, there's something wrong with him. We call it cerebral palsy. It's impossible for any doctor to determine at this early stage just how badly he's affected.' He threw them the sop of vain hope of limited damage, just as he had done to Andrew earlier.

'You're telling us that Bethan's child, our grandchild, is a cripple?' Elizabeth turned a stony face to his.

'Cripple isn't a word I'd choose, Mrs Powell.'

'How's Bethan?' Evan's voice was quiet, restrained.

'She's fine.' Trevor was glad of an opportunity to turn the conversation away from the baby. 'She's upset of course, but physically she's fine. Andrew told me to tell you they'll write soon.' He twisted the brim of his hat in his hands. 'I'm sorry I can't stay. I've promised to call in on a patient.'

'Thank you for coming to tell us yourself.' Evan opened the door. Elizabeth still sat, sphinx-like in front of the fire.

'Goodbye, Mrs Powell.' If she heard Trevor she gave no sign of it.

'I'll see you out.' Evan followed him into the passage and closed the door behind them.

'If there's anything I can do for Mrs Powell . . .' Trevor ventured, concerned by Elizabeth's unnatural composure. She'd always struck him as a cold woman. But surely no one could be as indifferent to the plight of a first grandchild as she appeared to be.

'I'll send for you, Doctor Lewis.'

'I could come tomorrow. After I've finished in the hospital.'

'There's no need.' Evan didn't trust himself to say more. His thoughts were with his eldest daughter. Alone in a hospital bed in an impersonal, unsympathetic cry. Too far for him to visit. But no, she wasn't alone. She had a baby to care for. A baby that would be a burden to her for the rest of its life. He didn't spare a thought for her husband. The responsibility of caring for children, especially ones that 'weren't right', always fell squarely on the mother.

Trevor turned right at the foot of the steps to Evan's house, and walked up Graig Avenue towards the patch of scrubland that marked the beginning of the mountain. Regretting the impulse that had led him to leave his car, he turned up the collar on his thin raincoat and tried to ignore the hailstones bouncing off his back. He had walked to the Avenue via his garden, stepping over the wall straight on to the mountain. He had lied to Evan: there was no patient waiting for him. Barring an emergency, he was free for the rest of the day, but he didn't want to go home. Not yet. He didn't want to face Laura. He felt helpless, ill-equipped to deal with her misery, as well as his own.

Andrew and Bethan were their closest friends, and he valued their friendship, particularly that of Bethan, for whom he had a very definite soft spot. Andrew – well, Andrew was Andrew. Everything had always come easy to him. He had been born into a comfortable moneyed home. He hadn't had to fight for a thing in his life. Charming, good-looking, easygoing, generous to a fault, Andrew's good points were enough to make everyone, or at least almost everyone, forgive his occasional irresponsibility, thoughtlessness and selfishness. Still, Trevor couldn't help wondering how Andrew would cope with misfortune of such a magnitude.

He stumbled over a stone into a freezing puddle that covered his shoe. Icy water seeped through the patches on his sole as he asked himself the terrible question, 'How would I cope if it was Laura who'd given birth to a child with palsy?' He shuddered. Feeling the need to touch wood he found a pencil in his pocket and gripped it tightly. It was the ultimate irony, he thought bitterly. Giving a man arrogant enough to call himself healer a child who could not be healed.

He recalled the pitiful scraps of humanity that lay in the cots of J ward in the Graig hospital. Babies abandoned to workhouses and institutions by parents who could not cope with the physical demands or emotional pressures of bringing up a child whose disability made it an outcast. But then, perhaps those who had been through the experience knew best. Perhaps institutions offered the only solution for parents and child alike. He himself had counselled enough women facing the problem with cold logic, telling them that in time they would have other children who had the right to demand all of their attention, not the little that could be spared from caring for a member of the family who would never be able to care for itself. Reassuring them with the official maxim that institutions, not homes, were the best place for those born damaged.

He had said it, and often, but a visit to J ward invariably shook his faith. He had never discussed the matter with Andrew, but couldn't help wondering if Andrew felt the way he did. And if he did, where did that leave Andrew's son – and Bethan?

Much as he liked Andrew he suspected that his friend would try to ignore the problem – and the child. And that would mean Bethan coping with everything on her own, without any support. If only Pontypridd were closer to London!

He kicked a stone across the sodden, muddied grass of the mountainside. The hailstones had turned to an icy rain that teemed down relentlessly, soaking through his worn mac into the wool of his sweater. He didn't care. He looked up. The rock the Graig children called the slide gleamed, shining and grey on an outcrop of stone-spattered mountainside ahead. He resolved to walk there. Sit on it for a while and think.

He and Laura had been married for three months, and already she'd had three disappointments. She wanted a child much, much more than he did. He was happy with things the way they were and only wished she could be as content with him as he was with her. Change, as Andrew and Bethan were undoubtedly learning, was not always for the better. And there was no guarantee that a child born perfect would remain so. He'd never forgotten the pain of watching his sick, worn-out mother nursing one of his younger brothers through the final stages of meningitis. His feeling of helplessness then had been the driving force that had sustained him through the lean, and often lonely, years when he had studied medicine alongside those born better heeled and better connected.

He sat on the rock and looked over the town spread out below him, but his thoughts remained with Bethan. Was she lying in a hospital bed this very minute, blaming herself for her son's misfortune? Knowing Bethan, she would be. Punishing herself by recalling every mouthful of every bottle of brandy she had drunk during the early stages when she didn't know she was pregnant and believed that Andrew had abandoned her. Reliving every blow she had taken when she had fallen down the steep stone staircase of the maternity block of the Graig Hospital in a drunken stupor. Would Andrew have the sense to take her hand, hold it, look into her eyes and tell her – sincerely – that it would have happened anyway? That her son's flaws were none of her doing?

Trevor made a fist and slammed it impotently and painfully into the rockface beside him. Nursing his bruised fingers he stared at the grey waterlogged sky, tears mingling with the icy raindrops that fell on his cheeks.

Chapter Three

'Alma. Are you up there?'

'Yes. I'll be down now, Mam.' Although she hadn't slept, Alma was reluctant to leave her bed. Despite the chill in the air, it was warm beneath the quilt and coat. The pain in her stomach had subsided while she'd remained quietly curled in the foetal position on her mattress, but the memory of the agony remained, and she was wary that movement would precipitate its return. She crossed her fingers tightly, hoping that news hadn't travelled out of Goldman's about her losing her job. She didn't want to tell her mother, not yet. And not until she had to. Her mother already lived in terror of the paupers' ward in the Graig workhouse. Better she leave the house every morning as usual and use the time to hunt for work. The unemployment register in the town was overflowing with girls her age only too willing to take any job they could get, but armed with a reference from the Ronconis she might pick up something if she wasn't too fussy about money.

She put one foot on the floor, wincing as the pain returned to knife viciously at her stomach. Doubled up in agony she looked down at her skirt and saw, even in the half-light of the street lamp that filtered through her window, that it was hopelessly crumpled. She pulled down hard on the hem, smoothed the front panel with her fingers and checked the buttons on her blouse. Picking up her mac from the bed, she felt in the pockets for her comb. After tugging it blindly through her curls she poured water from the jug into the bowl and splashed her face, dried herself hastily with the towel that hung on the back of the chair and made her way downstairs.

The first thing she noticed when she entered the kitchen was that the stove was lit.

'We have a visitor.' Her mother stood nervously in front of the dresser, cups and saucers in hand.

'So I see.'

Mr Parry, the chapel minister, made a point of calling in on Mrs Moore whenever he was in the Morgan Street area, but despite his outwardly solicitous attitude towards her mother's welfare, Alma found it difficult to remain in the same room with the man, let alone be polite. Four years ago when she had begun working Sundays in Ronconi's café, he'd come to the door backed by a full complement of deacons, to tell her that she was no longer welcome among the congregation of the faithful. Distraught by the ostracism the decree implied, her mother had pleaded with them to reconsider their decision. She couldn't bear to think of her only daughter being denied, not only entry to chapel services, but also the social life that was an important part of chapel membership. The afternoon teas, evening concerts, drama and youth clubs, not to mention the annual outing to the seaside, had been closed to Alma from that day on. At the time Alma had borne the ban with equanimity, upset more for her mother than herself. She'd had Ronnie then, and believed, really believed, she needed no one else.

'Alma.' The minister acknowledged her presence with a brief nod of his long thin head.

'Mr Parry.' She couldn't bring herself to enquire after his health.

'Your mother tells me you've been in bed,' he commented critically.

'I was tired,' she replied shortly.

'A girl of your age shouldn't be tired.'

'I think that depends on how much work a girl of my age does.' She wondered how any man, let alone a chapel minister, could live and work in an area like Pontypridd without realising just how close to the bone most people lived. In winter there was little else for her to do except sleep between shifts at the tailor's and the café, especially on days when the stove wasn't lit.

'I didn't think that either of your jobs was particularly taxing.' The minister was sitting in her mother's chair, which he had pulled as close to the stove as was physically possible without actually moving into the hearth. 'If you don't mind me saying so Mrs Moore, this room is quite chilly.' He glanced accusingly at Alma as though she were to blame.

'This house is difficult to heat,' Lena acknowledged in a small voice.

Alma gritted her teeth, loathing her mother's deferential tone.

'Mrs Parry has found that draughtproofing the windows with rolls of newspaper helps enormously.' He imparted his wife's discovery as though they should be humbly grateful for such largesse.

'Our house is cold, Mr Parry, because we have precious little to burn, although I notice Mam always seems to find a few coals whenever you visit.'

'Alma, please!' her mother begged.

'There's many that find life hard these days, Alma,' he countered testily. 'Instead of looking for more, you should give daily thanks for what you already have. A kind and loving mother, a roof over your head—'

'If we've a roof over our head it's no thanks to anyone except ourselves!'

The minister shook his head. 'Unfortunately that is the kind of remark I've come to expect from you, Alma, since you embraced pagan ways. You have strayed far from the path on which you were brought up. I can only repeat what I have had cause to say on more than one occasion before now. I visit this house purely to see your mother, and I don't think it's unreasonable of me to expect politeness from you while I'm here.'

'Alma, please say you're sorry to Mr Parry.' Lena wrung her hands in her apron before opening up the hotplate to boil the kettle.

'I am sorry, Mr Parry.' Alma gave the apology in a tone that even her mother with her acute hearing couldn't fault, but she stared at the minister coolly as she lifted the lid on the saucepan simmering on the second hob. Her mother had made a thin soup from the chop bones and peelings of the Christmas vegetables. She picked up one of the bowls set on the warming rack above the stove and ladled out a tiny portion.

'Would you like some broth?' her mother ventured to the minister when she heard Alma replace the lid on the pot.

'No thank you, Mrs Moore. I've satisfied the inner man well over the festive season. I was at the workhouse yesterday, to help serve the paupers their dinners, and I have to say that the town did them proud. You should have seen the decorations, the table, the linen, the variety of meats,' he eulogised, hearing no humour in the words he used to a blind woman. 'There was a choice of roast pork, chicken or beef, three vegetables and all the trimmings—'

'I take it there was enough left over to feed the crache who'd been doling out their annual allowance of charity?' Alma couldn't resist the gibe. It was a tradition in the workhouse that the poor were served their Christmas dinners by the town's councillors and well-to-do businessmen.

'I won't deny we had a fair meal. But we hardly took food out of the paupers' mouths. I doubt that any of them could have managed another morsel.'

'If you'd given them a couple of hours I'm sure they would have, bearing in mind their diet the rest of the year.'

'I take it you think they're hard done by?' The minister raised his voice as though he was sermonising in chapel. 'These people aren't deserving of Christian charity or pity. Having contributed nothing to the town, they throw themselves on the parish demanding to be clothed, warmed and fed. They don't spare a thought for the decent, hard-working, thrifty people who find themselves having to work all the harder to keep the workhouse doors open. The inmates are nothing more than idle layabouts who've never done a day's work, or saved a farthing in their lives. And instead of punishing them for their laziness and lack of prudence as we should, what do we do? We give them Christmas presents,' he answered quickly, lest Alma interrupt. 'There wasn't a man yesterday who didn't get his ounce of tobacco, or a woman who didn't get a bar of chocolate and an orange. And as if that isn't enough, we feed them first-class food. The meal I saw yesterday was as good as you'll get for half a crown in the New Inn any day of the week.'

'Workhouse inmates don't get Christmas dinner every day of the week,' Alma pointed out.

'You will take a cup of tea with us, won't you Mr Parry?' Lena broke in hastily as the kettle began to boil.

'I don't think so, but thank you for offering, Mrs Moore.'

'Please don't go on my account. I have to be on my way.' Alma rose from the table.

'In that case, perhaps just one cup, Mrs Moore.'

Lena went to the pantry to get the sugar and milk, hoping Alma wouldn't say any more than had already been said.

Alma carried her soup bowl into the washhouse and managed to tip most of what little she'd taken down the sink without her mother hearing.

'Don't wait up for me.' She kissed her mother on the cheek as she prepared to leave. She said no goodbye to the minister.

The last thing she saw as she allowed the curtain to swing down over the doorway was the Christmas tree she'd set up in the alcove next to the stove. Christmas had only been yesterday, yet already it seemed like months ago. The sweets and fruits she'd bought had all disappeared from the boughs and the presents she'd wrapped for her mother had gone from underneath it. It looked ragged and forlorn, and she made a mental note to take it down as soon as she returned.

She smiled as she recalled the expression on her mother's face when she'd handed her two of the four chocolates she'd bought. Her mother had loved the coat, but Alma had learned as a child that it was the little things that made Christmas memorable. Upstairs she had a new jumper. Not the green lamb's-wool she'd coveted on Wilf's stall, but a grey one that her mother had re-knitted her from her father's last remaining garment.

As she closed her front door she thought of the picture the minister had painted of the workhouse Christmas. An abundance of food and presents! If it really was that marvellous why hadn't people been queuing up to admit themselves to the dreaded building?

Exhausted by the long walk to the Tumble, Alma paused for a moment outside Ronconi's café. Through the fog of condensation that misted the windows she could see shadows at virtually every table. Didn't people have anywhere else to go on Boxing night?

The thought of spending the evening ahead ferrying teas and snacks in the hot, crowded, noisy atmosphere loomed, an awful task, but with her morning job gone, the last thing she could afford was the luxury of illness. She laid her hand on the door and pushed.

'You look dreadful, Alma,' Tina Ronconi greeted her tactlessly as she walked behind the counter to hang up her coat. 'You feeling all right?'

'Just something I ate over Christmas,' Alma mumbled as she tied her apron around her waist.

A crash of dishes resounded from the kitchen, followed by the sound of Tony Ronconi's voice raised in anger.

'I take back everything I ever said about Ronnie before he went to Italy,' Tina whispered as she slid a hot pie out of the steamer on to a plate. 'Tony's ten times worse than Ronnie ever was. All he does is pick – pick – pick, from first thing in the morning till last thing at night. Finding fault with everything, and right in nothing, especially the things I do,' she added, raising her voice in the hope that her complaint would carry as far as the kitchen.

'It's a lot to take on a place like this when you're only nineteen. He's just a bit unsure of himself.' Alma stepped smartly aside as Tony barged out of the kitchen. 'I'll start clearing the tables in the back.' She picked up a tray.

'Thank you Alma,' Tony said loudly in a voice directed at his sister. 'I'm glad to see that at least one person around here knows how to work.'

Charlie and William were sitting in the back room drinking tea and playing dominoes with a few of the boys from the Graig. The dominoes were an innovation. On Sundays they risked playing cards, even if it was illegal.

'Alma, how about another tea?' Glan Richards, the Powells' next-door neighbour shouted.

'Oxo for me, Alma.'

'Pie and chips for me, love,' a tram driver called out as he passed her on his way to the table next to the fire.

Half an hour later the pain in Alma's stomach had grown, intensifying until it invaded every aspect of her entire being, mind as well as body. By then Tina was working flat out manning the till and serving the tables in the front room because Tony was too busy screaming at their younger brother, Angelo, in the kitchen to concern himself with what was happening in the café.

As fast as Alma cleared dirty dishes and wiped down the tables, new customers filled them.

'Looks like the whole town has come out for an airing tonight,' Tina grumbled as Alma opened the glass case on the counter and removed a Chelsea bun. 'So much for Tony's quiet Boxing night.'

'Miss, Miss we'll have two teas and two scones.'

Alma recognised the voice and glanced across the room. Mary Morris and Freda from the tailor's shop were sitting at one of her tables in the back, but they were shouting at Tina.

'Workmates throwing their weight around?' Tina raised her eyebrows as she clanged the till shut.

'Ex-workmates,' Alma replied through clenched teeth as she reached for the butter dish. 'And don't you serve them. I'll get around to them in my own good time.'

'You lose your job?'

Alma didn't reply. She finished buttering the Chelsea she had cut open and carried it through to William.

'You want to order?' She stood in front of Freda and Mary's table.

'Yes, but we don't want to be served by you.' Mary pitched her voice high enough to reach all the corners of the café.

'In that case perhaps you'd better go elsewhere.' A thick red mist of anger began to cloud Alma's vision.

'I think the manager will have something to say about one of his waitresses talking to a customer like that!' Mary countered indignantly.

William scraped his chair noisily over the tiled floor, sat back, and stared belligerently at Mary. He regarded the Ronconi café as his second home and everyone who worked in it as his friend. If a man insulted Alma he would have waded in, fists flying; but women were different, and he hesitated, not quite certain how to react. Charlie, who was sitting next to him, laid down the domino he was about to add to the snake angled across the table, and turned his chair until he, too, faced Mary.

'What's going on here?' Tina, hearing the word 'manager', abandoned the till and her tables and positioned herself protectively beside Alma.

'My friend and I,' Mary simpered in a false 'refined' voice, 'do not want to be served by the likes of her.' She pointed her finger at Alma.

'Tough,' Tina snapped. 'She's the waitress here. If you don't like it, you can lump it.'

Tony hearing his sister's voice raised in an anger that surpassed his own decibel level, left the kitchen and barged into the back room, towel and spatula in hand.

'I could hear you in the kitchen, Tina . . .'

'These ladies,' Tina almost spat the word as she indicated Mary and Freda, 'don't want to be served by our waitress.'

Alma retreated from the table and leaned white-faced against the wall close to William's chair.

'Miss Moore has been a waitress here for many years,' Tony began evenly. 'She is perfectly competent to deal with—'

'It's not her competency but her morals we're calling into question,' Mary snapped self-righteously. 'Decent women have the right to object to being served by someone who's carrying a . . . a . . .' she faltered, lowering her eyes while glancing slyly beneath her eyelashes to make sure she held the attention of everyone in the room '. . . a bastard,' she divulged triumphantly to the hushed café, revelling in the consternation she was creating. 'And if *you* aren't prepared to take our complaint seriously then we'll just have to take our custom elsewhere. Freda?' Pulling the lapels of her coat high around her throat she rose majestically from her seat. 'We may be the first, but I promise you, Mr Ronconi,' she swept the skirt of her coat from her chair, 'we won't be the last women of the town to refuse to eat here.'

Confused, Tony turned, just in time to see Alma collapse. Charlie dived out of his chair and caught her, but not before she hit her head on the kerb of the tiled hearth.

'I've got her.'

Alma recognised Charlie's accent. She opened her eyes briefly and stared up into the Russian's deep blue eyes. The last thing she was aware of before plunging into unconsciousness was his strong arms wrapped around her body.

'Run up to Graig Street and get Doctor Lewis,' Charlie ordered Tony as he took control of the situation. 'You've got the keys to the Trojan?'

'I have but . . .' Tony's cheeks reddened as he squirmed

in embarrassment. He didn't want to look ridiculous in front of the entire clientele of the café by admitting that he'd never got the hang of driving the van.

'Here, give them to me,' William shouted impatiently, holding out his hand as he stared at Alma's deathly pale face, now streaked by a single scarlet ribbon of blood trickling from her temple down to her chin.

'They're behind the counter.'

William ran to get them. Neither Charlie nor Tony thought to ask where he'd learned to drive.

'Is there anywhere private I can take her?' Charlie demanded as customers strained their necks in an effort to get a good look at what was going on.

'Upstairs,' Tony suggested, as Mary and Freda banged the front door behind them.

'Over here, Charlie.' Tina lifted the flap on the counter and preceded Charlie up the narrow flight of stairs. The air was freezing, musty with disuse. There was no electricity on the first floor of the café. The only light that illuminated the upper staircase came in from the street lamp outside, through the window of a landing littered with cardboard boxes and catering tins of coffee, beans and cocoa. Tina had to put her shoulder to the door before it finally grated over the damp, swollen floorboards.

'Put her on the bed. I'll get a glass of water.' Tina disappeared back down the stairs.

Charlie laid Alma on the bed, but as the cover felt damp he shrugged his shoulders out of his jacket and lifted Alma again to wrap it around her. He stared at the cheap flowered cotton curtains hanging limply at the window and the paper dangling loosely from the walls. The floorboards were bare, and apart from the bed and a single chair the room was empty. A stub of candle, glued by a puddle of wax to a saucer, balanced on the seat of the chair. He reached into his pocket for a box of matches.

'Ronnie?'

Charlie struck the match and held it to the wick. It flared briefly before settling into a small flame that

45

scuppered low, finally dying in a draught that blew in from the door.

'It's Charlie,' he answered softly.

'What happened?' Alma tried to sit up. Reaching out frantically she clutched at Charlie's shirt-sleeve before falling back on to the bed with a moan.

'You fainted. Try and rest.'

'You don't understand. I've got to work,' she insisted hysterically. 'You can't stop me. I need the job . . .'

'Has she come round?' Tina reappeared in the doorway with a glass of water.

'I'm fine. I . . .'

'You're not fine,' Tina answered without realising Alma was raving. 'You can't work like that, and I can't breathe in here. This room smells like a tomb. I don't think anyone's been up here since Ronnie left,' Tina said, anxiety making her even more tactless than usual. She handed Charlie the glass, walked over to the window and wrenched down the sash. 'I know it's freezing outside,' she babbled, 'but then it's freezing in here too, so I don't suppose it will make any difference to you, Alma.'

Neither Alma, nor Charlie who was busy with the candle, answered her. The second flame he'd nurtured flickered weakly as he sat beside Alma on the bed, propped her against his chest and held the glass to her lips.

'You're going to be fine, Alma. Isn't she, Charlie?' Tina demanded.

Charlie sensed that Tina was looking for reassurance, but he had never lied in his life, and wasn't about to begin now. He brushed Alma's hair away from her clammy forehead and pulled his jacket closer round her shoulders. Alma writhed in his arms but didn't open her eyes.

Tina crept closer and he handed her the glass.

'If you see to Alma, I'll wait outside.' Shivering in his thin shirt and waistcoat he left the room and sat on the top stair, conscious that it wasn't right for a man to be in a bedroom – any bedroom – with a woman who wasn't his wife.

'Has she come round yet?' Tony called from the kitchen as he heard Charlie's measured tread on the rickety floor.

'Not really,' Charlie answered.

'Tell Tina to stay with her. We'll manage somehow until Trevor gets here.'

Charlie settled his back against the cold wall and waited. Tina glanced at him from time to time, glad not to be alone with the unconscious Alma. His pale face and athletic body reminded her of the picture postcards of marble statues her Italian relatives sent her father on his birthday. She could read nothing in the dispassionate set of his features, but inside Charlie's head, thoughts and emotions spiralled and whirled like dead leaves in an autumn wind.

It had been a long, long time since he, Feodor Raschenko (in his thoughts he always referred to himself by his Russian name, never the nickname that had been bestowed on him in Pontypridd market), had held a woman. He was still young. Only twenty-eight, but sometimes, surrounded in his working and lodging life by younger men like William and Eddie Powell, he felt like a grandfather.

He'd compartmentalised his life into sections: the proscribed past, and the allowable present. (He *never* attempted to forecast what the future might hold.) The problems of childhood, adolescence and early manhood paled into insignificance when set against the traumatic events that had marked his entry into Russian adult life. Afterwards had come the numb, desensitised years of exile. Five long years during which he had tried valiantly, with varying degrees of success, not to feel anything of a remotely emotional or personal nature.

And now – now – the simple act of carrying a sick woman up a staircase had reminded him that life didn't have to be cold and solitary. That human existence could encompass warmth, physical contact with people – and even – the possibility hovered tantalisingly, almost beyond his present conception – a relationship with a woman.

He looked into the bedroom. Tina was sitting on the bed. All he could see of Alma was a mass of red hair lying on the pillow, the same hair that had flowed over his arm when he had carried her up the stairs. Perhaps that was it! The combination of red hair and green eyes. Nothing more. A passing physical resemblance. An attraction that was not born of his feelings for Alma, but Masha . . . Masha . . .

'Charlie?'

The shadowy figure of Trevor Lewis stood before him on the staircase. 'William tells me Alma collapsed.'

'Yes. I'm sorry, I'm in your way,' Charlie apologised, rising quickly.

'Hello Charlie.' Trevor's wife Laura, who had been a Ronconi before her marriage, acknowledged him before following her husband into the room. 'I'll take over here, Tina, you go and help Tony downstairs,' Laura Lewis murmured in her brisk no-nonsense nursing voice. Charlie waited for Tina, then followed her down the stairs into the café where Tony's raised voice and Angelo's intensified crashing of pots and pans testified to the chaos that the temporary shortage of staff had created.

'It's appendicitis and mild concussion,' Trevor announced through the open door at the foot of the stairs.

'That isn't too bad, is it?' Tina enquired uneasily from behind the counter.

'I don't think the mild concussion will present much of a problem, and appendicitis is usually straightforward,' Trevor agreed, 'but Alma's appendix is on the point of bursting. I'm going to have to operate right away.'

'Here?'

Even Trevor smiled at the panic on Tony's face. 'Not in that bedroom, with only the stub of a candle for light and the wind whistling in and flapping the wallpaper! But I could move her into the kitchen. You do have a scrub-down table and sharp knives to hand?'

'You're joking?' Tony wasn't absolutely sure, even after the smile.

'My car's outside. I'll take her up to the cottage hospital. I'll need help to carry her downstairs,' Trevor frowned, thinking of the narrow staircase.

'I'll carry her down for you Doctor Lewis.' Wanting to help, but uncertain how, Charlie had been hovering close to the counter.

'She has to be held steady,' Trevor warned.

'He took her up there without any trouble,' Tina replied for him.

'Then if you'll be kind enough, Charlie. The sooner we get started, the sooner I can operate.'

'Someone's going to have to tell Alma's mother.' Tina hoped it would be her. High drama was infinitely preferable to the boredom of waiting at tables.

'I'll go,' William offered. 'If I take the Trojan I can drive Mrs Moore to the hospital.'

'There won't be anything for her to do there,' Trevor protested. 'Better you stay with her until it's all over. I'll call in and see her on my way back.'

'A woman should go with him,' Tina pressed urgently. 'Mrs Moore will need some sympathy . . .' A fleeting expression of annoyance crossed Tony's face and Tina fell silent. Ever since her family had detected the signs of budding mutual infatuation between her and William Powell, her father and brothers had dedicated themselves to keeping the pair of them apart.

'If Charlie comes with me to the hospital, Laura can go with William to Mrs Moore's.' Trevor's attention was fixed on Charlie as he walked slowly down the stairs with Alma, still wrapped in his coat, in his arms.

'She's just regained consciousness.' Laura followed Charlie into the café.

'Go with William to her mother's house.' Trevor gave

49

his wife an absentminded peck on the lips much to the delight of the customers. 'You'll know what to say to her.' He held the door open for Charlie to carry Alma outside.

'I can't go to hospital,' Alma protested vehemently as Charlie deposited her gently on the back seat of Trevor's car before walking around and climbing in next to her.

'I don't think you have any choice in the matter, young lady.' Trevor extracted the starting handle from beneath the seat and handed it to Tony, who was fussing round them. 'You're very ill, and you'll be even worse if we don't sort you out – and quickly.'

The cottage hospital on the Common was a long, low, colonial-type structure built on the top of the hill that overlooked the town. Flanked by the big semis and detached houses of the crache it was high enough, and far enough away from the collieries to ensure a plentiful supply of good clean air – a commodity often in short supply in Pontypridd.

'I haven't paid a subscription to the Cottage,' Alma gasped, biting her lip and grasping Charlie's hand in an effort to control the pain.

Trevor turned the corner by the old bridge, pointed his ancient car up the hill and pressed the accelerator down to the floor. 'You pay me my penny a week.'

'Yes, and the penny a week for the Graig Hospital, but I've never been able to afford the guinea a week for the Cottage,' she repeated dogmatically, wondering why Trevor was finding it so difficult to understand. 'I should go to the workhouse.'

'There's a better operating theatre in the Cottage than the Graig. Your father was a miner, wasn't he?'

'The union membership doesn't cover widows and orphans my age and we're—' she clutched Charlie's hand again, crushing his fingers as the pain became almost too great to bear.

'Yes it does,' Trevor contradicted flatly turning a sharp

left through the gates of the hospital.

'Are you sure?' Alma's eyes were rolling and she could only speak in short staccato gasps, yet her primary concern was still money.

'You have my word. You will not get a bill either for the hospital or my services. Is that good enough for you?' Trevor wrenched the handbrake of the car. 'Can you manage?' he asked Charlie.

Charlie nodded, lifted Alma out of the car and followed Trevor up a short flight of steps on to a veranda and through a pair of glassed wooden double doors into the foyer. A nurse stepped briskly out of an adjoining room. The expression of annoyance on her face was replaced by a smile when she saw Trevor.

'Doctor Lewis,' she curtsyed to him as he explained the situation and called for a trolley and porter.

A few seconds later Charlie laid Alma on the trolley and watched as Trevor, the nurse and a porter wheeled it down a corridor that led to the hidden recesses of the hospital. Left to his own devices he paced across the hallway. Trying to ignore the overpowering smell of disinfectant, he hesitated below a brass plaque that commemorated the opening of the hospital. Concerned only for Alma, Trevor had disappeared without a word, and Charlie was uncertain whether he was expected to wait or not.

A clock set high on the wall in front of the window of the closed office ticked on. Five . . . ten minutes passed. He shivered, realising he was in his waistcoat and shirt-sleeves. Alma had still been wrapped in his jacket when he had laid her down on the trolley. The nurse who had greeted Trevor walked back down the corridor, smiled at Charlie then turned a corner and entered one of the rooms.

He turned his back on the plaque and continued to pace up and down, swinging his arms in an effort to ward off the cold, and, with nothing else to do, he began to think . . . and remember . . .

'It was on the point of bursting, but it stayed in one piece until I dropped it in the kidney dish, thank God. So that minimises the risk of infection. Lucky she fainted when she did, and Tony had the sense to send for me.' Trevor handed Charlie his jacket.

'Then she is going to be all right?'

'Thanks to all of you, yes I think so,' Trevor hazarded cautiously. 'Although it's early days and the wound may get infected yet. She'll have to stay in here for at least three weeks, and even then it'll be a couple more weeks before she'll be up to doing anything strenuous.'

'That's going to hit her hard. I've heard money is very tight in that household.'

'It's tight everywhere,' Trevor commented philosophically as he rolled down his cuffs. 'Want to come with me to see her mother?'

Charlie shook his head. 'I don't want to intrude.'

'Then I'll drop you off in town. Perhaps you could call into the café and tell them how she's going. Oh, and you'd better warn Tony that he's going to have to find a replacement waitress for a month or so, but I wouldn't mention that until you're half-way out of the door if I were you. You know what his temper is like.'

Chapter Four

'YOU REALLY ARE a terrible patient.' Tina reached out to the bedside locker and filched a strawberry cream from the box of chocolates she had ostensibly brought for Alma.

'How can you expect me to lie here doing nothing when there's no one at home to take care of my mother?'

'I told you,' Tina gave a sigh of exasperation as her fingers strayed into the box again, 'Mrs Lane next door is keeping an eye on her and the house. Not that it needs it,' she added. 'Your mother is a marvel at housework. When I saw her scrubbing your kitchen and washhouse floors I would never have guessed she was blind.'

'You don't understand. Even if Mam *is* coping at home, I still need to work. The bills won't stop coming in just because I'm lying here.' Alma tossed restlessly on the bed.

'Laura's seeing to all your bills,' Tina blurted out thoughtlessly as she studied the illustrations on the inside of the chocolate-box lid.

'Seeing to them! With what?'

'Money, I should imagine. I haven't heard of anyone taking buttons yet.'

'And how on earth am I supposed to pay her back?'

'By putting in extra hours at the café when you're well?' Tina suggested casually. 'Oh and by the way, Eddie Powell was asking after you. I think he's sweet on you.'

Alma wasn't to be put off by tales of Eddie Powell. 'I'm fit enough to leave here now . . .'

'You most certainly are not.' Trevor Lewis strode down the centre of the ward, his white doctor's coat flapping around his lean figure. He smiled and nodded to the occupants of the other beds in the women's ward as he headed towards Alma. 'After three weeks of complete bed rest it'll be as much as you can do to stagger to the bathroom.'

'I walked there just fine this morning.'

'I don't doubt you did, but as it's only one hour into the first afternoon I'll talk to you again tonight.'

'I still don't see why I can't go home. I can rest just as well there.'

'I've yet to meet the woman who can rest in her own home without bobbing up and down every five minutes to see to something,' Trevor replied tactfully. He had visited Alma's house several times during the past three weeks, and had seen for himself exactly how bare and comfortless it was. He knew himself precisely what it meant to live out every day fighting a constant shortage of coal and food; and as a doctor, the last thing he was prepared to do was discharge Alma Moore into a cold, hungry home, where she'd be looking for paid work before her operation scar had time to heal. 'You're here for at least one more week, Madam, whether you like it, or not.'

Alma's mouth set in a grim line as she turned her face to the wall. Pity and charity! Since she'd collapsed in the café they greeted her at every turn. She knew from what her mother had told her during her Sunday and Wednesday visits, that she had practically moved in with Betty Lane next door, supposedly 'to help out with the children'. She also knew that Laura Lewis called in every day to check that her mother was all right and had everything she needed. The kindness of neighbours and friends was proving very hard to take, particularly as she knew it was extremely unlikely she'd ever be able to reciprocate their favours.

'Laura'll be here in a minute with your mother.' Trevor picked up Alma's chart from the foot of her bed and studied it.

'See, you can stop worrying, we have everything under control,' Tina mumbled, her mouth full of chocolate cream.

'Including the disposal of any sweets that the patient is

54

given?' Trevor lifted an eyebrow. 'Did you remember to bring in two boxes, one for yourself and one for Alma?'

Tina stuck a chocolate-coated tongue out at him.

'Only thinking of your figure, dear sister-in-law,' he teased.

Alma looked towards the door. Leaning heavily on Laura's arm, her mother was walking slowly down the central aisle between the beds. Dressed in the second-hand coat, woollen hat, scarf and gloves Alma had given her for Christmas, she was carrying a brown string carrier bag.

'Here we are, Mrs Moore.' Laura led Alma's mother towards the chair Tina had vacated, and lined her up in front of the seat. 'You can sit here, right next to Alma's bed.'

Alma reached out and placed her mother's hand on the edge of the seat; only then did Lena Moore gingerly lower herself.

'Doctor Lewis tells me you're feeling better, Alma?' She felt for the bed and deposited her carrier bag on it.

'I'm fine.' Alma forced herself to sound bright and cheerful.

Using Alma's voice as a guide, Lena leaned forward and fumbled for her daughter's hand. 'Are you really?' she whispered intensely.

'Of course,' Alma reassured her, taking her hand.

'Tina and I have to visit the men's ward,' Laura said as she tapped her sister's arm. 'Our uncle was brought in last night.'

'Oh dear, nothing serious I hope.' Mrs Moore lifted her face in Laura's direction.

'He chopped his hand when he was chopping chips in his café last night,' Tina explained, gathering her coat and handbag from the floor. 'But it's all right. My cousin fished his finger out of the fat fryer.'

'You'll have to excuse Tina, Mrs Moore,' Laura apologised, as she kicked her sister's shin. 'She has a peculiar sense of humour.'

'Have you brought him a box of chocolates as well, Tina?' Trevor replaced Alma's chart on the rail at the foot of her bed.

'Of course,' Tina retorted. 'See you later, Alma.'

'I'll be back before visiting ends to fetch you, Mrs Moore,' Laura called over her shoulder as they walked away.

'Thank you,' Mrs Moore answered as she heard their footsteps echo down the ward. 'Mrs Lewis is a lovely person, and so kind,' she enthused as she turned her back to Alma. 'And you really are better, aren't you? I can hear it in your voice.'

'I can get out of bed whenever I feel like now.'

'Don't forget to take it slowly,' her mother cautioned. 'Doctor Lewis told me how ill you'd been. He said that even when you come home you are on no account to work for at least two weeks, and that's in the house, let alone outside work.'

'We'll see how I feel, Mam.'

'At least two weeks. He warned me of serious consequences if you don't heed his advice, Alma.' To Lena Moore the words of ministers and doctors were sacrosanct. Both professions she placed in a social stratum only marginally lower than God.

'I'd be bored silly at home all day.' Alma forced a laugh. 'You know what I'm like Mam, I can't sit still for a minute.'

'Well, for once you're going to have to.' Her mother opened the carrier bag and lifted out a clean nightdress. 'Besides, there's nothing for you to do at home. Mrs Lewis has seen to everything. The rent, the bills, the shopping – she even got that nice young man who works for the foreign butcher in the market – what's his name?'

'William Powell,' Alma said suspiciously.

'That's him. She even got him to put a load of coals into the coal-house for me.'

'And you let him? What did you pay him with?'

'It's all right Alma,' her mother smiled. 'Mrs Lewis is

paying for everything out of the insurance you took out in work in case you got sick. She's been collecting your full wages. And not just the café wages. It's twelve shillings, the same as it would be if you'd been able to carry on with both jobs. Although no one from Goldman's been near the house to ask after you. That's not very neighbourly of them I must say. You see, you don't have to worry about a thing. These last two weeks I've even been able to put a little aside. By the time you come out we'll have a few shillings spare. Maybe enough to buy a length of pretty cotton so you can sew yourself a new summer dress.'

Alma lay back on her pillows listening to her mother's tales of how marvellous everything was at home, and saying little except the odd 'yes' or 'no'. She knew her mother had been worried sick about her. Now, for the first time in almost three weeks, relief was evident in the relaxed lines of Lena Moore's face and voice. The last thing she could do was shatter her mother's illusions.

She'd wondered just how Laura had managed to get her mother to accept charity. Now she knew. Insurance! How would her mother feel if she told her there was no insurance. That there never had been. That even if such a policy existed, she'd never had money enough to spare to subscribe to one.

Bethan hovered at the 'dining end' of the one-reception, two-bedroomed flat, or 'apartment' as Andrew liked to call it. She checked the table in a desultory, absentminded fashion, straightening knives and forks that were already beautifully regimented, patting the bunch of violets she'd arranged in her smallest, prettiest crystal vase – a wedding present from Laura and Trevor – passing time while she waited, half in anticipation, half in fear, for the sound of Andrew's key in the door.

She'd taken a great deal of trouble with the table, using the best damask tablecloth that Andrew's sister Fiona and brother-in-law Alec had given them as a belated wedding present. She'd spent half an hour that afternoon polishing the silver cutlery that Andrew's parents had sent, along with a fine set of Doulton china, from Harrods. She could accuse them of antagonism towards her, but never meanness. Fiona, Alec, Laura, Trevor and Andrew's parents – the only thing on the table she could honestly say was the product of their own taste was the posy she'd bought from the flower seller outside their block of flats.

Andrew wouldn't have approved of her going downstairs with the baby in her arms. It upset him to think of people looking at the child. One glance in the shawl or under the hood of the pram he'd asked her to keep raised in all weathers would be enough for anyone to see that something was wrong with little Edmund. Even the baby's name wasn't right. Before the birth they'd decided if the child was a boy they'd name him Evan after her father, and if it was a girl, Isobel after Andrew's mother. But then, before the birth they'd both hoped that the baby would help to heal the rift that had existed between their families ever since she'd run off to London to be with Andrew. Andrew's parents had never really forgiven her for being a miner's daughter and six months pregnant with Andrew's child when they'd married, and her parents had never forgiven Andrew for making her pregnant in the first place.

She wandered into the inner hall and peeped through the open door of the darkened nursery she and Andrew had lavished a great deal of money, time and trouble on before the baby's birth – and a room Andrew hadn't entered since the day she'd carried Edmund into it.

The baby lay on his back, eyes closed. She listened hard. His breathing was soft, regular. It sounded so . . . so normal. If *only* she hadn't drunk so much brandy. She was a nurse: she knew full well that alcohol taken in excess in pregnancy leads to complications and birth palsy in infants. And then to go and fall down the stairs of the Graig Hospital in a drunken stupor – and afterwards . . .

She closed her eyes tightly, gripped the door and swallowed hard. Little Edmund was the way he was because she'd tried to kill him before he even had a chance of life. She had never thought of him as an individual – a living, breathing being in his own right – until Andrew had returned to Pontypridd and talked about the baby they were about to have. So much guilt – hers and hers alone – and poor, innocent Edmund was paying the penalty.

How could she forgive herself! Not only for what she'd done to Edmund, but for the pain she'd caused Andrew. He'd hardly said a word to her beyond the brief exchanges that have to be made since she'd defied him and brought Edmund home from hospital against his express wishes. He had pleaded with her to leave the child in the nursery at the hospital until he was old enough to go into an institution – if he lived that long.

Perhaps it was the brutal honesty of Andrew's final remark that decided her, activating the stubborn streak she'd inherited from her grandmother. If Edmund was going to have a short life she owed it to him to make it a happy one. She didn't need her nurse's training to see just how frail the baby was. His legs and arms were paralysed. His oversized head lolled alarmingly on his thin neck. And worst of all, the only response he made to her ministrations was ceasing to cry when she fed him.

Before she brought Edmund home, before the crushing silence had settled between her and Andrew, he'd tried to talk to her about suitable places for children like Edmund. He had shown her photographs of institutions that had been set up in converted manor houses with beautiful gardens. But her time in the Graig workhouse had taught her the exact worth of beautiful gardens. Most patients were never allowed to walk in them, or touch the flowers. The closest they got to the manicured lawns was to look at them through glass windows.

The unwritten rule in the medical world was that inmates of institutions had to be kept indoors, segregated from 'normal' people lest the sight of them offend and upset. She recalled the rows of utility iron cots in the

59

depressing, green-painted rooms of J ward in the Graig; the listless babies too used to neglect even to whimper, because they knew that crying wouldn't bring attention. She'd tried to make Andrew understand how she felt, taking all the blame squarely on herself, but none of her efforts had lessened his shame at the son they had produced, or his determination to remove all trace of the child from their lives as soon as possible.

She went into the bedroom they shared and glanced at the alarm clock. Not quite seven. She tiptoed back into the hall, and took one last look into the cot before closing the door.

Edmund was generally very good and had begun to sleep through until six in the morning. It was just as well; it irritated Andrew beyond measure when she left their bed to see to him.

Pulling her small, entirely useless 'fancy' lace-trimmed apron tight at the waist she checked her reflection in the hall mirror. She'd had no trouble in regaining her figure after the baby's birth. In fact she was probably too thin. She'd lost all appetite when Andrew had insisted on her taking salts to dry up her milk so Edmund could be bottle-fed. She stared at her eyes, rubbing the taut skin beneath them as though she could wipe away the dark shadows. Not wanting to get out her lipstick, in case Andrew noticed and made a comment about her 'dressing up' in the house, she bit her lips to make them redder, and patted her hair, which was neatly waved just the way her Aunt Megan had taught her to do it. She hesitated, impulsively returned to the bedroom to put one more dab of essence of violets behind her ears, then went into the tiny kitchen to check on the meal.

The potato soup was simmering on the gas stove. It was so much easier to cook with gas. She felt guilty just thinking of her mother and all the women on the Graig who had to cope with temperamental coal-fired ovens. The choice at home at this time of day would have been scorched or tepid soup. The only way to gently warm a saucepan was on the rack above the stove that was used for dishes.

Tomorrow morning there'd be no oven to rake out or blacklead, only the living-room fireplace to clean. The work in the flat was nothing compared to the work of keeping house in Graig Avenue. Perhaps that was part of the trouble. If she had more to do, she'd have less time to think. The only person other than Andrew and the doctors she'd talked to since leaving hospital was the flower seller. They had a telephone, but she knew no one in London except Andrew's sister Fiona; no one in Pontypridd, apart from Andrew's parents and Laura, had a telephone in the house. She was afraid of Fiona's sophistication, and she worried too much about the cost of the call to telephone Laura. Her only contact with her family was through the post, and she was finding it increasingly difficult to write about things that mattered, like the baby. Instead she filled the pages of her letters with questions about what they were doing, and descriptions of the park across the road. But then, considering the state of little Edmund, perhaps it was just as well that most of her family had proved poor correspondents, except of course her mother. And she gained as little information or comfort from her mother's cold epistles as her mother probably did from her own unsatisfactory communications.

She opened the door of the oven to check on the dinner, then went through the menu in her mind. She'd made the dessert – 'dessert', not afters, she had to be careful not to revert to the vocabulary of her home because she sensed it annoyed Andrew – of apple jelly and cheese creams earlier, and they were now cooling on the marble slab in the pantry.

A perfect meal – and all of it copied from the *Complete Illustrated Cookery* that her brothers had saved up and bought for her from a *News of the World* offer. All she needed was someone to eat it. The clock chimed the quarter-hour and she shuddered. Andrew was coming home from the hospital later and later, and that was something else that had to be her fault. He couldn't bear to watch her give Edmund his last feed. He was right. She was being selfish in refusing to give up the baby. As he had said in an angry outburst before she had left the hospital, 'How can people be expected to trust a doctor who's produced a son like Edmund?'

Tears burned her eyes at the thought of handing her son over to strangers who wouldn't recognise the difference between a cry that denoted a serious need, and one that didn't. She stood staring at her wavering reflection in the uncurtained, blackened window, trying to remember all the arguments Andrew had put forward.

Every doctor who had seen Edmund, including Andrew, predicted an early death for the child. They said it was for the best; but none of their predictions had assuaged her guilt, or prevented her from loving the poor mite.

Dr Floyd had told her to forget the baby and concentrate on having another. But how could she? Edmund was nearly two months old and Andrew still treated her as though she had the plague, sticking rigidly to his half of the bed, wearing pyjamas, when he had always slept naked. She knew that at the back of his mind, and hers, lay the thought that there was no guarantee that another baby would either help her to forget their first-born, or be any more whole and perfect than its brother.

She dried her tears and checked the clock again. Half-past seven. If he didn't come soon the meal would be spoiled. Perhaps he was already seeking solace in someone else's arms. He was very good-looking, and used to girls flinging themselves at him the way they had in Pontypridd. A sudden picture filled her mind of Andrew, his arms wrapped around a slim, blonde nurse.

'Good evening.'

She started at the sound of his voice. 'I'm sorry, I was miles away. I didn't hear you come in,' she said nervously, aware that she was saying too much, too quickly. 'The meal's ready whenever you are.' She hesitated, hoping he'd kiss her; even a meaningless touch on the cheek would be a step in the right direction.

'I'll wash my hands.' The apologetic tone in her voice, her eagerness to please, set his teeth on edge. He fought the urge to lash out and shake her. Why didn't she ask him where he'd been until now as any normal wife would do? Alec said Fe gave him hell if he was as much as ten minutes late. Instead, all he got was longsuffering martyrdom wrapped in a coating of sugar-sweet brightness. Why didn't she shout at him? Reproach him for his failure to come to terms with their child's disability? Tantrums and screaming matches would be more honest than this ridiculous pretence of blissful domesticity.

In the bathroom he washed his hands, deliberately replacing the immaculately folded towel at an angle. He picked up the tooth-powder and scrubbed his teeth, hoping to rid his mouth of the taste of the half a pint of beer and the cigar he'd spun out in the bar round the corner from the hospital. Only a few short weeks ago he'd rushed home at the end of every shift, literally counting the minutes until he could be with Bethan. Now he was the last out of the pub, staying on with the widowers and bachelors, who had no reason to leave until their clubs began to serve dinner.

If only she'd allow him to put the child elsewhere. The whole time he was home he was conscious that in the next room lay a mockery of humanity, a living reminder of his failure to look after her when she'd needed him most. If he hadn't left her alone when he had, she wouldn't have been working, and she wouldn't have fallen down the stairs of the hospital. Complications might not have arisen in labour – why hadn't he demanded a Caesarean earlier? He should have known her pains were more severe than normal labour pains from the start. A Caesarean would have been better for Edmund. He would have been born perfect . . .

He shut his mind against a heart-wrenching image of

him and Bethan with a beautiful, flawless child. His superiors had sympathised, told him that Edmund's condition was simply one of those medical 'accidents' that happened from time to time. Oxygen starvation during a difficult delivery. No one's fault. But cold, medical logic didn't stop him looking for a scapegoat, or finding one in himself.

He left the bathroom. Bethan had served the soup. It was steaming in a tureen in the centre of the table.

'Shall I dish out for you?' she asked, instantly angry with herself for saying 'dish out' instead of serve.

'I'll do it myself,' he said gruffly. Ladling the smallest possible portion on to his plate he sat down and began to eat. In silence. There didn't seem to be any safe topic left for them to discuss. If he asked about her day he'd run the risk of her telling him, and he didn't want to hear how she'd coped with their son. Not now. Not ever.

'How nice of you to call, Mrs Lewis. Alma dear, it's Mrs Lewis,' Lena Moore called from the kitchen into the washhouse where Alma was leaning on the stone sink peeling potatoes.

'I'll be there now.' Alma dropped her knife into the dirty water, went outside to rinse her hands under the tap, and returned to the kitchen, drying her hands on her apron as she walked.

'Would you like a cup of tea, Laura?' she asked, grateful that the oven was lit so she could offer. The coal stocks William had brought had lulled her mother into a false sense of security and she'd insisted on lighting the stove every day since Alma had come home from hospital.

'That would be nice, thank you.' Laura set her basket on the floor. 'I've brought you some fruit from the market.' She lifted half a dozen brown paper bags from the top of her basket and laid them on the table.

'Thank you. That really is very good of you,' Alma's mother chattered gratefully. 'As you well know, Alma isn't up to carrying anything heavy like shopping yet, and

I won't be going into town until Mrs Lane takes me on Saturday morning.' Lena picked up the kettle from the hearth and walked slowly but surely out into the yard. She filled it at the outside tap. Turning, she hesitated for a moment on the threshold of the washhouse. The onset of her blindness had brought with it a heightened sensitivity to the atmosphere people carried with them and she sensed strain between her daughter and Laura.

'I'll do it, Alma,' she murmured as Alma held out her hand to take the kettle when she finally returned to the kitchen. She picked up the iron hook they used to lift the hotplate and set the kettle to boil. 'I'm sorry Mrs Lewis, I hope you'll excuse me.' She scooped her knitting from the table. 'I was just on my way to see Mrs Lane next door. I promised to show her a cable stitch she needs to make up a sweater for her youngest.'

'In that case I'll see you next time Mrs Moore.' Laura reached out and touched the old woman's hand as she confidently walked the six paces along the passage to the front door.

'Sit down,' Alma invited as the door closed. She indicated the most comfortable chair, the rickety wooden upright that sported a home-made cushion padded with old shredded stockings.

'You're not overdoing it, are you?' Laura asked critically, looking Alma over with a professional eye. 'You have to remember that you only came out of hospital three days ago.'

'I'm fine,' Alma snapped.

Laura sat down and stared at the kettle hissing on the stove.

'I'm feeling fine,' Alma repeated, conscious of having spoken sharply.

'I'm glad to hear it.'

Alma poured a little hot water into the teapot, swirled it round and took it into the washhouse to empty it down the sink. Busying herself on her return, she refused to meet Laura's searching looks. She spooned tea into the pot, filled it and took two cups and saucers from the dresser.

'I've just come from the new café,' Laura volunteered.

'When will it be opening?'

'The way it's looking now the builders will be working there for at least another month.'

'Ronnie promised me a full-time job there when it opened. Head waitress.' Alma felt as though she was demeaning herself by begging for a position.

'There will be a job of one sort or another for you as long as the Ronconis run cafés,' Laura promised quietly.

'I was hoping there would, but after . . . well after what happened that night with Mary and Freda I wasn't too sure.' Alma's voice trailed away as she poured the tea. It was difficult to look Laura in the eye.

'Alma . . .'

'I've been wanting to talk to you,' Alma interrupted. Thrusting her hand into the pocket of her skirt she pulled out a piece of paper and handed it to Laura.

'What's this?' Laura unfolded it.

'A list of everything I owe you for the bills you've paid, and the money you gave my mother when I was in hospital. I make it two pounds seventeen and eightpence.'

Laura glanced down at the list. Alma had left out nothing. Four weeks' rent at nine shillings a week, two hundredweight of coal, four weeks' groceries from the corner shop. Even the fruit and chocolates Tina had taken into hospital had been added to the list.

'Look Alma—'

'No, you look!' Alma's green eyes blazed fiercely in the thin light that filtered into the room from the back yard. 'They're my bills. Mine and my mother's. Have you any idea how it makes me feel to have you pay them?'

'Alma, we employ you. We're your friends,' Laura protested.

'Friend or not I intend to pay you back. Every penny,' she mumbled.

'You don't have to.'

'Yes I do,' Alma countered, swallowing her tears.

'Alma, no matter how good you think you feel now, you're still recovering from a serious operation. You need to give yourself time. You're not fit for work.'

'If Tony'll have me I intend to go back tonight.'

'Alma please . . .'

'This—' Alma opened a drawer in the table and lifted out a small cloth purse. She emptied it and coins fell into a noisy heap on the table next to Laura. They represented the sum total of her and her mother's savings. All the pennies her mother had scrimped from the 'insurance' money Laura had given her – 'is the first instalment on what I owe.'

'I can't leave you penniless.'

'We can get credit in the shop at the end of the street until Saturday. And I can start back to work tonight. Can't I?' Alma's face was a study in determination and defiance.

Laura made no move to pick up the money.

'I can have my job back, can't I?' Alma repeated, raising her eyes.

'We had to do some reorganising after you left,' Laura murmured evasively. 'We don't need anyone out front any more, but Tony really could do with some help in the kitchen. If you take the job it'll be at a higher hourly rate because there won't be any tips.'

'I'm a waitress, not a kitchen hand.'

'It will only be for a short while.'

'You're afraid someone else will make a scene, like Mary and Freda?'

'There's no sense in meeting trouble half-way.'

'But you're still prepared to employ me?' Alma's heart pounded erratically. Laura couldn't let her go. She just couldn't . . .

'Speaking as a nurse, I'd rather you didn't go back for at least another week.'

'My mother and I need the money.'

'Alma please. Let us help you. You've worked for us

67

for a long time. I thought we were friends.'

'I won't take charity.'

'If you won't take help from us, you and your mother are going to end up in the workhouse,' Laura stated bluntly.

'If we do end up there it won't be for the want of trying to find work.'

'Alma, be realistic. If you go back to work tonight you could collapse again. And then where will you and your mother be?'

'I won't collapse.'

'Ronnie would never forgive me if he knew that I'd allowed you to go back to work straight after an operation.' If she hadn't been so desperate to make Alma see sense Laura would never have used her eldest brother's name.

'Is that why you want to help me? Because I was your brother's fancy woman?'

The silence in the kitchen closed in unbearably. Laura stood up and picked up her basket.

'I'll tell Tony to expect you tonight.'

'Take the money.'

'No. I'd rather you paid me back all at once.'

'That could take time.'

'I can wait.'

Laura walked towards the curtain that screened off the passage. 'You will come to us if you need help?' she pleaded one last time.

'Thank you for the offer, but I'll manage,' Alma replied stubbornly.

'I would never have moved you out of the café into the kitchen if I'd had any choice. You do know that, don't you?'

'I know what everyone in the town is saying about me.' Alma's cheeks flamed crimson but she still looked Laura in the eye.

'Alma, all this gossip started when Ronnie left you to marry Maud. As Ronnie isn't here, the rest of the family have to bear some responsibility for what's happening to you,' Laura said finally, weary of diplomacy and mincing words.

'No they don't.' Alma lifted her eyes to meet Laura's. 'If I've lost my reputation, it's my own fault. No one else's. And I'll sort things out my own way without charitable handouts. From anyone!'

Chapter Five

'**N**O ONE ELSE is sitting down.'

'What everyone else does is no concern of yours. I'm the manager of this café, and if you want work, the only job I have on offer is vegetable preparation. And from now on that's done sitting down.' Tony dumped a chair in front of the wooden preparation table. 'Are you going to make a start or not?'

'Yes,' Alma answered sullenly, pulling the chair towards her.

'Here's your knife. There's the potatoes.' Tony pointed to the massive stone sink at the end of the table that Angelo had filled with half a hundredweight of potatoes.

'Thank you.' Alma didn't even try to keep the sarcasm from her voice.

'You feel the slightest bit ill, you go home.'

'I feel fine.'

'Angelo,' he shouted to his brother who was browning toast over a gas flame.

'I'll keep my eye on her.'

When Tony had started to work in the family's cafés, it had been Alma, not his older brother Ronnie, who had shown him the ropes and eased him into the café routine, and he was embarrassed at having to play the part of boss to her kitchen maid now. Banging the door behind him, he returned to the café. It was a Saturday night, the busiest of the week and his sisters, Tina and Gina, were dashing back and forth between the tables and the counter like yo–yos. Neither of them was as skilful at waitressing as Alma, and he picked up murmurs of discontent as the girls slopped coffee and tea into saucers, and beans off plates as they dumped them down in front of the customers.

'Gina! Tina!' He called them to the counter.

'I *am* sorry. The management appears to be having a crisis,' Tina apologised to the bus crew she was about to serve.

'More haste, less speed,' Tony hissed as his sisters approached him.

'What?' Gina asked blankly.

'Both of you are rushing it. You're slopping up, not serving the customers' orders. They're not happy.'

'We're run off our feet and you call us over to tell us that?' Tina stared at him in disbelief.

'I overheard someone complaining.'

'Someone will always complain. If you hire waitresses who look like Anna May Wong and sing like Judy Garland they'll still find something to gripe about,' Gina said mutinously.

'That's not the attitude . . .' Tony began.

'Well, clever clogs, seeing as how you know all about attitudes as well as waiting tables, you can damn well run this place yourself.' Tina pulled the bow on the back of her apron, whipped it off and handed it together with her notebook to her brother.

'Don't be stupid,' Tony growled. 'And don't use language like that. I just thought you should know they're moaning.'

'Well let them moan,' she raised her voice. 'If they don't like the way Gina and I wait tables, they shouldn't have kicked up such a bloody fuss about Alma.'

'Come on now, who'll offer me twopence for this? There's got to be two full pounds in weight here.' William Powell held a sheet of newspaper piled high with creamy folds of tripe above his head so even those at the back of the crowd who'd gathered around Charlie's stall could see what he was auctioning. 'Did I hear anyone say twopence?'

'Penny,' a woman shouted from the centre of the throng.

'Penny-halfpenny,' another called.

'It's yours.' William wrapped the newspaper around the tripe and glanced down at the remaining meat on the display slab. Unlike some of the other butchers on the market, Charlie insisted on clearing his stall of stock every night. Opening as they did only on Wednesdays, Fridays and Saturdays he liked to start every trading day with fresh meat, which he spent Mondays, Tuesdays and Thursdays preparing in the slaughterhouse.

William shivered in the icy draught of the constantly opening door as he debated which of the remaining bundles to auction next.

'What about those chop bones?' Viv Richards, Evan Powell's next-door neighbour pushed his way to the front. 'You ever going to hold them up?'

William looked at what was left. Four beef hearts, three shin bones splattered with a few meat scrapings, and the single heap of small, splintered chop bones Viv wanted. With luck, they'd be able to pack up in another ten minutes. 'OK, Viv, how much you prepared to give me?'

'A penny.'

'I'll give you a penny-farthing,' a woman elbowed Viv aside.

'Penny halfpenny.'

'Twopence.'

At a nod from Charlie, who knew just how little meat there was on the bones, William knocked them down to Viv. 'Now who'll give me a shilling for a beef heart?'

It was a procedure they went through every Saturday night after nine o'clock 'auction bell', and every Saturday night the hearts were knocked down for tenpence. Very occasionally the last straggler was lucky enough to get a misshapen one for eight or ninepence, but never less. There was good eating in a beef heart, and everyone knew it. Sunday dinner for the family, and afterwards, thinly sliced, it provided sandwich fillings for the week for those fortunate enough to be working.

While William sold off the remaining meat Charlie lifted the lid on the meat safe and checked the shelves. They were bloodstained, but empty. Taking the zinc buckets from beneath the counter, he left the stall in William's charge while he prepared for the nightly scrub-down. Two plump women, dressed in the white overalls and caps of the cheese and bacon stalls, were gossiping as they filled their buckets in the market wash house, and Charlie held back, waiting politely, and silently for them to finish.

'It's right, I tell you,' one said to the other. 'The Ronconis have put her to work out of sight in the kitchen because she's expecting. It's all over town, and Ronnie Ronconi married to Maud Powell and in Italy. Well that's one poor bastard that will never see its father. You can be sure of that. Do you know Mostyn Goldman sacked her?'

'No!' the other gasped.

'Well he had to, didn't he. It's what the Ronconis would have done if they could have, but then seeing as how Ronnie's responsible they couldn't.'

'Why not?' The question was a valid one. Paternity suits were difficult to prove at the best of times, and even if the judge was satisfied, with the father in Italy it would be well nigh impossible to extract the one or two shillings a week Alma could hope to be awarded.

'Gossip!' The woman nodded her head sagely. 'Well would you want to eat there, knowing they'd abandoned their own flesh and blood, even if it will be born the wrong side of the blanket?'

'There's plenty that won't want to eat there knowing a woman like her is working in the back.'

'You're right.' The tap was turned off and the full bucket exchanged for an empty one. 'But then, it's her mother I feel sorry for. Blind or not, she'll never be able to hold her head up in this town again. I can't think what the girl was thinking of.'

'That's obvious isn't it? The café. If she'd caught

73

Ronnie she'd never have had to look for food for herself and her mother again.'

'Well from what I've seen lifting your skirt leads more often to the workhouse than to wedding rings. But it's a shame to think she'll take her mother down with her. Lena McIver was a smart girl in her day, but then she would go and marry a Moore. Good-looking fellows the Moores, but none of them lived long. Weak chests,' the woman nodded sagely.

'I thought Lena's husband died in the pit.'

'He did, but if he hadn't he wouldn't have lasted long. Not with the Moore chest.'

With the second bucket full, the two women turned around. They paled at the sight of Charlie.

'Mrs Rees. Mrs Pickering.' He nodded to them as he stepped forward with his own buckets. The women continued to talk, even before they'd moved out of earshot.

'He's always so quiet.'

'Sneaking around . . .'

'Never know when he's there . . .'

'Sly, like all foreigners.'

Wilf Horton turned up with a bucket and stood beside Charlie. 'Bloody dog messed up the front of my stall,' he complained. 'Just when I sent the boy off to the night safe.'

'That's always the way it is,' Charlie sympathised as he stood back from the water splashing up from his bucket.

'Bloody dogs. Oughtn't to be allowed . . .'

'Tell me, Mr Horton,' Charlie interrupted. 'Do you happen to know who owns that empty shop by the fountain?'

'Which empty shop?' Wilf growled. 'If you ask me, Taff Street has more empty shops than full ones. Ponty looks more like a ghost town every day.'

'The shop that used to sell china.'

'Meakins' shop. Little wonder he pulled out, what with people cutting back to the bone. Not many have food

74

these days, so there's no point in them buying plates. He's taken a stall on the outside market now. Less working days, less money, but then there's less overheads and—'

'Did he own the shop?' Charlie pressed.

'Does any trader own a shop in this one-horse town?' Wilf retorted, using a phrase from a Western he'd watched in the Palladium. 'That place is one of Fred the Dead's.'

'Thanks, Wilf.' Charlie swung the heavy buckets easily into his hands and left the washroom for his stall.

'Looks like that's about it for the day,' William greeted Charlie on his return. The last few customers were wandering between the stalls as they finally made their way outside. Like chickens searching for grubs they darted their heads first one way, then the other, scanning the counters in search of edible leftovers which the traders might be prepared to give away.

'Missus . . . hey Missus!' Charlie shouted to a woman who was bundled up in a grey ragged blanket tied with a length of twine at what passed for her waist. 'Do you want some bones for your dog?' he asked when he caught her attention.

She nodded, flaccid lips trembling around her toothless gums. He wrapped the shin bones and one small heart, all that was left on the counter, in newspaper, and handed them to her. She ran off clutching them close to her chest.

'You know old Patsy hasn't got a dog.' Will tipped soda into one of the buckets.

'Start with the meat safe.'

'You could have sold that heart back to the slaughterhouse for dog meat,' Will grumbled as he tossed a cloth into the hot water.

'It's not worth it for what we'd get.'

'It would have been enough for a pint. You're a soft touch Charlie and everyone around here knows it . . .'

He looked up from the counter he was wiping down. Charlie wasn't listening. He'd picked up the wooden box that contained the day's takings, and pulled out the notebook he kept in his shirt pocket. Piles of farthings, halfpennies, pennies, threepences, and silver sixpences were mounting up on the shelf at the back of the stall. Alongside them lay a few florins and half-crowns. There was even a ten-bob note, but only one.

'We do all right, Charlie?' William asked.

'All right,' Charlie agreed as he handed William his half a crown wages. They'd taken nearly ten pounds, six pounds of which was earmarked to buy the next stock of meat. His boss, the Cardiff butcher who owned the stall, paid him on a commission basis on trading days. Today's share would amount to twelve shillings, a good average for a Saturday. It made up for the weekdays when the stall was closed and he cut meat in the slaughterhouse on Broadway, for which he only got paid two and six a day, the same as William. Most weeks he cleared one pound ten shillings after he'd paid his lodge and expenses. He had a lot to be grateful for. There were plenty worse off than him, and because he had no wife or children to keep, he'd managed to save over a hundred pounds. Enough to rent a shop and employ someone to run it for a couple of months until the profits started coming in.

He poured the day's takings into a cloth bag and tucked it inside his shirt, tightening his belt so it nestled against his chest. Then he bent over his notebook, concentrating hard as he jotted down a set of figures. William watched him as he wrote, wondering just when he was going to lend a hand with the clearing up. Eventually Charlie straightened up, tore a page out of his notebook, and folded it carefully into his shirt pocket.

'Lock up for me.' He tossed his keys at William.

'You trust me?' William asked facetiously.

'Not entirely, but then once the knives are locked into the meat safe, there's not a lot worth stealing. You will clean the knives properly before you put them away?'

'Don't I always?'

'When I watch.' Charlie smiled one of his rare wry smiles.

'Thanks a lot. May I ask where you're off to that's so important?'

'The New Inn.' Charlie took off his blue-striped apron and white overalls. Straightening his tie, he slipped on his jacket and coat.

'Drinking with the crache. The rest of us not good enough for you now?'

'Something like that,' Charlie murmured as he left.

William bent his head and attacked the wooden chopping block with a wire brush. Experience had taught him that if Charlie didn't want to talk about his business, there was no power on God's earth that would make him.

Charlie found the undertaker, Fred Jones, known in the town as 'Fred the Dead' standing at the bar of the 'Gentleman's Only' in the New Inn. People who knew insisted Fred was over forty, but it was difficult to tell his exact age as unlike most men in Pontypridd, he'd worn well and was always immaculately groomed. His fair hair was styled matinée-idol fashion and creamed with expensive preparations. The suits he sported on his thickset, bull-necked frame were well cut, spotless, crisp and new. Mostyn Goldman's wares were not for Fred. He patronised a Cardiff tailor and set aside a day every spring and autumn just to travel there to be measured.

Fred had left Pontypridd as a young man to join the Indian army, and in ten years had worked his way up to the rank of Drill Sergeant. He'd left only when his father, still known in the town as 'Big Fred the Dead' had died. 'Little Fred', as no-one now dared call him to his face, had kept his healthy-looking tan and his military bearing. No one ever tangled willingly with him.

He employed three men and had sons of working age who helped him in the business of undertaking and property rental that he'd inherited from his father, but he still 'walked out' ahead of the hearse at all of the funerals 'F. Jones and Son' arranged. And it was nearly always Fred himself who made the first personal call, and laid out the bodies of the crache who had money enough to purchase the best that his firm had to offer.

Charlie ordered a pint of beer. Sipping it, he moved along the bar until he stood alongside Fred, who, foot on brass rail, arm extended, was holding forth on the depression and its causes to Ben Springer who owned a shoe shop in town. When Fred finally paused to finish his drink, Charlie stepped forward.

'Another, Mr Jones?'

The undertaker eyed Charlie suspiciously before replying. 'I don't mind if I do. Double brandy.'

Charlie ordered the brandy. He stuck to his beer; it had been a long time since he'd eaten, and he needed to keep a clear head. At least for the next half-hour.

'I know you,' Fred said as he picked up the glass the barman handed him. 'You're that foreign butcher who works the market.'

'I am.'

'Don't know why we have to import foreigners to run the town's businesses when there's so many local lads out of work,' Ben Springer grumbled nastily, aggrieved that he hadn't been included in the round of drinks.

'I manage the stall for a Cardiff butcher,' Charlie explained. 'It's not mine.'

'And I suppose you think that makes it all right. But it's still a job you've taken from those that need it.'

'Is the brandy all right, Mr Jones?' Charlie asked, turning his back on Ben Springer.

'Fine.' Fred drained his glass and motioned to the barman to refill it and pour Charlie another beer.

'Could I have a word with you in private, Mr Jones?' Charlie asked.

Fred led the way to a table in a secluded corner. New Inn prices were too steep for all but a handful of people in the town, and the bar wasn't crowded, even on a Saturday night.

'What are you after?' Fred asked bluntly as soon as they were seated.

'I'd like to know what rent you're asking for your shop in Taff Street.'

'I own a lot of shops in Taff Street. Which one you after?'

'The one at the bottom of Penuel Lane that used to be a china shop.'

'Good spot that, next to the entrance to the fruit market.' Fred picked up his replenished brandy glass and sipped it. 'You know an opportunity when you see it, young man. You after it for yourself?'

'I'll be employing others to run it.'

'And what would you be selling. Meat?'

'No. Fancy goods,' Charlie replied vaguely.

'You'd have to sell a lot of those to pay the rent I'm asking. That's an expensive shop you're looking at there. It's even got a nice little flat above it. Did you know that?'

'Yes. That's one of the reasons I'd like it. But if the rent is too much for the profit margin I expect to be making, I'll look elsewhere.' Charlie finished his first pint and picked up the one Fred had bought him. 'I counted thirty-five empty shops in town this morning.'

'Not all of them have backyards, or living accommodation above.'

'Not all of them have high rents either.'

Fred narrowed his eyes. 'What are you prepared to pay?'

'No more than a pound a week.'

'That's scandalous.'

'Not for a five-year lease.'

'You're not lacking in confidence, I'll say that for you.'

'Two hundred and sixty pounds over five years, for a shop that was probably only worth three hundred and fifty pounds before the depression, looks a pretty good option to me.'

'There'll be no let-out clause in the lease,' Fred warned. 'I'll have it sewn up tighter than my wife's corsets.'

'I won't sign unless there's an option to buy at the end of the five years. I understand that's usual practice.'

'Do you now.' Fred fingered his chin thoughtfully as he drained his glass. 'All right, I don't see any problem with that. Option to buy at the going rate five years hence.'

'At one hundred pounds.'

'That's daylight robbery!'

'You'll be getting three hundred and sixty pounds for a rundown shop that wouldn't fetch a hundred and fifty if it was put on the open market now.'

'I'm in no hurry to sell.'

Charlie finished his second glass and left his chair.

'Where are you going?'

'To see the solicitor Mr Spickett Monday morning. He's acting for the estate that owns the shop next to the Park Hotel.'

'My shop's by the entrance to the fruit market.'

'The one by the Park Hotel is close to the Taff Street park gates, it will get a fair amount of casual trade in the summer.'

'Mine will get it all the year round.'

'Word will soon get about. People will always go where there's a bargain to be had.'

'Tell you what.' Fred signalled to the barman to fill his own glass and Charlie's again. 'I'll give it to you for two hundred at the end of the lease.'

'I offered a hundred.' Charlie ignored the beer the barman carried to their table.

'A hundred and fifty.'

'One hundred and twenty-five, and that's my final offer.'

The undertaker stared into the Russian's cold blue eyes and saw the man meant exactly what he'd said.

'I'll get my solicitor to draw up the papers tomorrow.'

'In the meantime if you wouldn't mind signing this.' Charlie pulled the piece of paper he'd torn from his notebook out of his pocket and pushed it over the table. Only then did he pick up his glass.

'What's this?'

'Details of our agreement.'

Fred peered at the figures. 'Lease at fifty-two pounds a year, payable quarterly . . . you said nothing about quarterly!'

'Standard business practice.'

'Comes to something when a foreigner tells a man what's standard business practice in his own country.' There was a trace of humour in Fred's voice that had been absent from Ben Springer's. 'Buying at one hundred and twenty-five pounds . . . you had it all worked out before you walked in here!'

'I worked out what I could afford beforehand. Yes.'

'Even if I sign this, it wouldn't be witnessed, so it wouldn't be legal.'

'No,' Charlie acceded. 'But it would be legal enough to make a fuss should you try to pull out tomorrow morning.'

'What did your family do in Russia? Horse-trading?'

'Something along those lines,' Charlie agreed mildly.

Fred removed a fountain pen from his top pocket, and signed his name at the foot of the page. 'How soon do you want to be in?'

'Monday morning.'

'This week coming?'

Charlie nodded. 'There's some work that needs doing.'

'How do you know?'

'I took a good look before the china people moved out.'

'Snooping?'

'I used to deliver meat for Mrs Meakins.'

'I'm not paying out any money for repairs. You take the place as you find it.'

'That's why I knocked you down on price.' Charlie finished his beer. 'If I'm going to own the place eventually, I'd like to see the job done properly.'

'Ever had the feeling you've been had?' Fred muttered to the barman as he pushed his glass across the bar after Charlie left.

'Every night I work in this place, sir.' The barman

pulled the brandy bottle from beneath the counter.

As Fred picked up his refilled glass he smiled. At least he'd managed to rent his empty shop, which was more than the poor sod who owned the shop next to the Park Hotel had done.

William had never been in the market so late. If there were things that needed doing that warranted staying behind for more than half an hour, Charlie inevitably saw to them, an arrangement that suited William admirably. After all, Charlie was the one who managed the business. He was only the paid help, although he was more than prepared to put in whatever effort was needed. He was grateful to Charlie for employing him, grateful that he had somewhere to go six days a week, unlike his cousin Eddie who worked for Wilf Horton every Wednesday and Saturday and tried to make up the money he earned by helping his father out on the cart. It was an open secret between the men in the household that Evan and Eddie didn't bring in enough money tatting to keep one of them, let alone two.

After putting on his coat and cap, William slammed the wooden shutters that Charlie had hinged across the stall, secured the padlock and breathed a sigh of relief hoping that he'd thought of everything. Knives . . . emptying buckets . . . oh well, what wasn't done, wasn't. He was damned if he was going to open the shutters again. He glanced at the clock over the door. Ten o'clock. Too late to do anything except go to Ronconi's, drink chocolate, and hope that Tina would evade her brother's eagle eye long enough for them to exchange a word or two.

Hands in pocket, coat buttoned high against the wind, he whistled the opening bars of '*You were temptation*' as he walked towards the side door.

'Will?'

'Vera?' he stared at a girl he last remembered as a ragged, grubby ten-year-old who'd lived a couple of doors down from him in Leyshon Street. He looked up at the stall. 'You working for old George now?'

'He's left me to lock up and I can't lift the shutters. You wouldn't give me a hand would you?'

'For you, Vera, anything,' he winked. Pushing his cap to the back of his head he picked up the first of the square wooden shutters, which unlike those around Charlie's stall, needed to be hoisted up and slotted into place at the front of the counter.

'Where's George then?' he asked as he heaved the last into place.

'It's Saturday night,' she said disparagingly.

'Don't tell me, he's playing cards in the back room of the Queen's.'

'You've got it.'

'Bit unfair, leaving you to do all the work.' William secured the bar across the shutters and slipped on the open padlock. 'There, all done.' He turned and smiled at her. Vera was a couple of years younger than him. Sixteen, if he remembered rightly, the same age as his sister Diana; but he didn't recall her being as pretty as she was now. Her wild, unkempt matted curls had been tamed, and there was no sign of the spots that had earned her the nickname of Nettles. Her dark brown hair was neatly waved and glossy. It framed an oval face with a beautiful peaches-and-cream complexion that showed off her brow-shaped mouth and large brown eyes to fine advantage. But he didn't waste too much time looking at her face. Her figure had filled out, and his glance lingered on the full, rounded breasts, clearly outlined beneath her thin cotton overall. If she had anything on underneath, it certainly didn't show, and he admired her capacity to withstand the cold. He was shivering through the thick layers of his jacket and coat.

'George has left me to lock up four Saturdays running,' she grumbled. 'He never used to before we were married.'

'You married George Collins?' William couldn't keep the shock from his voice. George Collins was fat, bald . . . old. He had to be at least fifty.

'He's a good man, and he takes care of me. I want for nothing.' She might have been repeating a lesson she'd learned by heart, and William realised this wasn't the first time she'd had to defend her marriage. 'He was my father's oldest friend and when Dad died . . .'

'I heard about that. I'm sorry. And I'm sorry we lost touch after you moved from Leyshon Street.'

'Mam says we should never have moved. The house we rented in Wood Road was bigger, but Mam says there's no people in Ponty like the neighbours we had on the Graig.'

'So how long you been married?'

'Four months. George is so kind, and not only to me. He helps my mam out too. She's still got five at home, and it's been hard on her since Dad died. George's money makes all the difference . . .' she stopped suddenly, realising she was saying far too much.

'Who would have thought it,' William said tactlessly. 'Little Vera and old George.'

'I'm not little Vera any more, and George is not that old,' she countered indignantly. But her protest didn't fool William. He noticed her bottom lip tremble.

'Obviously not in the way that matters, seeing as how he married you,' William consoled clumsily.

'Thanks for the shutters.'

'Any time.' He took a step forward, but something made him turn back. Vera was holding on to the padlock she'd fastened, sobs shaking her shoulders, tears pouring down her cheeks.

'Hey. Come on,' William put his hand on her arm. 'Whatever it is, it can't be that bad.'

'I'm just being silly,' she wiped her eyes with the back of her hand, but tears still clung to her eyelashes. For the first time William saw that she wasn't simply pretty. She was beautiful. She even looked good when she cried, unlike his sister Diana, whose nose always turned bright red. 'Come on, I'll walk you home,' he offered.

'George's house is on the Parade, and I know you still

live on the Graig. I saw Diana and Tina Ronconi waiting in the queue to get into the pictures. George lets me go to the Palladium with my sister every week, because he doesn't like the pictures. Diana told me that you were both living with your aunt and uncle now after . . .'

'Come on. Pick up your coat. If we don't make a move we're going to be landed with the job of locking the whole market.' The last thing William wanted was to get caught up in a discussion on the events that had led to his mother's imprisonment.

'Do you remember all those picnics we had over Shoni's pond?' Vera asked as they walked out of Market Square into Taff Street. 'That time you and your cousin Haydn fell in when you tried to catch fish. You said you were going to cook them over the fire we'd lit on the bank.'

'Just as well it was the wrong time of year for tadpoles,' he said carelessly. 'I have a feeling they wouldn't have been very tasty.'

'And then there was that time you hid Miss Jones's glasses in Sunday School, and tied Mrs Edwards's cat—'

'How long have you been working on George's stall?' William didn't enjoy talking about his childhood in Leyshon Street. It reminded him of home, of his mother, and he had never really come to terms with the thought of her locked up in Cardiff prison day after day.

'Since two weeks before we got married.'

'I can't get over you and George.' He shook his head as they rounded the corner by the old bridge. 'I always used to think that you and Jimmy . . .'

'Jimmy's in Cornwall. When he couldn't get a job around here he went to the Labour Exchange and they found him a place on a farm. He wrote to me once or twice, he seems to like it there.'

'Jimmy would. He was only happy when he was outside on the mountain. Remember that time he tried to ride one of Jones's cows in Penycoedcae.' They both laughed as they turned into the Parade.

'I don't think you should walk me to the door,' she said falling serious.

'Why not?'

'I'm a married woman now, and well, it's George. You see he can be a bit jealous.'

'After you've only been married four months?'

'It's my fault,' she said earnestly, looking around to make sure the street was deserted. 'I'm so much younger than him, and as he says, I always want to be off doing things that married women shouldn't. Like going to the pictures. And dancing . . . I really miss those dances in the Catholic Hall in Treforest. Do you?'

'I still go to them.' William looked into her eyes, shining with reflected lamplight, and recalled one evening when he and Tina had managed to evade her brothers and they'd gone round the back of the hall only to see Jimmy and Vera, and to quote Tina afterwards, 'not just kissing'.

'Oh it is good talking to you about the old days,' she cried.

'Vera, you sound as if you're a hundred years old, not sixteen.'

'Married to George sometimes I feel I am a hundred. Look,' she glanced up and down the street again. 'How about if you go down the lane and come into the house the back way? I'll leave the door open in the wall so you'll know which house it is, and I'll pull the kitchen curtains and stand in front of the window so there'll be no mistake. That way we can have a cup of tea. Talk some more . . .'

'I thought you said George is the jealous type.'

'He is. But the card game in the Queen's never finishes before three in the morning. I should know,' she added bitterly. 'He plays there four times a week.'

'I don't know . . .'

'Come on, Will,' she coaxed. 'It's been so good talking to you, and the fire will be banked up. My mother sees to that. She lays out a little supper too.' She touched his hand with the tips of her gloved fingers and his mouth went dry. He loved Tina Ronconi. But then Vera knew

that, and she *was* lonely. A cup of tea, a chat, a sandwich
– what could be more innocent?

'All right.'

'It's the sixth house down from this end. Give me five
minutes and I'll open the door to the lane.'

'Five minutes,' he echoed. If it was all so innocent, why
was he perspiring when the air temperature was barely
above freezing?

The first thing William noticed as he crept after Vera
through the darkened washhouse into the brilliantly lit
back kitchen was that she had changed out of her cotton
overalls into the same kind of silk dressing gown he'd seen
Myrna Loy swanning around in on the screen in the
White Palace. It was cream coloured, pulled in at the waist
by a belt that Vera had tied *very* tightly. It clung to the
contours of her body, leaving absolutely nothing to his
imagination, and once again he was left with the
uncomfortable feeling that she was wearing very little, if
anything, beneath it.

'I've put the kettle on. Why don't you sit down.' She
closed, and locked the washhouse door behind him. He
looked round the room. The furniture was oak, old but
good; the covers on the easy chairs and the lino on the
floor new. The bright, clean and long-piled hearth-rug
clearly hadn't seen much coal dust.

'George said I could change anything I liked in the
house. He buys me whatever I ask for in the way of
furniture, and, as you can see, clothes.' She fingered the
skirt of her dressing gown, pulling it wide to display an
expanse of smooth white thigh that sent William's pulse
soaring. 'But then I don't see much point in change
simply for the sake of change, do you?'

'No,' he agreed thickly, without the faintest idea what
she was talking about. He was totally preoccupied with
the sight of her long, slim legs, and her full breasts. Were
they really that shape? Or was she wearing something that
made them point upwards?

'I know this furniture is old-fashioned, but George is very fond of it. It was his mother's. She only died last year.'

'He wasn't married before?' By concentrating on a print of Jesus recruiting the fishermen of Galilee that hung over the mantelpiece, William just about managed to get the gist of Vera's last sentence.

'George,' she laughed, clearly amused by the notion. 'Good Lord, no! My father always used to say that George was a born bachelor. Here, there's a gap in the curtains. I'd better close them in case someone sees you.'

'What if George just walks in?' William asked nervously, suddenly wishing he'd turned a deaf ear to her invitation.

'He won't. I've locked the front and back doors and bolted them from the inside. No one can walk in.'

'Won't that make him suspicious?' William's breath quickened as she leaned across his chair.

'Not George. I always lock them in the evening when he's not at home. He calls me a scaredy cat, but I don't care. It feels so lonely here. Just me rattling around this big house. I get afraid. After living in a houseful of people all my life I'm not used to being by myself.' She leaned back for a moment, studied the curtains, then reached out again. The ends of her silk belt fell across William's face, and as he brushed them aside he caught a heady whiff of rose-scented perfume.

'Don't you like being tickled?' she teased, falling forward, laughing, on to his lap.

'That depends on who's doing the tickling,' he whispered, his voice thickening to a hoarse whisper as the weight of her thighs pressed down on his.

'How about if we try this instead.' Locking her arms around his neck she pulled his head close to hers and kissed him. A deep, long-drawn-out, sensual kiss that sent his senses reeling.

He pushed her away. 'Vera, we shouldn't be doing this.' He couldn't believe what he was saying. Here he was in a warm room with a practically naked, and it seemed all too willing, woman on his lap. She'd assured him there was no likelihood of their being disturbed and he was running scared. Was there something wrong with him? After all wasn't this every boy's dream? According to his cousin Eddie it was. Eddie was three years younger than him, and over a year ago he'd been boasting of his fleshy experiences with a naked chorus girl. The sum total of William's expertise was two quick kisses stolen from Tina Ronconi on the one occasion she'd escaped her brothers' vigilance.

But then, experience wasn't what mattered. At least that's how he, and his equally unworldly cousin Haydn, had consoled one another. It was the woman who was important. And he loved Tina. He'd told her as much. But . . .

'Will,' Vera slipped from the chair and knelt on the floor in front of him, her hands still resting lightly in his lap. 'You have no idea what it's like for me. You see, George . . .' her eyes looked at him, enormous, trusting pools of innocence. 'He's . . . he . . .' tears welled into her eyes once more, all the more poignant and pathetic for the dignified silence in which they fell.

'He what, Vera?' She looked so young, practically a child. She couldn't possibly have any idea what she was doing to him; what powers of restraint he was having to call upon as her fingers played restlessly against the front panel of his trousers.

'I expected so much when we married,' she murmured softly. 'I knew he was old, of course, but at the time that seemed to make it all the more exciting. I thought he'd be experienced. That he'd know what to do. I was even looking forward to it in a funny kind of way. You know what I mean, half frightened, half curious, not really knowing what to expect. But all he did on our wedding night, all he ever does—' a faint blush stole over he cheeks and she averted her gaze, staring down at the floor – 'is undress me. Then when I'm completely naked . . .' she looked at him again, 'I mean completely naked, he makes me lie down and he looks at me. Sometimes he touches me,' she took William's hand and pressed it against her breast, 'here, and—' she slid his fingers down over the silk to the top of her thighs – 'here. It's awful. Sometimes on a Sunday he won't allow me to dress at all. He even makes me cook and eat the dinner with no clothes on. And all he ever does is look and stroke. In the same way you'd pet a cat. Nothing more – nothing normal. You have no idea how it upset me at first. For weeks I could not stop crying. My mam doesn't know what goes on behind our curtains, but she did think that something was wrong. But when I tried to tell her about it, she wouldn't listen. All she did was remind me that I had made a promise in chapel to obey George, and that meant in every way. I went to the doctor and tried to talk to him, but he said it was my husband's right to do whatever he wanted with me, and my duty to put up with it. Then I saw my married sister. She said it shouldn't be like that. That there was something more. Much, much more.'

She lay back on the hearth-rug, watching him as he watched her. Then slowly, very slowly, she undid the knot on her dressing-gown belt. Sighing, she parted the two panels of silk.

Heart pounding, paralysed, William felt a certain sympathy with George. He couldn't have moved at that moment to save his life. He had been right. She was wearing nothing underneath the gown. And she was beautiful. Very beautiful. He gazed, mesmerised by the first naked female form he had seen off a picture postcard. Her breasts did point upwards, her skin was white, so fine there wasn't a single blemish to mar the perfection. He coloured as she looked up at him, then very slowly, quite deliberately she parted her thighs.

The word 'shameless' sprang to mind as he tried, and failed, to stop himself from staring. Then he remembered the life she led with her old, perverted husband, and felt ashamed of himself. George obviously thought no more of

Vera than the boys did of the women who posed naked for the photographs that were handed around the gym's changing room to the accompaniment of sniggers.

'Will.' She lifted her arms. 'Please. Show me that some men can do more than look.'

The next instant he was on top of her, his hands exploring every inch of her body, his fingers probing, lingering over the soft skin of her nipples, plunging down between her thighs. She moaned, and he moved back, tearing off his own clothes. His last thought, as he thrust into her, was of Tina. It was better for Tina, for both of them, that he went to their marriage bed with some experience. And with Vera married he wasn't taking any risks. None at all.

Chapter Six

HUDDLED INTO THEIR winter coats and stamping their feet in an effort to keep warm, Charlie and Evan shuffled impatiently along the line of men waiting to go in through the door of the New Town Hall.

'Mind how you go in there, Evan,' Constable Huw Davies, his sister-in-law Megan Powell's brother, called out as they inched their way past the group of policemen who had gathered in front of the closed box-office.

'I always do, Huw.' Evan raced up the wide stone steps and down the long, sloping corridor that led into the packed hall.

Unlike variety shows, the seats had been taken on a first-come first-served basis, and although Evan and Charlie had left Graig Avenue at five for the six o'clock political meeting, it obviously hadn't been early enough.

'Here?' Evan suggested, pointing to a bank of four seats still vacant in the centre of the last row of the stalls. Charlie nodded.

'Didn't expect to see you here, Charlie,' Billy Morris, a miner who had been on Evan's 'gang' when they'd worked in the Maritime pit, commented as Charlie slid into the seat beside him. 'After all, this isn't your fight, or even your country.'

'I said I'd be here.' Charlie's voice was ominously restrained.

'Looks like all the men on the Graig and half the men in the town are here,' Evan chipped in.

'Most of them wondering what a man's got to say that's worth paying a hundred pounds instead of the usual ten to rent this place on a Sunday night.' Billy pulled out his tobacco tin and filched a cigarette paper from his top pocket.

'Red Dai's stirring it up down the front.' Evan shifted in his seat, searching for a comfortable position for his long legs.

'The only thing he's likely to stir up is trouble.' Charlie looked around. It was obvious that the audience wasn't in an attentive frame of mind. He glanced behind him, wondering how many more people would be allowed in. Uniformed constables were filing in through the door, forming a line that effectively sealed off the back of the hall. A protesting voice that echoed in from the corridor outside was silenced as the door slammed. Metal bolts grated home, sealing in the audience.

Charlie glanced uneasily at Evan. The icy relationship between Evan and his wife had deteriorated even further since Trevor Lewis had brought them the news of their grandchild's condition. Usually calm and equitable in the face of whatever misfortune life threw at him, Evan had withdrawn into a morose brooding mood that no one, not even Eddie, William or Diana had been able to penetrate.

The hubbub of voices died as the side door nearest to the stage opened, and another small army of men, this time dressed entirely in black, began to enter.

'Good God, there's got to be close on a hundred of them,' Billy gasped as the door finally shut behind the blackshirts who'd lined up facing the audience in front of the stage.

'What's the matter, Mosley?' Red Dai, who'd picked up his nickname because of his loyalty to the Communist party, heckled. 'Scared to face us without a bodyguard?' he jeered at the empty stage.

The blackshirts snapped smartly to attention, their stern, set features glaring beneath their peaked caps towards a point somewhere at the back of the hall. Charlie turned again. The constables, arms folded, truncheons hooked at their belts, were staring impassively back.

The stage curtains were already open. A grey backcloth had been draped over the back wall and a row of chairs was ranged before it. In front of these stood a box-like stand, topped by a microphone. Muffled clankings and high-pitched screeches resounded from the orchestra pit.

'What the hell does he want a bloody orchestra for?' Billy bawled. 'Is he going to do a tap dance?'

Charlie didn't answer. He had a very real sense of foreboding. The tense atmosphere had heightened until it smouldered, an emotionally charged time-bomb. The first heated exchange would probably set it off.

The blackshirts stood at ease to a shouted command from their unit commander. They were an impressive sight. Not one of them under six feet, they were smartly turned out in brushed black shirts fastened by gleaming, polished buttons. They paraded in glaring contrast to the unemployed, shabbily dressed, Communist and Socialist miners who had queued since midday to pack the front rows of the stalls.

Half a dozen men, also in black shirts and trousers, walked on to the stage. A man Evan recognised as Mosley from newspaper photographs stepped forward and the orchestra struck up the opening bars of 'God Save the King'.

'That's not our bloody national anthem!' Dai yelled from the front row. 'Come on boys, let's give them ours.' He stepped forward, turned his back to the stage and waved his arms in the air. The audience, who had determinedly and quite deliberately sat through the orchestral overture of 'God Save the King', rose to a man and soon 'Land of my Fathers' echoed to the rafters, drowning out the strains of the orchestra and the Fascist voices.

Charlie, whose hearing was more acute than most, heard the sergeant behind him murmur, 'Steady lads.' He turned his head. The older policemen like Huw Griffiths were still standing sedately by, truncheons dangling from their belts. The younger ones were not so cool and composed. Most had unclipped their weapons and were holding them in both hands.

'It's just a singing contest, boys,' the sergeant muttered as the audience paused for breath between the first and second verses. 'You've seen them often enough in the bandstand in Ponty Park. Just think of it as the chapel versus the working men's club choir.'

Huw Griffiths nudged a rookie who'd stepped out of line, and Charlie watched as the boy retreated into the shadows at the back of the hall. The blackshirts stopped singing. Even the orchestra gave up trying to compete half-way through the second verse, but the men on stage remained on their feet waiting patiently for the audience to finish. The impromptu choristers, triumphant in their victory, sang their hearts out when they reached the final lines, raising the roof and deafening those, who like Charlie, didn't know the Welsh words.

Afterwards, the silence brought an uneasy sense of anti-climax. The singers shuffled awkwardly on their feet and looked to Dai for leadership.

He bowed, shouted, 'Well done boys!' and returned to his seat. Everyone in the auditorium followed suit, but Mosley wasn't a party leader for nothing. He stepped up to the microphone, and waited centre stage for absolute quiet.

'Ladies . . .'

'There are no ladies here,' Billy yelled. 'We've more bloody sense than to let them loose near a man like you. They'd skin you alive.'

A burst of laughter rocked the auditorium, and again Mosley waited for quiet.

'Gentlemen . . .'

'Why are we here, listening to the likes of him in a Town Hall that's been built with blood money earned on the backs of men who've given their lives for coal?' Dai shouted.

'He's right,' another echoed. 'No blackshirt's got a right to come here. There's nothing that he or any of his henchmen could say that would interest us.'

A crescendo of voices joined in from the auditorium.

'Everyone has the right to free speech,' Evan was on his feet shouting as loud as any of them. 'Without it—'

'Without it he'd be put in a camp where his bloody mate Hitler is starving and beating the Communists and Jews in Germany,' a voice to Evan's left screamed.

'What about the Jews, Mosley?' Dai taunted.

'Fascism means taking a pride in your country. It means a rebirth of nationalism . . .'

'It means torturing Jews!' Dai stepped threateningly towards the stage and a blackshirt grabbed him by the collar. The whole of the front row surged forward.

'Break it up!' The sergeant's voice carried above the hubbub as he used the loud-hailer he'd kept hidden at his feet. 'Break it up.'

The blackshirt reluctantly released his hold on Dai's collar. A dozen policemen moved down the central aisle and motioned Mosley's bodyguard to the side of the hall. Half of them moved, dragging their heels to the accompaniment of boos and jeers from the angry crowd.

'You're not wanted here. Any of you,' Billy yelled as the first of the line drew alongside the back row. 'Why did you bother to come?'

'You want jobs don't you?' the blackshirt shouted back in a cockney accent. 'A vote for Fascism is a vote for prosperity. Work, houses and cars for all those who are prepared to graft—' Boos interrupted his impromptu speech. He waited until they died down. 'What's the matter?' he mocked as soon as he could make himself heard. 'Are the miners of South Wales afraid of hard work? Is that why you're not even prepared to listen to what we have to say?'

'You bastard! What do you know about hard work? You ever been underground?' Billy vaulted over his seat and dived forward in a rugby-style tackle. Catching the blackshirt off guard, he head-butted him in the chest, bowling him over. Pressing his advantage he thumped his fists into the soft part of the man's stomach. Seeing the mass of blackshirts closing in behind Billy, Evan leaped over the back of his seat. Charlie tried to follow, but found himself jammed in by a solid wall of policemen surging forward from the back.

The sight of one of their own in difficulties enraged the blackshirts. Billy was felled to his knees by a well-aimed kick to the back of his leg. Evan reached him just in time to see a uniformed bodyguard swing a punch at Billy's head. All the pent-up anger and frustration of the past months exploded as Evan looked into the small eyes, pursed lips and fat face of the blackshirt.

An ardent Communist who had never missed a meeting except for those that had coincided with his shifts when he had been working, Evan fervently believed that the miners of Wales had suffered nothing but injustice at the hands of the English government for years. The pit closures had sapped pride, broken spirits and brought poverty, starvation rations, cold, the means test and the very real threat of the workhouse, to his own and every miner's family in the valleys. He was angry with everyone and everything: the government, for allowing the valleys to suffer; the town councillors who had rented Mosley the Town Hall, allowing him to spread his filthy creed in Pontypridd; his wife for her constant sighs of martyrdom and for blaming him for the joyless, daily grind of their existence; and a fate that had brought sorrow to his beloved daughter at what should have been the happiest time of her life. His temper snapped. He could do nothing to ease the greater miseries of his life, but he could do something about the bastards who were moving in on Billy.

He arced his fist wide, intending to land the blackshirt immediately behind Billy a punch on the nose. A young policeman, also seeing the threat to Billy, moved in on the blackshirt, pulling him aside just in time to receive the full force of Evan's blow on his temple.

Apart from four porters who'd called in for beans on toast before their late shift in the workhouse, Ronconi's café was empty, unimaginable on any normal Sunday evening. Tony paced restlessly from the counter to the kitchen and back, checking the stock of pies, pasties and Welsh cakes, chivvying Alma to peel more chips, hoping they'd have enough food to meet the demand of the rush he expected at the end of the meeting. He'd just picked up a clean, boiled rag to polish the steam urn when Eddie Powell burst through the door.

'Is Dad or Charlie here?' Eddie's collar was turned up in an attempt to disguise his boxing strip, but it was obvious from the way his coat flapped loosely around him that he had very few clothes on underneath it.

'No. Why, is the meeting over?'

'There's no getting near the Town Hall, Eddie.' William ran in behind him. 'The police have blocked off Market Square.'

'What's happening?' Tony asked.

'Wyn Rees couldn't get into the Town Hall earlier, so he and a couple of the boys hung around outside for a while,' William explained. 'The sergeant moved them on when they sent up to the police station for reinforcements, so Wyn and the others called into the gym . . .'

'Then trouble's broken out.'

'And my father and Charlie are in the middle of it.' Shivering, Eddie pushed his hands into his pockets as he sat down on the nearest chair.

'Both of them have got enough sense to stay out of any punch-ups.' Tony poured two teas and carried them over to Eddie's table. 'Which is more than I can say for you. I don't know about your mam, Eddie, but mine would kill me for walking around with no clothes on like that.'

'I was sparring when Wyn came in. I grabbed my trousers and coat and came here hoping to find Dad.' Eddie took the tea and sipped it.

'And I was playing cards in the changing rooms,' William complained. 'Wyn couldn't have picked a worse moment. I was just about to take a tanner off Dai Pickles—'

'Eggs and vinegar pickles?' Tony referred to the trader who sold eggs and vinegar on the streets of the town from the back of a horse-drawn cart.

'That's the one, and he can well afford a tanner.'

Eddie looked through the window and down the deserted street. 'You haven't seen anyone from the meeting then, Tony?'

'No one's been in here. It's been dead all night.'

'What do you think?' Eddie looked at William. 'Go back to Market Square?'

'I can't see the coppers changing their minds about letting us through so there's no point.'

'Well I'd best go back to the gym and dress. I can't go around like this all night.' Eddie finished his tea and pushed his chair beneath the table.

'Not if you don't want to get arrested.' Tony picked up the empty cup. 'That'll be a penny.'

'For what?'

'The tea.'

'I thought . . .'

'You thought I was running a charity shop?'

Eddie put his hand into his pocket only to realise he'd left his money, along with the rest of his clothes, in the gym. 'Will?' He appealed to his cousin.

'What am I, a bloody bank?' Will grumbled.

'I'll give it back.'

'The question is when.'

Eddie opened the door to the café. 'Crowd coming,' he shouted excitedly as a solid tide of men, flanked on both sides by police, marched up the centre of the bridge below the New Theatre.

'Are Uncle Evan and Charlie with them?' William joined him in the doorway.

'Some hope of seeing them in the middle of that lot, even if they are.'

'What's been happening, Uncle Huw?' Will shouted to Huw Griffiths.

'What we expected, a bust-up.' Huw Griffiths stood back from the crowd of marching men, close to the café door. 'We're escorting everyone from out of town to the station before any more heads get broken.' He nodded to

99

one of the younger constables who moved into the middle of the road and directed the marching men to the right, into station yard.

'Have you seen Dad or Charlie?' Eddie asked.

'I saw them, but I've no idea where they are now.' Huw pushed back his helmet to reveal a massive, swollen bruise on his forehead.

'I bet that hurts,' Tony said as he joined them.

'It does, but not as much as the one I gave back.'

'To one of Mosley's blackshirts?' Will asked.

'To your next-door neighbour Viv Richards who was throwing out punches alongside them,' Huw answered sourly. 'That little fracas has really sorted out the black from the white sheep of this town.'

Andrew paused before his apartment. He bent his head and stared at the door for a moment before fumbling for his keys. It took him a full minute to find the right one. Lurching forward, he attempted to insert it into the lock. He missed – tried – and failed again. A door opened behind him. His neighbour peeped through the crack, her sleep-numbed face topped by a garish pink and green chiffon scarf wrapped round a mass of iron curlers.

'Good evening,' he slurred, his voice thickened by beer and whisky. The door slammed. 'Bloody neighbours,' he muttered without really knowing what he was saying. The truth of the matter was, even in his fuddled state he did care what the neighbours thought of him. But then London wasn't Pontypridd. No one ever spoke, not even to pass the time of day. Never said as much as 'Hello', 'Good morning' or 'Good-night'. The only consolation was they probably didn't speak to each other either. But then who would want to speak to him, he thought despondently, if they knew about his son.

Pushing a vision of the baby from his mind he swayed on his feet and squinted at his door again. It seemed to be moving. Normally he stuck to one, or at the most two beers in an evening, but this evening the pace had been set by his colleagues and he had found it difficult to resist the pressure to join in their rounds. They'd gone out to celebrate someone's impending marriage. He scarcely knew the bridegroom, but that didn't matter. It had seemed a good idea to go with the crowd after work instead of going home to Bethan.

He dived forward, dropping the coat which he had folded and slung over one shoulder. This time, more by luck than judgement, the key homed into the lock. He turned it and the door swung open. Scraping his coat from the floor he fell into the hallway. Switching on the light, he looked out to make sure he'd left nothing behind, then pulling out his key he unintentionally slammed the door noisily behind him.

He stood for a moment bracing himself, expecting a wail from the baby. When none came, he breathed a sigh of relief and opened the door to the living room. It was in darkness. He switched on the lamps and looked around. The fire had been banked down for the night and the guard hooked into place. The hearth was swept clean, the tiled fireplace sparkling, the cushions plumped up on the sofa. A vision of perfect domestic bliss; not much evidence of the luxury that came with the kind of wealth he aspired to, but all order and cleanliness. Damn Bethan for making him feel guilty, even now when he was falling down drunk!

He threw his coat and hat on the sofa and backed out of the door, hitting his shoulder painfully on the jamb. Cursing, he went into the bathroom, reached for the tooth mug and dropped it. It shattered on the tiled floor. He salvaged his toothbrush from the mess, rinsed it under the tap and scrubbed his teeth. He ran a sink full of cold water and plunged his face into it, soaking the front of his hair, but it didn't do any good. The room still revolved around him when he pulled out the plug.

Bethan lay in bed and listened to Andrew moving around the flat. From the curses and sounds of shattering glass she knew something was wrong. When he'd telephoned earlier to say he'd be late, he'd mentioned something about a stag party, but she didn't even recognise the name of the groom, and she'd realised then that he was simply making excuses again. It hurt knowing that he'd rather spend an evening with strangers than with her, but she hadn't protested. Merely told him to have a good time. After he'd hung up, she scraped the dinner she'd prepared into the bin and went to bed. Not that she'd slept. Dr Floyd, Andrew's superior, had also telephoned earlier in the evening to ask if she'd decided where to put the baby. If she hadn't, he knew of a suitable place in the West Country, and could arrange an introduction to the matron. Uncertain whether or not Andrew had spoken to Dr Floyd, she'd thanked him for his concern, told him the situation would soon be resolved and hung up. But as she listened to Andrew retching in the bathroom she knew it wasn't going to be resolved soon – or ever – unless she did something to resolve it.

She left the bed and wrapped her blue silk dressing gown around herself. Heart pounding, she padded softly towards the bathroom. Andrew hadn't closed the door. He was sitting on the side of the bath, the shattered mug on the floor at his feet, his head in his hands, tears oozing between his fingers.

She stepped back quickly, and went into the kitchen. Filling the kettle she put it on the gas stove to boil, then ground a handful of coffee beans. It was later than she'd thought. Three in the morning. Andrew was on duty at eight, and he'd have to be sober by then. The door swung open and she started, almost dropping the coffee pot.

'I was making you some coffee,' she said apologetically. 'I thought you'd need it.'

'You don't have to wait hand and foot on me.' He kicked out a chair from beneath the kitchen table and sat on it.

'I know, it's just that—'

'You think I'm incapable?'

'No.' Her hand shook as she emptied the drawer of the grinder into the coffee pot. She looked at him and realised that as the result of his anger, or his retching, or possibly a combination of both, he wasn't as drunk as she'd thought. 'We need to talk, Andrew,' she said, grasping the opportunity.

'There's no point. You know my feelings about the—'

'I'm sorry,' she broke in hastily, not wanting to hear the cold, clinical adjectives he used to describe her son. 'Please, I just need more time.'

'I could give you all the time in the world, it wouldn't make any damned difference!'

The kettle hissed on the stove. She didn't answer him because she knew he was right. Time wouldn't make any difference. In fact it would probably only serve to strengthen the bond that had grown between her and the baby.

Andrew sat back and stared at her. It was the first time he'd looked at his wife, really looked at her, since the day the baby had been born. The light silk gown clung to her waist and hips, flaring out around her legs. The creamy lace collar highlighted what little colour there was in her face. Her dark hair gleamed, waved, shining and freshly brushed. He could even smell her perfume. She certainly hadn't let herself go, he allowed grudgingly, as he felt the faint stirrings of a desire that had lain dormant for what suddenly seemed like far too long. She looked clean, wholesome – and so very different from the grubby, peroxide blonde showgirls who had joined his party for supper.

He reached out and pulled her close to him. Her dressing gown brushed against his cheek as he clung to her. Emotions he'd held in check since the baby's birth flooded back, liberated by a sudden, overwhelming pang of pure lust. He was beset by an uncontrollable urge to lose himself and all his problems in her; yet at the same time he felt an acute sense of loss for the warm, loving familiarity he associated with the old pre-maternal

Bethan. Feelings he sensed were now beyond recapture.

'We had so much,' he rose and caressed her face, cradling it close to his chest. 'Don't destroy it, darling. Please, I need you . . .'

The warmth of his fingers seared her flesh through the light silk. She had prayed that he would come to her for months, never dreaming that it would be like this, with him pleading – and half drunk.

'I'm . . .' she looked down into his deep brown eyes and the pain she saw mirrored in their depths touched a raw nerve of conscience. He closed his mouth over hers. She steeled herself to return his kiss, suppressing her revulsion at the smell of stale tobacco smoke and beer that clung to his breath.

'Bethan,' he murmured when he finally released her. 'It could always be like this, if only . . .'

The hiss of the kettle turned to a high-pitched whistle. She broke away from him, not wanting to hear his 'if onlys', wishing with all her might that their problems would fade away, but knowing they wouldn't. Not until she finally gave in and handed her son over to an institution.

She switched off the gas and poured boiling water into the coffee pot. She sensed Andrew watching her, but she couldn't, simply couldn't, bring herself to look at him. As soon as she'd made his coffee she returned to the bedroom, closing the door behind her before getting into bed.

She needed time to think, to prepare herself for the arguments she knew he'd confront her with in the morning, but he gave her no time. He followed her, slumped on the edge of the bed and stripped off his clothes. He tumbled down beside her and planted a kiss on her cheek. She opened her arms to him, hoping he wouldn't say any more. It was easier to cope without words.

What followed wasn't lovemaking. Not on her part. It was grim, mechanical, loveless sex. She sensed Andrew was using her to forget his problems, just as he'd used drink earlier. It was as simple as that. She knew as he pierced her body with his own that he would never have contemplated making love to her if he had been sober. That it was a combination of the drink and some other woman, probably a nightclub dancer or singer who had momentarily aroused his interest, that she had to thank for his attentions.

Andrew fell asleep while he was still on top of her. She rolled him over. He lay on his back, arms outstretched, insensible to her presence and to the world. She envied him his unconsciousness as she lay quietly beside him, remembering . . . and thinking.

In the hours that followed, somewhere high above the clouds that blanketed London, dawn broke. The gloom in the bedroom lightened from dark to pale grey. Indistinct shapes of bedroom furniture crystallised and became recognisable.

Bethan turned on her side and watched her husband as he slept. His handsome features relaxed, his lips slightly parted, his hair ruffled, falling low over his forehead. Drunk, careless of her feelings, too weak to cope with their child – she loved him with all her heart. Would always love him. But she also loved another. One who had no one else, and who needed her more.

Chapter Seven

'WHAT DO YOU reckon?' Viv Richards paced the cell in the basement of Pontypridd police station where he, Evan, Billy and Charlie had been held for the past two hours. 'Charge us, or let us off with a caution?'

Neither Evan Powell nor Billy answered him. Billy sat slumped in the corner, nursing his battered head in his hands. Evan was kneeling on the stone floor next to the bunk on which the police had dumped Charlie's semi-conscious figure.

'Well they can't do much to us, can they?' Viv argued. 'After all it was provocation. It would have been a peaceful meeting if it hadn't been for the police.'

'The police? It was those bloody blackshirts,' Billy began heatedly.

'Considering no one was listening to what they had to say . . .'

'They have nothing to say that's of any interest to us in the valleys.'

'Of course they do!' Viv contradicted him vehemently. 'We're working men with no work, aren't we? There were enough of those in Germany before Herr Hitler took over and look at the difference Fascism has made to their lives. We won the Great War, but they're the ones with the work, houses and if what I've heard is right, even cars. You won't find any bloody means tests, starvation wages or depression over there!'

'We'll have less of that language or you'll be facing more than one charge, Richards,' a constable's voice blasted into the cell from the corridor outside.

'If life's so grand over there, why don't you . . . go and

live there?' Billy demanded irately, only just stopping himself from swearing.

'I would if I could . . .'

'Doctor!' the same officious voice announced sharply as a key grated the lock. Evan looked up to see Doctor John, Bethan's father-in-law, follow a constable into the cell.

'Everyone who's fit outside,' the constable said gruffly.

Viv Richards immediately stepped out into the corridor. The doctor walked over to Billy and prodded a swollen cut above his eye.

'Does that hurt?'

'Yes.'

'And this?'

'Yes.'

'Follow my finger with your eyes.'

'Nothing seriously wrong with this one,' Doctor John pronounced a few moments later.

'Outside,' the constable commanded.

'Mr Powell, isn't it?' Evan heard the contempt in the doctor's voice.

'It is,' Evan lifted his chin defiantly.

'Are you hurt?'

'Just bruised.' Evan rose stiffly to his feet. The full force of one of the blackshirt's punches had landed on his chest. Every time he breathed he felt as though a knife was being twisted between his ribs.

'Strip off and I'll take a look.'

'It's nothing.' Evan would rather put up with his discomfort than submit to an examination by the man.

'Then outside,' the constable directed brusquely.

'I'm concerned about my friend,' Evan protested.

'He's the only one not facing any charges,' the constable volunteered to the doctor.

'Don't worry, Mr Powell. I'll take care of him,' Doctor John reassured him coldly.

Hearing voices, Charlie opened his eyes. He looked at Evan.

'Tell the family where I am,' Evan whispered as the

constable gripped the top of his arm ready to haul him away. 'All of them. And tell them not to worry,' he added wryly, remembering the punch he had let fly which had floored the young copper.

It was as much as Charlie could do to nod agreement as he swung his legs to the floor.

'Charlie?' Tony stared in horror at the apparition hovering in the doorway of the café. One sleeve of the Russian's overcoat was hanging off, attached to the shoulder only by the lining. A white bandage, only marginally lighter in colour than his face, was wrapped low around his forehead, completely covering his left eye. Dried blood streaked his blond hair and the left-hand side of his face, his lower lip was split and swollen, the shredded skin already turning a dark, bruised blue.

'Are Eddie and William here?' he mumbled, looking around the café with his uncovered eye.

'They're in the back. They've been looking for you. Alma!' Tony called out urgently as Charlie walked unsteadily forward.

'Bloody hell, what happened to you?' William dropped the cards he was holding in a fan, face up on the table much to Glan Richards's delight.

'Here, sit down.' Eddie pulled a chair out close to the fire. 'Can I get you something?' Wanting to ask after his father, but afraid of the answer he'd get, he tried to remember what Charlie preferred. 'Tea? Coffee?'

'I think he needs something stronger than tea.' Tony appeared with a small glass of amber-coloured liquid. Alma followed with a bowl of cold water and a cloth.

'I'm all right.' Despite his protestation Charlie took the glass Tony offered.

'Where's Uncle Evan?' William asked.

'And my father?' Glan Richards demanded.

'They're holding six men including Evan and Mr Richards until the magistrates' court opens tomorrow morning. They were about to charge them when they let me go.' Charlie jerked his head to one side as Alma dabbed at the dried blood on his cheek.

'I'm only trying to clean it up, it's still bleeding,' she protested.

'That's because the doctor reopened it when he dressed it,' Charlie replied, pain making him even terser than usual.

Rebuffed, she wrung the cloth out and handed it to him. All she could think of was the gossip, and her outcast status. Feeling more like a leper than ever, she picked up the bowl and returned to the kitchen.

'What are they charging them with?' Glan asked.

'No doubt we'll find out tomorrow.'

'What happened?' William demanded, wanting to hear all the gory details.

'There was a fight.'

'You don't have to tell me. Red Dai started it.' Glan clenched his fists as though he was ready to take on the entire Communist party single-handed.

'Billy did when he attacked a blackshirt.'

'Billy from Dad's gang?'

Charlie nodded. 'The other blackshirts moved in—'

'And of course everyone went to Billy's aid,' William chimed in derisively. 'Even Uncle Evan who'd normally walk a mile out of his way to avoid a fight. And he calls me hot-headed.'

'Did Dad get hurt?' Now it was Eddie who looked as though he was ready to take on the world.

'No, but he hit a policeman.'

'A policeman?'

'He meant to hit a blackshirt,' Charlie explained briefly.

'And my father?' Glan persisted, wishing anyone other than Charlie was sitting there. It was easier to get money out of the dole than words out of Charlie.

'I only know they're holding him.'

'What will they do to Dad, Charlie?' Eddie ventured, dreading the answer. 'They can't put him away, can they?'

'I don't know Eddie,' Charlie replied slowly. 'I really don't know.'

At half-past five the milk cart rattled past the apartment block and the baby began to whimper. Bethan had been lying in bed, awake, waiting for the cry. Carefully, so as not to disturb Andrew, she stole from between the sheets and out of the bed. Picking up her nightdress and dressing gown from the floor she crept into the bathroom to wash her hands before making up the baby's feed. She put the kettle on to boil, then went into the nursery. He was lying just as she'd left him the night before, on his back in the bottom of the cot, his eyes open but unfocused as he made the soft mewing noises that normally preceded his cry.

She lowered the side of the cot and lifted him out, cuddling him close as she laid a rubber sheet over his eiderdown. Despite Edmund's lack of response she took her time over changing him: tickling his tummy, kissing his hand, reciting the same nursery rhymes and Welsh words of endearment that her grandmother had sung to her. When she'd finished she picked him up again and left him to kick on the floor while she took the soiled nappy to the bucket she kept outside on the balcony. After washing her hands yet again, she returned with his bottle and settled into the comfortable rocking chair that she and Andrew had bought together in that happier time, when it had not occurred to either of them that the child they were expecting would be born any way other than perfect.

The baby fell asleep in her arms before he finished half of the four ounces of milk. Usually she left him, but today was different. The events of the night preoccupied her. The late-night conversation and the lacklustre sex that had followed made her strangely reluctant to face Andrew. So for once she remained in her chair, quietly rocking the sleeping baby, wishing some miracle could make him well and strong.

At six o'clock the baby went rigid in her arms. She knew what to do. Fighting the urge to panic she rushed into the bathroom and ran a sinkful of warm water. She plunged him into it, clothes and all, careful to hold his head above the water.

'Convulsions?'

She didn't look away from Edmund, but she was conscious of Andrew standing behind her.

'Yes,' she admitted.

'You want me to look at him?'

'No. This always works.'

'He might need an injection of morphine.'

'They're never bad enough for that.'

'Then this isn't the first?'

'I mentioned them to the paediatrician when I took Edmund back to the hospital for his check-up,' she replied defensively.

'If you hadn't been a nurse you would have had to give him up at birth. You do know that, don't you?'

'But I am a nurse. And these convulsions are not that bad . . .'

'They're not good either, Bethan. Neither is his prognosis. When will you listen to sense?'

'Andrew please, we've been through all this before.' Tears fell from her eyes into the water that lapped around the relaxing figure of the baby.

'And we'll continue to go through it until you make the right decision. For his—' he pointed to the baby — 'welfare as well as your own. Tonight,' he insisted firmly, 'when I come home we'll discuss it. No more excuses, no more putting off what has to be done. You'll make your choice of place. God only knows I've brought enough brochures home. And when you've decided, we'll take him there. Together.'

He turned on his heel and returned to their bedroom. She lifted Edmund from the sink on to her lap, pulled out the plug and wrapped a towel round him. Retreating to the nursery she undressed and dried him, covering him with a thick, clean towel and blanket. She sought the sanctuary of the rocking chair, holding the baby close while she listened to Andrew moving around in their bedroom.

Obviously he hadn't gone back to sleep. When the alarm clock rang at six-thirty it was promptly switched off. She heard his footsteps in the small hall as he went to run his bath. She followed his movements in her mind's eye as he washed, shaved, dressed, combed his hair and splashed cologne on his chin; all the small routine tasks she had loved to watch when they had first been married.

She waited for him to go into the kitchen. Normally she would have cooked him bacon, eggs and toast by now. Before the baby had been born, this had been one of her favourite times of the day. They had sat and talked while Andrew ate. Discussing everything – and nothing in particular: the headlines in the paper, childhood reminiscences, amusing stories about his patients and the internal politics of the hospital he worked in. But they hadn't enjoyed a breakfast like that in months. Since the birth of the baby he had taken to eating in a silence she hadn't found the courage to brave.

Eventually the front door banged. A pang of guilt beset her as she realised he had left without eating anything. But still she lingered in the chair. Andrew might have forgotten something, he might return . . . The minutes ticked by. Five . . . ten . . . only then did she rise and return her sleeping child to his cot with an anxious check, just to make sure he was breathing.

She picked up the half-finished bottle and went into the kitchen. The coffee she had made the night before stood, cold and untouched in the pot. She emptied it down the sink. She had to think, plan out exactly what she was going to do. She tidied the kitchen and walked through the small inner hallway. The doors to all the rooms except the baby's were open. She saw their unmade bed, a thin patina of dust on the linoleum beneath it. The fire had gone out in the living room and the hearth was covered with ashes and coal dust. She couldn't leave the flat untidy for Andrew to return to after a hard day's work. That simply wouldn't be fair. But it would mean her catching a later train and not getting home until late in the evening . . .

Home – a train journey away. Money! Everything she had was in her purse. Seventeen shillings and sixpence housekeeping that was supposed to last her until Friday. Third class to Pontypridd was at least twice that amount. She could hardly go around the transport cafés looking for a lift with the baby. All the bank and cheque books were in Andrew's name.

Her heart sank at the thought of having to stay here until Andrew came home to coldly, calmly and logically discuss the removal of Edmund from their daily lives. She must have something she could sell or pawn. Her wedding ring caught the light, gleaming on her left hand. She could hardly carry a baby home without a ring, but she did have a gold and blue enamelled antique locket that Andrew had given her. It had cost twenty pounds, and she loved it, not because it had been expensive and was the only piece of good jewellery she possessed, but because Andrew had given it to her before she had become pregnant. If she pawned it, she could lose it for ever, but she consoled herself with the thought that she could send the ticket to Andrew. If it meant as much to him as it did to her he would redeem it; if it didn't, then it might be as well that she had no tangible memento of their early relationship. Either way, she had no choice. She couldn't stay here knowing how much the baby's presence upset Andrew, any more than she could abandon Edmund.

Still in her nightdress and dressing gown she picked up a duster and mop and attacked the bedroom. Stripping the bed, she cleaned the room thoroughly before remaking the mattress with fresh sheets. Filling the bath with water and soapsuds she threw the sheets and all the white washing she could find into it and left them to soak. Then she tackled the feeding bottles. It was a long journey from Paddington to Pontypridd: it might mean six or even more hours travelling. She had four bottles, and to be on the safe side she decided to fill them all.

The baby woke again at eight, taking her completely by surprise. She was on the balcony, pegging the sheets, nappies and collars on the washing line and hadn't realised it was so late. Not only had she finished the washing, she had also laid the fire in the living room. All that Andrew need do when he came home was put a match to it.

She lifted Edmund's small tin bath into the larger bath and filled it, deciding to wash him before giving him his feed. She splashed water over his fingers and toes and told him about the trip they were about to make as he lay back listless and unresponsive on her arm. Another four ounces of milk and she could have her own bath, and begin packing.

As she lifted down her old cardboard suitcase from the top of the wardrobe she remembered Andrew's dinner. He would be hungry when he came home. She ran to the pantry. There was a cold meat and potato pie she had made yesterday for his supper. If she peeled some fresh vegetable to go with it he could eat that. She looked along the shelves: a madeira cake and half a loaf of bread, fresh fruit, butter in the butter dish – he had enough to see him through tonight and knowing Andrew, he'd make other arrangements tomorrow, with his sister Fiona, or with one of the clubs his colleagues belonged to.

Packing didn't take long. Setting aside one of her three sets of underclothes and the coat and dress Andrew had bought for her wedding outfit, which she intended wearing, all she had left to fold in the suitcase was a blue serge skirt, a white blouse, her remaining underclothes and her old ringed black velvet dance dress. She looked at the two maternity dresses in the wardrobe. Deciding they could be cut down, she tossed them into the case. There was still room for a dozen of the baby's nappies and his spare towel. She closed the case and looked around for something to pack the baby's clothes in. There were only

Andrew's leather suitcases and she didn't want to take anything of his, so she settled on a roomy shopping bag. Carrying it into the baby's bedroom she folded the contents of his chest of drawers into it.

She bathed, dressed, combed her hair, and put on a little make-up, then prowled restlessly around the flat, checking for dust with her finger, making doubly sure that everything was neat and tidy. Finally she stood in the middle of the living room, holding her hat and coat, imagining Andrew walking through the door. Would he call her name? Look for her? Would he open the door to the baby's room, the room he hadn't entered since Edmund had occupied it? Would he wonder where she was? Miss her even?

She went to the sideboard drawer and pulled out the writing pad she used to write her letters home. Opening her handbag she took out the fountain pen her father had bought her the day she'd passed her eleven-plus and been accepted for grammar school. He had been so proud of her then. If only he were here now, to hug her, and tell her that she was doing the right thing. She poised the nib over the pad, and her mind went blank. It was ridiculous. She and Andrew were married, had made a child together, she loved him. There had to be something she could say. She began to write

Dear Andrew
There is a meat pie in the oven that can be heated up, and vegetables prepared on the stove. All you have to do is light the gas. I'm sorry I'm not here, but I am taking the baby home with me for a while. Should you want to get in touch you can write to me at my father's house. Please don't follow me, it's probably best that we both have some time away from one another to think things out.
I love you.
Bethan

The baby began to cry. Bethan laid the pad with her

note turned uppermost in the centre of the table and went to him. She fed and changed him, dressing him in a warm set of hand-knitted clothes that Laura had made, the only present anyone had sent her after he had been born. Wrapping him in the bedclothes from the cot she tucked him into his pram and wheeled him through to the outer hall. She laid the shopping bag at his feet, put on her coat and hat, and picked up her suitcase and handbag.

Her wedding ring was on her finger, her locket safely tucked in its box in her handbag. She was ready. The clock in the living room struck the hour. If she was to reach home today she'd better get going. She wheeled the pram through the front door and closed it behind her. She looked at the keys in her hand, then pushed them through the letterbox. There was no turning back. Not now.

'Six months' hard labour.'

'What?' Eddie turned his shocked face to Huw Griffiths.

'The magistrates' verdict. The others got six months for assault, your father got the same with hard labour because he hit a policeman as opposed to a blackshirt.'

'How come they've been sentenced already?' Eddie demanded. 'I thought the courts didn't open until ten o'clock.'

'They were expecting trouble, so they convened at six to deal with the cases from the Town Hall.'

'Where's Dad now?' Eddie asked.

'Waiting to be taken to Cardiff prison.'

'Can we see him?' Charlie spoke slowly. His head was still aching from the pounding he'd received the day before.

'Officially the answer's no, but I'll see what kind of a mood the Super's in.' Huw left the high counter in the reception area of the police station, and disappeared into the back. He emerged a few moments later. 'Super says you can have five minutes. But I warn you, the Black Maria's expected any minute, and when it comes you'll have to go.' He opened the flap in the counter, and Charlie stepped back to allow Eddie through first. They didn't have far to walk. Evan, Billy and Viv Richards were sitting in a row with three others on a hard bench in the corridor outside the reception room, their wrists linked together with cuffs, a policeman on guard duty beside them.

'Evan?'

Evan looked up. He tried to smile when he saw Charlie and Eddie behind Huw.

'You're the last people I expected to see,' Evan murmured. 'Not that I didn't hope you'd come.' He rose to his feet, but the handcuffs hampered the movement of his arms.

'No touching the prisoner,' the duty constable commanded sharply.

'Sorry, my fault.' Evan sank back down on the bench.

'Dad we'll get a solicitor . . . we'll . . .' Eddie clenched and unclenched his hands. Used to settling his problems with his fists, he felt helpless in the presence of so many policemen.

'You'll do no such thing, boy. No sense in throwing good money away.' He looked past Eddie to Charlie. 'There's nothing to be done. I hit him, I pleaded guilty, and the least I can do now is take my punishment like a man.'

'But Dad . . .'

'Six months will soon pass. You'll tell everyone I'm fine?'

'Everyone,' Eddie echoed dully, not realising his father was speaking to Charlie.

'All the family?' Evan repeated.

'I'll tell them,' Charlie promised.

'How is Elizabeth taking it?'

'Mam, like all of us thought you were only going to be kept in overnight,' Eddie murmured miserably.

'Then she's going to have to wait a while before giving me what for. That's almost worth serving six months' hard labour.' Evan smiled wryly. 'And you,' he nodded to his son. 'No late nights for six months. You take the cart out every day, rain or shine, and make enough to keep the mortgage paid. Nothing else matters, do you hear me? We'll be all right as long as we keep a roof over our heads.'

'I'll try, Dad.'

'Don't worry,' Charlie pushed his hands deep into his pockets. 'I'll see it's paid.'

'With *my* money,' Evan insisted. 'You're a good mate, Charlie, but we've borrowed too much off you already.'

'You've always paid me back.'

The steel double doors at the end of the corridor opened. The duty constable stepped out and pegged them against the outside wall. A van drew close to the opening, obliterating the small square of grey concrete yard and blue sky. The back door of the van opened from the inside and another constable stepped out.

'Move along there. Look sharp.'

Eddie stared at the steel cage inside the van; at the utility metal benches bolted to the floor either side of the back.

'Time you were gone.' Huw Griffiths laid a hand on Eddie's shoulder.

'We'll visit you, Dad. Just as soon as we're able,' he called out as Evan shuffled into the van with the others.

'Don't worry about me. Just keep the bills paid.'

'Someone's going to have to tell Mam,' Eddie said as he and Charlie walked outside into the thin, early spring sunshine.

'It would be best coming from you.'

'But you'll be with me?'

'If you want.'

'Not now.' Eddie balked at the idea of walking back up the Graig hill to tell his mother the news. He would have nothing to do for the rest of the day except sit around the house and listen to her moans. 'Later. I'll take out a cart . . .'

'They'll have all gone for the day.' Charlie led the way across the road and down the Co-op Arcade.

'The best rigs will have,' Eddie conceded. 'But if I take out whatever's left I can stick close to home. Do Maesycoed. Anything I make has got to be better than nothing.'

'It'll have to be better than sixpence or you'll be worse off,' Charlie pointed out practically. 'And your mother won't be very happy if she finds out about your father from someone else.'

'She won't. No one else knows except us.'

'It'll soon be all over town.'

'I may stop off home for dinner.'

Seeing that Eddie wasn't to be dissuaded, Charlie put his hand in his pocket. 'Here's sixpence,' he said, handing Eddie the rental money for the cart.

'It's all right, I've got some left from the money I get for cleaning the gym.'

'You sure?'

'I'm sure. You going back to the slaughterhouse?'

'I've some business to see to first.' Charlie turned left at the foot of the arcade. 'Are you all right?'

'I'm fine.'

Eddie thought about the look on his father's face as they had led him away. Despite Charlie's support he had never missed his brother and sisters so much. Seventeen years of age, an experienced boxer who had the reputation for never turning down or backing away from a fight, he was still absolutely terrified of facing his mother's wrath alone.

Chapter Eight

'YOU DON'T SEEM to know what to do with yourself, Vera.' Mondays had been special to George Collins since he was seventeen and his father had died, forcing him to take over the family business. It was his only real day of rest, one on which he didn't even have to go to chapel. A day which set him up for the busy week ahead. He worked from dawn until after nine on market days running his cheese stall, and delivering dairy goods to the valley corner shops in his van on the others. Monday he could put his feet up, read his library books, have a sort through his stamp collection, or play with the train set he had bought himself for his fortieth birthday and hadn't dared look at since Vera had moved into the house, lest she mock his childishness.

'I'm bored, George,' Vera complained, swinging her long legs over the arm of the easy chair she was sitting in. She screwed the top back on a bottle of nail varnish. Blowing on her fingers she wiggled them in front of his eyes. 'Scarlet passion, do you like it?'

'Very nice.' He pushed his glasses further up his nose and returned to his stirring tale of a shootout in downtown Dodge City.

'George?'

'Yes?' He wrenched himself away just as the hero had been forced to pull out his gun in response to the villain's threatening behaviour towards the schoolmarm.

'Take me somewhere.'

'You mean a ride. Out in the van?'

'I don't like the van,' she sighed impatiently. 'I wish we had a car.'

'We'll be able to afford one soon, if we're careful with money,' he said tersely.

'Well it's not very nice for me, is it? Sitting up on display in the front seat of a van for all the world to see. I don't know why you had to buy a van instead of a car in the first place.'

'I bought it to make deliveries, Vera. I need the loading space in the back.'

'I suppose you do.' She stood up, turned her back to him, and looked out of the window. 'It's chilly in here.' She walked over to the fire and lifted her skirt to her thighs, warming the backs of her legs in front of the flames.

'We could go up to Llanwonno for a walk. It's a quiet run and there won't be many around to see you sitting in the van. It's a pretty place.' He gave up on his book and shut it. 'Mother liked going there. There's a pretty church, old too, and some of the tombstones—'

'I don't want to see tombstones, George.' Vera plucked her skirt higher so he could see the fine lace that trimmed the legs of her French silk knickers. 'I want to see life while I'm still young enough to enjoy it.'

'If it was summer we could go to Barry, or Porth-cawl . . .' his voice tailed away. She *was* his wife, and they were alone. But after his mother's puritanical propriety he found Vera's blatant exhibitionism embarrassing.

'But it's not summer, George.'

'No I suppose it isn't.' He swallowed hard as she adjusted a stocking top. 'I know, how about we go down to Cardiff? I could buy you tea in the Lyons.'

'And take me to the shops?' she asked excitedly.

'If you want to,' he agreed doubtfully. Vera certainly wasn't the manager his mother had been. He hadn't saved a penny of his weekly income since the day they'd married. He'd even had to dip into his hard-earned capital, and that worried him. The van wouldn't last for ever. And he really ought to invest in one of those new cool-boxes to keep the stock fresh, and then there was that car she was always on about . . .

'There's a darling spring outfit advertised in the *South Wales Echo*. It's London made. You can see it in the cut of the cloth. Real crache. Real style. Howell's are stocking it . . .'

He blanched. Howell's was the most expensive shop in Cardiff. He couldn't understand why Vera didn't buy her clothes in the Co-op. His mother had, and everyone had always said she was a smart woman. Everyone, that is, except Vera. The first thing she'd done after they'd got married was give his mother's entire wardrobe to her mother. And although he couldn't be sure, he had his suspicions that some of the clothes had ended up on Wilf Horton's stall.

'. . . and it's only eight pounds, George.'

'Eight pounds!'

'You *do* want your wife to look nice, don't you George?' She leaned forward and twiddled her fingers in the short hair at the nape of his neck.

'Of course I do.' He couldn't resist her, that was the problem. He left his chair and slipped his hands around her waist.

'Not now, George. Not if we're going to Cardiff. Besides, you know I don't like you touching me in the kitchen. What if one of the neighbours looks in through the window?'

'I know,' he sighed. Twice in four months. All the touching she'd allowed him. Still, he had to be patient. She *was* very young. He had no right to expect too much. Not all at once. And perhaps if he bought her the outfit . . .

'Where did you spring from?' Elizabeth asked her daughter as Bethan walked into the kitchen carrying her baby.

'The station.' Bethan laid Edmund down on the easy chair closest to the stove.

'You travelled up on the train today?'

'All day, and it feels like weeks,' Bethan answered wearily.

'How did you get up here from the station?'

'I walked as far as Laura and Trevor's. He was in, so he brought me up in the car.'

'You called in on them before coming here?'

'The pram wouldn't fit in the station taxi. Trevor only just got it into his boot, and then he couldn't close it.'

'I can see you're used to London ways, thinking nothing of throwing your money away on a taxi. I only wish I had a shilling for every time I had to push a pram up and down that hill, and not with just one tired baby in it either.'

Bethan was too tired to snipe back. It had taken longer than she'd expected to find a pawn shop willing to give her anything for her locket, and even then she'd had to settle for six pounds, not the ten she'd hoped for. She had caught the eleven o'clock train out of London but it had been delayed in Reading, and having to change in Bristol had seemed like the last straw. She had spent an hour huddled on a bench close to the fire in the ladies' waiting room waiting for the next train to Cardiff. And there she'd had to change, not only trains but platforms, humping the pram and suitcase up and down two flights of stairs with the help of a passing stranger.

She had negotiated the top step of the Rhondda and Pontypridd platform just in time to see the engine steaming gently out of the station. She had felt like screaming, but forced to accept the inevitable, she had wheeled the pram into yet another miserable 'Ladies Only' waiting room, and fed and changed Edmund while waiting.

Exhausted and reckless enough to order a taxi when she finally reached Pontypridd, she had almost resorted to tears when the pram refused to fit into the cab. Strapping her suitcase to the pram handle with the belt from her dress, she balanced the shopping bag and pushed the pram up the Graig hill, practically falling into Laura's arms when she reached Graig Street. And despite the stew and sympathy Laura and Trevor had fed her, she still felt on the verge of collapse.

'I expect you could do with a cup of tea?' Elizabeth moved slightly so she could sneak a look into the bundle of shawl and blankets Bethan had set on the chair, but all she could make out was the top of a small head covered in light, downy hair.

'Tea would be nice,' Bethan murmured, sitting down.

'You staying long?'

'For a while.'

'Something wrong between you and Andrew?' Elizabeth asked bluntly.

'No. I just wanted to come home for a few days. London isn't like Pontypridd. It's noisy. There's no fresh air there. I felt as though I couldn't breathe.'

'Well, if it's fresh air you want there's plenty of that around here, but precious little else is being given away for nothing. I hope you can support yourself while you're here. Your father still doesn't bring in enough to keep the house going.'

'I can support myself and the baby.' Bethan looked down at her wedding ring and wondered what she'd get for it in Arthur Faller the pawnbroker's in Pontypridd.

'Elizabeth!'

'That's Mrs Richards from next door. I don't doubt she saw you coming in here and wants a look at the baby. Being the way he is I'd keep him covered up if I were you,' Elizabeth advised. She opened the passage door and called down to her neighbour, 'Come in.' That in itself was a novelty on the Graig where most of the neighbours were in and out of each other's back kitchens at all hours of the day and night. It was a practice Elizabeth had actively discouraged, and as a concession her neighbours generally came no further than the hall unless they knew Evan was in.

'What do you think?' Mrs Richards walked into the kitchen. She paused, taken aback by the sight of Bethan sitting with the baby on her lap in Evan's chair, but she wasn't to be put off her stride by asking questions that could wait. 'They tried our men early this morning. They all got six months, your Evan and my Viv included.'

'Six months?' Elizabeth echoed uncomprehendingly. Charlie had told her Evan was being kept in the cells overnight so the police could get to the bottom of what had happened in the Mosley meeting. She'd assumed he'd witnessed a fight, nothing more.

'Not that my Viv got hard labour, mind.' Mrs Richards folded her arms across her ample bosom. 'Your Evan did. But then he hit a policeman.'

'My father hit a policeman?' This time it was Bethan who was shocked.

'Oh Elizabeth,' Mrs Richards flopped her ample body down on the nearest chair. 'What are we going to do?' she wailed theatrically.

'At least your Glan is in work,' Elizabeth said acidly, her thoughts turning to money. They had just about scraped by on what Evan brought in from his carting round. How on earth was she going to manage with just the lodgers' money coming in?

'Do you want to see the costume and hat on me?'

'Seeing as how I've paid for them, I suppose I may as well.'

George was angry. His wallet was twenty, not eight pounds, lighter because Vera had seen a hat, shoes, handbag, gloves and bracelet that she'd wanted every bit as much as the costume. She'd pleaded so eloquently he hadn't really minded. Not when he was handing the money over, but then he'd turned just in time to see one of the male floorwalkers looking up Vera's skirt as he bent to pick up the handkerchief she'd dropped at his feet. And as if that hadn't been enough, Vera had stepped quite deliberately forward, in his opinion, to give the man an even better view. There'd been no question of tea in Lyons. He'd felt like hitting Vera for the first time in his married life. Restraining himself, he'd frogmarched her to the van, pushed her inside and driven straight home. And even now the minx had the gall to behave as though nothing had happened.

'Why don't you come up to the bedroom, George?' Vera called out seductively as she climbed the stairs. Despite her brave front, she realised she'd gone too far. It wasn't like George to sulk for so long.

'You come down here,' he replied gruffly, returning to his seat in the kitchen and his book.

'I'll only be a minute.'

She thought rapidly as she closed the curtains in the bedroom. Her mother had promised to leave an Irish stew and an apple tart in the pantry. All she had to do was warm them up in the oven. She was absolutely hopeless at all things domestic, a fact she only managed to keep from George with the complicity of her mother. All the cooking and cleaning in the household was done by her mother in exchange for a more than generous remuneration. But judging by the look on George's face, it was going to take a lot more than an Irish stew and apple tart to make him happy this time.

She stripped down to her stockings, suspender belt and French knickers. Slipping on the formal tailored jacket and skirt, she admired her profile in the cheval glass. The suit was pale grey with navy blue edging. 'Very chic,' she murmured repeating a phrase the salesgirl had used. She balanced the hat on her head, picked up her new handbag and gloves, slipped on her shoes and walked down the stairs.

'What do you think?' She paraded in front of George.

'All right.' He barely glanced up from the page.

'George.' She went to him, took his book from his hands and sat on his lap. 'Please, don't be a grumplestilskin,' she pleaded in a squeaky childish voice that had charmed him when she'd been younger.

'I've every right to be furious,' he replied refusing to be mollified.

'Not over this outfit. It will last for years and years . . .'

'Have you made tea?'

'Irish stew and apple tart. They're in the pantry. I'll put them in the oven now. They only need warming up.'

'When did you make them?'

'This morning. When you were putting the coal in,' she lied.

He looked over her head trying to ignore the warmth of her body on his lap. She might be a spendthrift, but at least she managed to keep the house clean and decent food on the table, he decided grudgingly. Pity she couldn't keep away from other men.

'George.' Her lips pouted very close to his. 'George, please don't be angry. I didn't know that man was looking up my skirt. Honestly!'

'But you should have realised . . .'

'You know how trusting I am. I expect all men to be like you, George.' She wriggled on his legs until her skirt rode high over her thighs. It was going to crease, but her mother could always iron it. She saw him staring at the expanse of white flesh above her stocking top. 'See what I mean, George,' she cooed. 'Most men would be taking advantage of me by now. You never have. And you're the only man I've ever really known. If I'm too trusting it's your fault.'

'You got a petticoat on?'

'I wore a thick flannel one to Cardiff. I had to take it off to try this on. The skirt wouldn't have hung right with it underneath.' She moved again, slipping precariously. He put his hand on her hip to catch her before she fell.

'You're not wearing any bloomers either,' he said accusingly.

'Yes I am. I'm wearing the silk ones my sister gave me for Christmas. See.' Like a little girl showing off, she lifted her skirt above her waist.

'Vera . . .' he babbled, aroused beyond logic.

'Do you want your Irish stew now, George?' she asked innocently.

'I think I want something else.'

She hung her head modestly.

'I *am* your husband Vera,' he reminded her.

'Of course you are, George. And I promised to obey

you. It's just that I don't like you talking about anything . . . like that.'

'Nor should any decent woman,' he reassured her as she climbed from his lap. 'Vera?'

'Yes George,' she murmured as she preceded him up the stairs.

'Do you think you could take all your clothes off this time?'

'Oh George.'

He felt an absolute brute as he heard a tremor in her voice. 'It doesn't matter.' He resigned himself to having to deal with her modesty.

'Well, perhaps if you switch the light out, George,' she agreed meekly as she turned back the blankets on the bed.

Elizabeth sat on one of the hard, upright kitchen chairs, her hands clasped together on the table, knuckles white with strain.

'I'll never be able to hold my head up in this town again. And to think my own son allowed Maggie Richards to be the one to tell me! Why didn't Eddie come back this morning? That was the least he could have done.'

'Mrs Richards has only just heard about the sentence, and her husband's involved just as much as Dad. Perhaps Eddie didn't find out anything this morning, and maybe he still doesn't know,' Bethan suggested mildly, her sympathies lying entirely with her brother. If she had been given the choice between carrying news of her father's trial and imprisonment to her mother, or running off to wherever Eddie was hiding, she knew which she would have chosen.

'Eddie must have known about the sentence,' Elizabeth protested. 'He and Charlie left here at seven for the police station.'

'It's possible the court hadn't finished by then—'

'Then they should have gone on to the court!'

Knowing there'd be no reasoning with Elizabeth in her present mood, Bethan opened the kitchen door and went down the passage. The pram and her suitcase were still outside under the bay window where she had left them. The bag containing the baby's things was just inside the front door. Edmund needed to be changed and fed, and his bottles were dirty. The soiled nappies from the journey were wrapped in a rubber sheet. So much had to be done, and she was absolutely and completely exhausted.

'You've always taken your father's and the boys' part against me,' Elizabeth said angrily when Bethan returned to the kitchen with the shopping bag.

'Mam, we won't know anything for certain until Eddie comes home.' She glanced at the baby to make sure he was in no danger of rolling off the chair, then she picked up the kettle.

'I suppose you want tea? A time like this and all you can think about is your stomach.'

'The baby needs changing and feeding. I need boiling water to wash his bottles.'

'There's plenty in the boiler in the stove, but then, I suppose that won't be good enough for you.'

'I'd prefer it on the boil,' Bethan said. 'It sterilises better.'

'There's no bed made up for you,' Elizabeth announced, almost triumphantly. 'Diana's in your old room.'

'Then I'll share with her.'

'You and the baby?' Elizabeth scorned. 'I can't see Diana being enamoured with the thought of sharing with a baby that cries every four hours.'

'He's slept right through for the last month.' Bethan struggled to keep her temper in check.

'I suppose Diana could move back into the box room. But don't expect me to start changing bedclothes around at this time of day.'

'If there's a bed in the box room I'll make it up as soon as I've seen to the baby.'

'There's nowhere for him to sleep, either down here or

up there,' Elizabeth persisted, venting her frustration on her daughter. 'I kept the cot you all slept in as babies, but your father threw it out when he cleared the box room so Diana could move into the house.'

'I have a pram,' Bethan said coldly, more angry with Elizabeth's indifference towards Edmund than with the cold reception she was extending towards her.

'A pram? How big a pram? One of those ridiculous coach jobs that will scratch all the paintwork in the hall, I suppose.'

'It is big,' Bethan conceded.

'Where is it now?'

'Outside the front door.'

'For all the neighbours to see that you've left your husband and come running home. As if they won't have enough to talk about with your father's doings.'

'I haven't left Andrew,' Bethan remonstrated.

'Well I know the neighbours around here, Miss, even if you don't. And that's what they'll be saying, especially with you producing a child like that . . .'

'I'll see to the bottles.'

Not trusting herself to remain in the same room as her mother a moment longer, Bethan carried her bag into the washhouse. She didn't know what she'd expected when she'd run home on impulse. Her thoughts had all been centred on her father; his strength, his support. Now that he wasn't here and she was faced with her mother's carping about everything from her father to their lack of money, she didn't know what to do, or where to turn. She only knew she was too drained to spare a thought for the appalling predicament her father was in, let alone cope with what was expected of her. Even the simple, mechanical things like seeing to the baby, feeding him, bathing him, washing his clothes, loomed over her, chores that demanded far more energy than she possessed.

She rinsed out the bottles with cold water and left them to soak, delaying her return to the kitchen until the mounting steam began to rattle the kettle lid. Thankfully there was no sign of her mother, and when she heard a creak overhead she assumed that Elizabeth had taken refuge in her bedroom. The baby was lying where she had left him on the chair. The one good thing about having a child like Edmund, she thought bitterly, was he always stayed where he was put.

She washed and scalded the bottles and made up two feeds before venturing back down the passage and opening the front and parlour doors. Moving her mother's prized octagonal mahogany table aside, she wheeled her pram into the parlour and dumped her suitcase next to it. One thing at a time . . . wash . . . change . . . feed and afterwards if there was time before she had to begin all over again – rest.

'Beth? Is that really you?' Eddie flicked on the light as he walked into the kitchen. Bethan started, clutching the baby closer to her. He wailed and Eddie smiled.

'I knew it had to be you when I saw the pram and suitcase in the parlour. Did you come because of Dad? How did you know about it? How did you get here so quickly? It's great to see you, sis.' Eddie's questions tumbled out faster than she could answer them. She looked past him at the old, grease-stained clock on the wall. The hands pointed to eight o'clock. She had slept for over an hour.

'Where's Mam?' Eddie asked, noticing the empty table and stove. Mindful of her duty towards her lodgers, his mother always had tea cooked and ready, and the table laid when they came in.

'She went upstairs after Mrs Richards told us that Dad had been sentenced to six months' hard labour.' The nap had restored Bethan enough for her to appreciate the full enormity of her father's plight. 'Is she right Eddie? Is Dad in gaol?'

He nodded, pulled a chair out from under the table and sat down. He wanted to move closer to the fire, but he'd just spent the last hour offloading his day's pickings in the rag-sorting sheds down Factory Lane, and an itch told him that he was probably carrying an unwelcome boarder that would just love the upholstery.

'What did he do?' Bethan demanded. 'Mrs Richards said something about Dad hitting a policeman, but I can't see him doing anything like that.'

'He did,' Eddie said shortly. 'He and Charlie went to a Mosley meeting yesterday—'

'And they got into a fight?'

'With Mosley's blackshirts. According to Charlie a policeman got between Dad and one of the thugs. He took the full force of a blow Dad intended to land on the Fascist. The last thing Dad said to me this morning was to tell everyone that he's all right. That he'll be fine, and six months will soon pass.'

'Then you knew about the sentence this morning?'

Eddie nodded sheepishly. 'If I'd known Mam would take to her bed I might have come back. But you know what she can be like, Beth.'

'I know.'

'But even so, it's not like Mam not to have tea ready.'

'No it isn't. Perhaps she went to sleep. Either way I don't think we should disturb her. There's bound to be something in the pantry that I can cook.'

'Give me ten minutes to wash and change, and I'll mind the little fellow for you while you sort it out.'

'Would you? You know he's delicate?'

'Trevor told me.'

'And you're not afraid of nursing him?'

'Of course not. I'm looking forward to getting to know him. After all he is my nephew.'

Eddie was bewildered by the expression on Bethan's face. He wasn't to know that it was the first time anyone had offered to hold the baby for her since the day she'd left the maternity ward.

Bethan opened the pantry door and switched on the light. Everything was neat, orderly and immaculate, just as she'd expected. The Welsh maxim, 'She was so clean you could eat off her floor' had always applied to her mother's housekeeping. As a child, equating love and warmth with the slightly chaotic domestic disorder of her Aunt Megan's home, she had often wished that her mother hadn't been quite so obsessive about the house. It might have made for a happier childhood but now, when she was about to make a meal, in what felt like a strange house, she was grateful for her mother's strict regimentation.

She opened the meat safe and peered inside: two breasts of lamb, already boned, rolled and larded, were stacked on a soup plate. As they'd take at least two hours to cook and everyone was expected home within the next half-hour she assumed that the news about her father had done the unthinkable – made her mother forget her duty as a housewife. She sniffed the meat and put it aside; it would keep until tomorrow. Behind the lamb she found two strings of sausages hanging on a hook. Hoping her mother wasn't keeping them for the lodgers' breakfast she took them out and looked around for something she could cook with them.

Elizabeth had always preferred to go without rather than risk wastage of food. And with money being short, her pantry was under a tighter and sparser control than Bethan remembered. Half a sack of potatoes, one of carrots, a slab of margarine, a pound of butter, a full milk jug, a loaf of uncut bread and a three-inch crust of another, a dozen eggs, two cake tins, one of Welsh cakes, one of scones, bags of flour, and sugar, packets of tea and cocoa, a row of pots of home-made blackberry jam, two dripping pots, one with pale skimmings of the best quality, the other speckled with the brown jelly that settled on the bottom, which her mother used as a sandwich spread.

'How does toad-in-the-hole sound to you?' Bethan called to her brother, settling on something that wouldn't require too much effort.

'Sounds fine.'

Lifting down the ingredients Bethan stepped back into the kitchen.

'Who's a fine fellow then. Look at me. Come on, look. Say hello. I'm your uncle.' Eddie was holding the baby firmly upright in his two hands, supporting Edmund's lolling head with his outstretched fingers as he dangled him on his knee.

Bethan almost dropped the mixing bowl in amazement. 'I had no idea you were good with babies,' she commented.

'Which proves you don't know everything about me.' Eddie tucked the baby into the crook of his arm and started tickling him gently under the chin. 'Joey Rees always gets me to look after his granddaughter when he brings her down the gym.'

'A baby? In the gym?' Bethan smiled at the notion as she broke an egg into the bowl.

'Joey has no choice but to bring her. His son gassed himself when the means test people refused to give him any money until he'd sold off his radio and furniture. A week later his son's widow ran off with a commercial salesman and left the baby with a neighbour. Joey's wife died years ago, so Joey had to either take in his granddaughter or put her in the workhouse.'

'How old is she?' Bethan asked.

'Eighteen months. And she's so bright for a dot of her age. You should see her spar . . .'

'Spar! Don't tell me you lot are teaching her to box?'

'Of course. What else do you expect us to teach her in a gym?'

Bethan shook her head in despair as she began beating the batter.

'I'm home, and I'm starving. Charlie worked every last ounce of sweat out of me today.' William slammed the front door and walked down the passage into the kitchen.

'Good God!' He stared in amazement at Bethan who stood, dressed in her mother's overall, at the kitchen table. 'When did the wind blow you in, Beth?'

'A couple of hours ago.'

'And this is my little nephew?' He walked across to Eddie and joined him in tickling the baby.

'He can't be your nephew, you're not my brother,' Bethan pointed out tartly.

'He'll forgive you for not having the sense to be born into the right family. Won't you, butch?' William addressed the baby gravely. 'Take a good long look at your Uncle William now. I'm easy to remember. I'm the handsomest one you'll see around here.'

Eddie snorted. Bethan cut the sausages, laid them in her mother's biggest baking tin and poured the batter over them. Despite her exhaustion she was content for the first time in months. Who would have thought that the boys, of all people, would have accepted her son so completely, and unquestioningly? The front door opened and closed again, quietly this time, and Diana, closely followed by Charlie walked in, bringing with them the cold, fresh smell of rain and the outside.

'Bethan!' Diana wrapped her arms around her cousin and hugged her tightly. 'It's great to see you. I was so upset when Will stopped off to tell me about Uncle Evan. Is there anything I can do to help?' she asked scanning the cooking debris on the table. 'Where's Aunt Elizabeth?'

'Upstairs resting,' Bethan replied, 'I'm afraid tea's going to be late.'

'And this is your baby. Here, you haven't got a clue, Eddie Powell.' Diana lifted the baby gently from Eddie's arms, and stood in front of the stove swaying from side to side as she rocked him in her arms.

A lump rose in Bethan's throat as she carried the dirty mixing bowl into the washhouse. Used to Andrew regarding the baby as a disgrace, she was now finding it hard to accept everyone's support.

'Is there anything I can do to help, Bethan?' Charlie, who'd hung back while Diana had greeted her, stepped into the washhouse.

'Nothing thanks, Charlie,' Bethan answered, struggling to keep the emotion from her voice.

'I could wash that for you.'

'It can wait until I do the dishes.' She turned and smiled at him, reassured by the solid strength that radiated from his heavily muscled, blessedly familiar figure. Charlie had once told her that neither she nor anyone else in Pontypridd could depend on him. That he was a drifter, a wanderer, 'here today, gone tomorrow'. But she was astute enough to realise that although that might be the way he saw himself, he was in reality very different. For as long as she'd known him he'd been there, quietly but staunchly lending his strength and support to his friends in times of need. It had been Charlie who'd helped William pick up the pieces after William's mother, her Aunt Megan, had been jailed. Charlie, who'd given William a job when he needed one. Charlie who'd lent her father the money he needed to start his rag and bone round. 'It's good to see you,' she said, meaning it.

'It's good to see you too,' he replied giving her one of his rare smiles.

'I'm off then!'

Bethan looked into the kitchen. Her mother was standing in the open doorway. The warm air of the kitchen was blowing out around her into the passage as a freezing cold draught whistled in from the rest of the unheated house. Standing in the open doorway of the kitchen was a cardinal sin Elizabeth would have taken anyone else severely to task over.

'Mam, where are you going?'

'I'm leaving, and I won't be back.'

For the first time Bethan noticed that her mother was dressed in her old grey coat, the only coat she remembered seeing her wear. Her black felt hat and the jet-headed pin she had inherited from her own mother were in her hands. Her handbag and a battered brown leather suitcase that had seen better days stood at her feet. Elizabeth jammed her hat on her head, skewering it firmly in place with the pin. 'I'm leaving,' she repeated in a voice pitched perilously close to hysteria. 'I wasn't brought up to criminal dealings. My father was a minister of God. He would turn in his grave if he could see just how low his daughter has been brought by the man she was blind and foolish enough to marry.'

'But where will you go at this time of night?' Bethan ventured practically, unnerved by the peculiar look in her mother's eyes. Elizabeth was inevitably cutting and dismissive of any behaviour that deviated from her own rigid standards. But she had always behaved rationally. Bethan felt as though the woman in front of her was a stranger. A ranting, wild-eyed stranger.

'I am going to throw myself on the mercy of my Uncle John Joseph Bull in the hope that he doesn't close his door against me in my hour of need.'

'Mam, you know what he's like,' Eddie protested.

'I *do* know what he's like,' she shouted, turning viciously on Eddie. 'He's unlike you. He's a minister of God. A good Christian, God-fearing man who knows the path of righteousness. He would never allow the Devil to lead him astray as your father has done. He—'

'Mam, it's late. Why don't you stay here just for tonight,' Bethan pleaded. 'We'll have tea soon. You can get a good night's rest, then if you still want to go, I'll take you to Uncle Bull's first thing in the morning.'

'I won't spend another night under the roof of a disciple of the Devil. My family warned me. So help me God, Uncle Joseph himself told me the day I married your father that it would come to this. And he was right. I sacrificed the best years of my life to that man. Bore his children, reared them, and look at my reward! You've all ignored my teachings to follow in your father's evil ways. Every one of you. Haydn, my eldest son, the one I had such hopes for. Did he enter the ministry as I brought him up to do? Oh no, not him! He had to go "on stage". Singing, dancing like a fool for the amusement of those who know no better than to watch the antics of a half-wit. Consorting with naked women—'

'Mam!' Bethan interjected.

'And you can talk, Miss, or is it Mrs now? Your child bears the hallmark of God's punishment for your sins. The retribution of the Lord may be slow in coming, but it comes, and when it does it is always just. You may count on that.'

'Mam, that's a cruel thing to say.' Eddie was on his feet, fists clenched.

'You dare talk to me about cruelty? You, whose only thoughts are of money and how to get it by beating people to a pulp. I wouldn't be surprised if even Maud's lung sickness stems from the rottenness that abounds in this family. Look where she is now, living in a heathen land among papists . . .'

'If you're set on going Mam, I'll carry your case.' Seething with barely suppressed anger, Eddie stepped forward and picked up his mother's bags.

'I can go alone.'

'Not at this hour of the night you can't.' Eddie glanced at Bethan and knew the same thought was in both their minds. John Joseph was as hard and unforgiving as their mother. If he refused to open his door, Elizabeth would be left on the streets of the Rhondda too late to catch the last bus back to Pontypridd. And it was a very long walk from the Rhondda to the Graig.

'I could go down to the café and ask Tony if I can borrow the Trojan,' Will offered.

'You will do no such thing,' Elizabeth retorted. 'As if it isn't bad enough that the whole town knows about my disgrace.'

Turning up the collar on his coat, Eddie walked to the front door with the case.

Elizabeth looked at her daughter. 'Goodbye,' she said sternly. 'Don't forget to tell your father what I've said. I will never set foot in this house again as long as I live. My only desire is to never clap eyes on him again. He has burdened this camel with the final back-breaking straw. I have made my last sacrifice for him.' She walked away stiffly. Bethan stood and watched her go. The door closed. It was left to Diana to break the silence.

'Here.' She handed William the baby.

'I don't know what to do with a baby,' he objected.

'Time you learnt.' She picked up the toad-in-the-hole and put it in the oven. 'Have you made up beds for yourself and the baby, Beth?'

'No. I fell asleep earlier and I didn't get around to doing them.'

'Well there's no time like the present. Charlie lay the table please, and keep an eye on the tea, or is it supper now. What do you say we make up your parents' bed with clean sheets Beth, seeing as how the room's empty now?'

Chapter Nine

'WHAT ABOUT EDDIE?' Diana protested as Bethan cut the toad-in-the-hole into four and shared it among them, giving herself the smallest portion.

'There's nothing worse than a meal like this that's been kept warm for hours. The pudding part turns to leather. I'll make him an omelette when he gets back.'

As Diana cut into the crisp batter and well-browned sausages she tried to think of something she could say to lighten the atmosphere. Elizabeth's outburst had affected them all. Except perhaps Charlie, who sat eating his meal as self-possessed and remote as ever.

'Will, do you remember seeing a cot when Uncle Evan and Eddie cleared the box room for me?' Diana asked her brother, finally settling on a safe topic.

'I wasn't around when they cleared it,' William replied.

'I'm sure there was one,' Diana mused. 'I'm not happy with the idea of you sharing your bed with the baby, Beth.' She sliced her sausage daintily into small pieces as she spoke. 'I know you. You'll be so afraid of rolling on him during the night, you won't close your eyes. And by the look of you you haven't had a good night's sleep in months.'

'I sleep well enough. And we'll manage. I think he's as worn out by the travelling as I am.' Bethan looked across to where Edmund lay on her father's easy chair, held securely in place by a makeshift contraption William had ingeniously constructed out of cushions and the kitchen stool.

'I wonder if they put it in the loft.'

'What?' William shovelled the last of the food on his plate into his mouth. The hollow in his stomach after a hard day's work had been a great deal larger than either the toad or the hole. He looked around hopefully for signs of something sweet and substantial. Fruit pie or jam roly-poly and custard, perhaps?

'The cot of course,' Diana answered irritably.

'I'll climb up the attic when we've finished eating and take a look.'

'As long as you're careful,' Bethan warned.

'You remember the time Haydn and Eddie fell through the rafters?'

'They told my mother they were looking for treasure. She wasn't very amused. It cost a fortune in plasterboard to repair the ceiling to my bedroom,' Bethan explained to Diana and Charlie.

'I'll go up there if you like,' Charlie offered.

'Thank you.'

'That's great, Beth. You let him go not me,' William grumbled.

'He's lighter on his feet than you,' Diana pointed out.

'He may be lighter on his feet but he's heavier overall.'

Despite Diana's brave attempts, the mood remained strained. Exhaustion coupled with the emotional upset of her mother's leaving had made Bethan lightheaded, and when Diana suggested, to William's chagrin, that she clear the dishes, Bethan was happy to take her up on the offer. She changed Edmund and gave him his last feed while William and Charlie went rummaging upstairs. William emerged triumphant ten minutes later, with cobwebs in his hair, dust streaked down his nose and a large parcel wrapped in an old sheet.

'We've put the big cot in your dad's bedroom, Bethan,' he said, self-consciously omitting Elizabeth's name. 'It was in pieces so Charlie's screwing it together. But look what else I found.' He pulled the sheet back to reveal a beautiful hand-carved oak cot. Set low on wide bowed rockers it had high sides and an overhanging fretwork canopy to shield the precious occupier from draughts.

'Mam Powell's old family cot!' Bethan exclaimed in

delight. 'I'd forgotten all about it. I remember you sleeping in it and Diana, and Maud. Mam Powell told me her grandfather carved it for her mother when she was born.'

'Then it must be a fair old age now.' William held it up to the light and looked it over with a keen eye. 'The wood's split in one or two places, but there's nothing serious that I can see. A clean-up, oiling, a bit of polish, a good dry-out in front of the fire and it will be as good as new. In fact if I get to work on it right away you'll probably be able to use it tomorrow.'

'The perfect day cot for down here. Will, you're a genius.' Bethan was so pleased she kissed him on the cheek.

'No slop please.' He made a wry face as he rubbed the spot she'd kissed with his handkerchief. 'You're a married woman now, and I'm a very handsome eligible bachelor. What *would* cashmere coat say if he could see you?'

Bethan fell silent. The cot wasn't the only thing she'd forgotten about. The nickname her brothers and William had bestowed on her husband held just the right ring of valley contempt for the crache. Exactly the kind of contempt the younger male Powells had reserved for Andrew.

'Will the other cot need airing?' Diana asked as she walked in from the washhouse with the dishcloth in her hand.

'It's painted iron. Does that need airing? It's certainly cold enough.'

'Iron doesn't need airing, you fool.'

'The mattress will though. It's been wrapped in rubber sheeting, but it still feels damp to me.'

'Of course it's damp,' Diana countered impatiently. 'It's been in the attic, you stupid boy.'

'I am neither a boy nor stupid . . .'

'Did you bring the mattress downstairs?' Bethan asked tactfully in an attempt to divert her cousins' attention.

'No, I couldn't carry it and this at the same time.'

William set the cot down on the hearth-rug.

'I'll go up and take a look at it.' Diana opened the door.

'I didn't mean for you to go running about,' Bethan protested. 'You've been working all day.'

'You sit there and feed the baby,' Diana smiled. 'You look very pretty, like an advertisement for motherhood.'

An hour later Diana had organised everything. Both cots had been washed and disinfected, inside and out. The mattress Elizabeth had so carefully stored in rubber sheets had been placed in front of the stove to air. Diana had made up the baby's bed, substituting a folded bolster for the mattress, and using pillowcases instead of sheets.

'It's only for one night,' she told Bethan as she came downstairs with the slop bucket. 'And now everything's ready, I suggest you take yourself and your baby up the wooden hill and get a good night's sleep.'

'I should wait for Eddie to get back.'

'I'll wait up for Eddie.'

'But you've got work in the morning.'

'One late night isn't going to kill me. Go on, off with you.'

'I really should talk to Eddie.'

'The kind of talking you two have to do is probably best left until morning. Neither of you can set the world, or your mam and dad, to rights tonight.'

'Yes mother,' Bethan joked, relieved to offload her problems on to Diana's willing shoulders for one night.

'See you in the morning.' Diana took the baby's bottle from Bethan's hand. 'I'll wash this, and in case you start looking for it, I've carried your case upstairs. All you have to do is undress and get into bed.'

Bethan glanced at the clock as she left her chair. It was half-past nine, way past the bedtime hour she had made Edmund adhere to in London. 'Thanks a million, Diana. What would I do without you?' she murmured, exhaustion and emotion making her tearful.

'You'd be just fine,' Diana retorted firmly. 'Everything will seem a whole lot better in the morning, Beth. You'll see.'

'It can't be any worse, and that's for sure,' William muttered darkly from behind the detective novel Evan had borrowed from the Central Lending Library.

Charlie sat quietly in one of the easy chairs until Bethan went upstairs, then he walked down the hall and picked up his coat from a hook behind the front door.

'Pint in the Graig?' Will asked, looking up from the book he was only half reading, in the hope Charlie would ask him along. Normally he would have gone down the gym with Eddie, not to box, but for company and a card game. No one had the money to do very much on a week night and it was easy for boredom to set in. But he knew better than to try to go anywhere with Charlie uninvited.

'Just a walk,' Charlie answered flatly as he went outside. He closed the door behind him and stood on the doorstep for a moment. It was a cold, crisp, clear night. Stars shone down, glittering spangles in a navy blue velvet sky. A sharp new moon silvered gossamer wisps of clouds as they drifted slowly across its pitted surface. The perfect night for a walk. After the strain of the day, Charlie had a sudden craving for clean, fresh air.

Reaching into his pocket for a cigarette, he descended the steps and walked out on to the unmade road. Iced by a thin layer of frost, the bare earth crunched beneath his feet as he turned right towards the end of the Avenue and the beginning of the mountain. If it hadn't been for the glow of the street lamps and the distant whine of a bus battling to climb up the Graig hill he could have been the last man left on earth. The thought wasn't an unpleasant one.

The front windows of the houses he passed were shrouded in darkness. Everyone in Graig Avenue lived out their waking lives in the warmth of their back kitchens, leaving bedtime and their freezing bedrooms until the last possible moment. He bent his head and struck a match. Inhaling deeply on the strong tobacco, he climbed towards the crest of the mountain. He had always

144

sought peace and solace in nature rather than the company of other men, and after witnessing Elizabeth's savage outburst he felt he didn't have to justify his preference to himself, or others, ever again.

As his eyes grew accustomed to the darkness, his pace quickened. He reached a large flat stone lightly padded by coarse, wiry whinberry plants. It made the ideal seat. Wrapping his arms around his knees, he propped his chin on his hands and continued to smoke. Below him, lit by street and kitchen lamps, lay the backs of the houses that ribboned the lower slopes of the Graig. The cubes of coal-houses and ty bachs, divided by garden walls and fogged by smoke from low-built chimneys, stood in regimented rows. An ex-miner walked into a backyard in Danygraig Street. Charlie knew he'd worked on the coal-face by the sound – a foul, lung-wrenching cough that could never ruffle the surface of the thick layer of dust that had settled on his chest. He counted himself fortunate that he hadn't had to resort to making a living in the pits.

If only he could be sure he was doing the right thing. Opening the shop meant working for himself, tying himself to a building, putting down roots, making himself responsible for the welfare and well-being of others. Something he had sworn he would never do again. And he didn't have to look far for the motive that had caused him, if not to forget, then at least to set aside his promise to himself.

Alma? He pictured her slim figure bending, swaying to avoid people as she walked through the crowded market. She reminded him of reeds wavering in the winds that had blown around a lake, where – 'back home'? He had to stop thinking of back home. He had no home now.

He shivered and pulled the lapels of his coat high around his neck, wishing he'd brought his muffler. Winters had been cold in Russia too. But not damp. Never damp, with this insidious chill that permeated the bones and joints, making the middle-aged creak like ninety-year-olds. Would that happen to him if he remained in Pontypridd?

No matter how he tried to look at it, one of the reasons for renting the shop and setting up in business was Alma. Ever since he'd held her in his arms he hadn't been able to stop thinking about her. The gossip he'd overheard in the market worried him. He knew just how harsh and unforgiving a face the town could present to a girl who'd lost her reputation. He'd seen it with Bethan Powell before Andrew John had come back to Pontypridd to get her. How much closer had the loss of her morning job put Alma to the breadline? Was she really making ends meet?

Strange, when she'd been Ronnie Ronconi's girl he'd scarcely given her a second thought. She'd simply been the pleasant waitress who'd served him every time he went into the café. After Ronnie left he'd noticed she'd lost weight, looked ill, but her plight hadn't really touched him. Not until the night she'd collapsed.

He wanted to offer Alma a full-time job in his shop. Afraid that something might go wrong, he'd put off approaching her until everything was signed and sealed, but as of that morning the place was his. He was stuck with it – but what if she wouldn't work for him? There were plenty of others who would jump at the chance. The problem was, another girl wouldn't be the same as Alma.

Charlie tried to examine his motives objectively. Didn't he simply want to make some money to put behind him against – against what? The time he returned to Russia? There was no going back. He had known that the day he'd jumped ship in Cardiff docks. But it wasn't as if he was thinking of settling down with the girl. He had, after all, only signed a lease. It was simply a matter of getting the shop on its feet. Six months, a year at the most, then if he wanted to he could sell it as a going concern, and sign the lease over at a profit. He had checked that the solicitor had put a transfer clause into the document. William was a good lad, a bit headstrong but he was a hard worker. If he signed the business over to William, he'd get his money back – eventually.

So what was he worried about? He didn't have to

stay in Pontypridd one day longer than he wanted to. There was nothing more to keep him in Wales today than there had been yesterday. Nothing except a reed-slim girl with red hair, witching green eyes, and pride enough to hold her head high, even when the whole town condemned her for falling in love with a man who had deserted her.

He dropped his cigarette and trod on it. If he wasn't careful Alma Moore could become a problem. But then, he hadn't offered her the job yet, and when he did there was a chance she might not take it. But if she did? The little devil voice echoed in his mind as he rose stiffly to his feet and descended the hill. If she did, he'd have to watch himself, that was all. He had survived eight years without getting too close to people. He could survive a few years more until – when?

The future loomed cold, empty, terrifying in its grey solitude. He shivered. He hadn't allowed himself to think about where he was going for eight long years. He dare not break that habit. Not now.

Graig Avenue was still peaceful and deserted. Charlie walked swiftly and quietly close to the high wall that enclosed the back gardens of Phillips Street. Pausing outside the door of the house opposite the Powells' he listened. A dog barked in the distance. Boots rang over the paved area around the corner in Llantrisant Road. Even if whoever was making the noise was turning into Graig Avenue, he still had a few minutes. Pressing down the latch he stepped down into the back garden of the first house in Phillips Street and closed the door quickly behind him. He walked down the well-trodden centre path that bisected the tiny area, negotiated a narrow flight of steps and lowered himself into a small enclosed yard. To his left, fine threads of light peeped between the folds of a pair of unusually thick curtains. In front of him the greyish white paint of the washhouse door glimmered in the darkness. He knocked before opening it.

'Mrs Pugh, Miss Harry,' he called so they wouldn't be alarmed. 'It's Charlie.'

The kitchen door opened and a cloud of warmth gusted out to greet him. Phyllis Harry, middle height, thin faced, appeared in the doorway. She smiled as she ran her fingers through her greying, mousy hair.

'Come in, Charlie. It's good to see you. Can I get you a cup of tea?'

'No thank you, Miss Harry.' He followed her into Rhiannon Pugh's kitchen, ducking his head below the low lintel of the washhouse door. The room was bright and cosy, a hard-working poor woman's room, glowing with multicoloured rag rugs, hand-knitted cushion covers and patchwork curtains. A cardboard box of home-made rag dolls and knitted animals stood in the corner.

'Charlie.' Rhiannon Pugh, well into her seventies and crippled by arthritis and bronchitis, nodded to him. Charlie looked from her to Phyllis and saw they already knew what he had come to tell them.

'Mr Roberts from next door called in this morning. He told us that Evan has been sentenced to six months' hard labour.'

'I saw Evan before they took him away. He told me to tell you he's fine, and six months will soon pass.'

'Typical Evan,' Phyllis smiled as she shook her head fondly.

'It will be hard on Elizabeth,' Rhiannon wheezed. Much as she loved Phyllis, who was more like a daughter than a lodger, she couldn't resist reminding her that the love of her life and father of her child also had a wife.

'She has taken it hard,' Charlie agreed shortly without elaborating.

'Will you be walking through?' Phyllis asked. Rhiannon had lived all her live in Phillips Street, and to spare her neighbours the long walk around Vicarage Corner allowed her house to be used as a thoroughfare between Graig Avenue and the streets below her own. It was a shortcut that had served Phyllis well. It was impossible to watch the front and back doors of the house at the same time, and even the most determined gossip had been unable to hazard a guess as to the identity of the father of her child.

'If that's all right with you, Mrs Pugh,' Charlie said, thinking that a beer with a whisky chaser drunk in the warm, masculine atmosphere of the bar of the Graig Hotel would go down extremely well.

'I'll see you out.' Phyllis closed the kitchen door behind her as she led the way to the front of the house.

'Miss Harry . . .'

'Phyllis.' She had told Charlie to call her by her Christian name at least a dozen times, but he never did.

'If you and the boy need anything, you will ask me?'

Phyllis looked at him proudly. 'We're fine Charlie, but thank you for the offer.'

Charlie'd had enough of stubborn Welsh pride in one day to last him a lifetime. He put his hand in his pocket and pulled out a ten-pound note. It was one of five he'd taken out of the bank to buy essential building materials and stock for his shop, and represented a tenth of his capital. 'Evan asked me to give you this.'

Phyllis stared at it in disbelief. 'Where did Evan get ten pounds from?' she demanded suspiciously.

'He's been saving. He wanted you to have it.'

'Not his wife?' Phyllis asked wryly.

'Eddie can keep the business going and the bills paid until Evan gets out.'

'I suppose he can.' Phyllis didn't want to take the money, but she had little choice. The savings she'd put by in the Post Office during twenty years of work as a cinema usherette in the White Palace were almost at an end. Now that Evan was out of reach he wouldn't be able to pay her the five shillings he had slipped her every week without fail since their son's birth. And although Rhiannon was very generous, her widow's pension didn't go far.

Charlie thrust the note into her hand.

'Will you be seeing him?'

'I hope to.'

'Thank him for me, and explain why I won't visit.'

'I will.'

'I'd write, only it might cause complications. They do open letters addressed to prisoners, don't they?'

'Probably.'

'You'll call in again?' she pressed, reluctant to let him go. He was a link, albeit a tenuous one, with Evan. And she was dreading the next six months without Evan Powell's nightly visits.

'Yes. You may see Bethan walking through,' he added, remembering that Bethan had often stopped to talk to Phyllis even when others had passed by.

'Bethan's home?' Phyllis smiled broadly. 'Tell her to call in when she has time.'

'I will. Goodnight.'

Charlie walked down the front steps and along the road towards the Graig hotel. He wondered why life in the Welsh valleys always had to be so complicated. It had been a great deal simpler in his home village in Russia. When Igor the bootmaker had left his attractive, shrewish wife for a plain, but gentle and kind widow, no one had blamed him. The gossips had targeted the shrew, not the widow, and he was sure if Evan made a similar move he would receive the same absolution from his neighbours. Elizabeth Powell's character was well known on the Graig, and Graig people were more inclined to sympathise with a man's ungodly mistress than a hard, unforgiving saint of a wife.

If he'd been offered the choice of living with Elizabeth or Phyllis he knew which he'd prefer. It was strange: physically the two women weren't dissimilar. Poverty had drawn the same angles and thin, spare features into Phyllis's frame as Elizabeth's, but their characters couldn't have been more unalike. Phyllis Harry's wasted cheeks and tired eyes radiated a warmth and compassion that Elizabeth was incapable of feeling. A warmth all the Powells could benefit from, especially Bethan.

*

Head down, a woollen scarf wrapped high around her neck and a cotton one tied cornerwise over her hair to protect it from the rain, Alma walked quickly down the dark street. The road gleamed like polished pewter and the fine drizzle haloed the lamplights, but Alma was too nervous to appreciate the beauty of the scene. She had never liked walking through the town late at night, but now that the gossips were shredding her reputation she hated it even more. What if someone should recognise her? Say something to her face? Or start denouncing her as Freda and Mary had done? A scene late at night in town was bound to be heard by the people who lived above their shops.

She slowed her steps as she heard the ringing of a pair of heels on the pavement and looked nervously over her shoulder. Blank panes of glass gleamed from the darkened shop windows. All she could hear was the pulsating drumbeat of blood in her veins, and the sound of her own laboured breath. She fought to subdue panic, straining her eyes as she peered into a cluster of shadows in the doorway of Heath's piano shop. Were they really shadows? Or a tall man wearing a trilby? She stepped up her pace, the throbbing of her heartbeat vying with the tapping of her steps on the pavement.

If Tony had mastered driving the Trojan she would have swallowed her pride and asked him to give her a lift home as Ronnie had done every night she had worked late. It was barely five minutes' drive in the slow, lumbering van, but a good fifteen minutes on foot. She had a sudden, very real picture of herself sitting in the van next to Ronnie, his left hand resting on her knee, a cigarette dangling carelessly from his lips. It conjured up memories of sweet, loving intimacy. But even if Tony had mastered driving the van, he might not want to take her home. Particularly if his parents were aware of the gossip.

What she hated most about Ronnie's desertion was that she'd been left with no real friend to turn to. Ronnie had been everything to her: lover, friend, holder of her deepest, and most private secrets. Now there was only her mother, who had been more burden than help to her for the last few years. She pulled herself up sharply; how could she ever consider her mother a burden? If she was in trouble, it was her own stupid fault. If she had no friends, it was because she had relied on Ronnie too much – for everything. Even now she had him to thank for her job, the food on her table and the roof over her head. Laura would never have helped her when she'd been in hospital if it hadn't been for Ronnie. If only she didn't miss him so much! His physical presence, his caustic wit, sarcastic repartee, but most of all the close, loving, physical relationship they had shared. It was hard for her to remember, even now when he was in Italy married to Maud, that she had loved him so much more than he had loved her.

The clock on St Catherine's struck twelve as she reached the corner by the YMCA building. She had to stop thinking about Ronnie. The past was past. She had more immediate problems to solve, like how to keep the worst of the gossip from her mother, and how to pay the bills on half a wage. She'd started back to work; that was the first positive step. Laura had said something about more money but she hadn't said how much more, and like a fool Alma hadn't thought to ask. She had to start saving as well to pay Laura what she owed, but how could she?

Her mother's pension of five shillings a week didn't even cover the rent. And now she was down to eight shillings – maybe nine if Tony was generous – a week. Where could they cut back? A cheaper house? They didn't come much cheaper than Morgan Street. Coals? Her mother usually only lit the range three days a week and they needed it to cook on. Clothes? They only bought them now as presents on birthdays and at Christmas. Food? It had to be food, but it was difficult to see where . . .

'Walk you round the corner, Alma?'

She whirled round. Bobby Thomas was standing behind her.

'You been following me, Bobby?' she demanded.

'Would I do a thing like that?'

'Yes.'

'You were going my way so I thought I'd just check to make sure you get home all right.'

'I'm fine thank you,' she said icily, walking on.

'Proper Miss Hoity Toity, aren't you?' He took hold of her arm. She struggled to free herself from his grip but he propelled her across the road.

'If you don't let go of me, now, this minute, I'll scream,' she threatened.

'What and wake up all the good people who are asleep in their beds? You don't want to do that, Alma. It would only give them something else to say about you.'

'I don't know what you mean.'

'Don't play the wide-eyed innocent with me.' He kept a firm grasp on her arm above her elbow as they walked up the hill towards Morgan Street. 'Mary and Freda have been telling everyone in town about you.'

'Telling them what?'

'As if you didn't know! How about it, Alma? I might not have a café, but I do have a lot of other things to offer.'

'How about you let go of me?' she said coldly, still trying to shrug off his grip.

'I'm Fred Jones's right-hand man,' he whispered. 'I can always put a word in if you can't make your rent.'

'My rent is paid up to date.'

'Only because your old boyfriend's sister has been paying it. Sooner or later she's going to get tired of forking out for someone else's bills. Take my word for it.' His hand travelled up to her chin as he pulled down the scarf she had wound around her throat. 'What you need, Alma, is a bit of security.' He caressed the nape of her neck with his thumb and forefinger. 'I'd be only too happy to look after you.'

'I can look after myself.'

'Not that well from what I've heard. Come on Alma,' he wheedled. 'You've put a smile on a few fellows' faces, what's one more? You'll not find me ungrateful, I promise.'

'And what would your wife say if she could hear you now, Bobby Thomas?' Unequal to struggling against his strength she finally stopped walking and faced him, hoping to shame him into leaving her alone.

'What the eye don't see, the heart don't grieve. Now how about you invite me in for a quick cup of tea. Your mam's gone to bed.' He nodded towards the dark windows in her house lower down the street.

'There's no point in lighting lamps for the blind.'

'She's always in bed by nine. I know. I collect the rent, remember.'

'I wouldn't invite you over our front doorstep if you were the last man on earth.'

'That's because you don't know me yet the way I'd like you to.' He inched his hand inside the top of her coat.

'Let go of me, or I swear to God I'll scream loud enough to bring the police running.'

'Well if you're prepared to risk it.' He heaved her towards him, tearing the buttons from her coat. He bent his head to kiss her but she turned aside, and his lips brushed wetly against her hair. 'A few liberties are nothing to a girl like you.' He thrust his hand inside her open coat and squeezed her breast. 'After all it's not as if I'm going to get you in the family way, you're already there. Come on, ten minutes with me will clear your rent for a week.'

She thrust her hand into his thinning hair, gripped and yanked hard.

'Ow!' he yelped. 'You little bitch . . .'

She kicked his shin, turned and ran towards her front door. For the first time in her life she bolted it behind her, but she could still hear him calling after her.

'You turn your rent in just one hour late, and you'll find out what's what, Alma Moore. Just one hour late and you'll wish you'd come crawling to me when you had the chance.'

'Alma,' her mother's querulous voice floated down the stairs.

'Coming, Mam.' She straightened her coat, too flustered to remember that her mother couldn't see it, and climbed the stairs, feeling her way in the darkness. 'Can I get you anything?' She pushed open the door to her mother's bedroom.

'You all right Alma? I heard shouting.'

'I'm fine, Mam.' She struggled to keep her voice calm and even, knowing that her mother was sensitive to the slightest tremor.

'Was there someone out there with you?'

'Only Bobby Thomas the rent man.'

'We don't owe anything do we?' Mrs Moore asked anxiously.

'Nothing,' Alma replied firmly. 'If you don't want anything I'll go to bed, Mam. I'm tired.'

'Alma, are you in the family way?'

'No!'

'Mrs Lane told me you were. She heard it in the shop tonight. She said she thought she ought to tell me before someone else did. I would have rather heard it from you.'

'I'm sorry people are telling you lies, Mam. But I promise you, I'm not anything of the kind.'

'Then why are people saying that you are?'

'Because I was ill. Because I went into hospital, and,' she took a deep breath, 'because Ronnie Ronconi has gone to Italy.'

'But Alma you can't just let people say what they like about you. You've got to do something. Otherwise your reputation—'

'Mam if you can think of something I can do, I'll do it,' Alma interrupted angrily.

'Ronnie Ronconi – you didn't do anything you shouldn't have with him, did you? I warned you how dangerous talk can be to a young girl like you, with no father to care for her. If men think you're not a decent woman they'll try to take advantage . . . they'll . . .'

'I'm beginning to find out just what *they'll* do, Mam.'

'I suppose there's nothing you can do except brazen it out.' Lena Moore's voice was tired, resigned, tremulous with unshed tears. 'I only hope the minister doesn't get to hear any of this.'

'I couldn't give a damn if he does.'

'Alma, your language. If you talk like that no wonder people are gossiping. They say there's no smoke without fire. Mr Ronconi never did anything to you, did he? I mean . . .'

'He never did anything to me that I didn't want him to,' Alma interrupted shortly.

'What kind of an answer is that?'

'Whatever he did, it's not important now. He's gone and he won't be back.'

'Well I suppose there's nothing for it. I'll have to stand by you no matter what. A lot wouldn't. Mrs Higgins down the road had her daughter put away for less.'

'I know, Mam.'

Alma stood in silence for a moment listening to the mattress creak and groan as her mother turned over.

'There never was any insurance money, was there?' her mother whispered as she settled back on her pillows.

'No there wasn't,' Alma admitted harshly.

'Then how are we going to live?'

'As best we can, Mam.' Alma closed the door and went into her own bedroom. 'As best we can,' she repeated as she arranged the threadbare curtains over her window.

Chapter Ten

'DON'T WORRY, SIS, we'll manage somehow, we always do.' Evan pinched Bethan's cheek gently as she scooped fried bread on to his plate.

'I wish I could be as optimistic as you. You sure Mam didn't say any more to you last night?'

'Not a word. I told you, she wouldn't even sit next to me on either of the buses. I carried her case to Uncle Joe's door for her. She rang the bell, he opened it, they went inside, and that's the last I saw of her. No goodbye, nothing.'

'You sure he didn't throw her out later?'

'I waited ten minutes. Any longer and I would have missed the last bus home. Look Beth, we'll manage without Mam. We'll be fine.'

'It's not us I'm worried about.'

'After what she said to you about the baby, you're worried about Mam?'

She tried to smile at him as she sat on the chair that had been hers. What was it her grandmother used to say? 'Count your blessings.' Well she'd better start now.

The first night without Elizabeth had gone remarkably peacefully, and already she could detect an absence of strain without her mother's presence lying like a frost over the household. Even the morning rush had gone well. Will, Diana and Charlie had raced around the kitchen like whirlwinds while she'd fed the baby, making their own breakfasts, cleaning their shoes, and all in a mad dash that would have had her mother shouting at them a dozen times over about opening doors, causing draughts and carrying dirt through to the kitchen from the outside yard.

'Well even if we're going to be "all right" I still need to know what the bills are on this place if I'm going to manage the money,' she said at last. 'Do you know what the mortgage is?'

'Seventeen bob a week.'

'Seventeen shillings! But Dad's been paying it off for years and his father before him.'

'He remortgaged it to buy out his mother and brother, and . . .' Eddie concentrated intently on the bread on his plate, slicing it into small triangles.

'And?' Bethan demanded.

'You're not to tell a soul this.' Eddie looked over his shoulder, even though he'd heard the others leave for work. 'He borrowed another twenty a while back. I only know about it because he dropped the papers when he was climbing down from the cart one day. I salvaged them out of the gutter for him.'

'And you didn't ask what he needed that kind of money for?'

'Come on, Beth. Would you have?'

'Was he in trouble of any kind? Had he been backing horses?'

'Dad!'

'It must have gone somewhere!'

'Wherever it went, there wasn't any obvious sign of it that I could see.'

'How much have you and Dad been clearing on the round?' she enquired, giving up on the subject.

'Thirty bob in a good week. Twenty to twenty-five shillings on the not so good.'

'Is that all?' Andrew gave her a pound a week house-keeping, and she hadn't had to pay rent or electricity out of that.

'Don't forget we've got nineteen shillings a week coming in from the lodgers. Charlie and Will pay seven and six each and Diana pays four shillings. She pays less because she used to help Mam with the housework.'

Bethan did some rapid calculations in her head.

Looking on the black side, if Eddie only brought in a pound, she'd have one pound one and sixpence a week to feed four adults and one baby, and that was without taking things like coal and electricity into consideration. She'd never do it. What had she been thinking of when she'd decided to come home? The only money she had, or was likely to have for some time, was in her purse. And that wouldn't be enough to keep her and Edmund for more than a month. If her father had been around it might have been different, but she could hardly expect her brother to support her.

'Post.' Eddie mopped up the last drops of grease with his bread before going to the door. He returned with two letters. 'Bloody electricity bill,' he swore.

'We'll have less of that language in the house, thank you.'

'Since when have you taken after Mam? Here, there's one for you.' He tossed a white envelope with a London late-evening postmark on to her lap. 'You didn't say how long you'd be staying Beth,' he probed as she stared at the handwriting. She'd know it anywhere as Andrew's.

'Mm . . . oh as long as you need me, I suppose.'

'Have you left him?' Eddie asked earnestly.

'Who?' she replied unthinkingly as she ripped the envelope open with her thumbnail.

'Cashmere coat.'

'Do you know I'd forgotten about that nickname until Will mentioned it last night.' She looked up. Eddie was watching her. In London it had been easy to ignore her brother's antagonism towards Andrew, but here it wouldn't be so simple. 'No, I haven't left him,' she answered.

'Then when are you going back?'

'When I've sorted a few things out.'

'Powell family things, or John family things?'

'Bit of both I suppose.' She glanced across to the little cot, bright and gleaming with polish, snugly furnished with an assortment of crocheted woollen blankets Diana had unearthed from the deepest recesses of her mother's ottoman. 'We've got a few problems,' she admitted reluctantly.

'Little ones by the look of it,' he said astutely, following her line of vision.

'It's nothing we can't work out. And,' she laid her hand over his, 'it is good to be home, and with you.'

'Don't try to soft-soap me, Beth. It won't wash. Good God is that the time! If I don't get a move on I'll miss the good rigs in Factory Lane again. See you, sis.'

'Don't forget to find out about prison visiting times if you can,' she shouted as he picked up his boots and tore down the passage.

'I won't. Bye.'

The door closed and she was alone. Blessedly, wonderfully alone. Broke, and a burden on her family. She pulled out two pieces of paper from the envelope. Andrew hadn't written her a long letter. In fact it was more of a note.

Dear Bethan,
You're probably right about us needing to take a break from one another. I'll send you one of these every month.
Take care of yourself,
Love Andrew.

The second piece of paper was a cheque for five pounds. Her pride told her to send it back. But if she did, what would she and the baby live on? Besides, he'd written that he'd loved her, hadn't he?

'I'm no builder, Charlie, but even I can see it's in a bad way in places.' William looked up at the ceiling of the largest room over the shop. Charlie had opened it up with a key he'd signed for at the solicitor's. 'Roof must have gone. That's more than just the damp of disuse coming in there.' William pointed to a corner where dark green patches were sprouting mould.

'The floorboards are sound.' Charlie stamped his feet

as he walked across the empty room.

'The windows haven't seen a lick of paint in years.'

Charlie fingered the blackened sash. 'But the wood's still solid. There's no sign of rot.'

'You thinking of renting this, then?' William was used to Charlie's mysterious ways, but even he had been a little bewildered by his boss's insistence on viewing the shop as soon as they'd finished for the day in the slaughterhouse.

'Yes.'

'Going to do it up yourself?'

'Not the roof.' Charlie pushed up the window and sat on the windowsill. Leaning out backwards, he looked up at the slates.

'But you'll paint the inside?'

'There's nothing here that you and I can't manage.' Charlie ducked back inside and slammed the window shut. 'I may even get Eddie to help.'

'Why this shop, Charlie?' William asked as he followed Charlie into a tiny, dark kitchen at the back. 'The town's full of places in better nick than this.'

'The solicitor handling them wouldn't drop the price.'

'And Fred the Dead gave you a good deal!' William exclaimed sceptically. Fred's reputation for driving a hard bargain was legendary.

'Eventually,' Charlie replied vaguely.

'I suppose it could be a good spot for trade,' William admitted grudgingly as they walked out on to a small landing and opened the doors to three other rooms. Two were as small, and as they were built at the back of the building, as dark as the kitchen. The third was a bathroom with a sink, bath and toilet, all in need of a good scrub.

'My godfathers. A bathroom!' When Charlie made no comment, William went to the front window again and looked down on the shuttered entrance to the fruit market.

'You'll get the town as well as the market traffic,' he commented, 'and depending on your prices, the idlers hanging around the fountain.'

'Do you want to manage this place?'

'This shop?'

'What do you think we've been talking about?'

'You've signed the lease?'

'Yesterday.'

'You bought it?'

'Sort of. It will be mine in five years.'

'What happens if you don't make a go of it?'

'I'll be broke.'

'I don't know the town can stand another butcher's shop,' William said doubtfully. 'It's getting hard enough on the market with most people only being able to afford the odd half-pound of tripe or brains.'

'It's not going to be a butcher's shop. At least, not like the one on the market.' Charlie led the way down the stairs and into the shop.

'Then what are you going to sell?' William asked, irritated at having to drag every word out of Charlie.

'Cooked meats. Meat pies and pasties. Sausage rolls, brawn, cold tongue, slices of stuffed belly pork, cooked beef and chicken. And every day of the week, not just market days.'

'There isn't another shop in Ponty that specialises in savoury baking,' William said thoughtfully.

'Exactly. And although people can't afford a joint of meat, most will be able to afford a slice or two if it's ready cooked, and cold enough to slice thin. We have lots of shops like that in Russia. They did well, even when people had very little money.'

'So that's why you wanted this place. Because it was a bakery years ago.'

Charlie opened a door in the back wall behind the counter. Two huge black iron ovens faced him; in front were three zinc-coated tables and two wooden ones. There were even dusty mixing bowls on the open wooden shelves, and rows of grimy metal utensils.

'They went bankrupt,' he explained. 'Fred Jones was the main creditor.'

'And he didn't think it was worth emptying this place before renting it to Meakins. Charlie you're a genius.'

'Not a word about what we're going to sell to anyone,' Charlie warned, well acquainted with Will's garrulous tongue.

'Not until we open. You crafty old devil,' William looked at the counter, which despite the years spent displaying china still showed the grey residue of old flour mixed with dust in the cracks around the glass front and marble serving slabs.

'Then you'll manage the shop?'

'Of course. Thank you for asking, but I warn you now I'm no cook.'

'I want you to sell, not cook. I have someone else in mind for that.'

'But what about the stall? I won't be able to do the two. Or are you giving that up?'

'Not for the moment.'

'You'll never manage it on your own.'

'I'll get Eddie to help.'

'He won't like that. He'll miss the cart.'

'He can still take that out on the days I don't need him.'

'But you'll be cutting more meat than ever in the slaughterhouse.'

'*We'll* be cutting more meat,' Charlie corrected. 'I forgot to tell you, the manager of this shop works long hours. He has to start work in the slaughterhouse at five in the morning, and doesn't finish in the shop much before eight at night.'

After a discussion on priorities, Charlie and William set about scrubbing down the ovens and water boilers in the old bakehouse kitchen. Although Charlie began with a better will and more energy than William it soon became obvious that his mind wasn't on the task. His hand slowed as he rubbed the brown patina of rust from the ironwork. He paused frequently, staring into space as he visualised

Alma dressed in a white overall and hat, moving around the kitchen as it would look once he'd transformed it. She would be busy cooking, cleaning, lifting trays out of the oven on to the tables, smiling at him as he worked alongside her, in that same distant, preoccupied way she had once smiled at Ronnie Ronconi. Perhaps she'd talk to him as they worked – but what about? Trade in the shop. The weather? If she learned to trust him, something more personal? What had he talked about with Masha when they had sat side by side in front of the stove every night after the day's work? Everything and nothing. The past – the future. His grandfather's funeral, what their unborn children would look like . . .

'Know anything about cooking meats then, Charlie?' William asked after he'd watched Charlie idle away a good ten minutes of working time.

'A little.' Charlie reluctantly faced the stove again.

'Seems to me you've got to know more than a little to cook on the scale you've been talking about.'

'You're right.' Charlie dropped his scouring pad on to the stove, and went to the tap. He turned it on but no water came out.

'Stopcock's off,' William informed him as Charlie stared blankly at the dry tap.

Charlie bent below the sink and turned the small wheel set there. Water gushed fiercely downwards, splashing out of the sink over his neck.

'Not with it are you, mate? You feeling all right after that blow to the head?'

'I'm fine. I have to see someone.' Charlie unfastened his overall, now stained with black filth from the cooker as well as dried blood from the slaughterhouse.

'Want me along?' William asked hopefully, fed up with scrubbing at the rusted ironwork.

'No.'

William watched as Charlie rubbed the dirt from his square, capable hands in the stream of water that flowed into the sink. When they were as clean as he could get them, he replaced the collar and tie he'd removed before starting work, and buttoned his waistcoat and jacket. Taking a comb out of his pocket he flicked his thick blond hair straight back from his forehead before putting on his overcoat. William had observed Charlie transform himself from worker into well-dressed businessman many times, and never ceased to marvel at how he could do it so proficiently without the aid of a mirror.

'You've got a big black smut on the end of your nose.'

Charlie removed a spotless white linen handkerchief from the breast pocket of his jacket and rubbed at his nose.

'Fooled you,' William laughed as he turned the pad of wire wool over in his hand.

'Keep working. I won't be long.'

'Give her my love.'

'Who?' Charlie paused by the door and looked back.

'Whoever she is. It must be love, I've never seen you so half-soaked before.'

'If it's love, you're looking at it,' Charlie said unsmilingly, indicating the shop as he closed the door.

'As if you could be in love with this bloody filthy place,' William muttered, staring miserably at the thick layer of grime that coated everything in sight, and wishing that Vera would walk through the door.

Charlie turned left and headed towards the Fairfield end of town.

'You moving in next door then, Charlie?'

'Yes.' Charlie paused in front of Frank Clayton's radio shop, the one shop in town that was always bursting at the seams with people, who, unfortunately for Frank, only came to listen to his radios and radiograms, not to buy them.

'Meat won't go down well here,' Frank warned sternly. 'It's one thing for people to come across pig's heads and tripe in the butcher's market where they expect to find such things, quite another for them to see offal in a window next to a luxury goods shop like mine.'

'I expect they'll get used to it, Mr Clayton.'

'In summer you'll bring nothing but smells and flies around here. It'll be unhygienic. Don't intend to do your killing out the back in the yard, do you?'

'No, Mr Clayton.' Charlie smiled wryly. Frank Clayton knew as well as him that if he tried to slaughter anything at the back of the shop the authorities would close him down overnight.

'Well I'm telling you now, the first whiff of a stink that upsets one of my customers, and I'll be reporting you to the Public Health.'

'I wouldn't have it any other way, Mr Clayton.' Charlie placidly tipped his hat.

'Bloody foreigners,' Frank swore to his son, inadvertently slamming the door in a customer's face as he retreated inside his shop. 'You'd think we'd have the sense to keep them out of this country. Instead what do we do? We let them in, give them the best shops in the prime trading positions, allow them to make money off the backs of people who were born and bred here and can ill afford to keep body and soul together as it is. Our own starve, while the likes of Russian Charlie grow fat. You mark my words lad, that man'll be riding around in a car soon if he isn't stopped.'

Outwardly oblivious to the town's interest in his affairs Charlie carried on walking down Taff Street, tipping his hat to customers and acquaintances, nodding gravely to the traders who were standing on their doorsteps looking out for potential customers. He turned the corner by the YMCA building, and a few moments later found himself the other side of Gelliwastad Road. He remembered someone saying the night Alma had been taken into hospital that she lived in Morgan Street, and although he'd never had cause to go into that area, he found it without too much trouble.

Though it hadn't rained that day, the unmade stretch that separated the double terrace of houses was covered with a thick layer of sticky mud, peppered with surprisingly deep puddles. Ducking his head to avoid hitting a washing line laden with sheets stretched between the houses, he almost fell over two small street urchins who were sailing newspaper 'ships' across an unwholesome-looking 'sea' speckled with mountainous islands constructed from stones and rubbish.

'Haven't seen you around here before, Mister.' The boy was thin, ragged and small. He was dressed in patched grey short trousers, and a jersey that was more holes than wool; his feet and legs were bare. His sharp, ferret-like face looked older than Charlie would have expected to see on a child of his size.

'That's because I haven't been here before.'

'You don't talk as though you come from round here either.' The second boy was as emaciated and threadbare as the first, and his hands and face were encrusted with thick brown running sores.

'That's because I come from another country.' Charlie pulled two halfpennies from his pocket and held them high, just out of the boys' reach. 'Can you tell me where Alma Moore lives?'

'My mam says she's a tart. You one of her fancy men?'

The boy with the sores wasn't interested in scandal. His attention was firmly fixed on Charlie's money. 'Over there, Mister.' He jumped up and snatched the coins from Charlie's hand. Holding them out of his friend's reach, he pointed to a house with a dilapidated front door.

Trying to avoid the mud by stepping carefully around the puddles, Charlie walked towards it. Seeing no knocker, he tapped lightly on the door.

'Come in.'

He pushed gingerly at the wood around the knob. The door opened into a cold passageway, floored in well-scrubbed, almost white flagstones, amazingly free from the taint of the mud that coated the street. He scraped his shoes on a sacking mat, and seeing a door to his left he pushed it. It swung open to reveal a bare room: no rug, furniture, nothing except a pair of faded curtains hanging at the window. He closed the door and walked down the passage. A piece of sheeting at the far end twitched aside and Alma's face, drained of colour by her vivid red hair and bright green eyes, peered suspiciously at him.

'Charlie? You're the last person I expected to see.' For the first time she wished she could call him by something other than the nickname that served him as both Christian and surname. 'Charlie' seemed appropriate enough in the café, particularly when he sat with the boys like Glan, William and Eddie, but here, in her own home, it sounded insulting and disrespectful. 'Won't you come in?' She pulled back the curtain.

'Thank you.' The smell of soapsuds and washing soda assailed his nostrils. Then he picked up on something else; something he recognised from the last year he had spent in Russia. Cold, clean poverty. The kind of poverty that is spawned when proud people try to hang on to their sense of decency in the face of overwhelming odds. He shivered involuntarily as he entered the chill atmosphere of the kitchen. It was colder than the street, with a damp, wintry frostiness that had been stored in the unheated stone walls of the old house for years.

Flustered, Alma pulled the chair with the cushion into the centre of the room. 'Won't you sit down?'

He took the seat she offered.

'I'd like to offer you tea, but I'm afraid I can't. Today's my day for cleaning out the range, and we don't have a gas stove, so I can't boil water.'

He glanced at the range. The brass fenders and rails were brightly polished, the ironwork newly blackleaded. It was spotless and, he suspected, ready for lighting, if there had been any coal.

'Would you like a biscuit?' Alma opened a tin that contained three oatmeal biscuits that were left from the trayful her mother had made when the stove had last been lit.

'No thank you.'

'You look better than you did on Sunday.'

'I'm fine.' He fingered the plaster that had replaced the bandage on his head.

She stood in front of him, wiping her hands on her apron, feeling unsettled and awkward, wishing he'd say whatever he'd come to say, then go away and leave her in peace.

'I heard you lost your job in the tailor's,' he said apprehensively, wary of provoking a scene.

'That's old news,' she retorted.

'Are you looking for full-time work?'

'Of course. It's impossible for my mother and me to live on what I bring in working in the café.'

'That's what I thought. I'm opening a shop.'

'I don't think I'd be able to run a shop,' she broke in swiftly. 'You saw what happened in the café.'

'I wasn't going to ask you to run it.l I already have a manager. What I need is someone to supervise the cooking.'

'Cooking? You're opening a café then?'

'No. A cooked meats shop.'

She laughed mirthlessly as she waved her hand around the sparsely equipped and furnished kitchen, 'I know very little about cooking the kind of meat you'd find in a shop.'

'You can read, write and follow a recipe, can't you?'

'Yes, but—'

'It will be quite straightforward. Cooking, pressing, pickling, curing, potting, collaring, smoking and boiling meats,' Charlie recited, automatically going through the full range he had envisaged stocking and selling. 'Slicing them when they're cold. Making faggots, croquettes, pies, pasties, rolls and brawn from offcuts and offal. Arranging everything on display plates ready for sale.'

'But I've never done any cooking professionally.' Alma could have kicked herself. Here was Charlie offering her an opportunity to make ends meet and she was putting obstacles in his path.

'I've seen you in the café. Like all good workers you learn fast. Ronnie . . . the Ronconis,' he amended diplomatically, 'have always thought a lot of you. You're conscientious, honest, not afraid of hard work, and—' he turned to face her – 'I thought you might like to leave the café.' He didn't elaborate on his reasons for coming to that conclusion. Colour flooded into her cheeks as he continued. 'I was hoping to turn the Ronconis' loss to my gain.'

'But I—'

'I'm not afraid of the gossips,' he said simply. 'Do you want the job or don't you?'

She remained silent, wondering if Charlie realised the importance most people in Pontypridd attached to the rumours being spread about her. What was it her mother had said? 'No smoke without fire.' Her presence could result in a boycott of Charlie's shop, but she needed full-time work.

'I'm not having a baby, Charlie,' she said at last, lifting her chin defiantly, her green eyes glittering antagonistically.

'I never thought you were. Do you want the job, or not?'

'You really don't give a damn about gossip, do you?' she asked incredulously.

'I don't have to listen to it.' He rose from his seat unable to stand the cold a moment longer without moving. 'My father always used to say that the best and most loyal workers are the ones who need the money the most, and from what I can see, you need the money,' he said with devastating simplicity. He walked over to the window that overlooked the tiny back yard. 'There is one problem, however.'

'What?' She steeled herself, half expecting him to make the same obscene overtures that Bobby had.

'Anything to do with cooking demands an early start. I was thinking of five at the latest. Four would be better. That would give us a couple of hours to do the cooking and set out the counter before the first customers come in at six. You could probably finish by midday as there'd only be the shop to run after that, but it would mean that you couldn't work late nights at the café.'

'I could if I had a rest in the afternoon.'

'I'd rather you didn't. Tired staff are inefficient. And as I'd be paying you a pound a week . . .'

'A pound a week?' Her eyes grew round in disbelief.

'It's not as generous as it sounds. I'd be taking eight shillings back for the rent and meat allowance.'

'You mean you want me to live in this shop of yours?'

'There's three rooms, a small kitchen and a bathroom on the second floor. I'm happy living on the Graig, but I can't afford to leave the place empty, and as you'd have an early start every morning it would make sense for you to live on the premises.'

'Let's get this straight.' Alma stiffened her back and looked him straight in the eye. 'You're offering me twelve shillings a week, meat and rent paid . . .'

'And electricity and fuel.'

'This shop of yours has electricity, even upstairs?'

'Even upstairs,' he echoed drily.

'You want to give me all that for eight hours' work a day?'

'It will be for six days a week,' he reminded her. 'Early closing on Thursday won't affect the cooking you'll have to do. If anything, there might be more as we'll have the weekend rush ahead of us. And I'll expect you to do all the cleaning. The shop and bakehouse as well as the flat and stairs.'

'I've already been accused of being the kept woman of one businessman in town. I'm not about to move on to another,' she snapped.

'Take it or leave it.' He met her look of suspicion with equanimity. 'The job is there if you want it. If you turn it down I'll advertise it in the Labour Exchange.'

'You'd offer the same pay and conditions to anyone?'

'They go with the job.'

'How do I know you don't want anything else from me?'

'You don't.' He crossed the room and pulled aside the curtain. 'Let me know what you decide. I hope to have the shop open and trading within the month. That only gives you a week to make up your mind.'

Chapter Eleven

ANDREW PASSED HIS neighbour on the communal staircase. It was the same woman who'd spied on him the night he'd come home drunk. He recognised the sharp, beaky features beneath the glossy waved hair and thick bright red lipstick. Her Eau-de-Cologne wafted around him, the clip of her heels on the marble treads of the stairs resounded in his ears, a door opened and closed, there was quiet, and she was gone. She had looked right through him. Either her eyesight was failing, or she had seen him and hadn't felt the need to acknowledge his presence. But then, neither had he attempted to acknowledge hers. He should be proud of himself, he decided sourly: he had taken the first major step towards becoming a Londoner.

He let himself into the apartment, threw his coat and hat on the empty table in the living room and walked through to the kitchen. Dirty glasses and plates were stacked haphazardly in the sink just as he'd left them that morning. The remains of the pie Bethan had left for him days ago stood congealing and mouldy in a Pyrex dish. He scraped the remains into the waste bin. Was he hungry? Most people ate at this time of day. He did, because it was expected of him. He came home, sat down and ate the meal his wife had prepared and cooked. Only now there was no wife. And because there was no wife, he had bypassed the bachelors and dubious attractions of their company for the first time in months to come straight home from the hospital. If Bethan had still been in London he would be in the pub now, nursing his half-pint, trying to make it last until the stragglers from his group left to dine in their clubs.

He opened the pantry door: half a loaf of rock-hard bread, a tray of eggs, a vegetable rack filled with potatoes, and the yellowed leaves of a cabbage of advancing age. A bowl of wrinkling apples. He picked one up and bit into it. It would do for now. He would have a bath, listen to the radio. There was a play due to be transmitted at half-past eight that someone had mentioned at the lunch table. Afterwards he could go to the Italian restaurant round the corner. He couldn't afford to make a habit of it, but just this once wouldn't hurt. Tomorrow he'd ask around the hospital, find out what the clubs charged for membership and dinner. He would explain that Bethan had returned to Wales to sort out a problem with her family. It was truth – of a sort.

In the bathroom he stripped off and ran a bath. When he opened the linen basket he was mildly surprised to find it crammed full of his dirty clothes. Yet another tangible reminder of Bethan's flight, and yet another domestic problem he'd have to tackle himself. Bethan had made a point of washing their clothes daily, even before she'd had the baby's nappies to deal with.

Suddenly and furiously aware of her absence, from the apartment and from his life, he sat on the edge of the bath and thought about what he was doing. Immersing himself in domestic trivia so he wouldn't have to dwell on the defection of his wife, or the child that suffered because of his shortcomings. What had been the use of all the study, all the training when he hadn't been able to lift a finger to help his own family? His superior had stopped him again today to assure him that no one was to blame, least of all himself. But then that was easy for Doctor Floyd to say. He hadn't had to watch impotently while his wife had fought to bring a child who was already half dead into the world. Why hadn't he demanded a Caesarean when things had first begun to go wrong?

He shuddered, damning himself for going over the events of that day yet again. It was no use. What was done, was done. The child had been a hopeless case from the start because he had failed Bethan at the birth – and before. Compounding neglect with negligence. She had deserved better. Much better.

An image of her invaded his mind. Smiling, laughing, her brown eyes shining with the sheer pleasure of life, as they had done the first time he had danced with her. If she had listened to him and placed the child in the care of professionals it could be like that again. Both of them happy, free to enjoy their marriage and all the attractions London had to offer.

Overwhelmed by a sudden acute sense of loss, he forgot his anger for a moment, and remembered how much he missed that young, beautiful, smiling Bethan. The pain of separation was intense, the dependency it suggested terrifying to one who had always prided himself on cool self-sufficiency, especially in matters of the heart.

If she truly loved him she would have been happy to have given the child up instead of deserting him, leaving him to fend for himself in this empty apartment. Was she trying to make him more aware of the love and passion they had once shared? Didn't she already know how he felt? Even the note she'd left, which he had read and reread until he had memorised every line, had ended 'Love Bethan'. Did she really love him – or were they simply idle words written out of habit? He had never received a letter from her before. Not even a note, so he had no way of knowing.

He still loved her. With a love he had tried to deny once before, only to cause both of them misery and heartache. But now the situation was reversed. It was he who needed her, and she who had walked away. Why hadn't she seen his need, his desire for her . . . for happiness. Why had she persisted in taking everything they had and throwing it away?

The baby had come between them, and would always lie between them. A child he couldn't bear to look at. And while she insisted on keeping it there was no hope of them picking up the threads of their life. Couldn't she see that she wouldn't have to do it alone? He would support her every step of the way. Together they would walk the long, flower-bordered drive of the gabled Tudor manor house Doctor Floyd had given him photographs of. The door would open, they'd be shown inside. A white and blue gowned nurse would be waiting in an ante-room to take the bundle Bethan carried in her arms. They would walk back down the drive together arm in arm: Bethan would be free from burden for the first time in five months. And so would he. He would no longer have to face a daily reminder of the guilt he carried.

The picture he'd painted was vivid, real; so real that tears started in his eyes when he looked around the bathroom and realised he'd been daydreaming. He took off his watch. He was hungry. Tonight he could drive to the fish and chip shop down the road and he could eat in the restaurant tomorrow. He wouldn't have to ask about clubs until the day after. Two days could change a great deal – perhaps even Bethan's mind. Tomorrow he might return from work to find her here. Then he wouldn't have to ask about clubs at all.

He switched off the taps and stepped into the bath. As the water flowed around him he began to relax. It was only a matter of time. She had written that she loved him. She'd be back. Wouldn't she?

'Rent man.'

Alma's hands turned clammy when she heard Bobby's clumsy footsteps in the passageway. She jumped from her chair, dropping her library book and the blanket she'd been huddling under. She was alone in the house. Her mother was out, shopping with Betty Lane. She wouldn't have put it past Bobby to wait for them to leave; it was common knowledge in the street that Mrs Lane took her mother down to the post office every Thursday to cash her pension. From there they went to Betty's sister's house for tea. What had started as a favour had become a weekly routine since Alma's stay in hospital. One for which Alma was grateful. After a culmination of minor incidents of the Mary and Freda type she had stopped walking out with her mother, and rarely by herself, unless it was absolutely necessary. Especially in broad daylight.

In fact she never went anywhere now except the café, and she had taken to walking as much of the way down the quieter Gelliwastad Road as was possible. 'Decent' women, especially chapelgoers would cross the road when they saw her approaching, and despite Tony and Laura's stout denials, she knew that trade in the café was suffering. She might be out of sight in the kitchen, but she certainly wasn't out of the minds of the townsfolk. She had even heard mutterings among her neighbours in Morgan Street about disgraced girls who were brazen enough to show themselves in public. She would have been only too delighted to keep herself hidden behind the walls of her home, if only she could have thought of some other way of earning money.

'Rent's due.' Bobby pulled back the curtain and grinned at her. Leaving the blanket and library book where they lay on the floor, she shrank back towards the washhouse door.

'I don't get paid until tonight.'

'Is that so?' He stepped into the room, kicking aside the book and blanket with the toe of his muddy boot.

'You can pick it up from me in Ronconi's tonight. I'll be there from six o'clock on.' She could have swallowed her tongue. Now he knew what time her shift started.

'The last thing I want to do on a Friday night is visit a temperance bar.'

'If you give me your address I'll bring it round to your house first thing tomorrow,' she pleaded, resolving to ask Tony if he'd pay her on Thursday nights in future. Far better to risk upsetting Tony than Bobby.

'I'm disappointed in you, Alma. I thought you'd remember our little chat about keeping your rent book up to date.'

'I do. And I've always paid on time before.'

'This is how it starts.' He walked over to the mantelpiece and picked up a framed photograph of her father. 'With one slip. Pay late once and it's easier to pay late the next time, and the next, until before you know it you've missed a week. Then one week becomes two . . .'

'Not with me. Please Bobby . . .' she began, hoping he'd leave without making a scene, or worse still, attempting to touch her.

'Oh it's "please Bobby" now, is it?' he smiled unpleasantly. 'Come down off our high horse now we can't pay our rent, have we, Miss Hoity Toity?'

'I told you. You'll get it tomorrow,' she repeated harshly, trying not to think about what her mother was spending in town.

'Alma?' He replaced the photograph and drew closer to her. Reaching out, he fingered one of her red curls. Stretching and pulling it between his fingers, he stroked her cheek. She recoiled, crashing into the washhouse door.

'I said you'd have it tomorrow.'

'I could give you longer,' he murmured.

'Get out.' Her voice rose precariously.

'Alma.' His face was close to hers. Very close. His tongue slicked wetly across his lips.

'If you don't get out now I'll scream for Mr Lane,' she threatened, fumbling blindly behind her for the knob of the door.

'I'm terrified. Do you mean that the wheezing old geezer from next door is actually likely to burst in here to . . . to what, Alma?' He frowned in feigned perplexity. 'Protect your virtue?' he suggested. 'Even you have to admit it *is* somewhat tarnished. I don't think there's a man or woman in Pontypridd who'd believe anything you have to say about a situation like this. Let's be practical.' He walked to the chair, sat down and propped his boots on the polished brass rail of the fender. 'How many years did you work for Ronnie Ronconi getting paid for more than your waitressing? You did well for yourself there, Alma.

That is until a decent girl caught his eye and he took himself a wife.'

'I said you'd have your money.'

'Come on, Alma, don't play games with me. Everyone knows how destitute you are. You could barely make ends meet when you earned money from two jobs. Not that I've heard anyone blaming Goldman for sacking you. After all, he can't afford to have any gossip, either about his business or himself. He's a family man, with a wife. Unlike Tony Ronconi who's only a kid and not at all worldly wise. Not yet.'

He sat forward, eyeing her up and down as he tapped a cigarette from a packet he'd taken from the top pocket of his tweed sports coat. 'But then I'd bet a pound to a penny that you'd be only too willing to educate him in the ways of the world . . . for a consideration. Always supposing of course that he doesn't mind taking up with his brother's cast-offs.'

'You foul . . .'

'I'm only spelling out what people are thinking about you, Alma. But as I said before, I can help you. In the same way Ronnie Ronconi did.' He paused for a moment, giving her the opportunity to speak. When she didn't he continued. 'You're an attractive woman. Bit thin for my taste, but then that'll soon alter. And when it does no one will be around to make the kind of offer I'm making to you. Make hay while the sun shines as they say, and seeing as how I happen to know that your mother won't be back for a while how about showing me the upstairs . . .'

She turned abruptly and pulled up the sash on the kitchen window, breaking her fingernails as she did so.

'Mr Lane!' she yelled.

'Tomorrow morning, no later than ten. I'll be here. If you haven't the money I'll be in the bailiffs' office first thing Monday morning, and then it'll be time for you to walk up the Graig.' Bobby rose to his feet, kicked the chair into the hearth and left the room.

Trembling, Alma sat at the table and sank her head on

to her arms. What was she doing? A theatrical bout of self-pity was a luxury she couldn't afford. Especially now. Opening the drawer in the rickety table she removed a stub of pencil and an old paper bag, and frantically began to jot down figures. She had been putting off this task for far too long, terrified of what her calculations might reveal.

Tony was paying her eight shillings a week. Her mother had five shillings a week pension. The rent was nine shillings. The doctor and the hospital took another penny a week each, and that was something she dare not cut back on, not with her mother growing frailer every passing year. Although they only lit the stove three days a week, a shilling went on coals. Soap was ninepence, washing blue a penny. Her mother paid eightpence a week burial insurance so there'd be enough for a decent funeral for herself and mourning clothes for Alma. That was something else they had to keep paying: her mother was terrified of the prospect of a pauper's grave. Tenpence went on a beef heart, the only meat they ate all week. A loaf of bread a day and marge to put on it took another two and sixpence. Tea worked out at elevenpence halfpenny. Milk came to a shilling . . . she was over eighteen shillings and that was without potatoes, fruit, vegetables, jam, flour, sugar, lard . . . With only thirteen shillings a week coming in they had to cut back. But where?

She owed Laura nearly three pounds, and their tab at Hopkins' corner shop stood at ten shillings. She took a deep breath. Bobby was right. They were getting deeper and deeper into debt and she could take one of two ways out. On the basis of the figures she'd just worked out, if she opted for the workhouse they might as well walk out of the house and up to Courthouse Street tonight. There was no need even to pack a bag. They wouldn't be allowed their own things. Her mother would have to wear the grey uniform of the women's geriatric ward, and she would be set to scrubbing floors in the coarse overalls of the women's ward until they found her outside domestic work. Either way she probably wouldn't be allowed to see her mother except on high days and holidays ever again.

And the alternative? It was merely a question of who she preferred: Charlie or Bobby? After all, as Bobby had so crudely put it, it wouldn't be that big a step to take. She had played the part of the fancy woman already, she thought resentfully, remembering Ronnie Ronconi and the French letters he had bought to use in the cold bedroom above the café, before Maud Powell had come on the scene. But it had been different with Ronnie. She couldn't even remember deciding to sleep with him. It had just happened as a natural result of the passion he had engendered within her. She had lived for the moments when she and Ronnie had been alone, naked in one another's arms . . . But now there was no Ronnie, only Bobby Thomas, married, his breath and clothes smelling of drink.

Bobby's sly insinuations and leering looks unnerved and frightened her. At least Russian Charlie was clean, and the wages he offered meant she and her mother could leave worries about rent and Morgan Street behind them. If he kept his word about the meat, fuel and rent it would also mean that in time she would be able to pay off every penny they owed.

Charlie would probably call into the café some time over the weekend. She resolved to ask Tony to tell him to wait for her after work. The sooner she took him up on his offer the better. And if he expected her to sleep with him as part of the arrangement, what did it matter? One man couldn't be that different from another.

William was the first tradesman into the butchers' market on Friday morning. For three weeks, ever since Charlie had picked up the key to the shop, he seemed to have done nothing but work. Scrub, clean and paint until late at night after his stints in the slaughterhouse. Run the stall single-handed while Charlie negotiated meat at wholesale prices, or checked out the cost of repairing the roof. He'd even put four extra hours in at the slaughterhouse late last night to help Charlie cut all the meat they needed for the weekend so Charlie could take this morning off to meet the builder he'd finally chosen to carry out the repairs.

It had been hard work, but it had been worth it. At least it enabled him to steal an extra ten minutes in bed.

He dumped the pig he was carrying, feet down. Propping its back against the side of the closed shutters, he pulled Charlie's keys out of his overall pocket and heaved on the padlock. He glanced down the aisle of stalls, peering into the dairy market in the hope of catching a glimpse of Vera. He'd spent the last four Saturday nights on the hearth-rug in her kitchen, and was already shivering in anticipation. The hands of the clock over the door pointed to five. Another forty-one hours and he'd be there.

He spent all his waking hours thinking about Vera, and the things they did to one another. She was even beginning to haunt his dreams, naked except for creamy silk stockings and a white satin and lace suspender belt, her breasts beautifully, deliciously bare, her arms extended, waiting to accept his embrace, her thighs parted – ready. Last night he'd woken to find Eddie pounding him viciously in the chest, telling him to stop moaning, or else.

'Will.'

'Good God, where did you spring from?' His mouth went dry as he stepped closer to the shutters, shielding her with his body to minimise the risk of anyone seeing them.

'I came in through the clothes market.' She smiled coyly, looking up at him from beneath lowered lashes with an expression that sent his pulse rate soaring. 'George thinks I'm having breakfast with my mother. He had to drive up to the farm because he sold out of clotted cream yesterday. He won't be here for at least another half-hour. No one will.'

William forgot all the promises he'd made to Charlie

about jointing carcasses and preparing the stall. He wanted Vera. Now. This minute. He couldn't wait until Saturday night. He looked around. Someone was moving down in the second-hand clothes market, but they were too far away to see anything.

'Quick.' He unlocked the shutters and pulled her towards him. 'Crawl in there before anyone sees you.'

Vera needed no second bidding. Dropping to her hands and knees she crept through the gap in the side of the boards. William relocked the shutters and after a second check, ducked beneath the shutters himself. Pushing the door shut, he wedged it with his foot.

'You are clever. No one would know we're here,' Vera giggled. Her voice sounded eerie in the darkness. All he could see were one or two cracks of grey light through chinks in the thick wooden shutters. The smell was overpowering: washing soda and stale meat, strongly and improbably perfumed with attar of roses, Vera's favourite scent, or so she had told him three times before he'd finally taken the hint and gone out and bought her a bottle.

'Ssh!' he commanded, suddenly terrified as footsteps echoed towards them. They halted just outside the stall. He could even hear someone breathing. As he crouched there, quivering in the darkness, he cursed the madness that had overtaken him. If George tore the shutters open above their heads now, what could he say?

'I dropped my keys and Vera was helping me find them?' Or, 'We're playing hide and seek, do you want a game?'

After an eternity, whoever it was moved, walking with sluggish steps towards the dairy market. William breathed again. He opened his mouth ready to tell Vera to go, then felt her fingers working to unfasten the buttons on his overall. Seconds later they were at his fly. She pulled him on top of her. He fell forward, but was careful to keep the soles of his feet firmly against the half-door let into the side of the stall. She'd hitched the skirt of her overall high, and as he slid his hand between her stockinged legs he realised she wasn't wearing any underclothes. She moaned softly, shifting beneath his weight.

'No noise,' he hissed into where he thought her ear should be. 'For God's sake, no noise.'

He didn't enjoy what followed. Fearful of every footfall, every bang of neighbouring shutters opening. And when it was over and he crawled outside to check the lie of the land he saw that his overall was covered with sawdust.

'Been rolling around in the hay, Will?' Eddie laughed as he carried a bucket of water over to Wilf Horton's stall.

'Dropped my keys,' he shouted back. As soon as Eddie'd gone he whispered to Vera. 'Out now. Quick.'

She tripped over her high-heeled shoes as she emerged.

'Your overall is filthy,' he groaned as she struggled to her feet.

'Thank you for helping me up, Mr Powell,' she said in a loud voice as Mrs Walker passed them. 'It was stupid of me to trip. And I think you're right. I will have to go home to change.'

Ostensibly unlocking the stall, he watched as she tottered away. The seams of her stockings were crooked. There was a ladder in the back of her heel, and her white overall was covered in black smuts and sawdust; but dirty and dishevelled, she still exuded sex as she swung her hips enticingly, allowing the cloth to flow over thighs he alone among the men in the market knew were naked. As he lusted after her retreating figure he vowed never again to take such a risk. Saturday nights with George down the road in the Queen's were dangerous enough; Charlie's stall on a Friday morning was sheer lunacy.

He folded back the shutters and clipped them to the sides of the stall. He opened the meat safe, and taking out the largest knife went to get the pig. He stared in disbelief at the vacant space where he had left it. Panic-stricken, he walked around the stall. It was nowhere to be seen.

Feeling sick, he locked himself behind the counter and began to unpack the safe of the meat they'd prepared the night before. A whole pig represented three trading days' profits. Charlie would kill him. Particularly now when the shop was taking every penny of his spare cash. It would take a month of overtime and working for nothing to pay Charlie back. And he hadn't even been able to take a good look at Vera.

'Here you are, Alma, your wages. You wanted them a day early.'

'For the rent, yes. Thanks Tony.' She took the three half-crowns and sixpence he handed her and secreted them in her purse.

'You managing all right?' he asked, thinking she looked even paler and thinner in the face than usual.

'I'm managing fine,' she answered quickly. Too quickly, judging by the fleeting expression of concern that crossed his face. 'See you usual time tomorrow.' She put on her coat, checked her tam was straight in the mirror that hung behind the counter and went out. It was raining heavily again, she noticed miserably as she hesitated to tie a headscarf over her hat. Putting her head down into the wind, looking neither to the left nor right, she began to walk.

It was the tail end of a long, hard week. She had waited impatiently for Charlie to appear in the café. Tony had begun to give her odd looks when she came in every night asking the same question. 'Has Charlie been in?' No one had seen him, or, for that matter, William or Eddie Powell around anywhere except the market for two weeks. And tonight had been the last straw. Glan Richards had overheard her asking Tina about Charlie yet again, and shouted through to the kitchen from the café 'Will I do?' The cheap gibe had earned him a laugh, and done nothing to increase her self-respect, or standing with the Ronconis. Rightly or wrongly, she was beginning to feel they would be happy to show her the door as Mostyn

Goldman had done. Whatever strings were attached to Charlie's offer of a job and accommodation, she now saw it as the only escape from the deepening pit of debt. But no matter how she tried to explain or dismiss his absence to herself, Charlie's disappearance from his usual haunts worried her. She lacked the courage to go looking for him in the market, and couldn't understand why he had forsaken the café, unless . . . unless he had taken her less than enthusiastic response to his offer as a refusal. She could well be building her future on a job Charlie had already given to someone else. And if he had? What would she do then?

It had taken her entire wages and the remnants of her mother's pension to pay off last week's rent, less one and six that despite all her efforts she had failed to raise. Terrified of what Bobby might do, she had tried to cover the difference by pawning the blankets and pillows off her bed, but Arthur Faller had refused to take them, saying they were too worn. She was dreading tonight, or tomorrow morning at the latest, when she would have to sit her mother down and explain exactly how things stood. She had to put a stop to the Lane children's daily trips to the corner shop to pick up her mother's bread, marge, tea and sugar. Every morning this week she had listened while her mother have given them her order, and every morning she had clenched her fists and grit her teeth dreading their return, waiting for them to say, 'Sorry Auntie Moore, but Mrs Hopkins says your tab's full, and we can't bring you anything else until it's paid off.'

Food – she wished she could stop thinking about it. It had become an obsession since the beginning of last week when she'd cut down severely on her own meals in the hope of making a saving on their grocery bill. She limited herself to half a piece of bread and margarine at breakfast, half at dinner and half before she went to work in the café. But she'd waited in vain for the hunger pangs to subside as her stomach shrank. If anything, the pangs had begun to dominate her waking thoughts, not to mention her sleeping ones. Last night she'd dreamed of cream cakes and chocolates like the ones she drooled over every time she passed the display window of St Catherine's café in the Arcade. She had even caught herself looking longingly at the scrapings left on the plates that came into the kitchen to be washed. It was just as well that she spent most of her time on vegetable preparation, not dish-washing or cooking, otherwise she might be tempted to put more than the odd lump of raw carrot or raw potato in her mouth when she could be sure Angelo and Tony weren't looking. But no matter how she cut back, the bill in the corner shop mounted alarmingly higher with every passing day, and the rent loomed too. They formed a double-edged sword of Damocles, poised, ready to fall at any moment and wreak destruction on what little remained of their home.

She had to talk to her mother first thing in the morning. But it would help if her bad news could be softened by some good. If only she'd been able to see Charlie first and be sure of the job – perhaps if she sent one of the Lane children to him with a note? The market opened very early . . .

A cat-call echoed across the empty street. Terror prickled down her spine as she remembered Bobby and his foul propositions. Staring at the pavement and walking in the shadow of the buildings, she hurried forward. It had been twelve o'clock when she had left the café. The pubs had disgorged their last customers over an hour ago. No one but shift workers and the police should be on the streets now, and of course tramps. She wasn't sure who she was most afraid of meeting, Bobby or a tramp.

She glanced furtively over her shoulder. If it hadn't been for the whistling cat-call she could have sworn that the street was empty. Perhaps it *was* a tramp? Like the awful hobo she had seen in the American second feature that had played with *The Scarlet Pimpernel*. It had been over six months since she had treated herself to a visit to the cinema, but she could recall every detail, not only of the main film, but also of the short, cartoon, second feature and newsreel. And that tramp had terrified her. He had broken into the heroine's house, tied up her mother, eaten everything in the kitchen and then climbed the stairs to the heroine's bedroom . . .

Her thoughts froze as she heard it again: a mocking sound that set the hairs on the back of her neck crawling. It seemed to come from up ahead. The ornate fountain? She darted into a doorway and studied the grey stone edifice. A figure swayed out from behind it. Stumbling clumsily, it staggered towards her.

'Rent day tomorrow.'

'I know, Bobby.' Quickening her pace she dodged him and crossed to the left-hand side of the road. To her dismay he followed.

'You want me to reduce it for you?'

'No thank you, Bobby.' If she remained polite, carried on walking, he might leave her alone.

'Go on, you know you can't pay. The reduction I'm offering would be more than worth your while.' He reached out and clasped her arm.

'You'll get your rent!' She snatched her arm away but he lurched forwards. Wrapping both his arms around her waist he fell on top of her, dragging them both to the ground.

'Let me go!' She fought with every ounce of strength she could muster, kicking out at his legs, lashing him with clenched fists. He rolled on top of her and started to laugh, with the inane cackle of the truly drunk.

She heaved him off and attempted to rise, but his hand had closed like a steel vice round her right wrist, pinning it to the pavement.

'If you don't let me go, Bobby, I'll scream. And after last time you know I will,' she hissed, terror muting her voice to a whisper.

He struggled to his knees and peered up and down the

deserted street. 'I don't see anyone who'll hear you, so go ahead,' he slurred. He sat back on his heels, his eyes rolling as he strained to focus on her. 'Come on, Alma,' he wheedled. 'Be a sport. You know you want it. Everyone knows girls like you miss it when it's taken off them suddenly. After all, how long is it since Ronnie Ronconi left? Five . . . six months?' He tried to dive on top of her again, but she moved quicker than he did, rolling away from him at the last moment. He landed heavily on his knees.

'Alma!' he chanted, laughing again as he closed his fingers even tighter around her wrist and carried her hand to his mouth. 'Alma . . .'

Desperate to get away, she sank her teeth as hard as she could into the soft fleshy part of his hand below the thumb.

'You cow!' He released his grip just long enough for her to regain her feet. She raced forward and he flung himself after her in a rugby tackle. She crashed heavily to the ground, and this time she did scream. Long, loud and clearly, a piercing echo that resounded around the deserted buildings as her head and chest connected painfully with the pavement.

An explosion of black burst in her brain. Through a thick mist she watched helplessly while Bobby, still laughing, locked his hands around her ankles and dragged her by her legs along the pavement into the doorway of Heath's piano shop.

'Leave me alone!' She struggled to pull her clothes down, conscious he was able to look up her skirt. 'Leave me—'

A hand materialised above Bobby's head. Even in her confused state she realised it couldn't be Bobby's because both of his gripped her ankles. She watched spellbound as luminous white fingers sank into Bobby's black curls. His head jerked back sharply, his grasp on her ankles relaxed, then finally loosened. He rose slowly, infinitely slowly into the air above her, like a marionette being manipulated by a dark, shadowy puppeteer. He swung away, his legs dangling ineffectually above the ground.

Heaving for breath and shaking in terror, Alma crawled to the display window of the shop behind her. She tried to stand, but a sharp pain in her ribs felled her to her knees. The pane of glass at her back shuddered in its frame as she stumbled against it. The fingers had formed a fist. It connected with Bobby's jaw and he shot backwards, landing with a dull thud on the ground beside her.

The only silhouette that remained standing was thickset, stocky, with wide shoulders and a cap pulled down low over its face, but she could see the white blond hair escaping its confines.

Chapter Twelve

'ARE YOU ALL right?' Charlie was bending over her, his hand extended. She took it and tried to pull herself up, but she tumbled back again, sliding weakly over the tiled floor of the piano shop porchway.

'I . . . I . . .'

The dark street whirled in a kaleidoscope as he scooped her into his arms and carried her through the open doorway of the shop next door.

'I was working late. I heard a noise outside,' he explained as he looked around for somewhere to put her.

The shop was no longer the series of grimy, filthy rooms Charlie had shown to William. The walls, floors and work surfaces were clean and shining; the atmosphere eye-stinging, redolent with the mixed odours of paint, varnish and turpentine. In the corner was a pile of dustsheets, dry, if none too clean. He lowered Alma gently on to them, but she locked her hands around his neck, clinging to him, refusing to allow him to move away from her.

'You're safe here with me, I promise you,' he murmured soothingly, recognising the terror in her eyes. He reached around to the back of his neck and prised her fingers apart. Then he went into the kitchen to fetch his coat. 'You're shivering.' He laid it over her.

'You always seem to be coming to my rescue.' She tried to smile but a grimace froze on her lips as pain shot through her head.

'You're hurt.' He returned to the kitchen and looked around. He and William had worked hard to clean the place up but there was precious little in it that was any use to him now. He spotted two mugs they'd used to drink lemonade because they hadn't wanted to waste coal by lighting the stove just to make tea. Lifting one down from the window-sill, he rinsed it under the tap and filled it with cold water. As an afterthought he pulled a clean handkerchief out of his overall pocket and soaked that as well before returning to Alma in the shop.

Sitting on the floor next to her and propping her against his chest he helped her to drink. Still dizzy and disorientated she hung on to him in an effort to steady herself. Charlie gently but firmly disentangled himself from her grasp, and placed the wet handkerchief over an angry red mark on her forehead.

'Your skin isn't broken, only swollen,' he reassured her.

She held the handkerchief over her temple. It was cool, although it smelt nauseatingly of paint.

'This is your shop?'

'Yes.'

'You were painting it now, at this time of night?'

'I hope to open next month, and as I work most days that only leaves the evenings.'

'Is that why you haven't been in the café?'

He nodded.

'I tried to get a message to you about the job,' she mumbled. She closed her eyes. Everything was swimming around her in a turgid, chemically tainted atmosphere.

'You're all right now,' he said, and for the first time in her life she actually believed the platitude. She leaned against him and allowed herself to relax. He smelt clean. A strange combination of bleach, soda and honestly won sweat. She would be able to stand him touching her. But not Bobby. *Never* Bobby. She opened her eyes and lifted her face to his, expecting a kiss. Charlie looked at her for a moment, then moved away.

'I'll be back in a moment.'

'Don't leave me,' she pleaded, hysteria mounting at the thought of being left alone.

'I have to go outside.'

She watched, feeling very small, alone and abandoned as he went to the door.

The pavement outside his shop was empty. He looked into the doorway of the piano shop. That too was empty. Whoever had attacked Alma hadn't stayed around. He returned to the shop, this time closing and locking the door behind him. Alma was still lying, white, frightened and tearful where he had left her on the dustsheets, his coat spread over her like a blanket.

'I'll lock you in and get the police. I won't be long.'

'No.' Her hand shook as she put the mug of water he'd given her on the floor.

'The next person he attacks might not be as lucky as you.'

'He won't attack anyone else.' She wanted him to come to her and take her in his arms, so she could feel warm, secure and comfortable again.

'Do you know who he is?'

'Yes.' Charlie was keeping his distance. Did that mean he didn't like her? But he'd offered her a job. Too confused to analyse the situation, she only knew that for the first time since Ronnie had left her for Maud, she had felt safe in a man's arms. She even felt safe now. Charlie's presence in the room was enough, even when he wasn't physically close to her. 'He's my rent man,' she replied, wanting to explain everything. Suddenly it seemed very important that Charlie knew the truth, not the rumours being spread about her. 'Since I lost my morning job in the tailor's I've had trouble paying my bills. He wants me to make up the difference with something other than money,' she said baldly.

'He attacked you. He deserves to be punished.'

'By who? The police couldn't care less about people like me.'

'He broke the law.'

'A law that says everyone should pay their debts. All he'd have to say is he threatened me with the bailiffs for not paying my rent and I attacked him.'

'I saw different.'

'He'd only make even more trouble for me if I went to the police. Please, my mother and I are lucky to have a roof over our heads as it is. Can't we just drop the subject?'

'How much do you owe him?'

'Why do you want to know?' she demanded, suddenly suspicious. A few moments ago she would have done anything he'd wanted her to, but that had been when he'd held her in his arms. Now, as he interrogated her across the empty shop, he didn't seem to be the same man. Was he going to proposition her, coldly, unemotionally as Bobby had? Other women got caresses, kisses and promises. Was there something about her that made all men want to treat her like a worthless slut?

'If you're going to work for me, I should know what trouble I'm taking on.'

'Damned sure I'm going to take the job, aren't you?' She closed her eyes, wishing the ground would swallow her up. Charlie was her only hope of leading a decent life. He'd saved her from Bobby and his odious intentions, and here she was throwing the opportunity he offered back in his face.

'No,' he answered quietly.

'Tomorrow I'll owe two shillings and sixpence on my rent,' she capitulated. 'But as well as the rent, there's our tab in Hopkins' shop. It'll only be a matter of time before they stop our credit, and as if that's not enough, I owe Laura two pounds seventeen shillings and eightpence.' Tears started in the corner of her eyes. The whole lot didn't amount to five pounds. But on an income of thirteen shillings a week it might as well have been fifty-five.

'You can move in here as soon as you like.'

'If I do, I suppose I could sign notes . . .'

'I'll lend you what you need to settle your debts against your future earnings.' Charlie still made no attempt to move from the door.

'Why would you do that?'

'You are going to work for me aren't you?' he asked, weary of fencing words.

'That still doesn't explain why you'd want to help me beforehand.'

'I told you last time I saw you. You're a good worker.'

'And because I jumped in Ronnie Ronconi's bed you want me to jump in yours?' She was glad she'd found the courage to ask the question outright. For once in her life everything was open and above board.

'The last thing I want or need at the moment, Miss Moore, is a woman in my bed. But thank you for the offer.'

She had expected a reply along the lines of, 'Seeing as how you brought up the subject, I'll take you up on that.' His rebuff left her speechless.

'I'll lend you ten pounds. That should be enough to cover your debts and keep you and your mother until you get your first wage packet from this shop.'

'I don't need that much.'

'Let's say ten pounds just to be on the safe side. That way you can pay off everything you owe and have a little to spare. You can pay me back at two shillings a week.'

'But that will take me—' her head ached as she frantically added up the figures – 'a year to pay back, and that's without interest.'

'There won't be any interest, now, if you feel up to it, I'll take you home.' He walked towards her and gently pulled back the handkerchief. A huge lump had broken out on the surface of her forehead. Red and swollen, it looked extremely painful.

'That hurts,' she protested.

'I'm not surprised. But better out than in.'

'What do you mean?'

'If the swelling occurs on the inside it can cause dangerous pressure, which could do considerable damage.'

'I didn't know that.' She bit her lip hard.

'Can you walk?' he asked, aware of how the sight of the two of them, alone in his shop at this time of night, could be misconstrued.

'I think so.' She rose stiffly to her feet. 'Here's your coat.'

'Keep it around your shoulders. It's cold outside.'

He didn't offer her his arm, but he watched carefully as she stumbled to the door. He switched off the light and locked the door behind her.

'I hate owing anyone money,' Alma murmured as he walked alongside her up Taff Street.

'You seem to have little option at the moment.'

'When I'm straight, I'm going to save every penny I can so I'll never get in this mess again,' she said vehemently. The effort of speaking made her feel dizzy again and she clutched at Charlie's arm. He lent her his support, but she still felt a distance she was convinced hadn't existed earlier when he'd carried her into the shop. She glanced up at his face. His eyes didn't even seem to be focused on the surroundings. They were looking inward with an expression that further chilled her icy body.

She wasn't to know that he was back in another time, another place. Walking out on a cold night just like this one, with a young girl clinging to his arm. One who, like her, had red hair and deep green eyes that a man could look into and lose his soul.

'What are you thinking about, Feo?'

She had been wearing a thick black wool coat and a bright red hand-knitted scarf. He'd had to bend down to kiss the tip of her frozen nose.

'You're not my mother,' she'd protested.

'I don't want to be your mother. But I want to make sure that you're around to share that future I've been dreaming about.'

'When we'll have our own house . . . just like my brother Dmitri and his wife,' she began, laughing at him a little.

'Not like Dmitri. Ours will be grander.'

'Grander?'

'Grander,' he repeated, refusing to acknowledge her scepticism. 'It will have a veranda downstairs and a balcony upstairs that you'll be able to sit out on and pick cherries from the trees that I'll plant all around the garden. There'll be stoves in all the rooms, not just the kitchen, with flues going up into the bedrooms to keep them warm.'

'I won't need flues. I'll have the feather bed my grand-mother is making us, and,' she arced her eyebrows, 'you to keep me warm Feo.'

Her smile bewitching, mischievous. Her lips beneath his, warm, enticing.

'Masha . . .'

'The others won't be back from my uncle's name day for hours. The barn is warm, we could go in for just a little while.'

'Don't you know what you're doing to me?'

'Spring will soon break, then we'll be married.'

'A few weeks.'

'In which to practise.'

'Masha!' He'd pretended to be shocked.

'Come on Feo, you're wasting time. The barn is dry . . .'

Dry and warm, just as she'd promised. Smelling of hay and the chickens that nested between the bales. And her hair, sweet, fragrant loosed from the bond of the net she wore. He wanted no woman in his bed. None except Masha . . .

'This is it?'

Charlie looked about him and realised Alma had led him to her front door.

'Thank you for walking me home.' She removed her arm from his and handed back his coat. 'Won't you come inside?'

'I don't think so. It's very late.'

She hesitated, her hand on the doorknob.

'Are you afraid to go in?' he asked intuitively.

'I know it's silly of me. It's just that Bobby collects my rent. He knows where I live.'

'Do you want me to check your house?'

Although he'd visited her before, she was torn between a desire to keep her poverty private, and her fear of Bobby. The fear won. 'Please, come in, just for a moment.' She opened the door and walked down the passage. Charlie closed the door behind him and instinctively reached out and felt for an electric light switch, then he saw the faint, brief flare of a match, followed by the soft glow of a candle through the thin curtain up ahead. Alma pushed aside the curtain, and he followed her into the kitchen.

'The back door is in the washhouse.' She lit another stub of candle from the flame of the one she held in her hand.

He took the candle she offered, lifted the latch and checked the washhouse thoroughly before opening the back door and looking into the yard, outhouse and coal-house.

'Nothing out there. Do you want me to bolt the door?'

'Please.'

He did as she asked, then followed her back into the cold kitchen.

'I'll stay here while you check the upstairs,' he said, handing her the candle.

Charlie stood, gazing out of the small kitchen window, listening to her footsteps as they echoed over the flag-stones in the passage. They paused for a moment, and he heard her checking the empty front room before walking up the uncarpeted staircase.

After Russia he'd believed himself immune to the wretchedness poverty trailed in its wake. Now he knew he wasn't. The house even smelt of poverty, an odour compiled from shame and the humiliation of not having two halfpennies to rub together. The last time he'd stood in the kitchen he'd noticed only the obvious: the lack of fire, cushions, rugs, small comforts that those who had the luxury of work took for granted. Now he had time to study the room at length without Alma's eagle eye watching him, he was appalled by its bleakness.

The battered and patched tin bucket in front of the stove contained barely half an inch of small coal. There was no sign of wood, only newspapers. The scrubbed surfaces of the pine-topped deal table and breadboard were devoid of the smallest crumb. He couldn't even smell food, and he had a shrewd suspicion that if he were to open the doors of the pantry and dresser they'd be bare. If any mouse was foolhardy enough to enter this house it would probably starve to death along with the occupants. The dresser held two cups, two saucers and two plates, if there had been more he didn't doubt they'd been sold or pawned. A single clean but patched saucepan hung upside down on the drying rack above the cold stove. Even the stub of candle Alma had lit was the last on the mantelpiece. A framed photograph stood incongruously next to it. Pushing the candle closer, he studied it.

'My father.'

Alma was standing in front of the curtain.

'He died when I was small. Pit accident.' She walked over to the photograph and picked it up. 'What I hate more than anything is not being able to remember him. Only the funeral, and my mother crying. Endlessly crying.'

He reached inside his shirt and took out the bag he kept his takings in. Carrying them and the stub of candle over to the table he counted out five pounds.

'That's for the rent and the corner shop. I'll stop by tomorrow with another five.'

He replaced the bag inside his shirt and slipped his arms into the sleeves of his coat. It smelt of the household soap she used and the cooking he associated with Ronconi's café.

'I don't need this much,' she protested as she looked

down at the mixed silver and ten-shilling note on the table.

'Take it. I'll see you tomorrow and we'll make arrangements for you to move into the flat above the shop. Don't forget to bolt the door behind me.'

She followed him but he stepped outside without a backward glance. She had been prepared to sleep with him. He'd rejected her, yet he'd given her money. The thought that floated uppermost in her mind as she rammed the bolt home on the door as that at least the women in station yard had the satisfaction of knowing that they'd earned their money.

It was strange how soon life, any life, eventually becomes a routine, Bethan thought as she carried buckets of water from the boiler in the stove to the enormous tub in the washhouse to do the weekly wash. She had been home for over five weeks and already it felt as though she and Edmund had never lived anywhere else. Strange too how, as if by tacit agreement, no one in the house ever brought up the subject of her mother.

Eddie had made a point of going calling for rags in the Rhondda the morning after Elizabeth Powell's departure, and on his return had mentioned that he had seen Elizabeth beating John Joseph's mats on his washing line. Eddie hadn't attempted to speak to his mother, but then neither had she said a word to him, although she must have heard the sound of his horn. From that scant piece of information Bethan presumed that Elizabeth had found a home with her uncle. The following day she wrote her mother a letter telling her that she and Eddie were going to try and keep the home going between them. Elizabeth had never replied, and as the household slipped easily and effortlessly into a new routine that eventually became an established pattern of life, Elizabeth became, if not exactly forgotten, at least relegated to a past that seldom warranted a thought, let alone a mention.

William, Eddie and Diana became more talkative in the

days following Elizabeth's dramatic exit and, although none of them tried to analyse their feelings, they all felt as though a smothering, suffocating fog had been blown from the house. Charlie alone remained as taciturn and preoccupied as ever, but Bethan put that down to the problems connected with opening his shop coupled with the financial loss of a whole pig. She'd lent William ten shillings to cover his carelessness, all that she could afford, but she knew that it went nowhere towards compensating Charlie for the loss of his unsold stock.

Despite Evan's absence which affected them all, William and Eddie took to whistling as they went about their chores. They filled the coal bucket, cleared the ashes from the stove and carried the vegetable peelings up to the compost heap at the top of the garden without Bethan ever having to nag for their help as Elizabeth had frequently resorted to doing. They also took to cleaning their shoes over old newspaper in the washhouse instead of the cold yard, ferrying cups of tea up to her and Diana in their bedrooms first thing in the morning, and dunking the biscuits Diana made in the evenings in their tea instead of nibbling them dry. Small things Elizabeth would have severely disapproved of and put a stop to at once.

Bethan knew that although the fabric of the house in Graig Avenue remained unchanged, there were subtle differences in the household as she ran it that her mother would have condemned as examples of degenerate, ungodly behaviour. For example, not one of them had set foot in a chapel since Elizabeth had left. Bethan had used the baby's condition as an excuse, but the boys and Diana hadn't even felt the need to fabricate one. Instead, for the boys and Charlie, Sunday had become a day for working on the shop, something they had the good sense to do quietly, concentrating on cleaning and decorating the back rooms where they couldn't be seen by the chapel contingent. For Diana and Bethan it became a day for reading, playing cards, and catching up with the hundred and one small jobs neither of them ever seemed to find time to do in the week.

If Bethan wasn't happy, she was at least contented, and for that she was grateful. Generally too busy to think about Elizabeth, or even her father, she only had cause to remember them when she dusted their wedding photograph which had been kept out of sight in the sacrosanct front parlour for as long as she could remember. But strangest of all was the way she had managed to banish all thoughts of Andrew from her mind, at least during her waking hours. Last Friday another money order had been delivered by the postman, accompanied by a brief note: 'Hope you are well. Best wishes, Andrew.' She had sent him the pawn ticket for her pendant with a brief explanation, finishing with the line, 'I am well', and although he hadn't asked after his son, 'Edmund is well too. Thank you for the money. Bethan.'

But in the cold, early hours of the morning she truly did miss him. She lay awake in her parents' great bed yearning for his presence with a fervour that could only have been soothed by his touch. It was then, when she watched the moon shining down on the back garden through the crack in the curtains as she listened to Edmund's slow, quiet breathing, that she remembered. The good times! There had been so many of them. When she had first met Andrew and gone out with him, when she had left Pontypridd to be with him in London. And the last days of her pregnancy when he had cared for her so tenderly and solicitously, in fact right up to the moment of Edmund's birth.

Pushing the memory of that painful moment from her mind she picked up half of the pile of sheets and pillowcases she had stacked on the floor and threw them into the tub. Five beds and a cot made for a lot of washing. And afterwards there'd be the boys' shirts and long johns, and her and Diana's petticoats and blouses, the baby's nightdresses, and if the water was still warm and clean enough, Charlie and William's butchers' overalls. They were so soiled she set them in a bucket of soda to soak overnight and washed them out separately before dumping them in with the rest of the wash prior to boiling and starching.

Bethan picked up the wooden dolly and started pounding. Her new maxim in life was quite simple: keep busy, take each task, and day, as it came. By the time she had cleaned the house, cooked the food, done the washing and shopping with the baby in a shawl wrapped Welsh fashion around him and her, so no one could take more than a sly peek at him, there wasn't much time left for thinking – all she had to do was try to find a way to sleep at night. If she succeeded in that, there would be no time for complex desires or introspection.

The dolly slipped in her wet hand and water slopped on to the flagstoned floor. She smiled, imagining the scolding Elizabeth would have doled out, as she tossed the floorcloth over the sudsy mess.

'Bethan! Bethan!'

'Mrs Richards, I'm in the washhouse,' she answered. Much as she appreciated the love and support of her family around her, she resented the interference of the neighbours more than ever after London, and Mrs Richards was by far and away the worst culprit. Annoying Bethan constantly by referring to Edmund as 'that poor mite', she was always trying to peek into the cot as though the child was an exhibit in a freak show.

'Bethan, what do you think?' Mrs Richards burst open the door to the washhouse. 'I saw Billy's wife down the market and . . .' she paused for breath as she laid her loaded shopping basket on the floor at her feet.

'And?' Bethan prompted as she concentrated on her washing.

'And she told me they're allowing visitors into Cardiff this Sunday. Your dad is in Cardiff?'

'Yes,' Bethan replied shortly.

'I thought they might have put him somewhere else, what with him getting hard labour and everything.' She made it sound a far deeper disgrace than mere prison. 'Where was I? Oh yes, visiting. Well I stopped off to get a message to my Glan in the workhouse. Of course we'll be going along with Billy's wife and his old mother, and I thought I should come right up here and tell you. You'll have to get a message to your mam, wherever she is.' She looked slyly at Bethan. 'I mean she'll want to see him, won't she? It being over a month since they were sent down,' she babbled, not really knowing, but guessing the cause of Elizabeth's flight from her home of over twenty years.

'This Sunday you say, Mrs Richards.' Bethan pulled the cumbersome free-standing mangle closer to the tub. 'What time?'

'Two o'clock. It's the first time anyone in our family has visited a prison, but it isn't for you, is it? Your Aunt Megan has been there quite a while now. Over a year?'

'William and Diana go to see their mother as often as they can,' Bethan said flatly in an attempt to shame Mrs Richards out of her tactless cross-examination.

'According to what Billy's wife told me, we won't be able to take much in for them. A few bits of food, that's all. They won't let them wear their own clothes or read anything except the one letter a month. They even cut up any cakes you bake, but at least we'll be able to see how they are for ourselves, won't we?'

'Thank you for calling in.' Bethan heaved the first of the sheets up to the mangle with the end of the wooden dolly. 'If you'll excuse me, I must get on with this before the baby wakes for his next feed.'

'Oh, bless him too, the poor little mite. Will you be going to see your dad?' Mrs Richards made no attempt to pick up her basket.

'Probably. I'll have to talk it over with my brother.'

'Oh yes of course, Eddie. It must be hard for you at a time like this not to have Haydn around. Such a nice sensible boy, Haydn. But then you must be missing your husband too. I was only saying to our Glan the other day what a good-looking young man Doctor John is. Will we be seeing him soon?'

'Possibly,' Bethan replied shortly, heaping the first sheet into the sink and starting to wring the second.

'Oh and I almost forgot in my hurry to tell you about the prison . . .' Mrs Richards leaned back against the wall, still hoping that Bethan would invite her to have a cup of tea so she could get a good look at the baby. A lot of people were wondering what he looked like, and as next-door neighbour, she thought it only fitting she should be the one to tell them. 'I heard down Griffiths' shop that Rhiannon Pugh's not expected to last the night. The poor old thing's done for. According to the doctor she's just plain worn out. But then, that's what comes of having the likes of Phyllis Harry in the house. Rhiannon's run herself ragged looking after Phyllis's bastard . . .'

'Rhiannon has been ill for years,' Bethan interposed quickly. She'd had a soft spot for Phyllis since the days when Phyllis had worked as an usherette in the White Palace and turned a blind eye to younger brothers and sisters who'd been smuggled into the back row of the chicken run through toilet windows; and she was very fond of Rhiannon, who had offered her tea and Welsh cakes – flat cakes baked on a griddle – every time she had used her house in Phillips Street as a short cut on the way to school, town and, later, to her work in the Graig Hospital.

'I know Rhiannon has been ill for years, but the Good Lord would have spared her for a bit longer if it hadn't been for all that worry over Phyllis. And now there's no saying what will happen to Phyllis and the boy. The house is rented in Rhiannon's name and I can't see Fred the Dead passing the rent book over to an unmarried mother, even if Phyllis could afford to keep it on, which I doubt she can.' Mrs Richards crossed her arms as though defying Bethan to tell her any different.

'She'll manage somehow, Mrs Richards, most of us do.'

'We manage. But the question is will we continue to

manage inside or outside the workhouse?'

'Let's hope it will be outside, for all of us.' Bethan dumped the last of the sheets into the water.

'So I pray to God every night.' Mrs Richards stooped and picked up her basket, finally accepting that she was not going to get a cup of tea, or a peek at the baby. 'I suppose it's time I went next door to start on my own washing. You've no idea of the state my Glan gets that porter's uniform of his into.'

'It's a nice drying day,' Bethan commented, hoping to finally edge Mrs Richards out. 'I'll see you to the door.'

'I know the way, dear. You stay and finish what you're doing.'

'No trouble, and thank you for the news about the prison.' Bethan followed Mrs Richards into the kitchen, positioning herself so as to ensure that Mrs Richards couldn't see Edmund. She opened the door. 'Thank you for calling in.'

'See you on Sunday then?'

'Perhaps.'

Mrs Richards walked down the Powells' front steps reflecting that although Elizabeth had left Graig Avenue, the welcome in her house was as cold as it had ever been.

Bethan rushed through her washing in record time, finishing it just before the baby woke for his feed. Eddie sometimes came home for dinner if he was calling the streets anywhere near home, but because she wanted him to come that particular day, he didn't show his face, and the bread and Welsh cakes she'd baked that morning remained locked in their tins in the pantry.

At two o'clock she picked up the spare bottle and nappy she had packed into a string carrier bag, put on her coat and hat and wrapped the baby and herself in a shawl. As an afterthought she filled an empty tin with her cakes and Diana's biscuits. She glanced around the kitchen before she left. It wasn't as smart or modern as the London flat, but it had been her home as a child, and it had become home again, providing a safe haven when she had needed one. It looked shabby and worn, but also clean, and cosy with the stove belching out heat. The warm, welcoming smell of fresh baking lingered in the air. She imagined the boys and Diana walking in, and the thought occurred to her that she didn't know how long she was going to be. She took a pencil from the marmalade jar on the windowsill and the back of one of Andrew's envelopes and scribbled, 'In Rhiannon's with Phyllis. Bethan.'

'Rent.' Bobby swaggered through the shabby door of Alma's house, purposely kicking the bottom panel as he went. It splintered from its supporting nails and fell in three large pieces on to the flagstones. Glancing up from the wreckage, he saw Alma standing in front of the curtained doorway of the kitchen, her green eyes contemptuous as she held out her rent book at arm's length.

'It's all there, folded inside. A ten-shilling note and a sixpence. Nine shillings for this week, plus the one and six I owe from last week.'

'It'll cost another ten shillings to mend this door. A pound for a new one if it can't be fixed.'

'You broke it. You pay.' For the first time she noticed the deep black and purple bruise that spread from his chin along his jawline up to his left ear. There was a cut on his eye too. She could see its bloody jagged edge beneath the plaster that was covering his left eyebrow.

'That rain guard fell off when I opened the door because you haven't given it a single lick of paint in the last ten years.'

'It was fine until you kicked it.'

'I say otherwise, and seeing as how the landlord pays me to check the houses and collect the rent I know who he'll believe.'

'Not after last night.'

'What happened last night, then?' He stared at her cockily as he wrenched the rent book from her outstretched hand.

'You know as well as I do.'

'I know nothing.'

'The mess on your face tells a different story.'

Bobby pushed past her, slamming her into the wall with his shoulder as he pulled back the curtain and walked into the kitchen. He laid the rent book down on the table and took a fountain pen from his pocket. He unscrewed the top with a flourish.

Although he had taken his time, waiting until he'd seen Alma's mother walk off to the market clinging to Mrs Lane's arm, he looked over his shoulder as he signed the book, just to make sure the house was really deserted. After last night he didn't entirely trust Alma not to have someone lying in wait.

'You Charlie the Russian's bit on the side then now?' he taunted after he'd ensured they were alone. 'Is that where this—' he stuffed the money that had been folded into her rent book into a bag – 'came from?'

'It's my money.'

'Not honestly earned I'll be bound, unless of course,' he sniggered, 'you count lying on your back working.'

She went to the window and opened it wide, letting in a draught of freezing air. 'Just sign the rent book and go, Bobby,' she said loudly.

'Or what?' Secure in the knowledge that not only was Mrs Lane out, but Mr Lane had taken advantage of his wife's absence to walk around the corner to visit the illicit bookie shop, he pushed his face close to Alma's. 'Or you'll go whining to your foreign friend and ask him to work me over again? Well, have I got news for you. I know a lot of funny people in this town, and Russian Charlie had better watch his back.'

'You touch him and I'll go straight to the police.'

'And tell them what? That I turned down your offer to pay the rent without handing over any money?' He caught her hair and twisted her head back. Planting his wet, greasy lips over hers, he kissed her. She kicked him on the shins and he yelped. This time she was quicker than him, fleeing down the passage and out through the front door before he managed to retrieve his pen from the table. She stood outside, trembling, waiting for him to leave. He followed her, kicking aside the pieces of wood then opening the door as wide as it would go.

'You'd better watch your Ps and Qs,' he warned softly as he walked into the street. 'You can start by having this door repaired,' he added in a louder voice. 'And if it isn't done by next week, I'll see you out of here for neglecting the terms of your lease.'

'You try that and I'll tell your wife all about you, Bobby Thomas,' Alma screamed after him, silencing the children who were playing in the street. 'And don't you come knocking at my door any more for the rent either. I'm walking up to Maesycoed to pay it to Mr Jones direct. And I'm telling him why.'

Chapter Thirteen

PHYLLIS WAS UPSTAIRS, sitting watching at Rhiannon's deathbed with her small son playing at her feet, when she heard Bethan call her name softly in the downstairs passage. She rose quietly from her chair and picked up her son. He looked anxiously up into her face from large brown frightened eyes as she smoothed the hair away from Rhiannon's face. He didn't understand what was happening, only that his mother and Mamgu were very quiet, and Mamgu didn't get out of bed or want to play with him any more.

'I heard about Rhiannon. I came as soon as I could. Can I look after the little one for you?' Bethan asked as Phyllis walked down the stairs.

Phyllis bit her lip in an effort to hold back her tears. Her shame at bearing a bastard had led her to expect ostracism, and the indifference she had affected after his birth had frustrated the efforts of even the most determinedly helpful of the women in the street.

'Please. You know that if my Aunt Megan were here, she'd be with you.' Bethan put a finger from her free hand into Phyllis's son's hand. He took it and smiled.

The smile decided Phyllis. Since Rhiannon had taken to her bed two days ago, she had felt more alone than she had ever done in her entire life. With Rhiannon lying unconscious, having to be washed, fed and changed as though she were a helpless baby, and without Evan's daily visits she had felt cut off from and neglected by the world.

'Thank you.' She set her son down on the floor close to Bethan.

Bethan held out her hand to him. 'What's his name?'

'Brian. I named him after my father,' Phyllis said as the child tottered unsteadily towards the kitchen door.

'Come on Brian, you can help me make some tea.' Bethan hesitated for a moment. 'Is there anyone I should send for, Phyllis?'

'Rhiannon has no family left.'

'What about you?'

'Charlie,' Phyllis said decisively without thinking who she was speaking to. 'Please, send for Charlie. He'll know what to do.' She turned and walked back upstairs.

Bethan was totally bewildered. If anyone had asked, she would have said that Charlie and Phyllis didn't even know one another. Keeping a firm grip on Brian's hand she opened the front door and walked out on to the top step. A ragged collection of boys were playing football with a tin can lower down the street. Three young girls were walking up and down following the game, taking it in turns to push a battered old pram containing a small baby. Cheaper and more readily available than a doll, Bethan thought wryly. She stared at the boys, hoping to see one she recognised, but it was difficult. A few months away in London and none of the faces looked familiar. Finally she settled on one she thought she recalled from Eddie's schooldays.

'Martin Gibbs?'

'That's not Martin, Nurse Powell. That's his brother Michael,' one of the young girls, dressed in a cotton dress that was too thin for the cold weather assured her knowledgeably.

'Run and get him for me would you please?'

'Our mam told us not to play near this house,' one of the girl's playmates commented gravely to Bethan. 'She said that old Mrs Pugh is dying and she deserves a bit of peace before she goes, without us yelling in the street outside.'

'She is dying,' Bethan murmured softly, clutching Brian's hand all the harder. 'And I'm sure she's grateful to you for keeping quiet.'

'You want me, Nurse Powell?' The boy Bethan thought was Martin ran towards her.

'I'd like you to run an errand for me.' Bethan pulled her purse out of her coat pocket.

'Down the shop?'

'No, down the market. You'd better tell your mam where you're going.'

'She's out gossiping, she won't miss me.'

'There's no one in your house?'

'My dad.'

'Then tell him.' She produced a penny. 'You can have this, and two more when you come back.'

His eyes grew round. Threepence was birthday money for a child on the Graig.

'I'll go with him, Missus.'

'And me.'

'And me . . .'

'Just you.' Bethan handed the penny to the boy. 'You know Charlie's stall in the meat market?'

'Course I do. Everyone knows Russian Charlie.'

'Ask him to . . . tell him . . .' Bethan thought for a moment, wondering how best to phrase Phyllis's message. 'Tell him Mrs John needs him in Rhiannon Pugh's house. And tell him it's urgent.'

Phyllis sat on one side of Rhiannon Pugh's bed holding her withered hand, and Bethan sat on the other. Bethan had helped Phyllis to change the old lady's bed earlier and remake it with rubber draw-sheets and the deep blue satin coverlet that had been kept for 'best'. Now it lay over the smoothed sheets and blankets, and the frail figure of the old lady who'd treasured it all her married life. Phyllis had hung the unbleached linen shroud and white stockings that Rhiannon had stitched against this day over the central mirror of the dressing table. The old lady had asked her to remove the garments from her chest when she had taken to her bed, and had also extracted a promise from Phyllis that she would dress her in them before the undertaker placed her in her coffin. In front of the grave clothes stood a blue vase inscribed with gold lettering that read, 'A present from Porthcawl'. It was filled with daffodils that Charlie had brought up from the market, a gesture that had amazed both Phyllis and Bethan. Neither of them had ever considered the Russian thoughtful before; although as Bethan watched him stand impassively at the foot of the bed next to the door, arms folded as he kept silent vigil with them, and remembered some of the things he had done for her family over the past three years she realised it was an adjective he well deserved.

He had arrived on Rhiannon's doorstep with the flowers in his hand and Trevor Lewis in tow. Respecting Phyllis's need to be with the old lady, Trevor had examined Mrs Pugh in her presence, shaking his head gravely as he tucked his stethoscope into his bag.

Bethan had given him tea afterwards, and he had taken the opportunity to check Edmund over, and to chastise her for not coming to visit him and Laura more often. She promised to do so as soon as time allowed, and he left, muttering something about coming back later. Diana had arrived at Rhiannon's door within five minutes of coming home from work and reading Bethan's note. Sizing up the situation, she took Edmund off Bethan's hands and went home to make Eddie and William's supper. Bethan washed the endless empty cups dotted around Rhiannon's kitchen, bathed Brian in Rhiannon's enormous stone sink, and put him to bed in the big double bed he shared with his mother.

Sensing something was wrong, Brian listened intently while Bethan sung him a lullaby, accepted her good-night kiss without a murmur, snuggled down with a knitted rabbit and fell quietly asleep, which was probably as well, because for the first time in his life his mother didn't come to kiss him goodnight.

Once Brian was asleep, Bethan's evening became a marathon of making endless cups of tea, ferrying them to Phyllis and Charlie upstairs . . . and waiting. And at eleven o'clock all was much as it had been when Bethan had arrived at two in the afternoon. Rhiannon hadn't stirred. Her eyelids hadn't even flickered when Bethan and Phyllis remade her bed around her. The cheese sandwiches Bethan had made stood, curling and untouched where she had left them on Rhiannon's dressing table at six o'clock. Phyllis hadn't drawn any of the curtains all day, and as dusk fell Charlie lit one of the stubs of candle on the dressing table. As in most of the houses on the Graig, Rhiannon's electrical lights only extended as far as the downstairs rooms.

The candle flickered, silence reigned, and the old tin alarm clock that had woken Rhiannon's husband every day of his working life continued to tick away the final minutes of Rhiannon's life.

Charlie watched the light of the candle flicker across the old woman's face and remembered another deathbed. It had been spring then too. But not a damp cold spring like this. Dry days had burst sunny and warm, melting snows into lifegiving water, coaxing buds to unfurl on the trees. And the curtains in the death room had been kept open so the occupant could see the apple-blossom cloud, pink and fragrant on the branches outside the window.

He remembered the fragile weight of his grandfather's wasted hand in his. 'It is your time now, Feodor. Enjoy it. Enjoy it while you can. Every minute, boy. Life is wonderful. But for me now, it is over.'

He stepped from the doorway towards the bed. He trod softly, and if the rickety floorboards hadn't creaked beneath his weight Bethan wouldn't have noticed he'd moved. She shook herself from her reverie and watched as he laid his hand lightly on Rhiannon's neck, just as a doctor would have done. The action was so fluid, so natural, she didn't even think about it.

'She's gone,' he murmured, wrapping his arm around Phyllis's shoulder. Phyllis turned to him and he helped her to her feet. She stood there, head buried in his chest while Bethan went to Rhiannon. Charlie was right: the spirit that had animated the frail bundle of bones had left.

'It's not right,' Phyllis sobbed. 'Saying nothing . . . going without a word, like that . . .'

Bethan recalled some of the deaths she had witnessed as a nurse. Deaths lacking in dignity where people had gone out fighting, rattling and screaming to the last.

'It's the kindest way, Phyllis,' she said quietly. 'Believe me, it's what I want for myself, and I'm sure it's what Rhiannon would have wanted if she'd been given the choice.'

Phyllis stifled her sobs, gripped Charlie's shoulders, and turned round to face Bethan. 'You'll help me lay her out?'

'I'd be honoured.' Bethan looked at Charlie.

'I'll go downstairs and bring up some hot water. Then I'll walk to the Graig Hotel and telephone Doctor Lewis.' He glanced at the clock. It had stopped. He pulled out his pocket watch. 'Half-past eleven. Rhiannon died at half-past eleven?'

Phyllis nodded. Picking up the grave clothes she held them tightly in her hands. Suddenly they seemed to be all she had left.

At midnight, Trevor Lewis arrived in response to Charlie's telephone call. A few minutes after he'd signed the death certificate in Rhiannon's bedroom, there was a knock at the front door.

'I called the undertaker,' Trevor explained apologetically to a startled Phyllis. 'I thought you'd need a coffin.'

Phyllis took one of Rhiannon's cold hands in her own and kissed it as Charlie went down to open the door. Outwardly Phyllis was composed, but inwardly she was desperately trying to cling to what little routine remained of her life. As long as the old lady lay here in her own bed she was at least an integral part of the household. Coffins had no part to play in life. They belonged to cemeteries, to the ceremonies that underlined the finality of the ultimate separation.

Phyllis realised that once Rhiannon was removed from this bed, she would never again see the woman who had been more of a mother to her than her own. She would be on her own, as she had never been before. Alone with sole responsibility for her son; the prospect terrified her.

'I wasn't sure which model you wanted. I've brought a standard pine with wooden fittings to be getting on with. If you want it replaced with mahogany and brass . . .' Fred Jones's voice floated up the stairs. Charlie murmured a reply, too low for Bethan and Phyllis to hear.

'If it's all right with you we'll set it up in place now, then carry the body down. I take it, she is in one of the bedrooms?'

Phyllis and Bethan considered Fred Jones's voice loud and insensitive for a house of death, but experience had taught the undertaker that it was easier to be mis-understood when you spoke in hushed tones.

Charlie looked at the narrow stairwell and nodded agreement. While he rearranged Rhiannon's heavy old Victorian furniture in the front parlour, the undertaker brought in trestles and set them up in pride of place in the centre of the room. After Charlie had given him a hand to carry in the coffin, he fussed around, inching the supports first one way, then the other in order to give anyone looking in from the passage the best possible view of the coffin, and its contents.

'Not that I suppose there'll be that many who'll come in to look at her,' Fred asserted when everything had been arranged to his satisfaction. 'From what I hear they led a quiet life in this house.'

In the end it was Charlie who carried Rhiannon's body, wrapped in the best bedcover, down the stairs, and Phyllis aided by Bethan who arranged the cheap machined cotton frill around the old lady's face and shroud.

'She looks peaceful, doesn't she?' Phyllis asked, seeking confirmation.

'I hate to get down to brass tacks at a time like this,' Fred interrupted in a rasping voice, before either Bethan or Charlie could answer. 'But the sooner the business side is tied up to everyone's satisfaction, the sooner you can get on with your mourning.'

'Can't it wait?' Phyllis pleaded as she folded Rhiannon's fingers around the gold crucifix her husband had bought to celebrate the birth of their only son over sixty years ago.

'I'll sit with Rhiannon while you talk to Mr Jones,' Bethan interposed, knowing how important 'corpse sitting' was to the women of the Graig, especially during the first night after death.

Phyllis reluctantly returned Rhiannon's hands to the coffin, and with one final backward glance, left the parlour. Trevor, Fred Jones and Charlie filed solemnly after her into the kitchen. Without thinking, Phyllis filled the kettle, put it on the stove to boil and counted heads. She went to the open-shelved dresser and lifted down three of Rhiannon's 'best' blue and gold cups and saucers for the men, then three more, one for herself, one for Bethan, and one for Rhiannon. When she'd realised what she'd done, the tears began to flow again. Charlie took the last cup gently from her trembling hands and replaced it on the shelf.

'I take it Mrs Pugh was insured?' It was after twelve. Fred had downed several brandies in the New Inn, and all he wanted now was his bed. Preferably warmed by the plump body of his wife. He resented being called out on a Saturday night. Any other night of the week he didn't mind, but a Saturday night was special. He found himself wondering, not for the first time, why people couldn't die during respectable daylight hours, say between eight in the morning and six in the evening.

'She was.' Phyllis dried her tears and set about spooning pungent black tea-leaves from Rhiannon's old tin caddy into the pot.

'Now, about the funeral . . .' He removed a notebook covered in shiny black cloth from his pocket and licked the lead on the pencil that had been tucked into its spine.

Phyllis stared at the book. She had only ever seen red notebooks before. Even the manager of the White Palace had carried a red one. She wondered if black ones were produced specially for undertakers.

'. . . how many cars besides the hearse?'

'Just one,' she answered instantly and decisively, much to Trevor and Charlie's admiration.

'One mourners' car. That's all? You sure?'

'There's no family, only me. Rhiannon had no one.' Phyllis picked up the boiling kettle and poured water into the brown china teapot.

'But there'll be friends and neighbours,' Fred urged softly.

'Who'll make their own way to Glyntaff.' Trevor had taken to calling Fred in on his final visit to a patient, to ensure that none of Fred's subtle pressure was exerted on families at a time when they were least able to cope with it.

The undertaker debated whether or not to press the point, and decided against it. Jones & Sons might be the biggest undertakers in town, but they weren't the only ones. 'I'll put you down for a hearse and one car. Grave?'

'She wants . . . wanted,' Phyllis corrected herself sharply as she handed out filled teacups, 'to be buried with her husband and her son. It is a grave for three. Rhiannon bought the plot in Glyntaff cemetery when they were killed in the pit accident.'

'I'll need the grave number.' He looked up from his notebook. Phyllis pulled out a bundle of papers neatly tied with black satin. 'These are the grave papers.'

He squinted at them and took down the number. 'There'll still be costs, you know,' he sniffed. Russian Charlie had made the decision that a standard pine coffin with wooden furniture would do without even consulting Phyllis, although heaven only knew where he fitted into the household. And with only one car and a hearse, and no new plot pickings were going to be slim – very slim indeed. The next thing they'd be saying was they wanted to cut back on flowers. 'The grave has to be opened so you'll still have to pay for the gravediggers' time. Twice. Once to open, and once to close the plot. I take it there will be a new engraving to be put on the headstone?'

'Only the date of death. Rhiannon put on her name, date of birth and "beloved wife of" when her husband died. How much will it all come to, Mr Jones?'

'Well it seems that you want a simple funeral, but even so, all things considered you won't get much change out of thirty pounds.'

'That will be fine, Mr Jones.' Phyllis breathed a sigh of relief. Rhiannon's insurance would come to exactly that sum, and in addition she had taken a penny a week policy out on her landlady's life which would pay her five pounds. More than enough for flowers and black mourning clothes for herself and her son, and extra tea and cake for the mourners.

'The insurance will cover all the costs?' the undertaker asked prudently.

'It will. Please go ahead and make the arrangements.'

Trevor handed Phyllis his empty cup. 'Well if you'll excuse me I must be going. There's a case of bronchitis I promised to visit in Penycoedcae last thing tonight. But I can call in again on my way down the hill.'

'There's no need, Doctor Lewis,' Phyllis said as she left her chair.

'Then I'll be back in the morning.'

'Thank you for everything you did for Rhiannon, Doctor Lewis, and thank you for coming out so late.'

'If it wasn't for the sad circumstances I'd say it was always a pleasure to visit this house.' He gripped Phyllis's hand firmly. 'Remember, if you need me for anything, just send. Any time, day or night.'

'I must be off too.' Fred scribbled a final line in his notebook and snapped it shut.

Charlie walked both men to the door. Trevor hung back for a moment to hand Charlie a small packet when the undertaker was outside and out of earshot.

'She'll probably insist on sitting up all night. If you stir this into her tea, she'll sleep. Don't worry, she won't taste it, and there's no after-effects.'

Charlie pocketed the envelope.

'Strange set-up back there,' Fred commented as Trevor walked past his hearse on the way to his car.

'In what way?' Trevor asked warily.

'Russian Charlie being there. You think he fathered her bastard?'

'I have no idea, Mr Jones,' Trevor replied frostily.

'Could be. She's a bit long in the tooth and thin in the face, but I'll say this much for her, she's not a bad-looking woman considering her age.'

Charlie walked back into the silent house and glanced into the parlour. Phyllis was sitting on one of the high-backed, heavily carved, Rexine-covered chairs. Bethan was standing behind her. The main light had been switched off, the thick green plush curtains were drawn, but the women had lit two red candles that had stood in Rhiannon's brass candlesticks on her mantelpiece for years; possibly saved for this very night. They had placed them on a small octagonal table at the head of the coffin. The flames flickered, creating shadows that danced and bowed in every corner of the room, lending the scene the sepia and gold effect of a Rembrandt.

Charlie stood and watched for a moment. Bethan was holding Phyllis's hand, but the older woman had clearly withdrawn into a world of private grief. In the kitchen the pot of tea was still warm, and Charlie poured out three cups. Stirring the powder Trevor had given him into one, he carried it into the parlour.

'Thank you. Both of you.' Emerging from her misery Phyllis took the cup Charlie handed her and wrapped her freezing fingers round it. A fire hadn't been lit in the parlour since the day of Rhiannon's husband's funeral. It was a perfect temperature for corpses but uncomfortable for the living. 'I don't know what I would have done without you,' Phyllis continued.

'You would have managed.' Bethan took her cup from Charlie. 'People always do when they have no choice.'

'It's easier when you have someone to help.'

'There's nothing more you can do tonight. Why don't you go to bed and try to get some sleep while you can?' Bethan suggested.

'I don't think I could sleep. Besides, my place is here.'

'I'll stay with Rhiannon tonight,' Bethan offered.

'No, it's all right, really . . .'

'You have a few more days to say your goodbyes. Why don't you sit in the kitchen for a while? Eat something. I doubt if you've eaten all day.'

'I haven't,' Phyllis admitted.

'I'll make you some fresh tea and toast,' Bethan offered.

Phyllis suddenly realised that she wasn't the only one who hadn't eaten for hours. 'I'll go and make us all something,' she said and finally left her chair.

'I'll sit with Rhiannon.'

It didn't occur to either of the women to consider Charlie's suggestion odd.

Phyllis found two toasting forks, Bethan opened the door to the stove and they set about making toast. As soon as the first piece was ready Bethan buttered it and handed it to Phyllis, who sat back in her easy chair to eat it. Her eyes closed before she'd finished chewing the second bite. Bethan plumped up a patchwork-covered cushion, pushed it beneath Phyllis's head and lifted her feet on to an ancient beadwork stool. The knitted blanket Rhiannon had used to cover her arthritic knees was still folded on her chair. Bethan tucked it around Phyllis's slumped figure.

'I've made you some toast and tea.' Bethan stood in the doorway of the parlour.

'Is Phyllis asleep?' Charlie asked.

Bethan nodded. 'In the kitchen.'

'I'll carry her upstairs.'

'You'll risk waking her,' Bethan warned.

Phyllis didn't wake. Charlie laid her next to her son,

and Bethan, who'd followed him, slipped off Phyllis's shoes and draped the bedcover around her.

'You eat and I'll sit with Rhiannon for a while,' Bethan whispered as they reached the foot of the stairs.

'If we leave the door open we'll be able to see the candles from the kitchen.'

'And that's all that matters?'

'I don't think Rhiannon is likely to tell us any different.'

In all of the four years she had been acquainted with him, Bethan had never known Charlie to be flippant or make light of any situation, but that didn't stop her from scrutinising him as they went into the kitchen. He took off his coat. Hanging it on the back of a chair he rolled up his sleeves and went outside to wash his hands and face.

'Remind me to replace the food I've used tomorrow,' Bethan's voice was soft, low, although there was no real need to whisper.

'You won't need reminding.' He sat down and took a piece of toast.

'No I suppose I won't.' She looked across the table as she poured out fresh tea for both of them, and smiled, suddenly blessing Charlie's presence here, in this house of death; his solid dependability and his habit of saying very little, but always what was short, important and to the point. 'Now that the worst is over why don't you go home and get some sleep?' she suggested.

'It's all right, I'll stay with you.'

'You'll be exhausted tomorrow.'

'Tomorrow's Sunday.'

'What about the stall?'

'It's too late to worry about that now. What William hasn't done will have to wait until Monday. Let's just hope he hasn't lost another pig.'

'Will you sack him if he has?'

'Maybe.' She still couldn't detect any trace of humour in his voice. He sat back and drank his tea. Bethan thought of all the times she'd sat in this kitchen as

Rhiannon's guest, talking to her, eating her Welsh cakes . . .

'It's strange to think I won't see her any more when I walk through here on my way to town,' Bethan said.

'Rhiannon?'

'Yes.' She pushed the plate with the remaining slices of toast over to him. 'Everything seems to be changing so quickly, and I'm powerless to stop it. I go away, come back and nothing is the same. My father's gone—'

'He'll be back soon.'

'And my mother?'

Charlie didn't answer that question.

'And it's not as if it's just Rhiannon and my father. It's Haydn and Maud as well. I turn my back for five minutes and the whole family splits up. Nothing will ever be the same again.'

'You grew up, left home and had a family of your own,' he pointed out logically.

'I suppose I did.' She was ashamed of the bitterness she could hear creeping into her voice. She felt as though she was condemning and betraying her own son simply for being born.

It was most peculiar, sitting here, in another woman's kitchen across the table from Charlie, she was thinking – and talking about more important things than she had ever dared to discuss with Andrew. Perhaps it was Charlie's undemanding, uncritical presence. His habitual silences had taken a great deal of getting used to, but now she was grateful for them.

Charlie lit a cigarette and moved from the table to one of the easy chairs. 'The candles are still lit,' he said.

'Corpse lights. We used to watch their flames flickering through the shadows of drawn curtains when we were children. My grandmother told us that they were lit to guide the soul to heaven. All it had to do was follow the line of the smoke.'

'That's a nice thought.'

'When my grandmother died and I sat up with her, I

watched the candles burn in my Aunt Megan's back bedroom for hours. I really felt as though I was watching her soul leave for a better place.'

'I wish I'd had the same thought when my grandfather died.' It was the first time she'd heard Charlie mention his family, and she waited, hoping he'd say more. He left his chair and opened the door to the stove. The fire was burning low. He picked up the tongs and heaped half a dozen large lumps of coal from the bucket into the embers.

'Russia is not so different from Wales.' He was speaking so quietly she had to strain to catch his voice. 'Not when it comes to matters of death. The corpse is watched. Everyone in the village comes into the house to view the body and pay their respects before the burial.' He replaced the tongs, closed the oven door, looked up and gave Bethan a rare smile. 'The village gossips count the funeral carriages, the cost of the headstone and the widow's clothes.'

'You have gossips in Russia too?'

'People may speak different languages and wear different clothes, but from what I've seen they're much the same the world over.'

'They weren't in London.'

'No gossips?' He brushed his hands through his thick hair and for the first time she noticed the layers of fair hairs on his lower arms.

'No gossips,' she repeated firmly. 'I would have been happy to have met just one. I would have had someone other than Andrew and myself to talk to.'

'Is that why you came back? Because you were lonely?'

'That and . . .' she faltered as she realised what she was saying, and who she was saying it to. If her father had been home she would have talked to him. As he wasn't, why not talk to Charlie? After all, she could be sure that her confidences would go no further. '. . . and the baby. Everyone in London wanted me to put him in an institution,' she stated harshly.

'A workhouse?' She had just told him that no one had talked to her in London. It didn't take a lot to deduce who the 'everyone' was.

'It would have been a workhouse in all but name. I just couldn't do it. I couldn't . . .'

'I can understand that.'

'You can?'

'I think that children like Edmund need their parents even more than healthy ones.'

'What happens to them in Russia?'

'Oh we have institutions in Russia too. Perhaps even more than here. It is peculiar, I've never really thought of it before. The well-educated people always send their crippled children to institutions, but not the peasants. They keep their children with them no matter how they turn out.'

'I don't suppose it matters so much on a farm. They won't get pointed or stared at, or disgrace the family.' She could hear resentment in her voice, but was powerless to stop it from surfacing.

'We don't have farms like you do here. Not family farms. We have collectives. It's something like a village,' he tried to explain, regretting the impulse that had led him to talk about his homeland because it brought memories only too vividly to the forefront of his mind. 'Everyone lives in one area and they all work the land, take what they need and the rest of the produce is sent off to the cities.'

'Then you can have more than one family living there?'

'Hundreds on the larger ones.'

A farm to Bethan was one of the hill farms on Penycoedcae or over in Maesycoed. She couldn't imagine a farm big enough to hold hundreds of families. 'Did you live on a farm?'

'No, but I grew up in a village that had many farmers.'

'And it became a . . . a collective?'

'Not exactly.' Charlie retreated into his shell. He wasn't ready to talk about his past, but didn't want to rebuff Bethan. He hadn't talked to anyone like this since Evan had been sent to jail, and he hadn't realised just how much he'd missed him. He returned to the easy chair and lit another cigarette. 'Have you heard about my shop?'

'I've heard about nothing else for weeks from Will.'

'I hope to open the doors next week. That way we can start trading, and hopefully making some money to offset my outlay.'

'William told me there's a flat with a bathroom upstairs.'

'Yes.'

'Are you moving in there?' She dreaded his reply. Money wasn't a problem at the moment. Between the lodgers' rent money, the little that Eddie brought in, and her pound a week they were managing. But she knew that without her money her father would be hard pushed to meet the mortgage, and the loss of Charlie's would be almost as disastrous. He was that rare being in Pontypridd: a lodger with a steady job who was also easygoing, and always ready to lend a hand. There were women who'd throw their husbands out of the house to make room for a steady, sober man like Charlie.

'No.' He looked at her in bewilderment, and she was relieved to see that the thought of leaving the Avenue hadn't crossed his mind.

'I'm glad to hear it. We'd hate to lose you.'

'If you want me to go . . .'

'I'd hate for you to go. We need you, Charlie, and I don't mean your money. With Dad away I don't know what we'd do without you. At times like this, for example.'

'I've asked Alma Moore if she'll work in the shop. In the back, superintending the cooking. I was hoping she and her mother would live in the flat.'

'You're going to rent the flat to Alma Moore?'

'She's always been a good worker for the Ronconis, I thought I could do worse.'

'You could do a lot worse,' Bethan said thoughtfully,

recalling the rumours Diana had talked about, 'but then, from what little William's told me about the flat, so could she.'

'I don't suppose you'd call into the shop and give me your opinion on what we've done so far and what needs doing before I open the doors?'

'I don't know anything about shops.'

'You do from a customer's point of view. I don't even know how many chairs I should have for shoppers to sit on.'

'If there's room, at least three.'

'Why three?'

'One for tired invalids, one for ladies who think they're important and one for children to climb on.'

'I wouldn't have thought of that.'

'Don't underestimate the children. They'll drag their parents into any shop where there's a chance of a free taste of food.'

'That's something else I hadn't thought of. It could prove expensive,' he mused, visualising slices of his best ham cut up into thin slivers as 'tasters' and disappearing down the throats of the town's half-starved urchins.

'What are you going to be selling?'

'Cooked meats, pies . . .'

'Pastry stars.'

He looked at her uncomprehendingly.

'Get whoever does the cooking for you to make shapes out of the leftover pastry. If you really want to attract a crowd, mix some stale leftover cheese with it. Lots of shops do them in London.'

'Cheap giveaway.'

'Provided you don't try to feed the town.'

'Thanks for the tip, but you'll still call into the shop?'

'As soon as I get a chance.'

'I'd better get back to the front parlour before Phyllis wakes up and finds Rhiannon alone.' He picked up his coat from the chair. Tucking it under one arm he pulled down his shirt-sleeves and buttoned them up.

'And I'd better clear the dishes.' She brushed past him as she went to the kitchen window and pulled the curtains open. A pale light shone low over the garden, peeling back the darkness from the ground. 'Another hour and dawn will break.'

'You've seen in the dawn before?'

'Often when I was working in the hospital.'

'Of course. I forgot you worked nights as a nurse.'

'I'd almost forgotten it myself.'

'I used to watch the dawn break over the sea when it was my turn to take watch. It's different out there. At least when it's not raining. Colder, clearer and brighter than it is on land, especially in the North Sea.'

'Were you a sailor long?'

'A while,' he answered evasively.

'In between living in Russia and here?'

'Yes.' He shrugged his coat over his massive shoulders and stepped into the hall. 'I'll close this door behind me. It's getting colder and you'll need to keep the heat in. Phyllis and the little one will be waking up soon.'

Bethan opened the drawer at the bottom of the stove. It was choked with white-hot, powdery ash. As she went out to the washhouse to look for the ash bin she wondered how well one human being ever really knew another. Particularly where a man like Charlie was concerned.

Chapter Fourteen

THEY STARTED ARRIVING before dawn. Small children, shabbily and inadequately dressed in torn jerseys, faded shorts and cotton skirts, knocked Rhiannon's front door and handed over plates of Welsh cakes and fruit cakes that were more flour and fat than fruit, with whispers of 'Mam says she's very sorry, and she'll be over later.'

Bethan stacked the cakes on plates in the pantry and marvelled at the speed of the Graig grapevine. Either Trevor had let something slip at the house of the bronchitis patient, or a neighbour had seen the undertaker's hearse and spread the word. It soon seemed as though every family on the Graig knew that Rhiannon had passed on. At eight o'clock the women began to arrive, and the gifts of food from their meagre stores mounted. Those who hadn't lit their stoves that day brought pots of home-made blackberry jam and cold bowls of 'cawl' made with the cheapest, scraggiest of scrag ends of lamb, 'to be heated up later to save the poor girl cooking at a time like this'.

By the time Phyllis had roused, washed and dressed herself and her son, the callers had begun to arrive in earnest. Bethan and Charlie took it in turns to corpse-sit and make tea, trying to look as though they were listening attentively as the neighbours repeated the same trite phrases over and over again.

'So sorry to hear the news.' 'But then she was a good age, wasn't she?' 'How old was she, by the way?' 'Would have been eighty next month!' 'Well then, that's all any of us can really expect, isn't it?'

Even the women who had shunned Phyllis came, but

they took care to make it abundantly clear that they called only out of respect for Rhiannon. The cakes in the pantry were brought out, cut and distributed on Rhiannon's best china plates. Brian, totally bewildered by the influx of alien people into his home, sat on his own small chair in the corner next to the stove, solemnly eating cake for breakfast and pocketing the halfpennies handed to him by one or two of the women who had working husbands. He knew from the quiver in his mother's voice and the tears that hovered perilously close to the surface of her red-rimmed eyes that he had to be extra good, so he bravely concealed his excitement at the very first money he'd ever owned.

'Well, I am sorry to hear the news and no mistake. Mind you, not that it's unexpected, but you must be devastated all the same.' Mrs Richards walked into the kitchen through the washhouse door just as Myra Jones, Phyllis's next-door neighbour was leaving, and just in time to take possession of the easy chair. Now she was enthroned as though she had taken root. 'Is there anything I can do to help?' she asked Phyllis, who sat white faced and drawn in the chair opposite.

'Not really, Mrs Richards,' Phyllis replied softly. 'Bethan and Charlie have done everything.'

'Well they won't be here to help this afternoon, but then neither will I,' Mrs Richards announced. She glanced at the women crowded into the room in the hope that someone would ask why she wouldn't be around. When no question came she volunteered the information in a piercing voice that made Bethan cringe. 'It's prison visiting. The first since they sentenced my Vivian and Evan Powell. Martyrs, that's what they are. Martyrs to the Communist cause,' she repeated, conveniently forgetting her husband's Fascist leanings, which would gain her no sympathy in this company.

'Bethan, you must be exhausted, and you must have things to do at home.' Phyllis followed Bethan as she went to fill the kettle and get away from the chattering throng in the kitchen. 'Thank you for all you've done. I don't know how I would have managed without you.'

'I will go now if you don't mind,' Bethan said wearily. 'But I'll be back tonight, and in the meantime I'll send Diana over.'

'There's no need . . .'

'You're going to need someone to organise that lot for you,' Bethan jerked her head towards the kitchen door. 'And I can't think of anyone better than Diana. She's her mother's daughter in more ways than one. If anyone can get Mrs Richards off the topic of her Viv, and out of that chair, it's Diana.' Bethan was cheered by the sight of a tight smile crossing Phyllis's face. It wasn't much, but it was the first sign of animation since Rhiannon had died.

There was barely time for Bethan to wash and change herself and the baby before they had to leave for Cardiff. She stumbled down the Graig hill between Charlie and Eddie like a sleepwalker, wondering how she had ever managed to work a full night shift in the Graig Hospital when she had been doing her midwifery, and then go out all day with Andrew. All she wanted now was to put her feet up. Even the prospect of a bus seat seemed like deep luxury, but because it was a Sunday with an uncertain local service they had to walk down to Broadway to be sure of getting a connection.

Edmund, normally so placid, became fretful as a cold wind whistled up the Cardiff Road and through the inadequate cover of the shelter. When the bus finally came, the only seats available were the hard wooden slatted ones at the back that were usually reserved for labourers dressed in their working clothes. They jolted painfully over every pot-hole in the road between Pontypridd and Cardiff, and long before they reached Taffs Well Bethan would have believed anyone who told her that the bus company had switched to wooden tyres to save money.

The closer they drew to Cardiff the more peevish the baby became. Worried in case he was sickening for something, Bethan became irritable herself. Eddie took Edmund from her to give her a break, and jiggled him up and down in his arms, but the child refused to be placated, and Bethan greeted the conductor's bell with heartfelt relief when they finally reached the stop closest to the prison. They walked up the road in silence, then Bethan stopped, stunned by the number of people who were standing outside waiting to go in. Mrs Richards and her son Glan must have caught an earlier bus, for they were well up the front of the queue. Behind them pale-faced mothers coped as best they could with children that ranged from clinging, whining babies to fully grown boys and girls who were passing the time by fighting and spitting at one another. Old women stood patiently in line as they dabbed at their eyes and noses with damp, grubby handkerchiefs. Young men, hands thrust deep in trouser pockets, talked loudly amongst themselves and tried to look nonchalant, as though visiting prison was nothing special, simply an everyday event in their lives and nothing to be ashamed of.

'Ten minutes to wait,' Eddie murmured as they halted at the end of the queue.

'Yoo-hoo! Bethan! Eddie! Charlie!' Mrs Richards waved vigorously from the head of the line.

'I'll kill that woman one of these days,' Eddie muttered darkly.

'They'll want to search us before they'll let us in,' Charlie warned.

'You've visited prison before?' Bethan asked.

'With Diana and William. They'll go through everything you've brought for Evan as well.'

'It's only tobacco and Welsh cakes.'

'They'll still want to examine them.'

A grating of bolts galvanised everyone. A small wooden door set in the left-hand side of one of the two massive wooden doors that closed off the prison yard opened, and an acid-faced, black-suited warder stepped over the wooden stoop on to the pavement.

'Form an orderly queue there. Step lively,' he shouted, and the ragged crowd of visitors lined up in tight formation.

'The sooner we do as he asks, the sooner we'll get in,' Eddie suggested hopefully, pushing into line.

Charlie, who knew better, stood protectively at Bethan's side. The warder watched as they waited what seemed like hours, although the hands on Charlie's pocket watch ticked off only five minutes. Finally the warder capitulated and allowed the first half a dozen people through the door.

The queue shuffled forward with interminable slowness. Bethan fixed her attention on the door and waited. She wasn't sure what she expected to see inside. To be shown straight into a room where her father would be sitting, waiting for them perhaps? A clean, bright airy room like the waiting room in the workhouse which was always being painted by the inmates in order to make a good impression on any influential visitors? Would she be allowed to hug her father? Hold his hand? Hand him the baby?

A second warder appeared in the gateway and ushered the small group that they were a part of into a bleak, empty, stone-lined ante-room to the left of the gate. A barred iron door crashed shut behind them, penning them in like sheep. Frustrated and disappointed she had to stand and wait again, trying to make sense of the noises that she could hear from the open yard she had caught a glimpse of on her way through the door.

A series of 'Move along there', 'What's this then?' and 'You can go' couched in brusque, masculine tones echoed into the room. After another ten minutes of frustrating inactivity the door finally opened and they were herded along a path that cut a straight line between raised flowerbeds adorned with the shrivelled, spidery arms of hibernating plants.

'Move along there.'

Charlie drew close to Bethan. Taking her arm he

steered her across an open yard hemmed in by the towering grey blocks of the prison.

'All bags, parcels and gifts for the prisoners to be left here.'

Bethan shivered despite the thick flannel shawl that was wrapped around the baby and herself. The yard was more sheltered than the pavement, but it was still icy with the chill of an atmosphere that was rarely, if ever, touched by the warmth of the sun. Charlie guided her and Eddie towards one of four tables set out in the bleak courtyard, and they stood in line yet again, waiting while the warders tore open the bundles and parcels of those in front of them.

Bethan watched as the warders broke a fruit cake into crumbs, turned a bible upside down and shook it until the pages fluttered free of the spine, and spread the contents of a tobacco tin so thinly over a sheet of white paper that half the strands were lost in the breeze that fluttered, trapped between the walls of the buildings.

'Your baby, Miss?'

Bethan stared uncomprehendingly at the hatchet-faced warder facing her.

'It's Mrs! Mrs John. Her husband's a doctor so you'd better watch your mouth,' Eddie snarled angrily.

'Didn't mean anything by the remark, son,' the warder said easily.

'And I'm not your son either.'

'Eddie, it's all right. They're just doing their job,' Charlie interrupted smoothly, realising that although Bethan and Eddie were both intimidated by the uniformed men and bleak surroundings, they were coping in very different ways. Bethan had sought refuge in silence and Eddie was, as usual, trying to conceal his feelings behind a front of open aggression.

'Your baby, madam,' the officer repeated with elaborate courtesy. 'I have to check his shawl and his clothes. Sorry, it's customary procedure.'

'Can't we go inside? He isn't well and it's freezing out here.'

'I'll be as quick as I can.'

Bethan reluctantly unwound the shawl and handed it to the man. He held it by the corner and shook it, while she opened her coat and pushed the baby inside, close to her shivering body.

'I'm sorry, madam, but I have to check the baby's clothes as well. You can keep hold of him.'

Bethan held out Edmund and the man ran his fingers over his tiny frame.

'Now you, madam.'

'Here, give the baby to me.' Charlie retrieved the shawl from the warder and wound it inexpertly around the baby, who'd begun to whimper. The warder ran his hands down the sides of Bethan's coat and asked her to empty her pockets. She laid a comb, handkerchief and sixpence in change on the table.

'You can go the other side of the table, madam, but you'll have to wait while I examine your bag and parcels.'

Bethan took the baby from Charlie, and huddling in what little shelter the wall afforded, wrapped both herself and Edmund in the shawl. She soon saw that the warder had been quick with her. He certainly took his time over inspecting her handbag and Eddie and Charlie's clothes, asking them to empty shirt, trouser and coat pockets, as well as checking and double-checking the turn-ups on their trousers. The parcel Bethan had prepared for her father received his attention last of all. The Welsh cakes she had wrapped so carefully between layers of greaseproof paper in an old biscuit tin were emptied out and broken up, every single one of them, into three pieces.

'For God's sake what do you think we're going to hide in a Welsh cake?' Eddie complained bitterly.

'You'd be surprised, lad. You'd be surprised,' the warder echoed, totally unaffected by Eddie's irritation. He fingered the crumbs then scooped them back into the tin. He opened the tobacco, peeled back the outer covering and prodded the contents, before stripping away the gold leaf and shifting the brown strands from one side of the pack to the other.

'Prisoner visitors through the double doors and along the corridor on the right,' he barked when he was finally satisfied that the tobacco and cakes were what they appeared to be.

Charlie took Bethan's arm as they walked through a doorway flanked by two more warders. The corridor was painted dark green; the walls and tiled floor looked clean but the air stank of male sweat and stale urine. The passage opened out into a small hallway bisected by a row of desks. Two warders sat behind each one, bellowing the same questions as the visitors approached.

'Name? Age? Address? Name of prisoner to be visited?'

'Damn it all, anyone would think we were the ones who'd committed a crime,' Eddie said as they joined yet another column of shuffling people.

'No more than two visitors to a prisoner,' a warder said sharply to Bethan, Eddie and Charlie when they finally reached the end of their line.

'Does the baby count?' Eddie countered truculently.

'Infants under one year don't count as visitors,' the man replied, straight-faced.

'Can we change over after ten minutes?' Charlie asked, knowing full well from visits to Megan that changeovers were allowed.

'You'll have to keep an eye on the time yourself. Next.'

They walked down yet another corridor, where floor and walls bore the scratch marks of hours of scrubbing. The deeper they went into the building, the more over-whelming the stench became. This time the sickly smell was overlaid with an odour of cooking, predominantly cabbage. At the end of the corridor they walked into a huge echoing hall. And for the first time since she'd entered the confines of the prison Bethan saw the prisoners.

A barricade of wire mesh stretched from one side of the room to the other. Supported by huge iron poles it effectively sliced the room into two: the visitors' side, and the prisoners'. On the prisoners' side, the fence was separated into small cubicles by tall, narrow wooden frames. Rows of hard upright metal chairs were ranged on both sides of the mesh, all of them chained to the floor, and on the far side Bethan saw a mass of grey-suited, grey-faced men who looked as though the sun hadn't shone on them in years.

'Prisoner?'

'Powell. Evan Powell.' Bethan heard Charlie answer the man, and tried to smile as she scanned the expectant faces of the inmates. Her father was probably watching her now, trusting the visit to give him the strength he needed to carry on living in this dreadful place.

The warden looked down his list. 'Prisoner number . . . 46 . . .' Bethan didn't hear any more. At that moment she spotted her father, thinner, and paler than she remembered as he made his way towards the barricade of wire.

'There he is!' Eddie was there before her. Grabbing two chairs, he pushed one in front of her before taking the second for himself.

'Thank you for your letter. It's good of you to come.' Her father smiled, but the smile didn't fool Bethan. She knew him too well.

'You've been ill, Dad?' she asked.

'It was nothing. Just a dose of flu. They looked after me well enough. Put me in the Infirmary.' His smile broadened. 'I get six months' hard labour and I spend the first four weeks in the Infirmary. How's that for fiddling the system?'

'You don't look at all well to me.'

'I'm well enough,' he answered cheerfully. 'Really. It's not that bad in here. They've put me on light work in the library for the next two weeks because of the flu. I get three square meals a day, which is more than a lot of people get outside.'

'And the hard labour?' Eddie asked.

'They say even that isn't so bad. But look, you haven't come all this way to talk about my boring life in here. How are you getting on?'

'We're managing fine,' Eddie answered, trying to sound optimistic in response to a nudge from Bethan. 'I'm keeping the round going like you told me to. Bethan's running the house . . .'

'Helping your mam, Beth?'

Bethan and Eddie exchanged guilty looks.

'What's wrong?' Evan demanded.

'Nothing, Dad,' Eddie began. 'It's just that . . .'

'Mam walked out when she heard about your sentence.' Bethan was too fond of her father to lie to him. Especially now.

'Where's she staying?' No flicker of expression betrayed his emotions.

'I took her to Uncle John Joseph's,' Eddie said flatly.

'He's keeping her?'

'He must be, Dad. I've written to her a couple of times but she hasn't written back.'

'Perhaps it's just as well, Beth.' Evan pulled the dog-end of a hand-rolled cigarette from behind his ear. 'I think I'm a great disappointment to her.'

'She got a bit het up when she found out. Mrs Richards came round just after I arrived and told both of us.' Bethan tried to soften the blow.

'Maggie Richards as a messenger must have gone down like a lead zeppelin with Elizabeth,' Evan said.

'It will be different when you get out and go and see her yourself, Dad.' Eddie forced a smile.

'That's if I bother. I don't think there was much left between us other than habit.' Evan turned to his neighbour and lit his stub of cigarette from a glowing end. What he couldn't say to his children was that there had never been much of anything between him and their mother except for one night of drunken fumblings that would never have occurred if he hadn't quarrelled with his childhood sweetheart. The result had been a quick marriage and Bethan, and although he didn't regret any of his children, he did regret every one of the miserable years he had spent tied to Elizabeth.

'This is my grandson then, Beth?' He peered at the baby through the mesh.

'Yes.'

'Hold him up love so I can take a look at him.'

Bethan did as he asked. Although her father looked away quickly, it wasn't quite quick enough. She saw the expression of pity and something else . . . something she couldn't quite fathom in the depths of his eyes.

'We brought you some Welsh cakes and tobacco, Dad. They took them off us. Cut up the cakes into small pieces . . .'

'That's all right,' Evan reassured Eddie. 'They do that to everything that's brought in. Don't worry I'll get the crumbs later.'

'Charlie's with us. He's opening a shop and he's asked me to work for him a couple of days a week, but don't worry. I won't let it interfere with the round, and he's offering me more money and better hours than Wilf Horton. And Haydn's written. He's having a great time in Brighton with all those chorus girls . . .'

The precious minutes trickled past consumed by Eddie's account of domestic trivia. And all the time Eddie gabbled Bethan longed to tear down the wire cage, reach out and stroke her father's pale, thin cheeks and ask how he really was.

'. . . oh, and Rhiannon Pugh died last night.' Beset by an onset of mixed emotion that he didn't dare examine too closely, Eddie moved on from the family's doings to an account of events on the Graig.

'Rhiannon?'

'Yes, last night,' Eddie repeated, surprised by the earnest look on his father's face. He hadn't realised he was so fond of the old lady. Of course they all knew her, walking through her house every day, the way half the street did . . .

'Is anyone with Phyllis?' Evan broke in. Something in the tone of his voice made Bethan look up.

'Charlie and I stayed with her last night, Diana's with her now.'

'That's why they both look so tired,' Eddie chipped in.

'How's Phyllis coping?' Evan asked. 'She had no one to turn to except Rhiannon, you know. She relied on her for everything.'

'She's coping,' Bethan murmured, a ghastly suspicion forming in her mind. 'Obviously she's upset, but she's bearing up under the strain, all things considered.'

Eddie looked from his father to his sister then back again at Charlie, who was hovering close to the door. 'It's time we changed over, that's if you want a word with Charlie.' Much as he loved his father he was glad of an excuse to leave the unnatural situation.

'I'd appreciate the chance of a word with him. Thanks for coming, son. You look after your sister and the house, and remember what I said about the round?'

'Of course.' Eddie pushed back his chair. 'And you don't mind about me taking the job Charlie offered? Just a couple of days a week.'

'No, I think it's a good idea. I'm not a believer in turning down regular money, you know that.' Evan watched his son walk away. 'You haven't left that husband of yours have you, Beth?' he asked when they only had strangers around them.

'No. He sends me money every week,' she said proudly.

'Then how come he isn't with you?' Evan raised his eyes until they looked into hers.

'Because he's having trouble coming to terms with Eddie. He wants to put him away.'

'And you don't?'

'He needs me,' she said simply.

'It must be a hard choice to make.'

'It doesn't have to be made at the moment,' she said practically. 'Not when I'm needed at home.'

'As long as you don't use our troubles as an excuse to run away from your own.'

'I'll try not to, Dad.' She sensed Charlie's presence behind her. 'Look after yourself.'

'I'm not about to get up to much in here love. Take care.'

Bethan nodded as she turned her back on the wire mesh and walked towards her brother. She could hear her father whispering to Charlie: low, solemn words that were too softly spoken to be deciphered, even if she'd been in a mood to do so. She was preoccupied with the strange look on her father's face when he had asked after Phyllis Harry. She remembered other things that had puzzled her. The way Phyllis had accepted Charlie's presence in the house as natural. The way she had leant on him, done everything he had suggested calmly, unquestioningly. And Phyllis's small son had such beautiful dark eyes and black curly hair, so different from Phyllis's fair hair and grey eyes – and so like her father's and Eddie's.

'You'll come again, next month?'

She turned. Her father's face was pressed against the wire, the forbidding presence of a warder behind him. Charlie hadn't had very long with him after all.

'As soon as they let us, Dad,' she called back. 'I promise.'

'I still don't understand why he's prepared to lend you the money to pay our rent and shop bill. It doesn't seem right to me.' Lena Moore sniffed as Alma ladled out a small tin of tomatoes on to two pieces of toast. As it was Sunday Alma had insisted on lighting the stove. For a few hours at least.

'I told you, Mam, he wants me to work for him,' Alma explained testily.

'If the wages he's promised you are straight and above board and all he expects from you is a week's worth in exchange, he can get any one of a number of girls with the money he's offering. So why you?'

'I've already answered that question, Mam,' Alma said impatiently. 'He's seen me work in the café and he thinks I'm a good worker—'

'And he's heard something of your reputation with the men?'

'It's not like that, Mam. Not with Charlie.'

'How do you know? Anything could happen once we're under his roof and in his power.'

'It won't. If you must know, I asked him outright if there was going to be any funny business and he said no.'

'What did you expect him to say? This whole arrangement doesn't sound right to me, Alma. It's too good to be true, and everyone is going to say so.'

'I've no choice but to take Charlie up on his offer.' Alma pushed a knife and fork into her mother's hand and guided her to her customary place at the table. 'If I hadn't, we would have already been put on the street by the bailiffs.'

'The chapel and the minister would never allow it to come to that, Alma. My father was a deacon . . .'

'The chapel's done precious little to help us until now. I can't see the minister or the deacons putting themselves out just because the bailiffs move in.'

'Of course they would help us. Look at what they did for poor old Mrs Edwards. They paid her house-keeper's wages when she was dying.' Her mother cut into the tomatoes and toast and ferried a forkful to her mouth.

'Poor old Mrs Edwards let it be known that she was leaving that great big house of hers to the chapel. They won't help us because there's nothing in it for them,' Alma commented caustically as she sat down by her mother.

'You're bitter because they banned you, Alma. But even if I say it myself, you were in the wrong. You work on the Lord's day of rest . . .'

'. . . to put food on this table. If I didn't we wouldn't even be able to afford this magnificent Sunday dinner.' Although she was hungry, Alma pushed her tomatoes aside in disgust.

'You don't even try to understand them, Alma. That's your trouble. They've been good to me over the years, particularly when your grandfather died. I wish he'd lived longer. Things wouldn't have come to this pass if he'd still been alive. He would never have allowed you to work on a Sunday for a start.'

'Rich, was he?' Alma enquired. She had heard the same stories before, many times, and steeled herself for the inevitable repetition.

'Only in a spiritual sense. You could have learned a lot from his example, Alma. He was religious, but forgiving and understanding as well. I upset him so much when I married your father. He tried, but no matter what he said, I wouldn't even listen. Now I know he was right. You've only got to look around this house to see how right he was.'

'My father kept us well enough until he was killed.'

'But he didn't really provide for us, and that's just what my father was worried about. I never understood until it was too late and I was left to bring you up on five shillings a week. But it's not just that.' Her mother reached across the table and laid her work-roughened hand over Alma's. 'It's these rumours. They would never have started if you'd done what the minister and deacons wanted. You should have listened to them, walked your grandfather's way as the minister wanted instead of . . .'

'Becoming a streetwalker!'

'Alma, how could you?'

'What, put the congregation's thoughts into words?'

'I'd rather you weren't beholden to any man,' her mother said sternly, suddenly finding her voice. 'This Russian? Who is he? Where does he come from? We don't know anything about him. Why is he living here instead of his own country? For all you know he could be a thief or a murderer.'

'The fact is, Mam, I can't see any other way I can support us.' Alma left the table and scraped her toast and tomatoes into the slop bucket.

'So in spite of everything I've said, you still intend to go ahead and work for him?'

'To keep a roof over our heads and food on the table. Yes.'

'Can't you see it should be this roof, Alma? Not his. People will talk.'

'Then let them. I won't be held responsible for their filthy minds.'

'I wish you wouldn't—'

Alma tried to block out the rest of her mother's speech as she left the kitchen. The biggest problem of all was that her mother was voicing her own doubts and fears. But she had made her decision. Anything Charlie offered her had to be better than Bobby Thomas or the workhouse. Didn't it?

Chapter Fifteen

'I MISSED YOU LAST Saturday night.'
   'George insisted on staying with me until we closed, then he walked me home before going to the Queen's,' Vera whispered as she pushed her bucket under the tap in the washroom of the market.

'Jealous?'

She nodded, not daring to turn round and face William lest someone see her.

'But he's leaving early tonight,' she mumbled. 'I overheard Albert from the bread stall asking him if he was going to the Queen's after work, and he said yes.'

'Then I can walk you home?' William's pulse raced at the thought.

'I don't know about that,' Vera leaned forward to check the level in the bucket. 'But . . .'

'Vera. How long is that water going to take?'

'Not long now, George.' She turned round and gave her husband a bright, artificial smile.

'Nice weather we're having for the time of year, Mr Collins,' William commented blithely.

'If you're a duck and like it wet,' he answered sullenly, eyeing his wife's shapely buttocks and legs as she bent over the pail. He really would have to have a word with her about the length of her overalls. They were far too short, and probably the reason she had a damned Powell sniffing around her like a dog after a bitch on heat. The Powell family always had produced men who'd been too good-looking for the peace of mind of fathers and husbands. He could remember William's father swaggering around town, attracting the attention of every girl for miles, never giving ordinary blokes like him a look in.

'Wet or not, it's warm enough to bring the customers out,' William smiled. 'Trade's up on the winter figures.'

'Maybe on the butchers' stalls, but not the dairy.' George turned from William to his wife. 'You can take that bucket over to the stall and start scrubbing, Vera,' he ordered sharply, making William's blood boil. 'I'll bring the other one over as soon as it's full.'

'Whatever you say George,' she answered meekly, picking up the bucket.

'My sister Diana often talks about Vera,' William ventured boldly. 'They were in school together. She's always admiring Vera's clothes.'

'And so she should, the price I pay for them,' George snapped. He stood back, arms folded, glaring at William. George Collins wasn't a tall man, five foot six inches at the most, but he was built like an ox, a good wrestler in his youth who still enjoyed a bout or two of arm-wrestling in the pub after the card game on a Saturday night. 'You taken over the Russian's stall now?'

'Only for today. He had to go to a funeral,' William explained, picking up his bucket.

'Rhiannon Pugh's?'

'That's right.'

'Heard he's doing all the sorting out for Phyllis Harry.'

'Him and my cousin Bethan,' William corrected, taking exception to George's tone. 'Mrs Pugh was good to us when we were children, and she had no family left.'

'So that's why he's doing it. As a favour,' George raised his eyebrows sceptically. He turned the water off and walked away without another word.

'Where have you been?' Eddie complained when William finally turned up.

'Waiting in the queue,' William moved to the left of the stall and began to scrub down the shelves. From there he could just about see the Collins' cheese stall.

'What about the shelves this side?' Eddie asked, his arm aching from scraping the wooden chopping block with a wire brush.

'You do those,' William answered flippantly. 'That's the way Charlie and I work it.' He braved a wink at Vera as George, dressed in his overcoat, walked out through the door.

'Seems a crazy way to me,' Eddie grumbled, picking up the second bucket.

'That's because you know nothing about working a butcher's stall.' William lifted down the box containing the money and counted it into piles. Noting the amount in a small book, he bagged it and thrust the bag into his shirt as Charlie always did. 'Finished?' he asked Eddie impatiently.

'Just about.'

'Then let's go.'

'To the café.'

'No.'

'You promised Charlie you'd give Alma that message.'

'Tell you what,' William handed Eddie his half-a-crown's wages plus an extra sixpence. 'You do it and I'll give you a tanner.'

'Why? What are you doing that's so important?'

'Man's work,' William said mysteriously as he locked the shutters.

'Who is she, Will?'

'Ask me no questions and I'll tell you no lies.'

'I bet Tina Ronconi will give me more than a tanner to find out.'

'You mention this to her and I'll regale Bethan with the full account of the chorus girl in Ponty Park as told by you. Noises and all.'

'You wouldn't?'

'Try me.'

William waited until Eddie was out of the door before sauntering past the cheese stall. Vera's shutters lay piled in a heap on the floor, exactly where they'd been the first time he'd noticed her.

'Want a hand with those, Vera?' he shouted.

'I'll give Mrs Collins a hand.' Carrie Hardy, a fishwife

with arms the size of hams rose from behind the counter and loomed over him. 'Mr Collins doesn't like young men hanging around his wife,' she said sharply. 'That's why I'm helping her.'

William looked over her head to where Vera stood, rolling her eyes heavenward.

'In that case I'll be off. Night, Mrs Hardy. *Mrs* Collins.' He touched his cap and kept on walking. A small boy caught up with him as he was kicking a path through the debris of the closed stalls in Market Square.

'Mister. Hey Mister! Lady told me to give you this. Said you'd give me a penny.'

William unfolded a scrap of the greaseproof paper George used to wrap his cheese in. The message had been scribbled in pencil and was difficult to read. He walked over to a lamp and held it up to the light.

Wait in the garden. I'll open the kitchen curtains when it's safe for you to come in.

He kissed the paper and tossed the boy a penny. She wouldn't have written if there'd been no chance of him seeing her. All he had to do was creep down the back lane into her garden and wait. A gust of wind blew through the square, snatching the paper from his hand. As he turned to retrieve it he saw the square solid form of Carrie Hardy marching alongside Vera's slender figure. Mrs Hardy had probably received orders from George to sit for a while with his wife. There was time enough for him to slip into the gym for a game of cards, or the Queen's . . . No – better not make it the Queen's, he thought, remembering George's card game – the Central for a pint. Which was it to be? Cards or beer? The beer won. Whistling, he went on his way.

Eddie pushed open the door to the café and looked inside. It was crowded, as it was every market night.

'Will not with you tonight, Eddie?' Tony asked.

'Not tonight.'

'More important fish to fry than he can find in here then?' Tony looked across at Tina who tossed her head haughtily as she loaded a tray with teas and coffees.

'He's seeing someone about business,' Eddie answered evasively. 'Any chance of a quick word with Alma?'

'She's in the back. Go on through.' Tony flipped up the hatch on the counter.

The kitchen was hot and steamy. Angelo, chef's hat pushed to the back of his head, was dipping a huge basket of chips into an open fat fryer. Alma was sitting on a stool as far away from him as she could get, buttering a stack of bread.

'Does Tony know you're in here?' Angelo asked.

'He knows. Charlie asked me to give Alma a message.'

'Charlie?' Hearing his name, Alma turned round and smiled, but her face fell when she saw Eddie.

'He couldn't come down himself. He had to see to Rhiannon Pugh's funeral.'

'The old lady who died on the Graig?'

'She didn't have anyone except her lodger, and it's a lot for her to manage on her own.'

Alma's back stiffened. She'd heard all about Phyllis Harry. Everyone in Pontypridd had. Phyllis had a reputation even worse than her own.

'Anyway, he said to tell you that if it's all right we'll move you into the shop tomorrow.'

'So soon?'

'If it's not all right it'll have to be Sunday or next Thursday. They're the quietest days for Will and me, and we're the ones Charlie hired to do the job.'

'I suppose we could move tomorrow,' Alma said doubt-fully, angry with Charlie because he couldn't be bothered to come down and tell her himself. She wondered why he'd arranged Rhiannon Pugh's funeral for Phyllis Harry. Was he the father of Phyllis's son? Was that why he didn't want her in his bed? Well if it was, it suited her. She'd have everything she wanted, a job, a home, money enough to live on and to spare, and all without strings attached.

'Eight in the morning suit you?'

'We'll be ready.'

'See you.' Eddie was glad to return to the warmth and companionship of the café. The more he saw of Alma the less reason he could find for Charlie to employ her. The woman was so damned spiky and miserable all the time.

It was cold behind George Collins's shed. Very cold, and very dark. Ianto Douglas next door came out to use his ty bach, and Will crouched low, holding his breath. He'd lost all track of time. He'd been staring at the closed curtains for what seemed an eternity. If they opened now he'd be too bloody frozen to move, let alone do anything. A washhouse door banged open and closed again. Ianto going in. Then he heard it, the unmistakable sound of the Collins washhouse door opening.

'Will?'

'Vera, I'm bloody frozen.'

'Ssh. I know, petal, but that horrid Hardy woman won't budge. George made her promise to stay with me until he got home.'

'Damn, he is suspicious, isn't he?'

'I've fed her three sherries and she's fallen asleep. If we're quiet we can go in here.'

'The shed?'

'Ssh . . .' Vera slipped the latch, and Will followed.

'What if she comes out?'

'I'll say I was looking for my tennis racket. The club's opening tomorrow. Come on Will, quick.' She straddled him, pulling her skirt to her waist.

His hands encountered warm, naked flesh. 'Don't you ever wear any underclothes?' he asked.

'I froze all day in the market hoping we'd have an opportunity to sneak into your stall like last time, but George wouldn't let me out of his sight for a moment.' She pulled at his belt buckle. 'He delivers to the valleys tomorrow. He goes every Tuesday and Thursday, if we found somewhere, we could . . .'

'What about here?' he whispered, nuzzling her neck.

'Too dangerous in daylight. We're bound to be seen by one of the gossips. But everyone says you're going to be working on Charlie's new shop. Isn't there a room there we could slip off to now and again? After all, you've got to have a midday break.' She slid her hand down the front of his trousers. 'Ooh you are cold.'

'Bloody frozen.' He racked his brains, then remembered the wooden storage shed in the shop yard. Charlie had dismissed it as a space to store rubbish. 'There is somewhere,' he murmured, struggling to speak coherently as her fingers slid teasingly, tantalisingly, between his thighs. 'But we're going to have to be careful.'

'Very careful, darling,' she echoed as he pulled her downwards. 'Very careful indeed.'

Charlie watched Eddie and William as they carried the last load of Alma's furniture up the stairs into the flat, and shook his head in despair.

'Checked it for woodworm?' he shouted.

'All of it,' William called back. 'It's firewood but it's clean firewood.'

'Alma wouldn't come on the cart with us, she's walking down with her mother.' Eddie looked down at him from over the stairwell.

'All right,' Charlie said absently as he returned to the closed shop. He'd brought a dozen large cuts of meat in from the slaughterhouse in the hope that he'd be able to cook them in preparation for the opening he'd planned for Saturday morning, but so far all he had done was succeed in lighting the two ranges, and after piling the coals into both chambers, he'd resolved to check on the price of running and buying a gas oven with Tony Ronconi. It was going to take an awful lot of meat sales to cover the cost of cooking by coal.

'Charlie?'

'Bethan! You came,' he smiled and walked round the counter to meet her.

'I had to do some shopping anyway.'

'On half-day?'

'It's quieter.' She tucked the shawl closer around herself and the baby.

'As you can see, I took your advice.' He pulled a chair out.

'Three chairs.' She looked around the room, noting the dark brown painted woodwork which provided a pleasing contrast to the cream walls. 'I like it.'

'Really?'

'It looks nice and new and clean. Just the sort of place a well-to-do housewife would patronise to buy cooked food for her family. You out to attract the crache, Charlie?'

'Not only the crache.' The Welsh colloquialism rolled oddly off his Russian tongue. 'I'm after the whole town, especially the people living on the dole. I'm hoping even they will be able to afford a slice or two of what I'm selling.'

'If you keep your prices low enough, they will. Well, I approve of the shop part.' She left her chair and walked round the counter. 'Mind you, you could do with something interesting on the wall.'

'Interesting?'

'Pictures. Something to stimulate their imaginations.'

'Appetites would be better. I'll see if I can find any prints of food. Would you like to see the kitchen?' He opened the door behind the counter.

'Who cleaned the range?'

'The boys. Why, haven't they done it properly?'

'If I'd realised they could clean a range like this, I would have set them to work on the one at home.'

He laughed and Bethan smiled.

'The shop's going to work out, Charlie. You do know that, don't you?'

'I hope so, otherwise I'm going to lose all the money I

have, and even some I don't,' he added remembering the five-year lease he'd signed. The rent would have to be paid on that every quarter whatever happened. A frown creased his forehead, and on impulse Bethan went to him and kissed him on the cheek.

'That's for luck,' she murmured as the door opened and Alma walked in.

'Sorry, I didn't know anyone was here.' Embarrassed, Alma backed out of the door.

'I'm just going.' Bethan put her hand into her shopping bag. 'I brought you something for your new home. I hope you like it.'

'Thank you.' Alma took the parcel, but made no move to open it.

'See you teatime, Charlie?' Bethan said as she left.

'See you,' he smiled, turning to a sour-faced Alma.

Bethan woke in complete darkness. She blinked, disorientated, and for one blissful unknowing moment she fumbled in the bed alongside her, seeking the reassurance of Andrew's presence. Surrounded by deafening silence she waited for the traffic noise of London to reverberate through the window from the street outside. Then she remembered: she was back home. In her parents' bedroom in Graig Avenue.

Fighting panic rooted in a fear she couldn't identify, she lay back aware of the thunder of her heartbeat, waiting for a repetition of whatever it was that had woken her. Something was wrong! She *knew* it. She listened hard, all her senses on the alert. Somewhere towards the mountain end of the street a dog barked, closely followed by the spitting, snarling sounds of fighting cats. Then the springs creaked in her grandmother's old double bed in the room next door as Diana turned in her sleep. Either William or Eddie coughed in their bedroom. None of the noises was in the least out of the ordinary. But there *had* been something. She was certain of it.

She sat up, swung her legs out of bed, and reached for

the old grey dressing gown she had left at home when she had fled to London. Wool, even scratchy worn wool, was more serviceable in the unheated bedrooms of the Graig than the silk and lace négligé Andrew had bought for her to wear in their centrally heated flat.

Edmund grunted, a muffling, snuffling sound unlike his normal steady breathing. In one single painful instant she knew what had woken her. She leaped from the bed and ran towards the door, feeling with her outstretched hand for the light switch. She flooded the room with a harsh light that brought tears to her eyes. Without giving herself time to become accustomed to the glare she darted towards the cot and picked up her baby. His tiny body was hot, fiery to the touch, so much she almost dropped him from shock. Holding him close, she carried him over to her bed and laid him down on the patchwork cover. He was rigid, his eyes staring blindly up into the bright light, but for the first time since his birth she was oblivious to his discomfort. She pulled up his soft flannel nightgown and carried out the routine checks she'd been taught under the eagle eye of Sister Church, who'd trained her in midwifery and infant care on the maternity ward of the Graig Hospital.

She ran her fingers over his chest. There was no rash. His nappy was dry. Was he dehydrated? His temperature! Holding him in one arm she went to the marble-topped washstand, poured cold water from the jug into the washing bowl and tossed in a flannel. Stripping Edmund, supporting his back and head with her hands, she plunged him into the bowl. He cried briefly as the chill of the water lapped around him, but even after she'd sponged him down, the fever still burned, flushing his skin a deep, unhealthy pink. Wrapping him in the sheet from the bottom of his cot she carried him, wet as he was, to Eddie's door and banged on it.

'What?' a sleepy voice mumbled.

'Eddie, run down the hill and get Trevor Lewis for me.' A crash came from the other side of the door, followed by a series of thuds. Eddie peered out sleepily. He was dressed in rumpled pyjama bottoms, his chest bare, spattered with the black and purple bruises of punches from his sparring sessions in the gym.

'Edmund's ill,' she explained, holding the damp bundle towards him.

'I'll go now.'

'I'll go Eddie, you stay with Beth.' William appeared in the doorway behind him. He'd already pulled his trousers over his pyjamas and was fastening the buttons. He reached out to the bottom of the bed, picked up his working shirt and thrust his naked feet into his boots. As Bethan retreated into her bedroom, she heard him clattering down the stairs.

She was sponging the baby down a second time when Eddie appeared, half dressed, in her bedroom.

'He is going to be all right, isn't he, Beth?' he asked urgently, staring at the tiny white figure laid out on a towel on her bed.

'I hope so, Eddie,' she breathed fervently as the baby wailed weakly. 'I really hope so.'

Even as he turned to go downstairs to make her a cup of tea he knew. One look into her eyes had been enough.

William had never flown in an aeroplane. He'd gone up to the field in Penycoedcae one Sunday when one had landed and offered trips over the town for half a crown, but he hadn't had the money. Now, as he raced headlong down the Graig Hill speeding past sleeping houses and empty streets, his footfalls ringing out on the metalled surface of Llantrisant Road, he felt as though the sensation couldn't be that different. He was whirling past a familiar world made strange. All life seemed to be extinguished. No lights burned except for the street lamps, and apart from a couple of cats fighting on the roof of a cottage he didn't see a living soul. But it was only when he passed the darkened window of Griffiths' shop on the corner of Factory Lane that he began to wonder just what time it was.

He placed his hands on his knees, bent over and took four or five deep breaths before sprinting on. Past the fish and chip shop, past the Temple chapel round the corner into Graig Street, up and over the triangular patch of rough grass to Laura and Trevor's front door. He hammered on it without pausing to catch his breath. Then he leaned back against the wall, gasping for air as he waited for his head to stop swimming and his heartbeat to steady.

'I'm coming.' He heard Trevor's voice from the bedroom overhead, the click of the landing light, the creak of the stairs as Trevor descended. The front door opened wide. No cracks, or peering around corners for a doctor used to night calls.

'William. Come in while I get my bag.'

'It's Bethan's baby,' William wheezed.

Trevor had already pulled his trousers over his pyjamas, but hadn't bothered with a shirt. He was wearing a leather patched sports coat over his striped open-necked jacket. He picked up a bunch of keys from the hall table next to the telephone and threw them to William, who was still in the doorway.

'Open the car and get out the starting handle.' He went into the front parlour to fetch his bag.

A few moments later they were chugging steadily up the Graig hill.

'Did Bethan say what it is?' Trevor asked.

'No. She just said to get you right away. I didn't see the baby. She had it wrapped in a wet sheet.'

'Fever.' Trevor slammed the car down a gear to climb the steep area past the fish and chip shop.

William was out of the car before Trevor drew to a halt. He raced up the front steps, turned the key in the door and held it open. 'She's in the main bedroom. The door facing you at the top of the stairs.'

Swinging his brown leather bag Trevor took the stairs two at a time, passing Eddie on the landing. Bethan was in the doorway waiting to meet him. William noticed that she'd dressed, and brushed her hair back from her face.

'High temperature,' Bethan announced without bothering with polite preliminaries. 'I've given him two cold baths and sponged him down three times, but it hasn't had any effect.'

'Convulsions?' Trevor asked.

'Yes, but he's had those before,' she explained as he followed her into the bedroom and closed the door.

William trailed behind Eddie into the kitchen. The light was on and he glanced up at the clock. The hands pointed to half-past three. No wonder he was tired. He opened the oven door, raked up the coals, recklessly adding another two pieces so that the kettle Eddie had already filled would boil quickly. Taking the easy chair opposite Eddie's, he sat back and waited; still, silent and impotent like his cousin, as they listened to the quiet murmurs percolating through the floorboards of the bedroom above.

'What is it?' Bethan's voice pitched high in urgency although she knew it was impossible for Trevor to make a firm diagnosis on the basis of Edmund's symptoms.

'I don't know.' He bent over Edmund and studied him closely. 'Frankly, I haven't a clue,' he added, irritated by his inadequacy. 'You know as well as I do how susceptible to infection children with palsy are. This could be anything from—'

'I took him out today, to town. And last Sunday we went to Cardiff. It was cold. He must have caught a chill while we waited in one of the bus shelters . . .'

'This isn't the result of a chill, Bethan. It's a deep-seated infection,' he said authoritatively as he laid his hand lightly on Edmund's stomach.

'You can't be sure of that. You—'

'Stop beating yourself with the stick of bad motherhood,' he admonished her. 'No matter what precautions you took this was bound to happen sooner or later. Didn't the paediatrician in the Cross warn you about the increased risk of infections for a child with palsy?'

'Yes.'

'I could admit him to the Graig. It would give you a break. You could rest . . .'

'What treatment would you prescribe?'

'At this stage only observation. I don't know enough to order otherwise.'

'I'd rather keep him here.'

'I couldn't stop you, but it might be better for Edmund, and for you, to have a shift of fresh nurses on hand rather than one tired mother.'

'I'll cope and I'd rather keep him,' she said firmly.

'You sure?'

'Perfectly.'

He knew Bethan too well to argue. 'I'll call in again before I do my morning rounds in the hospital. You obviously remember the drill. Try to keep the temperature down, and pour as much fluid into him as he will take. If he goes into convulsions again, even mild ones, send for me. Immediately! Laura always knows where I am.'

'Thank you for coming, Trevor.' Bethan wrapped the baby in a clean linen sheet. Although he still needed to be kept cool it didn't seem right for him to lie naked in the cold bedroom.

'That's what doctors do,' he replaced his stethoscope in his bag. 'Come when they're called. But for all of our training we can't help every patient the way we would like to.' He looked at her closely. She appeared composed, in complete control. But he'd worked with Bethan; seen her struggle through emotional traumas that would have felled a lesser person, only to collapse later when she'd believed herself alone. 'Do you want me to telephone Andrew?'

She looked down at her baby. 'If you like,' she answered dully.

'Bethan, surely it would be easier if Andrew were here, facing this with you.'

She bit her lower lip and shook her head, neither agreeing nor disagreeing.

'It's none of my business but if this was my son I'd want to be with him.'

'*You* would Trevor,' she said quietly. 'But Edmund's not your son, he's Andrew's.'

'Bethan, I couldn't live with myself if I kept something like this from any father, let alone Andrew who's a good friend . . .'

'Do what you think is right, Trevor. You're the doctor.' She sat on the bed and moved Edmund on to her lap.

'Then you won't mind if I call him?'

'He won't come.'

Eddie barged into the silence that had fallen between them, carrying two cups of tea that had slopped into the saucers.

'Keep it warm. I'll be back at half-past six before I go into the hospital.' Trevor picked up his bag.

Eddie dumped both cups on the bedside table. 'I'll see you out.'

'The baby?' Eddie whispered as soon as they were down the steps out of Bethan's earshot.

Trevor faced Eddie squarely. There was something infinitely pathetic about the boy who'd been forced to carry a man's load that wasn't even his, far too soon in life.

'I don't know what's going to happen to the baby,' he answered with more truth than diplomacy. 'If you're the praying sort you might try that.'

'I don't go to church, only the gym,' Eddie retorted drily.

'Pity we can't put whatever Edmund's got into a punchbag and give it a bloody good pounding.' Trevor opened his car door. 'That way we'd both be doing something useful.'

'That's all she said, "Do whatever you think is right"?' Laura turned the rashers of bacon she was frying.

'That and "He won't come."'

'And are you going to telephone him?'

'What do you think?'

'I think it's too early in the morning to play guessing games.' She clamped the lid back on the pan to prevent the fat from spitting over the stove.

'Truth is, Laura, I don't know what to do. I realise Bethan doesn't want me to telephone Andrew, but I can't help thinking of him, alone in that flat of theirs in London. He must miss them terribly . . .'

'The only thing Andrew John would miss in life is a good time. And, as he's living alone, it's my guess he isn't missing a thing.'

'That's a hard thing to say about any man.'

'If we were talking about any man I'd agree with you, but we're not, we're talking about Andrew John.' She lifted three eggs from the bowl on the dresser and placed them next to the frying pan. 'He never gave Bethan, or the baby she was carrying, a second thought when his parents sent him off to London because they didn't fancy the daughter of an unemployed miner joining the family.'

'He came back for her. He married her,' Trevor protested as he went out to wash his hands.

'So he did, but he isn't looking after her and that poor child now. Seems to me that whenever life gets tough Andrew runs.'

'We don't know for certain that he's running this time.'

'If he's a caring husband and father what is he doing in London while Bethan is coping all alone here?'

'Probably coming to terms with having a son like Edmund.'

'That's exactly my point.'

'Don't we all try to run away from the unpleasant things in life?' Trevor put his hands around Laura's waist and kissed the back of her neck.

'You don't,' she snapped irritably as she lifted the lid of the pan and received a spit burn on her finger.

'There have been times when I've wanted to.'

'Like now?'

'I've never wanted to run from you. But then you've never made it that tough on me.'

'I could. Especially if you carry on dilly-dallying about picking up that telephone.'

Trevor looked into the frying pan. The bacon still needed another few minutes before it became crispy, and Laura hadn't even broken the eggs yet. He had no excuse. If he *was* going to telephone Andrew he might as well do it now and get it over with.

He went into the hall, picked up the receiver and dialled the operator. He had to wait three minutes for her to make the connection, and when she finally did, the telephone at the other end seemed to ring with a hollow note as though it was trying to tell him there was no one around to pick it up.

He imagined the empty rooms, immaculately and exquisitely furnished in the modern, art deco blond wood pieces Andrew admired. Then he looked at his watch. Six o'clock. He should have asked Bethan what time Andrew went to the hospital. He didn't even know what department Andrew worked in, or if he was on call. For all he knew Andrew could be on night shift in casualty.

'Hello.'

The voice didn't even sound like Andrew's. Perhaps the operator had connected him to the wrong number.

'Could I speak to Doctor Andrew John, please?'

'Speaking.' The voice was curt. Trevor was beginning to regret his decision.

'I didn't recognise your voice. It's Trevor here.'

'Something's wrong with Bethan?'

'No.' Trevor took a deep breath. 'The baby.'

'It's bad.' It wasn't a question.

'It looks it.'

'I'll telephone the Cross and see if they can get someone to take over my shift. I'll be there as soon as I can.'

The line went dead. Trevor looked at the receiver for a moment before replacing it.

'Well?' Laura asked.

'He said he'd be down as soon as the hospital got a replacement for him.'

'Let's hope he'll be of some use to Bethan when he gets here. Do you want your eggs with runny or hard yolks?'

Chapter Sixteen

BETHAN SAT ON the edge of her bed, watching and waiting. She heard the alarm go off in the room Eddie shared with William. It continued to ring, and she realised that both boys must have remained downstairs. Seconds later it was joined by the tinny, angry sound of Charlie's alarm in the front room below her, but that was silenced almost as soon as it began. Nerves stretched to breaking point, she left Edmund lying in the centre of her bed and walked across the landing to Eddie's room. The clock with its cracked face stood on a chair next to the bed. She picked it up and silenced it just as Diana's clock started clanging. She felt like screaming. The same number of alarms went off in the house every morning. Today was no different. She couldn't expect the world to stop just because Edmund was ill. Edmund! She returned to her bedroom and laid her hand, yet again, on the baby's forehead. Was it her imagination? No! He was definitely a little cooler. Just a little. Did this mean that he was going to get better or . . .

'I've brought you another tea, Beth.'

'Thanks.' She tried, and failed to smile at Eddie.

'Friday's always a lousy day on the round,' he said awkwardly. 'So I thought I'd stay here. There's one or two things I've been meaning to get around to for a while. The shed needs tidying, and if there's any leftover paint in there I might give the outside walls a coat. And then again, if I stay I could help you with the housework,' he offered. 'I've watched Mam clean and blacklead the stove often enough to be able to do it myself. I can carry the rugs out and beat them on the line, and although I might not be a great cook, I can do a decent fry-up at a push. Ask

Charlie if you don't believe me. It was me who took over the cooking when Mam had to see to Uncle Joe last autumn when he went down with an attack of pleurisy.'

'It would be good to have you close at hand, Eddie,' she replied. It would be useful to have someone she could send to fetch Trevor at a moment's notice.

'I'll go and see to the breakfasts.'

'I'll be down in a moment.'

'You bringing the baby downstairs?'

'I think I'll have to. I don't want to leave him up here all alone. Do me a favour, move the day cot from the corner by the stove to the back corner next to the dresser. His temperature's dropping, but I still don't want him to get overheated.'

'Wouldn't both of you be better off up here until it's quiet? You know what it's like with everyone back and forth to the washhouse, doors opening and closing and draughts whistling everywhere.'

'You sure you can manage the breakfasts?'

'I'll bring you up some of my toast and porridge,' he boasted, hoping Diana would have time to show him how to make porridge. The last time he'd had a go, William had asked if he was trying to invent a new cement.

'I'd rather eat in the kitchen after everyone's left.'

'Don't forget to drink your tea,' he reminded her.

Bethan drank her tea and fought the temptation to pick up Edmund and nurse him. When the cup was empty, she left the bed, switched off the light, drew the curtains and pulled down the sash as far as it would go. Was the sky lighter than usual over the mountain? Perhaps spring was turning into summer after all. She had a sudden yearning for the warmth of the sun and the brightness of midsummer flowers.

She listened to the sound of water splashing as Diana washed in the bedroom next to hers. She heard footfalls descending the stairs and Eddie's voice hushed and self-important as he told Charlie and Diana about the baby's illness. She blessed him for taking the task upon himself.

It was far easier to sit and watch her baby in the growing light, doing nothing in particular, than face the family with the news.

She held her breath so she could monitor the baby's. Laying her fingers lightly on his forehead she felt his temperature steadily continue to decline in the face of the cool breeze that blew in through the window. She pulled the cotton sheet around him, laid his thin woollen shawl lightly on top, and continued to watch and wait, holding her breath every time he breathed in, only exhaling when she was certain that he'd breathed out. Silently praying until he drew his next breath. Hoping against hope that there'd be another . . . and another . . . and another.

'It's bad then?' Diana stirred a handful of salt into the porridge pot.

'I think so,' Eddie replied uncertainly, superstitiously hoping he wasn't precipitating anything dreadful by putting his worst fears into words. 'Doctor Lewis said he'd call again before he begins work in the hospital.'

'You know what a heavy sleeper I am. You should have woken me,' Diana said reproachfully.

'I would have if there'd been anything for you to do.'

Diana laid a burn-scarred wooden board in the centre of the table, carried the porridge saucepan over to it, and left it steaming while she went to the dresser to fetch bowls.

'Bethan said she'd eat later, but it might be better to take it up to her while it's hot,' Eddie said thoughtfully.

'Let me make up the baby's bottle first. She won't eat until Edmund's fed.'

'Have you got time?'

'I'll make time.' She jangled the keys in her skirt pocket. 'The only people likely to complain if I open up five minutes late are the customers, and they can wait. Wyn's too busy with the other shop to worry about what I do with mine.'

'Lucky you, having an easygoing boss,' William joked

in a voice loud enough to carry back to Charlie, who was cleaning his shoes in the yard. 'Mine's a slave-driver.'

'Four beef carcasses chopped and jointed for the boss's Cardiff shops by ten,' Charlie ordered as he washed his hands under the running tap. 'Then you can start on the lambs and lights we'll need for the stall tomorrow. And this afternoon you can slice all the cooked meats in the shop, and boil up those hams I bought.'

'See what I mean?' William moaned to his sister. He was deliberately avoiding the subject of Bethan and her baby, although he felt their presence in the room above him as keenly as the rest of them. Clowning around and banter had always been his way of coping.

'I could send a message to Wyn. Perhaps his sister could take over the High Street shop just for today,' Diana began doubtfully.

'There's no need,' Eddie interjected. 'I've already told Beth that I'll stay home today and help her.'

'Help her by all means,' William said warily. 'But please don't cook tea. My stomach hasn't recovered from the last bacon you fried. As a substitute for shoe leather it might have had a future, but as bacon . . .'

'Oh God, who's that now?' Diana complained as there was a loud rapping on the door.

'The doctor probably.' Eddie pushed his spoon into his porridge and left his chair. 'I'll let him in.'

Diana mixed the baby's milk powder in boiling water. Leaving the bottle to cool she picked up her own breakfast.

'Yoo-hoo, it's only me.'

'Mrs Richards, at this hour. Pity help us,' Diana muttered as she swallowed the last of her tea.

'Sorry to come over so early, but I thought you'd like to know.' Mrs Richards gave Charlie an arch look as he sat at the table in his shirt-sleeves with his collar hanging loose around his neck. 'The bailiffs are round Phyllis Harry's. They're throwing her and that baby of hers out on the street. Fred the Dead waited until he made his money

265

from the funeral, and not one day more. If you want my opinion, the man ought to be shot. Even if it is Phyllis Harry he's evicting.'

'Mam, I don't know why you want to see the minister. Every time you talk to him he upsets you.'

'I won't have anyone else telling him and the deacons what you've done, or where we're living.' Lena pulled her knitted hat firmly down over her head.

'Why? What's the difference? They've already forbidden me to enter the chapel, what else can they do?' Alma carried the new hand towels Bethan had bought her as a house-warming present from the kitchen into the bathroom.

'I need to talk over what you've done with someone I respect. I need to know what people will think of you . . .'

'Mam please, don't start that again.' Alma returned from the tiny bathroom to the equally small kitchen. 'Charlie has given me a job, and us a better roof over our head. There's no reason for people to talk. It's purely a business arrangement. He still intends to lodge with the Powells. He's happy there,' she emphasised, embroidering the brief conversations she'd had with Charlie.

'It's all very well for you to say he won't be living here. He'll be working downstairs every day. This is his flat, you're in his power. He can do whatever he wants with you . . .'

'Mam, you make him sound like Fu Manchu.'

Lena wasn't impressed by her daughter's attempt at humour. 'All I'm saying is that if the minister has a word with this new boss of yours, tells him what a decent girl you are, then he might be more inclined to stick to the bargain he's made.'

'The last thing I want is for anyone from the chapel to speak to him. Don't you see, it would ruin everything. Charlie overlooked a lot of gossip when he gave me this job.'

'But that still doesn't make moving in here right. Alma, please listen. My father was a deacon, well respected in the chapel. There are businessmen in the congregation. Some of them might be looking for help. Ben Springer who owns the shoe shop is always taking on girls. If I ask the minister to put in a word and Ben agrees, you could tell this man—'

'His name is Charlie,' Alma shouted angrily.

'What kind of a name is that! When I was a girl people called their employers sir. They showed respect.'

'Charlie's real name is unpronounceable, not that it matters. It isn't a person's name that's important, but the way they are; and I wouldn't work for that slimy toad Ben Springer if you paid me double wages, and neither will anyone else. That's why he's always looking for girls.'

'Working for a married man could go a long way to making you respectable again.'

'Respectable! Respectable! Is it respectable to live in the workhouse? Because that's where we'd be going if it was up to your damned minister.'

'Alma, your language,' Lena sat down heavily on the kitchen chair.

'When are you going to realise that the congregation of that chapel you think so much of would be quite happy to sit back and watch both of us be put out on the street. They wouldn't lift a finger to help. They'd enjoy it,' she added cruelly, wanting to make her mother face the facts. 'But if you want to, go and visit your minister. Just remember we don't have anywhere else to live, and this flat goes with the job I've taken.'

'You told me you'd paid the rent on Morgan Street until today,' her mother said.

'I have,' Alma agreed grimly. 'But that didn't stop Fred Jones from taking someone else's money from tomorrow. We couldn't go back to Morgan Street now even if I wanted to, which I don't. The house has already been let to someone else.'

*

'You can't walk through here.' Bobby Thomas fingered his bruises as he blocked the door set into the garden wall of Rhiannon's house when Charlie, flanked by William and Eddie, crossed Graig Avenue.

'I'd like to call in and see Miss Harry,' Charlie murmured softly. Eddie and William squared up threateningly behind his back.

'She's at the front of the house. If you want to see her you're going to have to walk round to Phillips Street.'

'Who says?' Eddie stepped in front of Charlie and thrust his nose close to Bobby's. Bobby didn't step back, he merely let out a long, low whistle that carried piercingly through the cool morning air. The garden door opened at his back and two more of Fred's rent collectors stepped out.

'We'll walk around, Eddie,' Charlie said evenly, tipping his cap to Bobby.

'But we've been walking through Mrs Pugh's house for—'

'It doesn't matter,' Charlie interrupted. 'We'll walk around now.'

William nudged his cousin in the back. 'The sooner we go the sooner we'll be there.'

Much as he saw the need to hurry, Charlie waited until he could be sure Eddie would follow. The three of them finally walked off down the rough road towards Vicarage corner.

'We saw them off,' Bobby laughed, crossing his arms over his chest.

'For the moment.' James, Fred's eldest son, leant against the wall wishing his father was around to see the havoc his eviction order was creating. But the one thing he had learned in the six months he had been working for the family firm was that his father was *never* around on eviction days. One of the perks of being boss was being able to stay away from the seamier side of working life.

'I can't believe that Fred Jones would put Phyllis out on

the street with Rhiannon only just in her grave.' Eddie burned with righteous indignation.

'Rumour was going around that Phyllis Harry's son is Fred's. His wife gave him an ultimatum Wednesday afternoon: either he put Phyllis out, or she left.'

'Where did you hear that?' Charlie asked.

'In the Central, Wednesday night. Williams the milk came in. He lives next door to the Joneses and when he left home to go out, Fred's wife was crying all over Mrs Williams telling her the story. Apparently Fred used to collect the rents in Phillips Street himself, just about the time Phyllis had to give up her job in the White Palace.'

'I didn't know you went to the Central,' Eddie said, kicking a stone across the road.

'Now and again,' William replied airily.

'Well you never said a word to me about it.'

'You weren't there to hear it when I got home. Sometimes I think you live in that bloody gym.'

Charlie quickened his pace. By the time they reached the Graig Hotel he was ahead of them. He paused on the corner of Llantrisant and Walters Roads and looked up the hill. The front door of Rhiannon's house was wide open, and a crowd had gathered. Two men were carrying out her prized china cabinet. Even from that distance he could hear the crashing and smashing of the ornaments it contained.

'The bastards haven't even emptied it.' Eddie clenched his fists.

Charlie sprinted up the hill, Eddie and William running behind him. A woman stepped out of the crowd and shook her fist furiously at Bobby, who had obviously walked through the house to face Charlie and the boys when they arrived.

'You and your boss will rot in hell for his, Bobby Thomas,' she screamed hysterically. 'You mark my words. God will see you rot in hell. Putting a woman and her baby out on the street like this.'

'You want to join her, Mavis?' Bobby asked. 'If you do, just carry on.'

'You wouldn't dare. I pay my rent on the nose, every week. I've got my rent book to prove it.'

'But your kids make a racket. Mr Jones's other tenants don't like it. And you and your old man are always at it, hammer and tongs. I keep a record of all the complaints I get on my round, Mavis. You live in a rented house. Mr Jones has every right to put you out if he sees fit.'

The woman fell silent. Phyllis sat hunched on a kitchen chair that stood incongruously at the foot of the steps, her little boy wrapped in a shawl on her lap. All that could be seen of him beneath the layers of cloth was his red, runny nose.

'Phyllis?' Charlie had to call her name twice before she answered him.

'We'll have to find somewhere for you to go.'

She looked up, recognised Charlie, and a torrent of words poured out on a tide of tears, washing away all pretence of stoicism.

'It's not as if it's just me and the baby, Charlie. It's Rhiannon's furniture and all her things,' she sobbed looking at Rhiannon's prized possessions scattered over the street.

'There's nothing in my front room,' Mavis announced with a defiant look at Bobby. 'We had to sell all our best sticks, even my grandmother's rugs, before they'd give us enough dole to feed the kids. You're welcome to use it.'

Charlie turned to William and Eddie. 'Get as much of this furniture off the street and into next door as you can,' he ordered.

'We'll help.' The cry came from a dozen people. Paralysed by a sense of impotence, they had stood idly by not knowing what to do or how to help. Despite Phyllis's outcast status, her plight had invoked their pity.

'Where you going, Charlie?' Eddie picked up Rhiannon's sewing box.

'I'm taking Phyllis and the baby to Bethan.'

'You do that,' Eddie shouted in a voice calculated to carry to Bobby Thomas. 'We can take them in, our house is our own. It's not rented off any man.'

'Take them through our house,' Mavis ordered, wrapping her arm around Phyllis and the baby.

'Thank you, Mrs Davies.' Charlie looked warily at two men who were carrying a chaise-longue down the steps.

'Charlie?' One of the bailiff's men stepped forward, mopping his sweating face with a handkerchief. Charlie recognised him as a miner who had once worked with Evan. 'I . . . we . . . none of us like doing this,' he said awkwardly. 'But we need the money and when all's said and done, a day's work is a day's work.'

'You don't have to explain anything to me,' Charlie said flatly.

'Well I just wanted to say, the lady's clothes, the baby's cot and his toys . . . Well the boys and me, we don't want to carry them out here.'

'Is it all right if some of the things are carried through the house up to the Powells' house in Graig Avenue, Mr Jones?' Charlie asked James, who was standing just inside the door.

James turned aside, feeling very sick and ashamed of himself. 'I'll get the men to do it, Charlie,' he mumbled. 'Just tell us which pieces you want.'

Belinda Lane led Alma's mother through the town towards Berw Road. Avenue might have been a more appropriate name, as all the houses were built on one side. The other side sloped down steeply towards the river. Close up the water was black, turgid with coal dust, but distance and the trees that grew along the banks lent the flow of water a certain enchantment, and the houses were sought after by those who couldn't afford the prices of the villas on the Common.

The minister's house was a brisk five-minute walk out of town, close to a large, pleasant, open green space. Belinda led Lena Moore carefully up the steep stone steps, knocked the door tentatively and waited. She had to knock a second time before they heard rubber-soled carpet slippers squeaking over the flagstoned passageway.

'I'll play on the green, Auntie Moore,' Belinda said nervously. 'You can call out when you want to leave. I'll hear you.' She'd been in the minister's house once and had hated the unnatural silence and the smell: a closed-in musty scent of damp plaster and books that reminded her of chapel, mixed together with beeswax polish and boiled fish.

'Mind you don't go far, Belinda.'

'I won't.' The girl skipped off.

The door opened and the minister's sister stood framed in the porchway. A tall, well-built God-fearing woman, she had devoted her life to the chapel and her brother. Regarding herself as the epitome of the women of the scriptures, she had little time or sympathy for those who, in her narrow opinion, had strayed from the path of righteousness, and had told Lena so, repeatedly.

'Mrs Moore.' She peered suspiciously at Lena. 'Did you want to see my brother?'

'I rather hoped I could,' Lena said apologetically. The minister's sister always made her feel nervous. 'But if it's not convenient . . .'

'It is rather early for a call. However, he's just finishing his breakfast, and if you'd care to wait in his study I'll see if he can spare you a moment or two.' Her voice told Lena exactly how much of a nuisance she was being.

The study was every bit as cold and cheerless as the kitchen in Morgan Street.

'Can I take your coat, Mrs Moore?'

'No thank you. I won't disturb the minister for long. I only need a minute of his time.'

'There's a chair behind you to your left. I'll just go and finish seeing to his breakfast.'

Lena stood in the doorway of the room and extended her hands. She took small steps, halting when her foot touched the chair. She crouched down, and felt for the seat and fell into the chair rather inelegantly, glad that no one was around to witness her fumblings. While she waited she amused herself by trying to recall the study. She could remember the house quite well from her frequent visits as a child, invited on the strength of her father's position as a deacon. There'd been Christmas tea parties with stewed tea and boiled fruit cake, Harvest Thanksgiving when the table had been laid with slabs of coarse brown bread and home-made sour milk cheese, and fund-raising coffee mornings which she had spent washing up with the 'girl' in the scullery.

'My brother will be with you in a moment, Mrs Moore.' Lena started, wondering how long the minister's sister had been in the room.

'Would you like a cup of tea?' she offered curtly.

'I've just had breakfast, but thank you.'

'As you wish.'

'Mrs Moore, this is a surprise!' The minister himself bustled in. Lena heard a chair creak as he sat down, then the door closed. She assumed his sister had shut it behind her.

'May I ask what brings you down here today, Mrs Moore?' the minister asked.

'Alma,' she admitted miserably.

'Your daughter.' He shook his head, then remembered that she couldn't see his gesture of disapproval. 'I might have known. What's the girl been up to now?'

'It's been hard since she lost her job in the tailor's shop.'

'That I can believe,' he said harshly. 'But then if what I've heard is right, she deserved to lose it. As you well know, I've little patience with the girl, but I must confess that after thinking it over I've come to the conclusion that perhaps Alma isn't the only one to blame for your troubles.'

Lena looked in the direction of his voice, and waited for more.

'As your father would no doubt have told you if he'd lived longer, you spoilt the girl when she was young. You allowed her to run wild.'

'I did the best I could,' she protested.

'I'm not saying you didn't,' he pursed his lips. 'All things considered I suppose we couldn't really expect any better. Your father told me a few things about your husband, and we must remember that Alma has her father's blood in her. But when I hear—'

'She's found herself another job,' Lena interrupted quickly. 'That's what I wanted to talk to you about.'

'What kind of job?'

'Working in a cooked meat and pie shop.'

'Serving?' he asked incredulously. 'A young girl who worked with Alma in the tailor's told me that decent women have refused to allow Alma to wait on them.'

'I'm sure that's not true,' Lena countered timidly. She'd never dared contradict Mr Parry before in her life.

'I assure you the girl is quite reliable, and respectable.'

'This job isn't behind the counter. It's in the back, cooking and baking,' Lena broke in, not wanting to hear any more about the 'girl' or what she'd said.

'I didn't know Alma had received training in domestic skills,' the minister commented drily.

'And because she'll be starting work really early every morning we've had to move into a flat over the shop,' Lena continued valiantly, sticking rigidly to the topic she wanted to discuss.

'Where is this shop?'

'On the corner between Taff Street and Penuel Lane, by the fountain. Opposite the entrance to the fruit market.'

'So you've left Morgan Street. You really should have let us know. One of the deacons could have wasted time looking for you.'

'Alma didn't tell me we were moving until late Wednesday night. I came as soon as I could.'

'You do realise that if Alma loses this job, you will both be out on the street,' he informed her coldly.

'That's what I came to talk to you about. I know my father always valued your advice, and I was hoping you could help us. I begged Alma not to give up the house in Morgan Street but she insisted we couldn't afford the rent without her money from the tailor's . . .'

'Am I right in thinking that the rent you will be paying for this flat will be deducted from your daughter's wages?'

'Yes.'

'Then what are you going to live on? Surely her earnings will barely cover the cost of the flat?'

'She's going to get ten shillings after the rent, coals and food are paid for.'

'She is going to be earning enough to cover all that by cooking?'

'It seems a lot to me, but then I've no idea of wages.'

'I have, and I'd like to know just what kind of duties warrant that level of salary. I am acquainted with many married men who bring home a good deal less.'

'But she insists it's straightforward work. Early start in the kitchen. Three to four o'clock most mornings, and then work through to midday. And because it's better pay than she's getting now, she won't have to work nights in the café. She said it will be a better life for both of us. It just doesn't sound quite right to me . . .'

'Or me. So why exactly have you come here?'

'I was hoping you could talk to her,' Lena pleaded. 'Make her see sense before it's too late.'

'But you've told me that you are already living in the flat tied to this job.'

'Yes,' Lena admitted miserably.

'Then it is too late. There's nothing I can do for you or your daughter now, Mrs Moore.'

'I suppose there isn't.' She gripped the arms of her chair tightly.

'Might I ask the name of the man Alma is working for?'

'I'm not sure. Alma calls him Charlie.'

'The foreign butcher on the market!'

'I think he's the one.'

'Another unmarried foreigner like the last. I feel for you in your sorrow, Mrs Moore.' He rose from his chair.

'But there is nothing I can do for you. I have my sister and her reputation to consider, so I'm afraid I am going to have to ask you to leave.'

'I'm sorry . . .'

'And until such time as you leave this man's house I'm afraid I will have to ask you to forgo attending chapel.'

'No!' This was one eventuality that hadn't occurred to Lena. Brought up to revere the chapel, she interpreted the minister's edict not only as social disgrace but also as eviction from heaven. 'Please . . .'

'It is not me you should be pleading with, Mrs Moore, but your daughter. How could you allow her to behave this way? Going from one man to another without a wedding ring in sight. All I can say is I'm glad your father isn't here to see what his granddaughter has become.'

Lena burst into tears.

'You had better get down on your knees and ask for God's forgiveness – but not in my chapel. I will pray for you. Goodbye Mrs Moore.'

Chapter Seventeen

CHARLIE STOOD BACK to allow Phyllis and her baby to walk into the house before him.

'I shouldn't be here. Not here. Of all the houses on the Graig . . .' For the first time in her life hysteria mounted as the finality of the move she was making hit her.

'You can sit in my room while I see Bethan,' Charlie said gently but firmly. He stepped ahead of her and led the way to his room, which was just in front of the kitchen. He ushered Phyllis in. 'I'll go and find Bethan. I won't be long.' He closed the door, leaving Phyllis and the baby alone.

The room was clean, orderly and sterile. A single bed with plain deal foot- and head-boards, neatly made, and covered by a smooth grey, blue and black piece of woven Welsh flannel, was pushed up against the wall to the right of the door. Opposite it a lavishly embroidered firescreen concealed the hearth of a polished iron firegrate, topped by a brass airing rail that hung just below the wooden mantelpiece. White-painted wooden planking doors fronted the alcoves, and Phyllis presumed they held Charlie's clothes and possessions.

The curtains were pulled wide in the bay window, giving a view of the garden wall of Rhiannon's house opposite, and the centre sash had been pulled down a couple of inches. The room was cold, but with the kitchen stove going full blast next door, not overly so. Phyllis pulled the checked flannel shawl closer around both herself and Brian as she sat on the only chair in the room. Placed in the exact centre of the bay window it faced inwards. She tried to imagine Charlie sitting here and doing . . . what? There were no books in evidence and she decided that they too must be in the cupboards. The bed, the chair, the firescreen and a small card table pushed up against the back wall facing her – there was nothing else. Even the mantelpiece was free of dust and photographs. Not even one of the dark, hurriedly developed snaps the beach photographers took in Barry Island and Porthcawl.

She looked around. The walls were papered in a busy rose trellis pattern that would have camouflaged any pictures. Not a single object gave a clue to Charlie's likes, dislikes or personality. She knew that he had lived with the Powells for nearly a year, and Megan Powell, Evan's sister-in-law, for two before that. Three years in Pontypridd, but he might well have moved in yesterday. She wondered if he was really close to anyone. Man or woman.

Man! Evan Powell. They frequently had a drink together, and Evan had told her how much he relied on Charlie's judgement and friendship. She shuddered as an image of Evan came to mind. She had promised herself that she would never lean on him, never demand anything of him, no matter what; and here she was, sitting helplessly while Charlie of all people pleaded with Evan's daughter to take her and her son in. She was reduced to begging charity from a woman who had more cause to dislike her than anyone, except perhaps Elizabeth. She sank back into the chair, clutched her baby and wondered if it would have been better to have walked down to the workhouse after all.

Bethan was still in her bedroom watching her baby when she heard Charlie's soft, muted voice floating up the stairs. She heard the door to his room open and close and wondered who he was talking to. When she heard footsteps on the stairs she stood up and smoothed her skirt with her hands. It had to be Trevor. Charlie hadn't come up since the day he'd moved into the house; he had no reason to. She opened her door, stepping back in amazement when she saw Charlie standing on the landing.

'I know your baby is very ill, and I'm sorry to disturb you, Bethan. But I need to talk to you. The bailiffs are putting Phyllis and her baby out on the street.'

'Bailiffs. But why?' She stared at him uncomprehendingly.

'Fred Jones wants her out now that Rhiannon is dead, and as the rent book was in Rhiannon's name they have the right to do it.'

'But the funeral was only the day before yesterday. There's all the furniture . . .'

'William and Eddie are carrying some of it next door. I hope you don't mind, I asked them to bring Phyllis's more personal possessions here.'

'Of course.' Bethan thought rapidly. 'The front parlour will need clearing—'

'I'll see to that,' Charlie broke in swiftly.

Bethan turned away, went to the bed and picked up Edmund. She laid his cheek against her own. He was still unnaturally warm, but not as hot as he had been in the night.

'Phyllis and the baby have nowhere to go.'

She had known what Charlie was going to say and had been prepared for it. 'This is my mother's as well as my father's house.'

She spoke so quietly Charlie had to strain to catch what she was saying. He cleared his throat awkwardly.

'When we were in prison, with your father, I thought you'd guessed.'

'I guessed all right. Only too well.'

'If you don't take her in no one else will. They're all too afraid of their landlord.'

'That's Phyllis's problem.'

'After nursing there you know better than anyone what it's like in the workhouse for an unmarried woman. Bethan please, can she stay here? Just until I can sort out something better?' he pleaded. 'She can have my bed. I'll sleep on the floor of Eddie and William's room.'

'How can you ask me, of all people, to take her in?'

'I'm asking because it's what your father would do if he were home.'

'Not if my mother were here.'

'But neither of them is, and Phyllis is downstairs—'

'You've brought her here!'

'She's in my room. She knows I've come upstairs to talk to you.'

'How could you put me in this position, Charlie!' She bit her lower lip in an attempt to contain her anger.

'Because I don't want to leave her nursing her baby in the street, surrounded by Rhiannon's furniture,' he said simply.

'But this, all of this,' she said wearily, glancing down at her baby, 'will just create more scandal and gossip. I . . .' her voice trailed miserably as she looked into Charlie's deep blue eyes. None of the contempt she felt for herself was mirrored in their patient depths. Here she was worrying about scandal and gossip, as if scandal and gossip would make any difference to her relationship with Andrew. Their marriage had fallen apart on the day Edmund was born. What did it matter if she took Phyllis in, or that Phyllis was her father's mistress? What did any of it matter?

Her thoughts went out to Phyllis and the solemnly beautiful little boy with the black curly hair just like Eddie . . . just like her father.

'Get the boys to clear the parlour for the things Phyllis wants to bring with her. She'll have to sleep with the baby in the box room for the time being. The furniture . . .'

'Don't worry about the furniture. I'll sort it out. Thank you, Bethan.'

She closed the door and sank back on the bed. Edmund had fallen asleep on her shoulder, and his small body felt limp and damp against hers. Had she done the right thing? Her father would undoubtedly think so, and thank her for it, but her mother would probably never speak to her again if she ever got to hear. But there were the boys. Haydn was away, but what if he should come home and find out? And Eddie, he was always too handy with his fists. How many fights would he feel honour bound to settle when the whole of the Graig found out who Brian Harry's father was, and began talking about it?

'Bethan says you're welcome to stay.' Charlie exaggerated the truth when he saw Phyllis sitting, like an anguished Madonna with her son on her lap, in the bay window of his room.

'She did? But . . .'

'She knows who fathered your child,' he interposed. 'Bethan's baby is very ill and she's waiting for the doctor, but she suggested that you and Brian sleep in the box room. I'm sorry, but Diana had to go to work. There's no one to help you make up the bed, or make you breakfast,' he apologised artfully, knowing that the best thing for her would be work.

'If someone could bring over the linen and my clothes, I'll make up the bed.' Now she was away from the street and prying eyes she couldn't bear the thought of going back.

'I'll see to it. Why don't you sit in the kitchen. It's warmer there.'

She picked up Brian and followed Charlie. One glance at the disorder in the room was enough. She took off her coat and shawl and sat the baby on the hearth-rug in front of the stove. He wailed and clutched at her leg.

'You've got to be good,' she said sternly, as she set about clearing the table of breakfast dishes. Something in the tone of her voice silenced him. Charlie disappeared into his room and returned with a wooden box. He knelt on the floor beside the baby, opened it and showed him the chess figures it contained. Phyllis realised that there were some personal things tucked away in the alcove cupboards after all.

'If those are valuable don't give them to him,' she warned. 'He's teething. He might bite them.'

'He wouldn't be the first child to cut his teeth on them.'
Charlie rose to his feet. 'I'll bring your clothes and linen over. You'll let the doctor in when he calls?'

'I will.' Phyllis was already soaking the burnt porridge saucepan in the washhouse.

Bobby Thomas was nowhere to be seen when James Jones allowed Charlie to walk through Rhiannon's house. It already had a deserted air, as if the occupants had moved out months ago. The washhouse was empty. Two broken dolly pegs lay abandoned in a corner. The big round washtub had been carried into the back kitchen, and one of the men was emptying the contents of the pantry into it: dishes, plates, bowls, a bag of potatoes, a bread bin, a crock with three eggs in it. The kitchen itself had already been stripped. There was no sign of Rhiannon's table and chairs, or the easy chairs with their bright patchwork cushions. Even the curtains had been taken down. Charlie walked through the passage. He glanced in at the two men who were denuding the parlour of its pictures.

The crowd's mood wasn't quite so ugly now that Phyllis had gone. Mavis had opened the doors of Rhiannon's prized inlaid china cabinet and she and two other women were removing the china, placing all the pieces into baskets: whole pieces one side, broken pieces the other.

'I'll get our Cath to fix them with good glue,' Mavis explained when she saw Charlie walking down the steps. 'She's a dab hand at it. Artistic, like my father. It's in the blood.'

'I'm sure Phyllis will be very grateful.'

'We've put the table, chairs, dresser and beds in Mrs Davies's front room, Charlie,' Eddie said as he and William scanned the pavement wondering what to take next.

'Bethan's agreed to have Phyllis,' Charlie murmured in a low tone as he stood close to the boys.

'Good for our Beth,' Eddie said loudly.

'Quiet!' Charlie said sharply. 'Now listen, both of you.' He looked around. 'See that blanket chest over there. Put all the clothes, sheets and blankets you can find into it and carry it into my room.'

'Your room?' William stared at him in amazement.

'There isn't space for anything that size in the box room, and we'll need the front parlour for Rhiannon's better pieces,' Charlie answered shortly, reading the expression on William's face and not liking what he saw. 'Phyllis can take what she wants out of it and carry it upstairs.'

'Beth's putting Phyllis and the baby in the box room?' Eddie asked.

'For the time being,' Charlie answered evasively. He looked round and saw the bailiff who had worked with Evan. 'Give us a hand to carry this china cabinet over the road?'

The man looked to James, who nodded.

'Be glad to, Charlie,' he replied.

'Just give us five minutes to make room for it in the house, then we'll be with you.'

'He *must* be,' Mrs Richards hissed, elbowing Mavis Davies out of the way, and peering into the washtub as the men carried it past her before dumping it on the pavement.

'Phyllis's little boy's got black hair and brown eyes, and Charlie's hair is as white as snow and his eyes are blue,' Mavis protested.

'But Phyllis Harry's father had dark eyes, and hair the colour of coal,' Mrs Richards reminded her. 'Phyllis got her colouring from her mother, God rest her soul, but black hair and dark eyes are in her blood. That child of hers could be a throwback to old Harry. Take my word for it.'

'Well, I suppose Charlie has taken charge here,' Mavis conceded reluctantly, not really wanting the paternity of Phyllis's child to be resolved. It had been a topic of great discussion with the gossips in the street, and once the mystery was solved it would lose all interest as a talking point.

'*And* seen Phyllis Harry all right,' Mrs Richards pronounced with a decisive nod of the head. 'Which he'd want to do if the baby was his, wouldn't he?'

'What I can't understand is why he didn't marry her. He can't be short of a few bob.'

'Men. They're all the same, have their fun then clear off first chance they get.'

'Then why is he helping her now?'

'Who knows? Perhaps he has a conscience. Mind you, I'm surprised at Bethan Powell taking her in.'

'Bethan Powell's taking her in?' The group of women all turned to Mrs Richards.

'Didn't you hear Charlie talking to the boys? I did,' she crowed. 'Bethan's putting her in the box room, and I must admit I never expected to see that. With her being married to a John, and a doctor and all. The Johns won't like the idea of someone like Phyllis and her bastard living under the same roof as their daughter-in-law and grandson.'

'Seems to me they don't like the idea of Bethan Powell as a daughter-in-law, or the idea of a grandson like the one they've been given, full stop,' Mrs Evans muttered as she passed them carrying a bundle of Rhiannon's curtains. 'If they did they would have come to see her by now. And there's been no car except Doctor Lewis's outside that house since the day she came back.'

'You can't expect the likes of Doctor John and his wife to come to the Graig,' Mrs Richards pronounced.

'Or the likes of Bethan Powell to go crawling to the Common crache,' Mavis countered.

'Eddie told me the baby's really ill,' Mrs Evans announced as William, Eddie and Charlie reappeared at the front of the house.

'Shame for her. She was such a nice girl too.'

'Well that's what you get for marrying above you,' Mrs Richards said enigmatically as the women went back to their fetching, carrying and sorting.

Trevor dropped his leather bag on to the floor next to the cot, opened it and removed his stethoscope.

'Sorry I'm late,' he apologised, as he sat beside the baby on the bed.

'Your other emergency?' she asked.

'Can't fool a nurse. You're just like Laura. How can you tell?'

'The expression in your eyes and around your mouth.'

'Mr Hughes died half an hour after I left here early this morning.'

'Poor you. You can't have had much sleep.'

'It happens. You must have found that out with Andrew.'

'Not really. It's different, working in a big London hospital. He does his twelve-hour shift then he comes home. That's it until the next shift. Occasionally the senior consultants get called out, but not the junior doctors like Andrew. There's always another one around who'll cover.'

'That must be nice for you. Able to make dinner knowing that Andrew will come home on time to eat it.' He warmed the disc of the stethoscope in his hands before laying it against Edmund's bare chest.

'It used to be,' she murmured absently as if talking about something that had happened a long time ago.

Concentrating on listening to the baby's heartbeat Trevor didn't hear her answer. He frowned, then he pressed his hand gently on Edmund's chest and abdomen. He picked him up, laid him across his knee and listened to his back.

'His temperature *has* dropped,' Bethan informed him eagerly as he removed the stethoscope from his ears.

'Slightly. But he has a chest infection, Beth.'

'Is it pneumonia?'

'I don't think so. Not yet.'

'What can I do?'

'Keep him in an even temperature. Get plenty of fluids

down him. Watch him. In short do all the things you are already doing.' He opened his bag wider and rummaged in its depths.

'It's bronchitis, isn't it?'

'Yes,' he said reluctantly. 'I wish you'd let me admit him to the hospital.'

'They wouldn't let me stay with him.'

'No, they wouldn't. But he'd be well looked after, I promise you.'

'No, Trevor. I know you're only trying to help, and thank you, but no.' Her reply was firm and final.

'I telephoned Andrew.' He rose wearily and looked at the bedside clock. Half-past nine. He should have been in the Graig Hospital at eight. Now he wouldn't finish on the wards much before three, and he'd still have all his house calls to make. Better to steal ten minutes as he drove down the Graig hill now, and warn Laura that he wouldn't be home for dinner, than incur her wrath when he turned up to a burnt dinner at teatime.

'Is Andrew well?' Bethan might have been enquiring after a stranger.

'I didn't think to ask and he didn't say. He told me to tell you he'll be here as soon as he finds someone to take over his shift in the hospital.'

Bethan picked up Edmund and wrapped him in the cool sheet again. 'Will it be all right if I take him downstairs to the kitchen? I have to do some work. Wash his bottles, make up his feeds. Make tea for everyone.'

'As long as you keep him out of strong direct heat.'

'I asked Eddie to move his cot to the corner next to the dresser in the far corner, opposite the stove.'

'That should be all right.' He picked up his bag. 'Beth,' he said, placing a hand on her shoulder. 'You don't have to be strong all the time. Let Andrew carry some of this load. He's obviously prepared to.'

She allowed herself the luxury of relaxing against Trevor's shoulder for a moment. The most marvellous thing about Trevor was his calm, steady reliability. She found herself envying Laura. Not her husband, but his dependability. Trevor would have accepted Edmund if he'd been his son, she was sure of it. She turned away and laid Edmund down in his cot.

'You don't understand, Trevor. Andrew doesn't want Edmund—'

'Of course he does,' he contradicted fiercely, loyal to his friend. 'You know what Andrew is, he's never been very good at expressing his feelings. Edmund's his son. He loves him, Beth, I'm sure of it, even if he hasn't told you in so many words.'

'The reason I'm here, not London, is that Andrew wanted to put him in an institution. Please, you will help me won't you? You won't let Andrew put Edmund in the Graig. You know as well as I do that they won't do any-thing there that I can't do for him here. Please, Trevor . . .'

'I'll try,' he promised, resolving to get Laura to call up as soon as possible. 'But Andrew's a doctor, Beth. He's going to think of both of you. And frankly I'm as worried about you as I am about the baby. You're white as a ghost, you're not resting properly. How long will it be before you fall ill too? Then we'll have both of you to look after.'

'There's a reason for that.' She looked up at him, her eyes dark-ringed, enormous in her pale face. 'I'm going to have another baby.' Her voice jerked as relief poured through her veins. It was wonderful to tell someone her secret.

'All the more reason to put the strain of nursing Edmund on to someone else.'

'No! And I don't want you to tell Andrew.'

'He doesn't know?'

'If he did he'd only use this baby as just one more excuse to put Edmund away. He'd say I couldn't look after two.'

'Edmund does need a lot of time and nursing,' Trevor reminded her.

'I don't want another child,' she said savagely. 'Not if it

means having to give up Edmund. You're just like Andrew. You don't understand.'

'I'm trying to, Beth.' He dropped his bag and sat next to her on the bed. 'I really am.'

'What a day,' William complained to Charlie as they walked along Taff Street. 'I seem to have been working forever. Humping all that furniture up and down steps. Chopping carcasses, cleaning the shop—'

'It was worth it,' Charlie interrupted. 'It's finally ready to open.'

'I still think you've spent far too much money fixing up the roof and painting the outside. The place is leasehold, for pity's sake.'

'A lease that's going to revert to me.'

'And that carpet you put down in the living room of the flat?'

'It was a bargain. Because Wilf doesn't normally deal in them he wanted to get it off his hands.' Charlie took a cigarette and offered one to William.

'How about we have tea in Ronconi's?' William suggested as they headed towards the Tumble.

'I think we should go home,' Charlie said, thinking about Phyllis, and Bethan's baby.

'I saw Diana when I bought those pies for our dinner. Told her not to wait for us. I knew you'd hold my nose to the grindstone until this hour. There's nothing we can do even if we do go back,' William said bluntly, not wanting to face the sick-room atmosphere of Graig Avenue. Not just yet. He knew Bethan's baby couldn't help being ill, and that Phyllis and her baby had to go somewhere, he just wished they hadn't had to come into his back kitchen. 'There's three women in the house and Eddie to run any errands. We'd only be in the way, particularly wanting tea.'

The prospect of a nice quiet meal in front of the fire in the back room of Ronconi's suddenly seemed very appetising and very pleasant to Charlie.

'All right,' he agreed.

'And seeing as how you squeezed every last ounce of work out of me today, I'm going to land you with the bill.'

'As long as you eat only one dinner,' Charlie warned as he pushed open the door to the café.

'Tony! Double portion of sausage, chips, beans and egg, four rounds of bread and butter and a mug of strong tea,' William shouted as he walked up to the counter. 'And he's paying,' he pointed to Charlie.

'That OK with you, Charlie?' Tony asked, pencil poised.

'Fine,' Charlie murmured.

'You having anything?'

'Single portion of sausage and chips, no beans, and one round of bread and butter. And tea.' Charlie looked around. The back room was hot, noisy and smoky.

'Pub crowd in there,' Tony warned, nodding towards the archway that separated the two rooms. 'If I were you I'd sit in here.'

'Good idea.' William took the table nearest to the stove, unwound his muffler and pulled the cap from his head. He caught sight of Tina Ronconi ferrying a plateful of chips and three teas out the back and winked at her.

'Leave those, Tina,' Tony ordered. 'I'll see to them.'

'It's only Bobby Thomas and his crowd,' she protested. 'I can handle them.'

'You don't have to while I'm here,' he answered brusquely. 'See to the orders I've written.' He took the tray from her hands and disappeared out the back.

'Do you need seeing to?' she asked, flirting outrageously with William.

'Depends what you have in mind.'

She looked at Tony's scribbles. 'Three sausage and chips coming up. Two on one plate.' She pushed the swing door open with her back and went into the kitchen shouting the order at Angelo.

Alma was at the sink washing dishes.

'Guess what?' Tina whispered as she crept up behind

her keeping half an eye on Angelo, who was as likely to order her back out to the café as Tony.

'What?' Alma whispered.

'Charlie's just come in.'

'Charlie?' Alma hoped he'd wait and walk her back to the flat. She wanted to discuss her mother's banning from chapel with him, and warn him that as well as making her mother hysterical it could adversely affect his trade. But most of all she wanted to hear his reassurance that, no matter what, the job would remain hers.

'And I saw Mrs Richards on the Graig hill when I walked down,' Tina continued. 'She told me that Charlie moved Phyllis Harry into the Powells' house earlier today when the bailiffs put her and her son out on the street. Mrs Richards said it was terrible until Charlie came and sorted everything out. Now everyone's saying that Phyllis's baby is his. After all, it's the first time he's ever put himself out for a woman.'

'Tina, where the hell are you? Charlie and Will are waiting for their tea.'

'Coming, Tony.'

'What do you think of that, eh?' Tina dug Alma in the ribs. 'Bet you'll never see your new boss in the same light again.'

Alma stared at the grey, soapy water. She felt as though someone had just hit the breath from her body, and she didn't know why. After all, it wasn't as though she cared for Charlie.

Bobby had been ugly drunk when he had come into the café, and the food had made no difference to either the drunkenness or the ugliness. His cronies, who appeared to be floating in a similar alcoholic haze, became quieter and quieter as the evening progressed, too wary of saying anything that was likely to make him even more aggressive. After a while Bobby's voice was the only one that could be heard. Loud, raucous, it held absolute sway in the tense atmosphere.

'I did debate whether to let them in,' Tony confided to Charlie and William as he refilled their teacups and carried them back to their table. 'I hoped the food would sober them up, but it doesn't seem to have had any effect.'

'You, Angelo and the girls couldn't have done much to stop them coming in,' Charlie pointed out logically. 'Looks like there's six . . .'

'Seven,' Tony corrected him.

'Those odds are way too high, even for me.' William let out a large satisfied burp as he ate the last of his sausage.

'Ronnie always tried to pacify rather than confront.' Concern creased Tony's forehead as he wished his older brother were here to advise him.

'Do you hear from Ronnie?' William asked, trying to take Tony's mind away from the troublesome group.

'Do you hear from Maud?'

'Two letters last week. One for Bethan redirected from London, and one for Uncle Evan and Aunt Elizabeth. Bethan's decided not to tell her that Uncle Evan's in jail.'

'Maud must write more than Ronnie. We've only had a card from him telling us they arrived safely. Did Maud say how Ronnie's liking it over there?'

'From what I saw she only wrote a lot of nonsense about Ronnie.'

'Mush?' Tony laughed.

'Mush and lovey-dovey,' William agreed, glancing slyly at Tina.

Bobby chose that moment to push aside the bead curtain that separated the front from the back room. He'd intended to leave for the Cross Keys pub on Broadway, but the sight of Charlie stopped him in his tracks.

'If it isn't my Russian friend.' He swaggered over to the table. Ignoring William and Tony, he pushed his bruised face close to Charlie's. 'See this!' he pointed to a cut above his left eye, 'and this!' His finger travelled across to a bruise on his cheekbone. 'Do you remember how I got them? I bloody well do.' He lunged forward but Charlie was on his feet and out of his chair before Bobby had time to form his hands into fists. The blow slammed into the back of Charlie's empty chair, splintering the bar between the uprights. 'You bloody coward!' Bobby hissed. He whirled round, but Charlie was heading towards the door in an attempt to draw Bobby outside and away from Tina, who was white with shock. Bobby moved swiftly after him. Wrapping his arm around Charlie's neck he pulled him back into the room towards the archway.

'I don't want to hurt you again,' Charlie gasped as he prised Bobby's arm away and thrust him into the thick of his friends, who were standing with bemused expressions on their faces. William stepped close to Bobby, fists clenched at the ready. Charlie shook his head, warning him and Tony to keep their distance. While the argument was just between Bobby and him there was hope that it could be taken outside.

'Bobby?' Alarmed by the noise, Alma had left the kitchen and was standing behind the counter next to Tina. 'Please . . .' she began, as he turned to face her.

'This is nothing to do with you, you little tart,' Bobby snarled. 'This is between me and Mr Big here, who thinks he can come to Ponty, throw his weight around and get away with it.' He dived head-first towards Charlie again. His head connected with Charlie's stomach. Winded, Charlie slammed back against the partition wall.

'This is my café and I order you to stop it. Now! Before I call the police.' Tony's command sounded ineffectual even to his own ears. He tried to push between Charlie and Bobby, but all he succeeded in doing was collecting a punch on the nose from one of Bobby's mates.

'Stay out of it!' the man yelled as blood poured from Tony's face.

Angelo vaulted over the counter and adopted the classic boxer's stance, right fist raised above left, but William caught him by the shoulder and thrust him towards the door.

'Police station, and quick,' William whispered to him.

Angelo took one look at the half-dozen men grouped in

the back room, and Charlie sandwiched between them and Bobby. Then he ran.

'Bobby, if you insist on having this out here and now, I think we should follow Marquess of Queensberry rules, don't you?' William tried his best to stop his hand from shaking as he held it up.

Bobby grunted something unintelligible as he stared belligerently at Charlie.

'Whatever's going on here is between Charlie and Bobby, right?' The most sober of Bobby's friends nodded assent and the others followed suit. 'In that case shouldn't this be taken outside before any more of the Ronconis' property is damaged?' William insisted.

Charlie looked at William. His attention was distracted just long enough for him to be caught unawares as Bobby slammed him against the back wall. Alma crammed her fingers into her mouth, but she still cried out as Charlie's back crashed into the hard surface with a sickening crunch.

The chimney in the back room hadn't been swept all winter so it was difficult to keep a fire burning without great clouds of soot falling, damping down the flames. Tony had banked up the wood, coal and paper with an icing of small coal and had left the poker wedged beneath it to create a through draught. Bobby saw the tip of the poker glowing red, dived forward and pulled it from the grate. Waving it in the air, he lurched towards Charlie.

'For Christ's sake, Bobby!' one of his cronies shouted. 'Think about what you're doing, man.'

'Thump me in the face, would you?' Bobby hissed, his face contorted with hatred. 'Smash me on the pavement, would you?'

'Bobby, put the poker down before someone gets hurt.' William's voice was calm, belying the fear that vibrated through his body.

'Will's right, Bobby. If you don't put it down someone will get hurt.' Alfie White, a friend of Bobby's that William recognised from schooldays, rashly put himself between Bobby and Charlie.

'Out of my way!' Demented with rage and drink, Bobby swished the red-hot end of the poker wildly in the air. Everyone's attention focused on the glowing arc of light that hovered in the centre of the room for a moment. The arc vanished as suddenly as it appeared. The poker fell and the searing smell of burning wool and flesh filled the café, closely followed by a long, loud bestial scream. Alf fell to his knees clutching his arm. William leaned forward and grabbed Alf's leg, dragging him into the front room. Tony locked his shoulder under Alf's, helped him to his feet, and steered him into the kitchen. Alf's moans filled the atmosphere, heightening the tension. The only one who appeared unaware of the noise was Bobby, who still circled threateningly around Charlie with the poker in his hand.

'Can't anyone do *anything*?' Alma pleaded hysterically. 'Please . . .'

Bobby turned and stared at her. His friends took the opportunity to move towards the door. One of them opened it and soon his footsteps could be heard pounding up Taff Street.

'Please?' Bobby mocked as he stepped closer to her with the poker. 'Please . . . Please *what*, Bobby?'

Charlie moved like lightning. Hurling himself between Bobby and Alma, he reached for the glowing end of the poker. Closing his fingers around it, he lifted it and lashed out. The steel handle sank into Bobby's fleshy stomach. As Bobby crumpled to his knees the smell of scorched flesh again permeated the air. Charlie turned and walked slowly into the back room. He didn't drop the poker until he reached the firegrate. As it clattered into the hearth William saw that the end was no longer glowing, but covered in a fine grey-white film of skin.

Chapter Eighteen

ANDREW REACHED CARDIFF station at nine o'clock in the evening. Refusing a porter's help, he carried his doctor's bag and small suitcase himself, walking briskly ahead of the crowd that surged away from the train, down the steep flight of stone steps and into the white-tiled tunnel that connected all the platforms. He reached the Rhondda Valley departure point just in time to hear a barely decipherable announcement that the train to the valleys had been delayed until nine forty-five. Tired, irritable, and unaccountably angry with the world in general, this came as the last straw. He took his luggage and stormed towards the refreshment room only to find the door bolted and the lights dimmed. He looked at the outside benches. The only unoccupied one was covered with black smuts. He dropped his bags on to it and patted his pockets in search of a cigarette. Finding one in a squashed packet in the breast pocket of his suit, he lit it with his lighter and inhaled deeply. Across the rails a huge billboard was dominated by the swashbuckling image of a sword-wielding pirate, dark-haired beautiful girl behind him, evil-faced villain in front. Below the picture in foot-high crimson letters was 'CAPTAIN BLOOD AT YOUR LOCAL PICTURE PALACE NOW'.

Whoever Captain Blood was, he envied him. His choices were simple and clear cut. All he had to do was draw his sword, fight evil and rescue the beautiful damsel in distress. If only the choices in his life were that easy to make.

As he drew on his cigarette again he wondered what exactly he was doing standing on this platform. Trevor Lewis had telephoned and he'd come running. For what?

To witness the death of a son he'd done his damnedest to ignore since birth? To comfort Bethan? If she'd really wanted him she would have telephoned him herself. It was hypocritical of him even to have left London. Trevor had once told him he always looked for the easy way out. Trevor had been right. He'd do anything to avoid direct emotional confrontation, and not only with Bethan. A brave man would have been honest when Trevor phoned, realising the futility of paying lip service to a dead marriage. Why didn't he turn round? Now! This minute. Walk down the steps to the London platform and take the first train back. The refreshment room might even be open over there. He could buy himself a hot cup of tea and a sandwich; perhaps there'd be a sleeper. The thought of stretching out and relaxing was very tempting. And in London he had work waiting. His patients needed him, even if his son and his wife didn't, and best of all, their ailments weren't the result of his neglect. On the wards of the Cross he was a healer, not the guilty party.

'Andrew. Andrew John! How marvellous. You're coming home? For good, I hope. All the young people have missed you. Especially in the tennis club. Anthea never stops talking about the good times she had when you were a member.'

'Mrs Llewellyn Jones.' Of all the people in Pontypridd the one he least wanted to see at that moment was Mrs Llewellyn Jones, the wife of the town's bank manager, and one of his mother's most patronising bosom friends. But well trained since childhood, he was too polite to allow his dislike of the woman to surface. Taking his cigarette from his mouth with his left hand, he extended his right.

'You *are* going home, Andrew?'

'Evidently.'

'Yes of course.' She laughed shrilly, attracting the attention of everyone on the platform. 'You could hardly be going anywhere else from this part of the station, could you?'

'I'd offer to buy you tea, but the refreshment room is closed.'

'So remiss of them. First they delay the train, then they close everything down. But what *can* you expect? The whole country has gone downhill. Just look at this station. No matter what time I travel, I've never once seen it in an acceptable state. Or anyone even attempting to clean it.'

'It's the trains,' he informed her gravely. 'Running on coal makes them very dirty.'

'I suppose it does,' she replied doubtfully, uncertain whether it was a joke, or not. 'But then it's not just this station, it's every public place,' she continued, repeating an observation that had been very well received by the Ladies' Section of the Pontypridd Golf Club. 'No one takes any pride in themselves or their work any more. You need look no further than your father-in-law,' she slipped in slyly. She paused, waiting for him to comment, but he remained obstinately silent.

'Well, the situation is so awkward, for *your* parents of course. As I said to your dear mother, sometimes the social gulf between the Common and the Graig simply isn't wide enough. Gossip travels all too quickly, and when he was sent to gaol . . .'

The news of Evan Powell's imprisonment came as a complete surprise to Andrew, but by dint of superhuman control he managed to keep the shock from registering on his face. Anger burned furiously, as he remained outwardly impassive. Why hadn't Bethan told him his father-in-law was in gaol? Why had she allowed him to find out like this? Didn't she love him? Didn't she consider him part of her family? Didn't she have any regard for his feelings at all?

'. . . well I mean to say it's hardly the sort of thing you want to broadcast around the town. That you're connected, even by marriage, to a man who's serving six months' hard labour for assaulting a police officer.' She looked up at Andrew, wondering why he didn't say something. Perhaps he didn't want to discuss his father-in-law in public, but then – she glanced around – it wasn't as if there was anyone who *mattered* near them. 'I met your wife that once when we dined with your parents. She did seem a very nice girl, but . . .'

'*But!*' There was always a 'but' with the Mrs Llewellyn Joneses of this world, Andrew reflected acidly.

'. . . it can't be at all *nice* for her having come from a family like that. My woman who comes in to do the heavy work does occasional ironing for Mrs Leyshon.' She smiled broadly at Andrew. 'You *must* know the Leyshons. They live in the house on the Graig,' she said as though there was only one. 'Danygraig House. From what I understand it's the only decent house on that hill. Not that I've ever been there,' she qualified, as though the Graig was in some way tainted. 'Well, my woman told me that Mrs Powell has moved out. Apparently she's living with her uncle, a minister, chapel of course, in the Rhondda, and who can blame her? It must be very difficult given the circumstances. Your wife is coping with the situation, I trust?'

'Yes,' Andrew answered shortly, not knowing whether his parents, let alone Mrs Llewellyn Jones, were aware that Bethan was in Pontypridd. If Mrs Llewellyn Jones's 'woman' was as much of a gossip as he suspected, they probably did. And that would give his father one more reason to be angry with him.

'As if she hasn't enough to do with the baby . . . poor little thing. Your mother told us all about it. So sad. Mr Llewellyn Jones and I were so sorry to hear—'

'Bethan is coping perfectly well. Thank you for your concern.' He dropped his cigarette and ground it to dust beneath the toe of his shoe.

'She's living in Pontypridd, and you're living in London now?'

Damn it. The woman did know.

'Temporarily.' He spat out the word as he fumbled in his pocket for another cigarette.

'I'm glad to hear it. Separation, no matter what the

cause, is never good for a marriage. But I suppose your wife felt obliged to go home after her father's disgrace. We can't always do what we want in life. Mr Llewellyn Jones did his duty and volunteered his services during the Great War. I hardly saw him for four years. He spent the duration in the Admiralty Office in London, you know.'

'It must have been a very harrowing time for both of you,' Andrew commented drily.

'Very,' she concurred, failing to see the irony in his remark. 'You staying in Pontypridd long?' she probed artlessly.

'Unfortunately not.'

'Then you are hoping to take Bethan back with you?'

'Eventually.'

'Your mother will be so pleased to see you. She doesn't say much, but I can tell,' she wagged her finger at Andrew as if he were a naughty schoolboy. 'She misses you dreadfully. You really should write or telephone home more often. I know you have a wife now, but you must spare an occasional thought for your mother. It's a sad fact of life that a mother can never entirely cut the bonds that bind her to her child, no matter how she may try. Take me and Anthea . . .'

Andrew didn't hear the story of Anthea's devotion. He was dwelling on his mother's sometimes irritating, always fussy, but undeniably deep and abiding love for him. Mrs Llewellyn Jones was right: the bonds of motherhood were never altogether severed, even in adulthood.

For the first time he realised the enormity of the demands he had made of Bethan. He saw their son as a reproach, a living reminder of his failure to look after both mother and son, but Bethan saw him as her child, and no mother would willingly give up her child. He had driven Bethan into choosing between Edmund and him, and she had chosen the most vulnerable. Knowing her as he did, how could he have expected her to have done otherwise?

He'd been a fool. Seeing an institution as an easy solution to the problem of the baby. Putting Edmund away would solve nothing for him or for Bethan. The baby was there. Would always be there. A part of both of them that Bethan would never willingly abandon to strangers. Maternal instinct had taken its powerful, insidious hold. He couldn't deny the strength of the bond between Bethan and the child, but he also knew that the blame he carried would never allow him to feel the same way.

'Why, here's our train at last.' Mrs Llewellyn Jones had to tap him on the arm with her umbrella before he saw the steam train pull in.

'Mrs Llewellyn Jones. Let me help you.' He took hold of her elbow and propelled her towards the door of a first-class carriage. Opening it, he pushed her inside. 'So nice to see you,' he murmured, smiling at her for the first time. 'Do give my regards to Anthea, and Mr Llewellyn Jones.'

'Won't you join me?' she asked, flustered by his sudden, unexpected attention. 'It would be *so* nice to continue our little chat. I haven't told you about Anthea's trip to France and her—'

'It will have to wait until some other time, I'm afraid. I only have a third-class ticket,' he lied as he went back to the bench to get his bags.

'Soon, I hope!' she shouted after him. 'Soon.'

'You want to prefer charges, Charlie?' Constable Huw Davies asked as Charlie sat slumped on a chair in the back room of the café, his arm extended across the table, lying on a bleached linen tea towel. Tina and Alma were sitting either side of him covering his hand with potato skins.

Charlie looked up at Alma. She shook her head. The movement was slight, so slight that anyone who hadn't been looking for it would have missed it. Charlie recalled her fear of attracting more slanderous gossip.

'No,' he answered between clenched teeth. For about ten minutes after he had gripped the poker and wrenched it out of Bobby's hands his whole arm had gone blessedly, blissfully numb but now it was returning, all too agonisingly, to life.

'Well I do,' Tony Ronconi declared angrily. 'Just look at the state of this place.'

'Criminal damage,' Huw wrote in his neat script in his notebook.

'And just think about the effect this is going to have on our custom once word gets out.'

'Violent, threatening behaviour,' Huw continued to write. 'I've got more than enough to keep him overnight. Can you call down the station tomorrow morning Tony. We'll try and get him before a magistrate then.'

'I'll be there.'

'You ought to go to hospital and get that hand seen to,' Huw said to Charlie.

'I'll take him,' Tony volunteered.

'I'll get the Trojan.' William was happy to have an excuse to leave the café. He didn't want to look at Charlie's hand, yet he couldn't look away. The fingers were flayed red raw, the palm was charred, blackened, the flesh hanging loose in long, thin, bloody shreds. And it seemed to have been in that state for hours. Huw had taken the names and addresses of Bobby's friends, told them they'd be called as witnesses, and warned them that if they didn't stay out of trouble it wouldn't be the witness box but the dock they'd be finding themselves in. When he finally allowed them to leave, they sloped off silently, grateful to Huw for allowing them to sleep in their own beds that night. Only Bobby remained in the café. Huw had handcuffed him to the brass rail in front of the counter, and he sat there, a glowering, threatening presence that William could quite cheerfully have knocked senseless.

'Alma, you come with us. Tina, you and Angelo close up. I think we've all had enough for one night.'

'Tina can go. I'll clear up here,' Alma volunteered.

'Sort it out amongst yourselves,' Tony said impatiently. 'It doesn't matter what you decide as long as we get away from here soon for Charlie's sake.'

'Boys!' Huw Davies greeted the reinforcements he'd sent Angelo to fetch from the station. 'We have one rather nasty drunk here who wants to take us up on our offer of free bed and breakfast.'

*

'Bethan?' Phyllis knocked timidly at the bedroom door. In response to Bethan's answering call she carried in a cup of tea. 'I've come to take down your supper dishes.' She looked at the tray Diana had brought up earlier. 'Oh, you haven't touched a thing!'

'I'm not hungry.' Bethan leaned over her son's cot so she wouldn't have to look Phyllis in the eye.

'I'm boiling water for his bottles now.'

'Thank you.'

'I can run the house for you until your baby is better, that's if you want me to of course,' she offered shyly. She watched as Bethan picked up her baby, waiting for her to answer. When she didn't, she continued. 'I want to say . . . want you to know,' she stammered clumsily, 'how grateful I am to you for taking me and my son in. I know it couldn't have been easy for you, especially as you're so crowded here already.'

'It's what my father would have wanted me to do,' Bethan said coldly, wishing Phyllis would go, and leave her in peace with Edmund.

'Thank you anyway.' Phyllis retrieved the tray and retreated downstairs.

Bethan felt guilty almost before Phyllis was out of the door. She should have made an effort, accepted Phyllis's gratitude more graciously. It was just that she felt so tired and drained. Far too exhausted to think about anything, or anyone other than Edmund. Later, when she didn't feel as though the world was crashing down around her shoulders she'd make a point of apologising for her coldness. But not now. Not when Edmund had to struggle so hard to take even the shallowest breath.

'What the hell happened to you?' Eddie demanded as

William ushered a bandaged, white-faced Charlie into the back kitchen.

'Ssh! Keep your voice down,' Diana ordered abruptly from the depths of the pantry where she was stacking newly washed dishes. 'Bethan's having a hard time nursing that baby as it is without you waking him every five minutes with your noise. What on earth . . .' She stepped out and put her hand to her mouth when she saw Charlie.

William took the burden of explanation upon himself, and while he talked, Phyllis set about making Edmund's bottles and putting the kettle back on the stove for tea.

'Is there anything we can do?' Diana asked, shocked by the size of the bandage on Charlie's arm.

'Make us both a cup of hot sweet tea to take away the shock, and if Uncle Evan's got something a bit stronger tucked away, so much the better.'

'There's a bottle of vodka in my room, Will.' Charlie rested his head wearily against the back of the easy chair. 'It's in the alcove to the right of the fireplace.'

'I didn't know you indulged,' William said, tearing himself away from the warmest spot in front of the stove.

'I don't. That's why I have a full bottle,' Charlie answered brusquely. His hand was painful despite the anaesthetic. And he wasn't at all happy with Doctor John's recommendation that he take at least two weeks off work, and refrain from cutting meat until the skin had completely healed, for the sake of both his customers' health and his own.

'Looks like I'll have to take over the stall and the slaughterhouse for a while,' William said returning with the bottle. He took a corkscrew and a set of six small glasses on a wooden stand from the dresser shelf.

'I can work one-handed,' Charlie growled.

'There's no need. Take a rest for once in your life. If you have to do something, you can take the money in the shop when it opens on Saturday. How much of this stuff do you put in a glass?' He pulled the cork that sealed the bottle.

'Fill it up, to the brim,' Charlie ordered, noting the size of the glasses.

'Anyone else?' William asked. 'Diana? Phyllis? Eddie?'

'Joey's arranged a sparring match for me tomorrow.'

'I'd prefer tea,' Phyllis said shyly.

'And so would I,' Diana snapped, concerned about Charlie.

'Would you take the baby's bottle upstairs, Diana?' Phyllis asked. 'I think his feed is about due.'

'Yes of course.' Diana stared at the tray Phyllis had brought down. 'I don't suppose she's eaten anything all day?' A knock at the door interrupted them.

'If that's Mrs Richards again, she can go to hell,' Eddie declared firmly.

'She never knocks, just walks in,' Diana pointed out.

'She knocked this morning,' Eddie said.

'Well I've had enough for one day,' William said. He handed Charlie a full glass of vodka and pulled Evan's chair close to the range for himself. 'Go and answer it, Di,' he ordered when a second knock sounded.

'What did your last slave die of?' Diana demanded.

'I've been working all day, and I've had a hard evening.'

'What the hell do you think I've been doing?' Diana picked up the baby's bottle.

Phyllis hoped they didn't expect her to open it. After the events of the morning it was much as she could do to face this roomful of people, let alone any others.

Eddie left his chair just as the front door opened.

'It's me Eddie,' Trevor called out as Eddie opened the kitchen door. He stood on the coconut mat and shook the rain from his coat.

'Hello Eddie,' Andrew said, following Trevor in.

'Bethan's upstairs,' Eddie informed him curtly. 'She hasn't left the bedroom all day.'

'I'll show Andrew the way,' Trevor said pleasantly. Eddie watched them climb the stairs, then retreated to the kitchen and slammed the door behind him.

'Who was it?' William asked.

304

'Bloody cashmere coat,' Eddie said angrily.

'That *is* his sick baby and wife upstairs,' William reminded him.

'I bloody well wish he'd never married her,' Eddie declared fervently. 'Bethan's troubles only started when she met him.'

Bethan was nursing the baby against her shoulder in the darkened bedroom, standing in front of the window. It wasn't much of a view in daylight, but darkness had softened the harsh aspect, shading broken walls and blanketing the evidence of poverty's dereliction with compassionate shadows. She looked out over the ty bach roof at her father's wire mesh dog run, the shed, the old stone wall that ran the width of the garden, dividing it from the lane behind, and beyond that the tops of the neighbours' chicken coops. High over everything a dark sliver of night sky, devoid of moon and stars, hovered above the crest of the blackened mountain.

Bethan preferred the room in darkness, and not just because of Edmund. She had always felt safer in the dark, cosier, more secure. Her brothers and sister had taken it in turns to fear the night, waking up and screaming at the formless, nameless terrors the darkness spawned. But she never had. Her mother hadn't allowed night lights, and it had fallen to her as the eldest to creep out of bed, first to Haydn, then later to Haydn and Eddie, to comfort and assure them that there was nothing to fear. It had been easier with Maud. They had shared the same bed.

The night had always brought other pleasures, principal among them being time to dream. Not the jumbled nightmares of sleep, but the peace and mental privacy that allowed her to refashion the events of her days into happier frameworks. Even now she was luxuriating in another world, one in which Edmund was strong, and perfect, her father was free . . . and Andrew? What did she wish for Andrew?

A tap at the door shattered the idyllic world she had created, bringing a bewildering sense of loss.

'Come in.' She hoped that whoever it was wouldn't stay long. Now she'd been rudely returned to reality she remembered her priorities, chief of which was cuddling Edmund while he could still feel her presence. She hadn't needed Trevor's diagnosis to know that very soon she wouldn't be able to.

She remained standing with her back to the door as it opened. She resented the light flooding in from the landing, and heard the unmistakable tread of masculine feet.

'Trevor?'

'It's not Trevor. It's me.'

She turned. Andrew's broad, tall frame was silhouetted in the doorway, the light behind him throwing his face into shadow.

'You didn't have to come.' Her voice was icy. Andrew didn't hear the emotional numbness that lay behind it, only the chill note that shut him out.

'I didn't have to, but I wanted to. How's the baby?' Even now he couldn't bring himself to call the child by the name she had given it.

'Have you seen Trevor?'

'Yes. He drove me here.'

'Didn't he tell you?'

The light had fallen on her face and figure, casting dark shadows. From what he could see of her above the shawl, she looked thinner, more gaunt than he remembered.

'He told me he's very ill. Bethan, won't you let me help?' Andrew pleaded. 'At least allow me to hire a night nurse so you can get a good night's sleep.'

If he had offered to sit up with the child himself she might have been kinder; as it was she saw his plea as a continuation of the demands he had made in London.

'No doubt you, like Trevor, think Edmund would be better off in the Graig Hospital,' she countered bitterly. 'Both of you have forgotten I've worked there. I *know* what it's like on the children's ward. He's my child, Andrew. I'll look after him.'

'He's my child too,' he reminded her pointedly, hurt by her rejection of his olive branch, and angry with himself for being peevish. Was it so hard for her to take help from him? She had undoubtedly accepted it from her family. Did she intend to shut him out of her life permanently? 'Can I at least look at him?' he asked when the silence in the room became too crushing for him to bear.

She unwound the shawl from her waist, removed Edmund and placed him, wrapped in his lighter shawl, in Andrew's arms. Then she switched on the light. Harsh, glaring, it shone directly down on to the baby's face.

Andrew lifted the shawl, holding it over the baby's eyes. 'He doesn't like the light,' he murmured.

'I thought you'd need it to make a medical examination.'

'I didn't want to examine him. Just hold him.'

'Trevor's told you that his bronchitis has developed into pneumonia?'

'Yes.'

She switched off the light, but not before Andrew had time to register the bluish tinge on the baby's skin as he laboured to draw breath into infected lungs. Andrew held him close to his chest. He could feel the erratic beat of the tiny heart beneath his hand. This was his child. His son, and this was the first time that he'd held him in his arms, or even looked at him for any length of time.

'Bethan I'm sorry . . .' the words sounded pitiful, shabby, totally inadequate. He wanted – no needed – to offer her more than sympathy. 'If you return to London with me, I'll find a specialist . . .'

'I think Edmund's seen enough specialists, don't you?' She held out her arms and he gently replaced the baby in them. Holding him against her shoulder she wrapped the shawl around them both. The baby cried, a thin weak wail, then recognising the smell and feel of his mother, settled again.

Andrew felt desperately tired, mentally and physically. He looked around for a chair; seeing none, he sank down on the corner of the bed.

'You're staying with your parents?'

'I hadn't really thought about it, I've only just come in on the train.'

'I'm sorry I can't offer you a bed. The house is packed. As you can see, the baby and I are both in here, and if you moved in as well, none of us would get any sleep.'

He wanted to break through the barrier of cold formality, reach out, stroke her cheek, ask her if she'd got any sleep at all the last few nights, but fear of rejection held him back, and his hands remained firmly locked in his pockets.

'The boys are sharing one bedroom,' she explained unnecessarily as though she had to justify her refusal to allow him to stay. 'Diana's in the other. Charlie's in the front room downstairs, and Phyllis Harry and her son are in the box room.'

'Phyllis Harry, do I know her?'

'Rhiannon Pugh who lived across the road died last week. This morning the bailiffs put her lodger Phyllis Harry and her baby out on the streets, so we've had to put them in the box room.'

'Wasn't she the woman who was stoned out of chapel?'

'You remember me telling you that?'

Was it his imagination or was there a glimmer of a smile on her lips? 'I do. Bethan, are you mad? Think of your reputation. Think of Diana . . .'

'She had nowhere else to go.'

'She could have gone to the Graig.'

'To the workhouse?' Bethan was speaking softly so as not to disturb the baby, but there was a venom in her voice that needed no raised tones. 'That probably seems an easy option to you, but then you've only worked in the place. You've never been under the threat of being sent there.'

He allowed the barb to pass without comment. He

thought of leaving her now, of going to his parents' house. Of relaxing with his mother, father and the inevitable after-dinner brandy in their tastefully overfurnished sitting room. His mother would no doubt fuss about Bethan living apart from him, and about Evan Powell's imprisonment, just as Mrs Llewellyn Jones had done. And if news had travelled to the Common about Bethan taking in Phyllis Harry as well . . . The thought of having to listen to more gossip decided him.

'I'll sleep downstairs in a chair in the kitchen.' He didn't frame it as a question lest she refuse him even that small privilege.

'You won't be comfortable.'

Did she really want him to leave that much? 'I'll manage,' he said testily. 'But until bedtime I'd like to stay here if I may?' He wished he could have said 'with you' so there would be no mistake, but again he choked on the words.

'There's nothing you can do.'

'I've brought my bag. It will save you sending for Trevor.'

She knew then that the end was nearer than she had thought.

'If you don't mind I'd like to rest for a while now.' She looked at him as he sat on the bed, and he rose. She didn't sit down until he was on his feet. He watched her for a moment. She was holding Edmund very close, her cheek pressed against the baby's, her hand wrapped around his tiny fingers, as though by holding him she hoped to ward off the inexorable advent of death.

'I'll go downstairs then.' He looked around the room, shadowy in the half-light, saw the cold cup of tea on the dressing table. 'Would you like me to bring you anything?'

'No thank you.'

There was nothing left for him to do there.

He had only ever been in the house once before, but he had been in a hundred like it when he had practised medicine in Pontypridd before taking up his London post. Leaving the landing light burning, he walked down to the back kitchen and opened the door. After the chill of the bedroom the room seemed hot, smoky and crowded. Charlie and William were slumped in easy chairs either side of the stove. Trevor and Eddie were sitting at the table talking, and Diana was stepping over outstretched legs and moving kitchen chairs in an effort to get near the stove. Phyllis Harry was nowhere to be seen, and Andrew was grateful. He hoped she'd gone to her room for the night. He could barely cope with the family let alone a stranger.

'Doctor John.' William was the only one to greet him as he opened the door.

'Hello William, it's good to see you,' he replied with a forced geniality.

'Wish we could say the same,' Eddie muttered audibly.

'Would you like a cup of tea, Doctor Lewis, Doctor John?' Diana asked, pushing a brown curl back from her flushed face as she lifted the boiling kettle from the hotplate.

'No thank you, Diana. I have to get back,' Trevor answered.

'On call?' Andrew asked, grateful for the one presence in the room that wasn't hostile.

'No. But I was last night and I only managed to sleep an hour. I'm whacked.'

'Who's on call tonight?' Andrew asked warily.

'Your father. But as I'm nearer Bethan knows that she only has to send and I'll come, whether I'm on duty or not.'

'I've told Bethan I'll stay.'

Trevor nodded.

Eddie stared at Andrew, dumbfounded. 'You're staying here?'

'Just for tonight,' Andrew said quietly. 'That's if it's all right with everyone.'

'We don't count,' Eddie snapped. 'It's Beth who matters.'

'It's Bethan I'm thinking of,' Andrew retorted quickly.

'Have you come straight here from London?' Diana asked.

'Yes.'

'In that case you'll be wanting more than a cup of tea.'

'Tea will be fine, thank you. I don't want to put you to any trouble.'

'No trouble. Bethan didn't eat her dinner. It will only take a moment to heat up.'

'In that case, thank you.' Andrew was too wary of offending to refuse the offer.

'I'll be off then. Remember, if you need me, send Eddie or William down. I'll be easier to get hold of than your father,' Trevor added tactfully.

Andrew followed Trevor and Eddie out into the passage. Eddie opened the door.

'It's good of you to keep calling in like this, Doctor Lewis,' Eddie said clumsily, donning the mantle of the man of the house again. 'I know our Beth appreciates it.'

'I just wish I could do more for the baby, Eddie.' Trevor held out his hand and Eddie shook it.

'I'll walk you to the car.' Andrew followed Trevor down the front steps. 'Not exactly the warmest of welcomes,' he murmured as Trevor opened the door of his car.

'They know the baby is dying. As you saw, Bethan's taking it badly, and that's put all of them under a lot of strain. They're all very fond of her,' Trevor added superfluously.

'I know,' Andrew answered irritably. 'What I can't understand is with all of this going on, why Bethan had to take someone else in today.'

'You don't understand . . .' Trevor only just stopped himself from saying 'us'. He hadn't grown up in the Graig but in a poverty-stricken household in the dock area of Cardiff. He knew better than any of the crache in Pontypridd just why the working classes needed to offer and accept support. Why they clung together more in times of stress and trouble. But he didn't know how to begin explaining it to Andrew.

'I am trying to understand,' Andrew protested.

'I know.' Trevor rubbed his eyes. He was so tired he was finding difficulty in focusing. 'But until you've gone through what these people have, it's not easy. You will send for me?'

'In the morning.'

'Either your father or I will have to sign the certificate.' Trevor climbed into his car. 'I'm sorry, Andrew.'

'I know.' Andrew turned his back and climbed the steps into the cold, unwelcoming house.

Chapter Nineteen

THE ROOM SWAM alarmingly around Charlie as he bent his head to unlace his boots. He kicked them off, then lay back on his bed without undressing. It wasn't just his arm that was throbbing, but also his head. He felt sick, tired and ill, but not all of his sickness was due to the pain that emanated from his burnt hand. He couldn't stop thinking about Alma. Her curt refusal to go to the hospital with him shouldn't have made any difference. It wasn't as if she was his . . .

Red-gold hair, green eyes, tall slim figure – so many similarities to Masha, and yet so different in disposition. Masha. A name he tried to forget, because the slightest whisper of it in his mind brought back the taste of her kisses, the feel of her body nestled close to him. Masha! Gentle yet playful. Like a kitten that hasn't yet learned to claw. Would she have turned into a shrew? Never. He smiled at the thought. Not his Masha.

'I love you, Feodor.'

She lay alongside him in the bed, the sheets and blankets billowing around their entwined bodies. Her head resting on his shoulder, her arms wrapped so tightly around his chest that he had difficulty breathing. He moved his finger over her arm, tracing on her skin the shadows that fell through the curtained window. She propped herself up on her elbows, and looked at him.

'It was more fun to be your mistress than your wife.'

The mischievous smile on her face begged for punishment. He reached out to tickle her, but she melted into his arms. He looked for her, called her name, begged her to return . . .

*

The cry woke Andrew. He had pulled the two easy chairs together fronts facing, in the kitchen, taken off his jacket and overcoat, covered himself with them as best he could, put his feet up, and slept. He hadn't meant to but the warmth of the stove, the aftermath of the tiresome journey, the strain of facing Bethan and his son, had all taken their toll. He tried to rise, got his long legs hopelessly tangled in the wooden arms of the chairs, and fell between the two seat cushions. Rising to his feet he slammed full force into the kitchen table, cursed and stood still for a moment trying to remember where he was. He saw the line of light beneath the door. Graig Avenue! William had said he would leave the lamp burning.

He stumbled against a wooden chair as he tried to negotiate the furniture. He heard the second cry as he opened the passage door. It sounded as though it had come from the room directly to his left. As he tapped lightly on the door, the stair creaked overhead.

'Are you all right?' He tried to recall just who Bethan had said slept there. The lodger, Charlie? He pushed open the door. Charlie was lying, stretched out on his bed fully clothed. His face was so white it blended with his pale hair, making him appear more phantom than living, breathing man.

'I heard a noise. If your hand is giving you a lot of pain I have something in my bag that might help.'

Charlie opened his eyes wider in an effort to focus. 'I'm fine, Doctor John,' he murmured unconvincingly.

Cold politeness again! Was that all he was ever going to get in this house?

'It's all right, Eddie. I just slept awkwardly. Rolled on my hand.'

Andrew glanced backwards. He started when he saw not only Eddie's face but William's inches away from his own.

'If you're sure you're all right?'

'I am, William,' Charlie insisted. 'Go back to bed.'

Andrew followed the boys out of the room but returned with his case a few moments later.

'I can give you a pill that will help you to sleep.'

Too emotionally drained to argue, Charlie nodded assent. Andrew went into the kitchen. Unable to find a glass he took a cup from the dresser and walked out to the washhouse to fill it with water. When he returned Charlie was sitting on the side of the bed, his feet resting on the floor.

'I wouldn't think of going for a walk just yet if I were you.' Andrew handed Charlie a pill and the cup of water. 'If you like I could take a look at it.'

'I have to go back to the hospital tomorrow to have it dressed again.'

'Then it must be bad.'

'It's not good.'

'How did it happen?'

'I picked up a poker by the hot end.'

'That seems a strange thing to do.'

'Someone was waving it close to a woman's face at the time.'

'I'm sorry, I didn't mean to pry. It's really none of my business.'

'You're not prying, and as it happened in Ronconi's café the story will be all over town tomorrow, if not tonight. I'm sorry Doctor John, I'm afraid I woke you.'

'I wish someone other than Bethan in this house would call me Andrew,' he said fervently as he sat on the chair in the bay. 'And I'm not tired. Not any more. I'm not even sure I was sleeping.'

'Your son won't live much longer.' It was a simple statement, spoken sympathetically.

'No he won't,' Andrew agreed dully.

'Bethan—' Charlie took a crushed packet of Players cigarettes from his top pocket and offered Andrew one. To his amazement it was accepted – 'has had a lot to do lately. Running this house, seeing to all of us, visiting her father in prison—'

'I wanted to ask you about that,' Andrew broke in quickly, hoping Charlie would answer the questions he hadn't found the courage to ask Bethan, 'and about her mother. Has Elizabeth really moved out?' He lit both their cigarettes, and Charlie sat forward, blowing smoke at the floor. 'Please,' Andrew pressed, hoping to find an ally in the Powell household. 'Bethan hasn't written about any of this to me, and I can hardly ask her what has happened now. Before I even reached Pontypridd I was given the full story of Evan's imprisonment. According to the gossips, that is,' he added caustically.

'Mrs Powell walked out the day Evan was sentenced to six months' hard labour. Eddie found out that she's living with her uncle in the Rhondda. She hasn't been back here since she left. Neither has she answered any of Bethan's letters.'

'And Evan? He struck me as being very even-tempered. I have difficulty imagining him doing anything that warranted a prison sentence, let alone hard labour.'

'Evan and I went to a Mosley meeting,' Charlie began. 'You know Bethan's father is a Communist?'

'I suspected as much from what he told me.'

'The ideology flourishes among people who have nothing to lose,' Charlie said dispassionately.

'You're Russian, you've lived in a Communist country. I take your word for it.' Andrew was left with the feeling that Charlie had said more than he'd understood, not only about Communism, but about his own history.

'Evan went to the Mosley meeting along with a lot of other miners to put forward the unemployed's point of view. Mosley brought his bodyguard. A fight broke out, Evan swung a punch, but unfortunately for him the blackshirt it was intended to land on ducked, and a policeman got it on the nose.'

Andrew laughed in spite of the misery that had settled like a black cloud over him since he had reached Wales. 'Good for Evan. Every time I see the newsreels I'd like to land a blackshirt one myself.'

'You'd probably feel differently if you were paying for the privilege with six months' hard labour.'

'I probably would,' Andrew agreed soberly. 'Has Evan appealed against his sentence?'

'He pleaded guilty. A solicitor costs money.'

'Why didn't Bethan come to me?'

'Perhaps she thought you had enough to worry about with the baby.'

'How can I worry about the baby when she took him out of our flat to bring him here?' Andrew paced uneasily to the empty fireplace.

'Bethan always does what she thinks best, not for herself, but for others.'

'You know her that well?' Andrew looked Charlie keenly in the eye.

'It's difficult not to know someone well when you live in the same back kitchen.'

Andrew was suddenly jealous. Of Charlie, Eddie, William, Diana – of all the men – and women – who were closer to his wife than he was.

'She's a very special woman,' Charlie said slowly, meeting Andrew's steady gaze. 'She has great inner strength, but that strength is being tested to the limit. She needs help . . .'

'Which you all give her.'

The irony wasn't lost on Charlie. 'When we can, and when she'll accept it,' he agreed cautiously. 'But I've never known her to forget she's married to you.'

'Pity her devotion didn't extend to sending for me herself when the baby became ill, instead of leaving it to Trevor.'

'You're here now. When it matters.'

'But I can't stay. My job, my apartment – everything's in London.'

'The one thing I've learned, Doctor John' – Andrew winced at hearing his surname yet again – 'is that places and work are unimportant. People you care about are the only things that matter in life.'

'I'm sure you're right. But I can't leave my job just like that.'

'It must be difficult, being a doctor.'

'Sometimes it is.'

'And it must be difficult being Bethan right now,' Charlie continued perceptively. 'Her father asked Eddie to keep the home going so he'd have something to come back to. She knows Eddie can't possibly earn enough to pay all the bills on his own. That's why she stayed.'

Of course! Why hadn't he thought of that? Without Evan bringing in any money, the Powells would probably lose this house. Bethan had told him that it was mortgaged. Perhaps she would have returned to him if things had been different here. If her father hadn't gone to prison, if her mother had stayed, if her elder brother hadn't been working away, if he hadn't sent her money . . .

Andrew heard the cry before Charlie, but then he'd been waiting for it. He rushed through the door and up the stairs. Eddie and William were already on the landing in their pyjamas, and Diana had opened her door. All of them were looking at Bethan as she stood in the open doorway of her bedroom. She was still holding the baby in her arms. But now his face was blue, the harsh rattling sound of laboured breathing finally quiet.

'Bethan?' Andrew called her name softly. A cold shiver ran down his spine as she looked through him as though he were invisible. Eddie stepped between them, held out his arms and she went to him.

Trevor took a death certificate from his bag on the back seat of the car, filled in the details, signed it and handed it to Andrew.

'Has the undertaker been?'

'William's gone to get him. There didn't seem much point in disturbing him last night.'

'They're used to it . . .'

'What are you saying, Trevor? That it will be better when we put the baby in a box, out of sight and out of mind?' He thrust open the passenger door of the car and walked up the street towards the mountain. Trevor waited a moment, and when Andrew didn't turn back, he climbed out. Buttoning his mac to his chin to protect himself from the downpour, he followed. His friend hadn't gone far. He'd walked past the houses, up the hill, past a levelled plot where a community club was being built, and was walking blindly along a narrow sheep track that led to the top of the mountain.

Fighting his instinct to retreat, Trevor caught up with him close to the summit.

'I want to help,' Trevor put his hand on Andrew's shoulder. 'Will you let me?'

When Andrew turned round his face was wet, but only from the rain. His eyes were wild, dry, burning in their intensity. 'I'm sorry. I just had to get away for a moment.'

'You don't have to justify yourself to me.'

'Perhaps that's the problem. I don't have to justify myself or my actions to anyone. Not you, not Bethan . . .'

'Bethan cares.'

'Not any more.'

'Not at the moment, perhaps,' Trevor conceded, 'but she will again. There's too much between you for it to be otherwise.'

'I have a lot of things to do,' Andrew said flatly. 'I have to discuss things with the undertaker when he gets here, telephone London, see my parents . . .'

'Would a car help?' Trevor asked.

'Doctors on call need them.'

'I'll be in the hospital at nine. You can have it for a couple of hours then.'

'Thank you.' Andrew reached out and clasped Trevor's arm. 'You've been a good friend, even when I've been a bloody fool.'

'Bethan does need you,' Trevor insisted as they began their descent.

When Andrew didn't answer he felt like shaking him. But Bethan had asked him to keep her secret and he had to respect her confidence, though he hated himself for doing so. 'You're right, Andrew,' he agreed as they walked into Graig Avenue.

'In what way?'

'There are times when you're a bloody fool.'

Careful to keep one step ahead of the patrolling policemen, Phyllis walked the side-streets around the workhouse. Up and down Grover Street, up and down Kirkhouse Street, all the time nursing her son in her arms. Eventually dawn would have to break. And then she'd do what she should have done when the bailiffs had knocked on Rhiannon's door the day before.

She'd heard what Doctor John had said about Bethan taking her in. She'd been putting her son to bed, and after he'd slept she'd cried herself to sleep, but not for long. She'd been awake when Charlie had shouted out in his sleep, she'd heard Bethan call Eddie, and afterwards she'd listened while Diana and Bethan had cried in Bethan's bedroom. It was then that she'd packed her son's best clothes and favourite rag dolls into a pillowcase.

If she stayed in Graig Avenue she'd focus gossip on Evan's family and she couldn't bear the thought of doing anything that would hurt him. But as she paced the cold, inhospitable streets, she wished with all her heart that there was somewhere for her and her son to go other than the workhouse.

'I've cooked all the meat that was here. I followed the recipe books, and it looks all right. But I haven't tasted any of it.'

Alma stood back doubtfully as Charlie inspected the hams, pork legs and sides of beef she'd roasted. 'William said something about pies and pastries . . .' she began, taking his silence as an ominous sign of disapproval.

'These look all right.' He slid a clean skewer into the beef and withdrew it slowly, prodding the area around the hole with the forefinger of his unbandaged hand to check the colour of the juices as they ran out. 'We'll find out what they taste like when they cool and we slice them.'

'I was going to do that after I made the pies and pasties. I've mixed the fillings.' She pointed to three huge saucepans simmering gently on the stove.

'I think we'd be taking on too much by attempting to do pastry goods as well now.' He glanced at her. She was pale and drawn, her green eyes glittering like enamel in the early morning sunlight. 'You look tired.'

'Just the after-effects of yesterday.'

'I know what you mean. Bethan Powell's baby died last night.'

'I'm so sorry.' She remembered Bethan smiling at her, and the towels she had given her as a house-warming present; she had written Bethan a note to thank her for them only yesterday. She had always found it hard to take kindness from others. Now was her chance to help someone else. 'Is there anything I can do?' she asked sincerely.

'Write to her, perhaps go and see her after the funeral.'

'You think she'd want to see me?'

'I'm sure she would. But in the meantime we're going to have our work cut out here.' He deliberately steered the conversation on to business matters. 'William has gone to fetch the undertaker, and then he and Eddie, if he can get away, are going to run the stall for me. After last night,' he held up the sling, 'I'm not going to be up to cutting meat or working on the market for a while.'

'Perhaps we could buy in pies,' Alma suggested.

He leaned heavily against the tiled wall.

'Here,' she pulled a chair out from under one of the zinc-covered tables. 'You should sit down.' Charlie took her advice, and it was then that she saw he was really ill. 'Look, the ingredients are all here. Seeing as how I've already started suppose you let me have a try.'

'You told me yourself you've never cooked professionally.'

'How hard can it be? Besides you're here to supervise.'

'I've never cooked professionally either.' He looked at her and she coloured.

'All right,' she said, lifting down a bag of flour. 'Let's give this a go.' To her surprise he made no attempt to leave, but continued to sit and watch her.

'I haven't said thank you for last night,' she said guiltily, feeling that it was her fault he was injured. 'Not only for stopping that maniac waving the poker in front of my eyes, but also for not pressing charges against him afterwards.'

He fell silent for a moment. 'I wasn't just thinking of you. He began by threatening me, remember. Then, like an idiot, I lost my temper.'

'After seeing you, I hope you never lose it with me.' She had meant it as a joke, but her words fell flat in the quiet atmosphere of the kitchen.

'Only fools lose their tempers,' he replied unequivocally. 'And all I've succeeded in doing is hurting this business before it's even opened, as well as jeopardising my job running the stall. William and I talked last night. He's going to take over the slaughterhouse and market with Eddie's help, and that, I'm afraid, leaves this place staffed with a one-armed man, and you. Unfortunately until I find out what kind of trade we're going to get here I can't afford to pay anyone else.'

'Which means?' She was terrified that he wasn't going to open the shop after all. She'd already handed in her notice to Tony.

'Which means that although William can help on the days when the market is closed once he's finished his stint in the slaughterhouse, it's mainly down to you; and if you want the job you'll have to do more than just the cooking. I know I said you could have the afternoons off, but if I can't cope, would you mind working in the shop as well? The only problem as I see it is the long hours . . .'

'You want me to serve behind the counter after what happened in the café?'

'I'll be there with you most of the time. All I need is another pair of hands to help me cut the meat and take the money.'

'But—'

'You can't allow the gossips to ruin your whole life, Alma,' he said irritably. 'If they come in, we'll just have to face them together.'

She hadn't had a chance to tell him about her mother and her trip to see the minister. But now, when he was ill, exhausted and worried, wasn't the time. He'd done so much for her.

'If you want me to serve in the shop, Charlie, I'll be happy to do it, and work whatever hours are needed to make a go of the business. I'll cope with the Marys and Fredas as best I can. And you don't have to worry about my health. I'm used to hard work and eighteen-hour days.'

He gave her one of his rare, tight smiles. 'I knew I'd picked the right girl for the job.'

'Name?'

'Phyllis Harry.'

'State your business.'

'We're homeless.' She held up her son, who was blue after the hours spent in the cold.

'Follow me.'

The lodge-keeper led her through the main gates into a small yard. To the right was the master's house; to the left, the gate lodge, both low-built and bordered by well-stocked, colourful flowerbeds. Facing her was an intimidatingly high building, a veritable wall of dour grey stone, and set in the centre of it was another set of gates, only marginally lower than the first. She walked towards them, expecting the porter to direct her into the yard she could see beyond the gates, but he halted at the entrance to the open passageway that cut through the block.

'You can wait here,' he ordered. He opened a door on her right that led into a low-ceilinged waiting room. Painted the inevitable institution shades of green and cream, it appeared to be crowded with people. Hugging her baby close she looked around warily. A whole family – mother, father and five small children – occupied one corner. A filthy old woman who stank of drink and urine sat in another, singing to herself. Three middle-aged men stood despondently close to the door. She clutched her son and crept as close as she could to the family. She stood there, leaning against the cold, stone wall for what seemed like hours, watching and waiting, fearful of what was to come because of the stories she'd heard, mainly from Mrs Richards.

'One night! That's all poor Martha lasted in there. They took her baby away from her, and she cried her eyes out. Dead of a broken heart by morning . . .'

'TB, more like it,' Harry Griffiths had contradicted. (She must have been in his corner shop.)

'You believe what you want to, Mr Griffiths. I know better,' Mrs Richards had crowed.

'Females and children follow me!'

Phyllis kissed the top of her baby's head, gripped her bundle tightly and followed a sister dressed in a dark blue uniform dress that was almost covered by a white apron, collar and cuffs. They walked through the gate into yet another yard dominated by a massive block, the largest she had yet seen.

'Males follow me,' a masculine voice commanded. 'Females to the left.'

The group Phyllis was with turned at the command. To her surprise they seemed to have picked up more children and women from somewhere. Behind her, she could hear the mother of the small children crying, her sobs accompanied by the low murmurs of her husband.

'Come on now, stop that for the children's sake. It's not for long. Only until we get on our feet again . . .'

'Males, to the right.' A male nurse directed the men away from the women. The mother lingered, clinging to her husband's arm.

'You're not doing yourself or your husband any good.' The male nurse peeled the woman's fingers away from her husband's shabby jacket.

'Females in line.' Phyllis shuffled along, taking her place in the queue that formed in front of a high, three-storey block of dressed stone. It began to rain, heavy spots that rapidly turned into a downpour. There was no shelter in the yard, and as no one had suggested walking in through the open door that faced them, Phyllis pulled Rhiannon's old shawl higher, covering her son's face and head.

'All infants under three to be handed over.'

'Your baby.'

Phyllis stared at the young nurse in front of her.

'Your baby,' she repeated. 'He can't be left out in the cold like this.' The nurse held out her arms.

'He's hungry.'

'He'll be fed and looked after.'

'When can I see him?' Phyllis shook uncontrollably as she slowly unwrapped the shawl with numbed fingers, and wrapped it around Brian.

'That will depend on you, and how you get on. If you work well and behave yourself, possibly a week Sunday,' the sister replied officiously, standing alongside the young nurse.

'Best hand him over without a fuss, love,' a woman murmured higher up the line. 'It'll go hard if you don't.'

'Infants three to eleven years of age.'

'Where are you taking them?' the woman who'd clung to her husband asked.

'Maesycoed Homes. They'll be well looked after. Eleven to sixteen, Church Village homes. Come on Sam,' the young nurse smiled at a gangling youth who was being led across the yard by a male nurse. 'You know you're only twelve.'

'I want to stay with my dad.'

'Not this time, Sam.'

'Bailiffs put us out again, Nurse Harding,' his mother said to the staff.

'Get these children out of here.'

Phyllis couldn't see where the harsh masculine voice came from, but it provoked an instant response. Brian was snatched from her arms so quickly that she barely had time to turn her head and check the direction he was being carried in.

'Name?'

'Phyllis Harry. I gave it to the porter . . .' She wouldn't have dreamed of protesting if she hadn't been so upset by the sound of Brian's screams growing fainter as he was carried from the female yard into the deeper recesses of the workhouse.

'And now you have to give it to me. Age?'

'Forty-one.' Someone had pushed her into the reception area of the female ward block. To her left was a huge tiled room with a row of baths set in the centre. She could smell the foul stink of disinfectant from where she was standing. She began to count them . . . three, four, five, six, seven . . .

'Last place of residence?'

'Danygraig Street.' She wouldn't implicate Evan, especially here.

'Reason for leaving?'

'The bailiffs evicted us.'

'Non-payment of rent?'

'No,' Phyllis replied indignantly. 'My landlady died.'

'Relatives?'

'Only my son.'

'Husband deceased or absent?'

She lowered her head. 'I'm not married.'

'I see.' The disapproving tone said it all.

'Last occupation?'

'Cinema usherette.'

'We have no cushy jobs like that here. It'll be domestic work. Plain and hard. If you prove satisfactory we may find you an outside situation. A portion of your wages will be deducted to support yourself and your son. I take it you have no money?'

Phyllis put her hand in her pocket and pulled out a threepenny piece and two pennies, all the money she had after paying for the funeral. Then she remembered her Post Office book. There was seven of the ten pounds Charlie had given her on it. She'd left it in the box room, in Rhiannon's jewellery box. How could she have been so stupid? It would have kept her and Brian for a week or two. Given her time to think of something. Now it was too late.

'Hand it over.'

'Are there any situations where I can keep my son with me?' Phyllis ventured, as she laid her pennies on the desk, hoping even at this late stage for a miracle.

'None.'

'When can I see him?'

'We'll consider a visit in a week or two. What's that you have there?'

Phyllis looked down and realised she was still holding the bundle she had made of Brian's rag doll and his clothes. 'They're my son's—'

'Inmates are not allowed personal possessions. Hand them over.'

'But . . .'

'I'll see your son gets them.' Another, younger, prettier nurse left the bathroom and took the bundle from Phyllis's hands.

'His name's Brian. Brian Harry. He's only a baby,' Phyllis called after her.

'Inmates are not allowed to speak to staff until they're spoken to,' the admitting sister admonished sternly. 'Any problems with you, woman, and you won't be seeing your child for quite some time. In there,' she indicated the bathroom. 'Next?'

'It's not so bad,' the younger nurse whispered in her ear. 'They're not all like Dragon-face. Now here's your uniform.'

She gave Phyllis a pair of wooden clogs and a long drab work dress stitched out of coarse Welsh flannel. 'Undress next to your bath. Leave your clothes in a neat pile on the floor. I'll take them.'

'But where?'

'You're not allowed to wear your own clothes in here, Phyllis isn't it?'

Phyllis shook the dress out in her hands. 'But what about underclothes?'

'You have your dress. It's modest enough.' She walked away holding the bundle out in front of her.

'It really isn't that bad when you get used to it. The first day is always the worst,' said the older woman whose son had pleaded to be allowed to stay with his father. She followed Phyllis into the bathroom with its row of waiting baths.

'No talking along there. Strip off.'

Colour flooding her cheeks, Phyllis hung her head and began to unbutton her blouse.

'They won't let you keep anything like that, love, and once they get their hands on it you'll never see it again,' the woman whispered as Phyllis fingered the gold chain with its heart-shaped locket that Evan had given her the day Brian had been born. 'Didn't you have anyone you could leave it with?'

Phyllis shook her head, tears stinging her eyes.

'Well then, you'd better hand it over first as last. Sad, but there you are. They sell things like that, you know. Set what they get against the cost of our keep, or so they say. Pity you didn't think of pawning it. You might have been able to stay out of here a bit longer if you had.'

'Hurry up there. There's others waiting to get in that bath.'

Phyllis stared down at the water, grey and scummy with something other than disinfectant.

'The inmates get to use them first, love,' the woman told her. 'New arrivals are always last in the queue.'

Phyllis felt that the final remnants of her dignity went

with her clothes. The last thing she did before stepping into the water was to unfasten the locket from around her neck and slip it into her mouth. Tucking it into the hollow of her cheek with her tongue she decided they'd have to kill her before she handed that over. As long as she held on to it, she still had Evan – and Brian. Their photographs were inside. And she had the feeling that she was going to need to look at their smiling images often in the days that lay ahead.

Chapter Twenty

'DARLING, I AM sorry,' Mrs John rang the bell for the maid and ordered an extra place to be laid at the breakfast table. 'It must have been a dreadful strain on you, and Bethan of course. How is she taking it?'

'As well as can be expected,' Andrew answered the standard question with the standard reply.

'Well, all I can say is it has to be for the best, darling. A child like that . . .'

Two days ago Andrew would have agreed with her sentiments, but after seeing the anguished expression on Bethan's face as she had nursed the child the night before he couldn't. Not any more.

'You must be absolutely worn out, all this—'

'Bethan's borne the brunt of it,' he interrupted.

'Yes, of course,' she agreed hastily. 'Being the mother, she must have.'

'How are you and Dad keeping?' He determinedly changed the subject.

'Oh, we're fine, right as rain.' She began to rearrange a posy of primroses on the side table next to her. 'Your father was upset of course when he saw Bethan's father in the police cells. And I can't say that either of us was exactly overjoyed when we heard that he'd been sent to prison. It's just like her aunt's case all over again, such a dreadful . . .'

As his mother chattered on, Andrew sat back and studied her as though she were a stranger. Peculiar really, how he'd had to leave home before he could evaluate his parents for what they really were. The foibles, the pettiness, the meticulous attention paid to dress and detail at the expense of humanity. Even the house seemed to epitomise their faults. Old-fashioned, cluttered and fussy, it grated on his nerves after the simple, clear-cut, modern lines of the furnishings he'd chosen for his own flat.

He found himself wondering what Bethan's taste was. He'd picked out all their furniture, even their cooking utensils and linen, invariably settling on the aesthetically pleasing lines of art deco. He'd asked Bethan several times if she had a preference, but as she'd constantly deferred to him and his taste, he'd taken her at her word and gone ahead and selected what he wanted for his home. Just as his mother had selected everything for this one. Was there no happy medium in marriage?

'. . . have you any idea why he did it, darling?'

'Why who did what?' He stared at his mother blankly.

'Bethan's father hit the policeman, of course,' she stressed irritably, lowering her voice as the maid came into the drawing room to announce that breakfast was waiting to be served in the dining room.

'It was an accident. He was trying to hit a blackshirt.'

'Really, dear. Are you absolutely sure?'

'Absolutely,' he echoed as he followed her into the hall.

'Andrew. Good to see you.' His father pumped his hand up and down enthusiastically. 'Sorry about the circumstances and all that.'

'Tea or coffee, darling.'

'Coffee please.'

His mother reached for the silver coffee pot on the sideboard. It stood next to the silver teapot, sugar bowl and milk jug. He found himself appraising the silverware in a way that he had never done before. The muffin-warmers, the butter dish, the cruet set, the hot-water jug, the trays, the spoons . . . how much money did they represent? For years he had taken all of this – the house, his parents, their money, the servants – for granted. How worthless it all seemed now he was faced with his son's death and Bethan's grief.

'Any chance of a job here?' he asked his father casually as he picked up his coffee and sipped it.

'What, here in Pontypridd?'

'I can't think of any other "here".'

'I thought you were settled in London.'

'I'm not.'

'But it's such a good opportunity for you. Working in the Cross with all those specialists and consultants. I would have given my eye teeth to have had the chance to do the same at your age.'

'Perhaps I'm not ambitious.'

'Bacon and kidneys, Andrew?' His mother interrupted their conversation to push the hot dish towards him.

He shook his head.

'Of course you're ambitious. It's poppycock to say you're not. Every fellow wants to get on in life. Look, I know things aren't going very well for you at the moment—'

Andrew burst out laughing. A harsh mirthless laughter as he pushed his clean plate aside. 'Not going very well,' he echoed. 'My son dies . . .'

'It's not as if it wasn't expected, or a blessing,' his father retorted angrily, retreating from what he sensed could become an 'emotional' scene. 'You're young. You can have others.'

'Having babies isn't quite like having puppies, you know. Besides, it must be obvious to everyone with eyes in their head that my marriage isn't exactly what you'd call "up to the mark".'

His parents exchanged telling looks and his mother reached out and placed her hand over his. 'We know, darling, believe me we know, but we warned you against marrying Bethan. It was obvious from the start that the two of you simply weren't suited. But it's not the end of the world,' she consoled him. 'You can divorce her. After all, this is the 1930s not the dark ages. No one thinks that badly of divorced people any more. You only have to read the papers. It happens in the best of families nowadays, even Royalty.'

'But not mine if I can help it,' he snapped. 'Well, Dad, is there any chance of a job?'

'Posts are always available in Pontypridd and the valleys, you know that,' his father replied testily. 'Doctors aren't exactly queuing up to work here. The junior working with Trevor at the moment is taking up a position in Cardiff Infirmary next month.'

'Then you'll put in a word for me?'

'Andrew really, it's what you were doing before you went to London. Four pounds a week in the hospital and whatever you can pick up from your share of the penny-a-week patients. You could do much better.'

'It's how you started out.'

'Yes and look at me now. Senior Medical Officer in a Welsh backwater.'

'If you'd wanted better or different, why didn't you try for it?'

'My father was here, and I thought my roots were. I freely admit I should have never returned to the town after college. But the last thing I want is for you to repeat my mistakes.'

'Suppose you let me run my own life.'

'Andrew!'

'Look, while we're discussing business I know Granny left me money . . .'

'You and Fiona,' his father broke in, wondering what was coming next. 'We never made any secret of it. It's invested, and the interest is added to the capital every year.'

'How much is there, and how long would it take to cash?'

'Why?' his father asked suspiciously.

'I want to buy a house.'

'Here in Pontypridd?' his mother said doubtfully. 'But that's such a final step.'

'The Hawthorns is for sale. If you're set on staying here I suppose that would do you.' His father heaped more bacon and toast on to his plate. 'Old Mrs Herbert died last month, and I happen to know that the family want a quick sale. You could probably get it for four hundred pounds.'

333

'And it's just down the road,' Mrs John smiled brightly, determinedly making the best of a bad situation. 'I could look out for Bethan, introduce her to all the right people, propose her for the Ladies' Guild . . .'

'How much did Gran leave me then, Dad?' Andrew asked, ignoring his mother's projections of his and Bethan's future. 'Is there enough to buy a house?'

'A great deal more, actually. Fifteen hundred pounds when I last looked.'

'Can you arrange for me to have access to . . .' Andrew thought for a moment. 'Six hundred.'

'But the house will . . .'

'Will need furnishing,' Andrew finished for his father. 'And I'll need to buy a car, and it wouldn't hurt to have a bit in the bank. Oh, and I'll probably need somewhere to store my things for a week or two when I give up the lease of the London flat. Can I use the rooms over the garage?'

'If you must,' his mother said. 'But darling . . .'

He looked at his watch. 'Is that the time! I have to go.'

'But you've only just got here,' his mother protested.

'Oh, and Dad could I have the second car for a couple of days? I borrowed Trevor's to get here but he needs it.'

'I suppose so,' his father consented ungraciously.

'Thank you. I'll get Trevor to drive me up later to pick it up.'

'Will you be staying?' his mother asked hopefully as he left the table.

'No, but thank you for the offer,' he called back.

He left the house through the french window in the drawing room and walked across the garden to the garage. He glanced up at the rooms he'd occupied when he'd been at home. It seemed like half a lifetime ago. He had some growing up to do, and the sooner he began the better, for him and Bethan.

Andrew had to wait for Trevor to finish his rounds in the

Graig Hospital before he could return to the Common to fetch his father's car. As a result it was midday before he arrived back at Graig Avenue. For the first time he walked straight into the house and through to the back kitchen without knocking the front door. Charlie and William were nowhere to be seen, but Eddie was there, spooning tea into the pot.

'Bethan's upstairs,' he said coldly when Andrew entered. 'Diana's with her. She's not going into work today. Do you want tea?' he asked gruffly.

'Yes please,' Andrew answered, chalking up another first. Eddie actually offering him something.

'You didn't see Phyllis Harry, did you, when you came up the hill?'

'Phyllis Harry? Oh, the woman Bethan took in yesterday. I'm sorry, I've never met her.'

'She's disappeared,' Eddie said as he poured boiling water on the tea. 'I can't find her anywhere. She would have been carrying her baby in a shawl,' he added as an afterthought, forgetting that half the women on the Graig had babies of an age to be carried in shawls.

'I didn't see anyone on the hill,' Andrew explained. 'I drove up. I've borrowed a car.'

'It must be nice to know people you can borrow things like that off,' Eddie retorted nastily.

'Well, if you'll excuse me I think I'll go and see Bethan. Shall I take her up her tea?'

'If you like. Tell Diana hers is poured down here.'

Andrew tapped quietly on the bedroom door before entering. Bethan and Diana were sitting side by side on the bed. Bethan had dressed Edmund in the suit Laura had given him and laid him out the night before. Now he was lying in a small white coffin placed on a trestle at the foot of the bed.

'I've brought you some tea, Bethan,' Andrew said, laying it down on the dressing table in front of her. 'Eddie said to tell you that yours is ready downstairs, Diana.'

'I'll be back in a few minutes, Beth.' Diana squeezed Bethan's hand before leaving the room.

'Bethan?'

She turned round slowly and faced him.

'Bethan . . .'

'You do know what the headstone and grave you agreed to this morning will cost?'

'A plot for three is always expensive,' he said pointedly.

'I haven't any money, Andrew.'

He reached out and touched her arm, gratified that she didn't shrug off his touch. 'Now is not the time or place to sort out our problems. Can't we just bury our dead—' he looked down at the tiny body in the coffin – 'and when it's all over start again?'

The eyes that looked into his were cold and spent.

'Please, Bethan.'

'There's nothing to start again, Andrew,' she said indifferently. 'Don't you realise that?'

Andrew waited until she finished her tea, then he carried both cups downstairs. Diana passed him in the hall, and he remembered hearing the boys move around the night before. There was very little privacy in a house like this. He laid the cups on the table, said goodbye to Eddie and left. As Bethan obviously didn't want him near her, there really didn't seem to be anything else for him to do. He climbed into his car, drove down the hill into town and parked in the police station yard. Both of his father's cars were well known, so no one would question the presence of this one, merely assume that his father had taken his mother shopping.

Saturday was the busiest day of the week in Pontypridd. Like Wednesday, both the indoor and outdoor markets were open, and it was traditionally the day when the whole town shopped for Sunday, their one day of rest. He knew he was unlikely to run into any of his parents' friends. The crache preferred to buy their fresh food on a Friday when only the indoor market was open.

It gave them first choice of the goods on offer, they didn't have to contend with Saturday's crowds, and although there were fewer bargains to be had and prices were higher, they didn't mind paying extra, for what they saw as better quality.

Andrew walked past the watchmaker's, down Penuel Lane, through the fruit market, bypassing the haberdashery stalls, and into the butcher's market. Bethan had mentioned that the Russian managed a stall there. He looked around, searching for a sight of his blond hair.

'After a bargain, Doctor John? Seeing as how you're almost family I can offer you a pound of rump steak at a knock-down price.'

William was standing behind one of the centre stalls watching him.

'I was looking for Charlie,' Andrew explained as he walked towards him.

'He's in his shop. He's leased the one opposite the fruit market on the corner of Penuel Lane.'

'Thanks. I'll go there.'

'Sure I can't tempt you with that steak?' William heaped a couple of bloody red pieces on to newspaper. 'One and six a pound. Go on, treat yourself, you can afford it.'

'I'd buy it if I thought you and Eddie would share it with me.'

William eyed him carefully. 'We might at that if Diana cooks it.'

'You're on.' Andrew dug in his pocket. 'Put enough in there for Charlie and the girls as well. I'll bring the beer.'

'I'm sorry about little Edmund,' William sympathised as he handed the parcel over. 'He was a nice little fellow. Quite a character in his own way, especially when he had the hiccups.'

'I'm glad he had you to care for him during his last weeks.'

Andrew walked away quickly not trusting himself to

say any more. He found the shop without any problems; the only wonder was he hadn't noticed it before, particularly as it had 'CHARLIE'S COOKED MEATS' painted in foot-high blue letters over the doors and window. He peered inside: it looked bright and clean and new. There was a small queue of customers at the counter. He pushed open the door and an attractive girl with bright, red-gold hair looked up from the till.

'Is Charlie here?' he asked.

She apologised to the woman she was serving and lifted the latch on a half-door set into the counter. 'He's in the kitchen, if you'd like to go through.' She opened a door in the back wall. 'It's Doctor John, isn't it?'

'I wish I knew everyone in Pontypridd who seems to know me.'

'I'm very sorry about your baby, Doctor.'

'Thank you,' he said awkwardly, feeling that Bethan should be receiving the condolences, not him.

In the kitchen Charlie was removing slices of beef from a cool cupboard on to a plate. As he was using only one hand it was long, slow work.

'You said last night that you had to go up to the cottage today to have your hand dressed. As it happens, I have to go that way so I wondered if you'd like a lift.'

'I went there first thing this morning.' Charlie turned to face Andrew as he spoke. He looked ghastly, even paler than usual.

'That isn't really why I called. I'd like to talk to you about Evan Powell if I may. It won't take long, only about half an hour.'

'I'll see if Alma can manage without me.' He checked that his collar was fastened and opened the door. Andrew heard him speaking to Alma through the hubbub of conversation in the shop. Then he returned.

'As long as it is only half an hour,' he said. 'We seem to be busy.'

'Business is good.'

'Too early to say. We only opened today.'

Andrew waited until he and Charlie were alone again before continuing.

'What you told me last night about Evan. Would you be prepared to sign a statement in a solicitor's office to that effect?'

'Of course. It's the truth.'

'Did anyone else see that Evan was aiming to hit a blackshirt?'

'Plenty.'

'Then why weren't they called to court?'

'The police were expecting trouble. They convened the magistrates' court at six in the morning. There wouldn't have been any time to call witnesses. Besides, Evan didn't want to incur any costs, so he pleaded guilty. All the magistrate had to do was sentence him.'

'He didn't even plead extenuating circumstances?'

'Not to my knowledge.'

'Then would you mind if we called into Spickett's the solicitor's? They're not far, only in Gelliwastad Road. I thought about it last night. There's a possibility that we may be able to get Evan out of jail before he serves his full sentence.'

Charlie looked at him, wondering if they had all misjudged Bethan's husband.

'Bethan's going to need him,' Andrew said as Charlie opened the back door of the shop. 'Now more than ever.'

'Ashes to ashes, dust to dust . . .'

To the disgust of Elizabeth and John Joseph Bull, who'd made a point of writing to Bethan to announce that they would be attending Edmund's funeral, Andrew had engaged the Anglican vicar, Tony Price, to conduct the service. Andrew had settled on Tony Price because Trevor had said he was a kindly and humane man, and because he couldn't have borne one of the hellfire and damnation services that John Joseph Bull was notorious for conducting, any more than he could have withstood one of the genteel Anglican services his mother was so enamoured of.

Organising the whole funeral had been a nightmare. Bethan was adamant that she wanted to attend the actual interment, breaking with the sacrosanct 'men only, women in the house' Welsh tradition. She'd also refused to have any food in the house, which meant that any women who wanted to pay their respects had to do so at the graveside or not at all. Elizabeth had been so appalled that she'd actually visited the house she'd sworn never to enter again in an effort to persuade Bethan to change her mind about having a 'funeral tea', but Bethan, to Andrew's admiration, had refused to be swayed. She hadn't even needed his support to face her mother, something he had mixed feelings about. Since Edmund's death he'd spent all of his days in Graig Avenue, and his nights close by in Trevor's house, in the vain hope that she would turn to him for comfort, instead of to her family.

She was standing opposite him now, flanked by her brothers and her father who'd been allowed out of prison for the occasion. Between them lay the open grave, a deep chasm that seemed to emphasise the depth and finality of their estrangement. He looked down at the small white coffin nestling in its depths and shivered despite the warm spring sunshine. It looked smaller than ever at the bottom of the dark pit, its surface overshadowed by two very separate wreaths. Bethan's simple posy of small white rosebuds set against a background of blue forget-me-nots made his expensive wreath of waxy-looking, trumpet-shaped lilies and overblown red roses appear vulgar and crass.

'In hope of the life everlasting . . .'

He had been right about his wife needing her father. Evan's arm was wrapped around her shoulder. Haydn, who'd handed his role over to his understudy for one night to be with his sister, held on to her right hand. Eddie was standing on her left, next to his father and close to William and Diana.

He wished he could see Bethan's face beneath the thick

veil she was wearing. Take some of her grief and burden himself with it. If only they were alone . . .

'Thank you, Reverend, a most moving service.' It was over. Evan was thanking the vicar while looking at Andrew, making him feel guilty for neglecting yet another duty.

'Andrew, we'll see you later?' His mother, dry-eyed, tight-lipped, tapped his arm. His father, resplendent in his dark made-to-measure suit alongside her, his uncles, his aunts, his cousins, even the Llewellyn Joneses – all here to mourn a child they had never known, because it was the 'right thing to do'; and across the other side of the grave from them, Bethan's family and friends, Laura, Trevor and Charlie firmly fixed among them. The separate halves of Pontypridd had come together at the graveside of a child who should have belonged to both worlds, yet even here they couldn't mix. Each stuck rigidly to its own side of the grave. And Eddie, big, tough, 'take on and fight the world Eddie', clutching a teddy bear Bethan had bought for the baby; holding it so tight he virtually wrenched an arm from its body before throwing it into the grave.

'So sorry, Andrew.'

'So sorry' . . . Handshakes . . . 'So sorry . . . So sorry . . .' Expressions of sympathy, but only from his own family and friends. Nothing from Bethan's side. Then his mother actually bridged the gulf, going over to Bethan.

'So sorry . . .'

Weren't there any other words in the English language?

'You and Andrew must come and dine with us soon.'

Bethan nodded her head without answering. Elizabeth moved closer, standing next to the tall, impressive figure of John Joseph Bull. Taking his courage in his hands, Andrew walked over to Bethan.

'I'll take you back. There's room for four, five at a push, in the car,' he said, looking at Eddie and Haydn.

Evan pushed Bethan gently towards Andrew.

'Go with him, love. I'll see you soon, and I'll be thinking of you.' It was only then that Andrew saw the uniformed warder standing at a discreet distance behind the funeral party. Evan stepped back and Elizabeth stepped forward.

'My sympathies and condolences, Bethan.'

There were other words in the English language after all.

'And mine.' John Joseph Bull extended his hand to his great-niece. 'But God's will be done. He finds ways of punishing the sinners and—'

'Excuse us.' Wrapping his arm round Bethan's shoulders, which were still warm from the weight of Evan's hand, Andrew led her down the long path to the cemetery gates and the car, Haydn, Eddie, William and Diana following close behind them.

'I'm not coming back, Evan.' Elizabeth confronted her husband as he stood alongside the warder. The prison officer tactfully retreated even deeper among the gravestones.

'When I heard that you'd left the house I didn't expect you to return,' Evan said flatly.

'That's just as well. I've put up with as much as I can. Uncle John Joseph is going to try and get me a teaching situation. They now allow women with widow status to teach.'

'Would it be more convenient for you if I died, Elizabeth?' Evan asked drily.

'As far as I'm concerned, Evan, you are dead.' She took her uncle's arm and followed Bethan, Andrew and the boys down the long straight path that cut across the graves to the gate.

'Ready, Evan?' the warder asked as the last of the party turned their backs on the open grave.

Evan saw the gravediggers waiting. 'As I'll ever be.' He held out his wrists in expectation of the cuffs that had been removed as a special concession.

'There's no need for that,' the man said. 'You aren't

thinking of going anywhere are you?'

'Not for a while,' Evan agreed softly. 'Not for a while.'

'Andrew, you can't leave Pontypridd. Not now!' Trevor said hotly.

'Just what are you thinking of?' Laura demanded as she slammed a steak and kidney pudding down on the table. 'Bethan needs . . .'

'Bethan has her brothers and Diana.'

'Brothers are no substitute for a husband. And don't go all big-headed on me because I said that,' Laura turned angrily on Trevor who was sitting quietly in his chair.

'They'll look after her, keep her busy, that's what she needs right now. Charlie even asked her if she'd help out in the kitchen of his shop for a week or two until his hand heals.'

'And you're happy with that?' Trevor asked, concerned for Bethan's condition, which she obviously hadn't seen fit to mention to Andrew.

'Not entirely. But then she won't be on her own, and they won't let her do too much . . .'

'And what happens when Charlie doesn't need her in the shop any more? What then?' Trevor asked.

'Then,' Andrew took the enormous serving spoon Trevor handed him and helped himself to a small portion of the pudding, 'I hope to be back. All I have to do is work my notice in the Cross and sort out the flat.'

'You're coming back to Pontypridd for good?'

'Yes.'

'To the Graig or the Common?' Laura demanded astutely.

'What would you say if I said neither?' he answered quietly.

For weeks after the funeral Bethan moved through her days like an automaton. She woke when the alarm went off on her bedside table, she called everyone in the house, she made breakfast, cooked, washed, cleaned, scarcely noticing that Eddie's working days became shorter and shorter on the three days when she didn't help out in Charlie's shop. Trevor Lewis had told everyone in the house to watch her, make sure she kept busy, but not enough to overtax herself. He made a point of calling in every day, as did Laura. And Laura took care to make sure that Bethan was never alone, not even for a minute. On the days Bethan stayed home, Eddie didn't leave the house until Laura came. If it was Laura's baking or washing day she took Bethan back down to her house with her for 'company'. It was Laura who persuaded Bethan to walk through the market with her for the first time two weeks after Edmund's death, and it was Laura who confronted embarrassed neighbours who turned their backs or went into shops when they saw her and Bethan walking together, because they didn't know quite what to say to a mother who'd lost a child who was 'different'.

Laura occasionally took Bethan to Pontypridd Park in the afternoons. They sat on benches and watched the sons and daughters of the crache play tennis, or they walked to the cricket field, or the bandstand, or along the river, but by tacit agreement they never went near the children's playground. That was perhaps the hardest thing of all for Laura, because she wanted a child so much. She would have liked nothing better than to discuss Bethan's pregnancy, to find out what it felt like to give birth to your own child, but one glance at the look of anguish that had never entirely left Bethan's face was enough. So she stuck to 'safe' topics: Haydn's career, Diana's working life, economical recipes, and the doings of her various brothers and sisters. And she continued to invite Bethan into her tiny house after their outings, making her cups of tea, insisting that she wait until Trevor arrived so he could drive her up the remainder of the Graig hill to Graig Avenue. Attentions Bethan accepted, thanked them for, and always in the same chill monotone.

When Trevor drove Bethan up the hill he asked how she felt and tried to talk to her about the coming baby, but without success. After he watched her get out of the car and walk up the steps to her house, he invariably drove away cursing Andrew, who had left Pontypridd the day after the funeral and not returned. Not even sending word of when he could be expected. Nothing, in over four weeks.

'Hello, girl!'

'Dad?' Bethan whirled round, staring dumbfounded at her father standing in the washhouse doorway. 'You're here . . . you . . . how . . . you haven't . . .'

'No, love,' he smiled, as he closed the door and sat in his chair. 'I haven't escaped. I've been back a couple of hours, and I've banked up the fire and made a nice pot of tea. Take off your hat and coat, and sit down. You look worn out.'

'Oh Dad.' Bethan flung her arms around his neck. Scalding hot tears fell from her eyes – the first she had shed since Edmund had died.

'They let me out this morning. Bail, pending an appeal.'

'I didn't know you were appealing.'

'Neither did I until Mr Spickett—'

'The solicitor in Ponty?'

'Engaged by and paid for by your husband, turned up yesterday afternoon to tell me that he'd arranged it all. Andrew even posted bail. Fifty pounds. Mr Spickett seems to think there's a very good chance I won't have to go back.'

'Andrew never said a word to me.' Bethan finally released her father and pulled the pins from her hat.

'Perhaps he didn't want to say anything in case it didn't work out.'

'That would be like Andrew,' she agreed.

'I have to report to the police every morning, but at least I'm home and I can work. Is Eddie out on the round?'

'The round's had to go, Dad. Charlie hurt himself and

345

Eddie helped out on the stall and in the shop for a while. Now Charlie says he can't manage without him.'

'Is that the shop Charlie was thinking of opening a while back?'

'It's open now. It *is* good to have you home.' She lifted the teapot down from the range. 'Aren't you hungry?'

'I had some bread and cheese when I came in.' Evan frowned. He didn't want to ask the next question but he had to.

'Where's Phyllis Harry? I went to walk through Rhiannon's and there's new people in the house.'

'They evicted her as soon as Rhiannon was buried.'

Evan's frown became a look of anguish, and Bethan's heart went out to him. For the first time since the death of her son she found herself feeling for the suffering of another, and despite the pain it exacted, it wasn't entirely unpleasant. Something akin to the hurt that was a part of giving birth, an agony that had a purpose.

'Charlie brought her here. It was the day Edmund died. She left in the early hours of the morning without saying anything. When we found out later that she'd admitted herself and Brian to the workhouse, Charlie went down to bring her back, but she wouldn't come. She insisted that she'd bring disgrace on all of us if she lived here. Charlie offered her a job in his shop, said she could sleep in one of the spare rooms above it, but she wouldn't leave . . . Dad, where are you going?'

'To bring her and the boy back where they belong.'

'I hope she comes.'

'You know, don't you?'

'I know Brian's your son. I also know that Mam will never come back once Phyllis is here.'

'She wouldn't have come back anyway,' he said with a grim smile. 'And even if she had, I'm not entirely sure that I could have lived with her any more. Not the way we were. Prison does funny things to you. Makes you value what you've got, think of what you want to do with the rest of your life.'

'I'll sort out the beds and make the tea. She'll be sharing with you, Dad?'

He stopped in his tracks. 'I . . .' he stammered, colouring in embarrassment for the first time in his life. He had been prepared for a lot of things, but not this much understanding from his daughter.

'She can go in the box room. It is empty, isn't it?'

'I'll make up your bed, and the box-room bed. That way Phyllis can choose whether she sleeps with you or Brian. I'll move in with Diana.'

'Love, about you and Andrew . . .'

'I don't want to talk about me yet, Dad. Let's get you and Phyllis sorted first.'

'Just one thing – when is that husband of yours coming back to get you?'

'I don't know,' she said carelessly.

'He loves you, Bethan,' he said earnestly. 'Just as much as you once loved him.'

She looked at her father in amazement. 'Yes, I suppose I did love him. Didn't I?'

Chapter Twenty-One

'NAME?'
    'Evan Powell.'
'Householder?'
'Yes.'
'Occupation?'
'Rag man.'
'Relationship to the inmate?'

Evan swallowed hard. 'Miss Harry is a friend of my family,' he answered eventually.

'You intend to offer the inmate a domestic position?'
'Yes.'
'You are married?'
'Yes.'

'As the inmate is an unmarried mother and deemed to be in moral danger, your wife should be the one making this application, Mr Powell, not you.'

'My wife is not living with me.'

The thin, sharp-featured clerk laid his pen down on an adjoining chair and stared disapprovingly at Evan. 'Do you really expect the authorities to release a woman into your care, Mr Powell, when by your own admission you are living apart from your wife . . . with . . .' he glanced at the paper in front of him, 'an extremely precarious way of making a living, to say the least.'

'Miss Harry is a friend of my daughter and my niece. They are both living in my home with me, and my niece and my son both work in shops in the town.'

'I see. You may have a reasonable income going into your household, Mr Powell, but if your daughter and your niece are not married, then I hardly think Miss Harry would be a suitable person for them to associate with.'

'My daughter is married.'

'Her name?'

'Bethan John.'

'Her husband's name?'

Evan debated whether or not to tell the man. His son-in-law had already done a great deal for him. He was loath to make free with the connection and risk embarrassing him further, although he knew full well that Andrew's name would probably accomplish what he had thought impossible a few moments ago. He looked up, saw the grey walls, remembered what it had been like for him in prison, and thought of what Phyllis was going through. The sight of the bars on the windows made the decision for him. 'Andrew John. Doctor Andrew John,' he added, so there could be no mistake.

'Doctor John's son?' The clerk's tone changed immediately to one of polite deference. Evan had disliked the official on sight; now, he decided, he hated him.

'He is Doctor John's son,' Evan agreed tersely.

'Can I take it that this woman's services will be required by your daughter?'

'By all of us, to run the household. We have three lodgers.'

'I see.' The clerk tapped his nose irritatingly with the stem of his pen. 'That puts an entirely different complexion on the matter, Mr Powell. I am sorry that I had to ask you those questions earlier, but you do understand that we can't be too careful when we hand over inmates to prospective employers.'

'I understand.'

'You realise of course that you will be accountable for her welfare while she is in your employ. That you will be responsible for paying her a fair wage, and for holding back a proportion to pay for the upkeep of her child . . .'

'I intend to remove the child from here as well.'

'That is most unorthodox, Mr Powell, and something the authorities would never recommend. The child will interfere with this woman's ability to carry out her duties.'

349

'Until she came in here, Miss Harry was an extremely efficient housekeeper. The child lived with her then and didn't interfere with her duties. It will be welcome in my house.'

'Yes . . . well. Without referring to the records I couldn't tell you if the child is still here . . .'

'Where else would he be?' Evan demanded, his blood running cold at the thought of something happening to his son while he was here, in the hands of strangers.

'We have been fortunate in placing some of the younger babies with families who are prepared to adopt them.'

'Surely you can't do that without the mother's permission?'

'Not if the mother is capable of making her own decisions,' the clerk hedged evasively as he left his chair and headed nervously for the door. 'But then Miss Harry may have consented . . .'

'I know Miss Harry. She would never willingly give her child up for adoption.'

'In that case he's probably still here. I'll look into it for you.' He wrenched open the door and practically ran outside. 'I also have to have this application checked. Placing inmates isn't entirely up to me, you know. If you would wait here.'

The clerk closed the door behind him. Evan stood up and paced the floor uneasily, unnerved by the talk of adoption. Just what *did* go on behind these walls? He hated asking for favours, even more than he'd hated using Andrew's name, but he began to wish that he'd thought of calling in and asking for Trevor Lewis's help on the way down the hill. Like all unemployed miners he lived in fear of the workhouse, knowing just how easy it was to end up in the poor ward. Plenty of his workmates, and their wives and children, had been forced to throw themselves on the mercy of the parish. When he'd heard about their plight he'd wished them better days, but then he'd had no idea that it was so damned difficult to get out of this building once you were inside it.

He could hear hammering coming from the carpenter's shop across the male yard to his right. He walked up to the door, put his hand on the knob and hesitated, debating whether or not to go in search of the clerk. Deciding against it, he turned and walked back to his chair. Time crawled by. He waited. And waited.

'If you'd like to come this way, Mr Powell?' The clerk appeared in the doorway. He led Evan across the entrance hall into a long, thin corridor. 'There are some papers you have to sign.' He tapped a door that had MASTER'S OFFICE on it in large black letters. 'They are release papers.' The man gave him a sickly little smile.

'For both Miss Harry and her son?'

'Yes. Her son was up for adoption, but he hadn't been placed.'

Five minutes later the formalities were over. Evan only hoped that Andrew John would never have cause to regret the free use he'd made of his name. He was returned to the waiting room and left alone. Ten minutes later Phyllis appeared in the company of a nurse.

He hardly recognised her. She was wearing a long, grey, shapeless woollen smock. Her hair was straight, cut short in a most unflattering style. She hobbled with difficulty in unwieldy wooden clogs, her face downcast, her hands, redder and more work roughened than he'd ever seen them, clasped in front of her.

'Phyllis.'

She raised her head. Forgetting the nurse who was standing beside her, she ran towards him, tripping headlong over the clogs into his arms. She fell, sobbing on his shoulder.

'I'll just get your son, Phyllis. I won't be long.' The nurse retreated tactfully, but neither Evan nor Phyllis heard her. They were holding on to one another as though they intended never to let go.

William was living in almost as much of a haze as Bethan, but for a very different reason. After an adolescent awakening to the pleasures of illicit 'dirty' photographs, two quick kisses with Tina, and years of wondering, he'd finally discovered all the joy, ecstasy and passion of sex. Totally obsessed with Vera, he lived for the moments she stole from George and so generously gave to him.

He'd heard one or two of the married boys down the gym complain that fun with women wasn't all it was cracked up to be. That the craving wore off after a couple of months. That wasn't his experience. As the weeks of his affair had turned into months so their lovemaking had become increasingly adventurous, urgent and frenzied. The moments they snatched together were all the sweeter for being forbidden – and fraught with danger. He held no illusions about George's jealousy, or the wrath that George would hail down on both their heads if he should ever discover what they were up to. But fear of George didn't stop him – or Vera – from becoming bolder, more careless, or increasing the risks they took.

They made wild, abandoned naked love in George's shed every Saturday and Wednesday night. George's sherry bottle took a hammering as Vera fed as much of it to Carry Hardy as she would down. And Carrie had never disappointed them. Sometimes it was one or half-past before Vera managed to creep outside, but whatever the time he was waiting and – as spring progressed and the nights warmed – ready. On Tuesdays and Thursdays Vera did her shopping in town, slipping into the shed at the back of Charlie's shop in between calls. At William's insistence they never repeated the insanity of retreating behind the shutters of Charlie's stall.

But for all of his obsession with Vera, or to be more precise, her body, William never considered himself and Vera a couple. On the rare occasions he thought about his future he saw himself with Tina Ronconi, although his commitment to Vera meant he rarely went to the café, and never on market nights. Sometimes days at a time passed without him seeing Tina. Constantly preoccupied with scheming and planning out his next meeting with Vera, he failed to see that Tina was cool towards him on the few occasions when he did go into Ronconi's.

In public he was careful — very careful indeed. He avoided looking into Vera's eyes; he tried not to say too much, or too little when he had occasion to pass George's stall, and he believed — really believed — Vera when she assured him that they were too clever to be found out. But neither of them had reckoned with the all-seeing eye and cunning of a jealous man who'd married a woman a third of his age.

For the first time in his life, George neglected his customers, watching every move his wife made instead of attending to their needs. He didn't worry about Wednesday and Saturday nights when he joined the card school in the Queen's, because he continued to pay Carrie, and pay her well, to walk home with his wife and stay there until he arrived. And sure enough, every time he staggered into his house in the early hours Carrie was snoring in the easy chair, and Vera was sleeping like a baby in their bed.

It was then that guilt beset him most. When he watched Vera as she slept, her fair curls falling across her face, her eyes closed, her mouth relaxed in a sweet innocent smile, he wondered how he could ever believe her capable of betraying the trust he had placed in her on their wedding day. Then the next morning she'd exchange a glance with one of the handsome young assistants who worked the market, and a murderous rage of jealousy would rise to consume him all over again. And none of the assistants on the market came any more handsome, charming or amenable than young William Powell.

All Vera had to do was make a detour around Charlie's stall on her way to the 'Ladies' and swing her hips provocatively within William Powell's sights, for all George's nagging doubts to surface. Gradually he became convinced, absolutely convinced, despite Carrie Hardy's watchful eye, that William Powell had his feet under Vera's table. But conviction wasn't enough. He wanted and needed proof. And he knew just how to get it.

*

A firm pattern of trade had been established within a short time of Charlie's shop opening. Alma knew that on Wednesdays, Fridays and Saturdays she would be run off her feet, so she was grateful when Bethan John came in to give them a hand, although she would have liked to know exactly what was 'going on' between Bethan and Charlie. Mondays they had the rush of people who'd eaten their pantries and cupboards bare on Sunday, which left Tuesday and Thursday mornings as quiet times. Both days William worked the morning in the slaughterhouse and the afternoons in either the shop or the kitchen. And every Tuesday and Thursday since the week Charlie had opened, William had asked her to keep an eye on things for half an hour or so and disappeared into the old shed at the back.

She'd look up from pushing pasties on to plates in the kitchen one Thursday afternoon to see William peeking round the door into the yard. Moments later Vera Collins had tiptoed out behind him, her face flushed, her curls in disarray. He'd straightened her hat, kissed her on the lips, slipped his hand under her skirt to give her a friendly squeeze, and let her out of the side door that led into Penuel Lane. Suddenly everything that had puzzled Alma about William fell into place. His absentmindedness, the times he hadn't heard what she'd said because he'd been too busy daydreaming, the stupid mistakes he made. It was too close to what she'd been like during the early days of her affair with Ronnie Ronconi. She knew exactly what William was going through. And she felt for him. Really felt for him.

'Want to go to a party?'

Alma looked up. She was alone in the shop with Charlie. His hand had healed and he was removing the empty plates from inside the glassed counter. Eddie was out the back slicing a whole ham ready for the late-night rush which inevitably came round about six on a Saturday.

354

'Are you asking me?'

'Yes.' Charlie straightened up and looked across at her. 'Diana, William and Eddie are coming and, if we can, we hope to persuade Bethan to join us.'

'What kind of a party?'

'A Russian one. Down in Bute Street.'

'Cardiff docks?'

'Don't believe all the stories you've heard about the place.'

'My mother would have a fit.'

'Then don't tell her.'

'Charlie!' She pretended to be shocked and he smiled. He'd grown accustomed to working with Alma and although the atmosphere between them was always professional, it wasn't professional enough to prevent her sharing the occasional joke with Eddie, William – and him.

'I lived down there for a while when I first came to Wales, and I have a friend who's celebrating his name day.'

'What's a name day?'

'The day of the saint he's named after.'

'How are we going to get there?'

'Bus. Everyone works in the week so Sunday is the best time. It will go on all day.'

She thought for a moment: William, Diana, Eddie, Bethan . . . with that number of people around, nothing could possibly happen to incite any gossip about her and this boss.

'All right, I'll come.'

'Meet you on Broadway bus stop at ten in the morning.'

'I'll be there.'

Bethan paced uneasily from room to room in Graig Avenue. Everything was neat and tidy, clean and orderly. Phyllis had proved to be a good housekeeper, and, after a strained beginning, was proving to be a good friend. Her son filled the house with his chatter, taking to the boys and Diana, and her and, through no fault of his own, making her heart ache even more for Edmund, and everything she had lost with him.

Her only regret about Phyllis was that it had taken Evan not Charlie to persuade her to leave the workhouse. So much time had been wasted when they could have been getting to know one another. The day her father had returned to the house with Phyllis and Brian, she had helped Phyllis put Brian to bed in the box room that was now his. While they had been occupied upstairs Evan had explained to the boys and Diana exactly whose son Brian was. Eddie hadn't liked the situation at first, but Phyllis's gentle diffidence had eventually won him over, and if the neighbours tittle-tattled about the latest additions to the Powell household, or thought Evan's relationship with Phyllis strange, none of them had yet found the courage to say anything openly to their faces.

Bethan opened the door to the front parlour and stared at the spot where she had kept Edmund's pram. After the funeral Eddie and Diana had bundled up all of Edmund's things and put them in the attic, but it hadn't helped. She only had to close her eyes to picture the day cot, his teddy bear, his clothes, his frail, tiny frame . . .

She turned her back on the parlour. Desperately trying to shut out the painful memories, she gazed blindly out of the window. The street was brilliant with sunlight. It was a warm, beautiful Sunday afternoon. The sort of day she had loved to walk out in dressed in a summer frock. Just the feel of light cotton against her skin after months of serge and wool had been enough to make her happy.

Evan had taken Phyllis and Brian for a walk up Shoni's pond. They had asked her to go with them, just as Charlie, Diana and Eddie had pleaded with her to go to Cardiff. She had told them that she preferred to stay at home, and reluctantly they had been forced to take her at her word. But for the first time since Edmund had died she was beginning to regret her decision to stay in the house. Perhaps it was not too late. She could put on her shoes – go up the mountain . . .

The front door opened and she turned. Andrew was standing before her, spruce as always in an open-necked white silk shirt, navy blue blazer and grey flannels. She remembered washing and ironing the shirt and suddenly, unaccountably, tears started in her eyes.

'Can I come in?'

She nodded, a thickness in her throat preventing her from speaking.

He closed the door and walked up to her. She was wearing a loose black and white cotton frock, a shapeless overall tied over it. She had put on weight since he had last seen her, but she still looked pale, tired and strained.

'I was hoping you'd come for a ride with me.'

'You have a car?'

'Didn't you see me pull up?'

She looked out. A shining new car was parked in front of the house, its black paintwork and chrome bumper glittering in the sunshine.

'I'm sorry, I really didn't see you coming. I was miles away.'

'Please—' he held out his hand but she didn't take it. 'Will you come?'

'Where to?'

'Does it have to be anywhere special? We need to talk.'

'There really doesn't seem to be a lot to say.'

'We're still married, Bethan.'

She wondered if he wanted to ask her for a divorce. She could hardly refuse him – not when she was living in Pontypridd and he was living in London. 'Give me a few moments to get my shoes and a cardigan.' She ran up the stairs, washed her hands and face, splashed lavender water on her neck and wrists, combed her hair and spread a little powder on her cheeks. She didn't bother with lipstick; her face was so pale it would have made her look like a clown. She took off the overall and buttoned up the cardigan to conceal her thickening waistline. Andrew waited for her to leave the house and followed her down the steps, opening the passenger door of the car for her.

As she expected he turned left at the bottom of Graig Avenue, went up over Penycoedcae and took the seaside road that ran through Beddau and Llantrisant.

'Are you going to Swansea or Porthcawl?' she asked when they reached a point half-way up Penycoedcae hill.

'You'll see in a moment,' he answered mysteriously, smiling at her.

She looked away from him, out of the window. 'When did you come back?' She didn't really want to know: it was simply talk to break the silence that had fallen between them.

'Late last night. I booked into the New Inn,' he added, not wanting her to think that he'd run back to his parents.

'And when are you leaving?'

'I'm not. I've given up my job in the Cross, the lease on the flat, and moved all the furniture back. It's being stored in my father's garage.'

'What are you going to do?'

'That—' he glanced across at her – 'depends entirely on you.'

She retreated into silence again, resenting the idea that she had to take responsibility for his life as well as her own. He turned left into a drive. To their right loomed a huge house that she had seen often from the road and admired. A veritable mansion, she had equated it with the big houses Jane Austen had written about in her books, but she had never been so close to it before.

Double bays swept up either side of the pillared front door, from the ground to the second floor. Above them was a neat row of small attic windows.

'What's this?'

'A house.'

'Whose house?'

He fished a key out of his blazer pocket. 'I can hardly expect you to live on the Common, and I'd rather not live on the Graig for reasons that have nothing to do with snobbery, but with your family's well-founded dislike of me. So I thought we'd compromise and settle on Penycoedcae. This place isn't so far up the hill that your family can't walk here a couple of times a week. And if you don't like the idea of trekking up and down to see them and Laura, you'll just have to learn to drive, won't you?'

'Drive. Me drive a car?'

'Why not? I've got enough money set aside to buy another one, and driving is nowhere near as difficult as nursing.' He climbed the steps to the front door and opened it. 'Please Bethan, just take a look inside. I've taken my old job back, in the Graig,' he said as she walked slowly towards him. 'Junior doctor, working under Trevor.'

'Andrew, I know you. You won't be happy with that for long.'

'What I do know is that I can't live without you. I've found out the hard way that my happiness depends on you. Please, Bethan, take me back. I know I've behaved like a fool, especially over Edmund. But after he was born I felt so guilty . . .'

'You felt guilty!'

'If I hadn't left you when you were pregnant, you wouldn't have had to carry on working, you wouldn't have fallen down the stairs in the Graig . . . you might not have had such a rough time when he was born. And even then I could have demanded a Caesarean but I didn't until it was too late . . . Bethan please, love. What's wrong? What have I said?' He reached out hesitantly and enveloped her in his arms as tears fell silently from her eyes.

'It was my fault Edmund was the way he was,' she sobbed. 'All my fault . . .'

'How can you say that? Bethan, it wasn't. Oh God I'm sorry. I made it so difficult for you. I'm sorry, darling. But it's not your fault, it's mine. Didn't you realise he was damaged by the birth? It was my fault, not yours. All my fault. I should have seen the problems coming. I'm sorry, darling. So very, very sorry. I know I don't deserve it, but won't you please give me one more chance?'

Through the tears and half-understood words a horrible suspicion formed in her mind. She wrenched herself out of his embrace. 'I suppose Trevor told you.'

'Told me what?'

'That's why you want me back, isn't it?' she continued, too angry to listen to him. 'Why you want to start all over again. Wipe the slate clean, pretend that Edmund didn't exist. Try to blot out one baby's life by having another. Well it won't work, Andrew . . .'

'You're pregnant!'

'You didn't know?' she whispered, seeing the truth in the stunned look in his eyes.

'How could you keep something like that from me, Beth?' He sat down suddenly on the doorstep.

'I left London, after . . . after that night. I didn't find out until I'd been in Pontypridd for a couple of months.'

'You could have written.'

'Why? To give you one more excuse to put Edmund away? To tell me that I couldn't look after him and the new baby?'

'I was there when Edmund died,' he reproached her.

'And you returned to London straight after the funeral.'

'Only because you shut me out. You never once said you wanted me to stay. You turned to your brother, your family . . .'

'Because they're always there when I need someone.'

'Oh God, what a mess. What a bloody awful mess.' He covered his eyes with his hands.

'You should have listened to your parents.' Her anger died as suddenly as it had flared. 'We were never really suited. It went wrong between us from the start. Perhaps my mother and Uncle Bull were right. Edmund was the way he was because of—'

'That's rubbish Beth, and you know it.'

He lowered his hands and continued to sit on the step

staring at the trees that shaded the rolling lawn he'd
envisaged sitting out on in summer, eating picnic teas,
playing tennis, croquet . . . He'd been so wrapped up in
his ideas of starting again, of being alone with her, making
up for all the pain and loss she'd suffered that it hadn't
once crossed his mind that they could have other
children. Even now he didn't want to consider the strain
they would put on a relationship that was so fragile, so
tenuous . . .

'It doesn't matter either way now. Not really,' she
murmured. 'It simply won't work. There's nothing left,
Andrew.'

'Bethan, I've changed,' he protested earnestly. 'I
promise you this time I've really changed.'

'So have I.'

'Please, won't you at least come inside, look at the
house. Please.'

'There's no point.'

'Then what? You're leaving me?'

'I left you months ago.'

He rose to his feet and wrapped his arms around her
again. This time she didn't pull away. Simply leaned her
head against his shoulder, breathing in the old familiar
scents she would always associate with him. Kay's soap,
Andrew's cologne, tobacco . . . Standing together in this
peaceful garden in the sunshine she wanted to believe that
they could begin again. But then she remembered
Edmund, their estrangement, the gulf between them that
no amount of talking would ever bridge.

'Andrew . . .'

His mouth was on hers, silencing her. She surrendered
to the magic of his touch, the sensation of his lips. It was
easier to allow herself to be swept along on the tide of his
passion than to resist it. After all, it was something she'd
done so many, many times before.

A cloud drifted across the face of the sun, the air grew
cooler, the kiss ended and the spell that had held her
shattered.

'It's hopeless, Andrew,' she protested as he finally released her.

'You want me, Bethan. If you didn't you wouldn't have kissed me like that. You . . .'

'I want you.' She looked up into his dark brown eyes, tawny and gold with reflected light. 'Oh I want you, but when the kissing stops the problems start, and we can't live out the rest of our lives in bed.'

'But I love you.'

'And I love you.' She looked away from him, unable to bear the pain and hurt reflected in his eyes. 'But sometimes love simply isn't enough.'

Chapter Twenty-Two

THE HOUSES WERE small, red and yellow brick set in a typical dockside terrace of two-up, two-downs with lean-to washhouses and outside ty bachs, but the minute Alma entered the street she sensed she'd moved into an alien world. Even the smell was different: spicy food, exotic perfume, strange drink and tobacco, and judging by the widest smile she had ever seen spread across Charlie's face, she knew that somehow the foreign atmosphere held a little of the essence of Russia.

More animated than even William had seen him before, Charlie wandered up and down the street, greeting people of all races and colours, introducing them to Negroes, Russians, Chinese and Norwegians, sampling food from the tables that the women had set up on the pavements, laughing and slapping men heartily across the back; the whole time speaking in a harsh guttural language that transformed the old familiar Charlie of Pontypridd into a gregarious native of this new and outlandish place.

'Feodor! Feodor Raschenko!' A burly man built like a bull, who towered above William by a head, gave Charlie a bear hug, swinging him high off his feet.

'Was that Charlie's ribs I heard cracking?' Diana asked as Charlie's blond head almost disappeared into the man's long black hair and beard.

'You old fool, where have you been hiding yourself?' The man kissed Charlie on both cheeks before setting him down on the pavement.

'I haven't been hiding anywhere,' Charlie protested. 'Your mother always knows where to find me. Come on you old rogue, meet some friends of mine.'

'Russian?' the man beamed at Diana and Alma as he strode over to where they were standing next to William and Eddie.

'Welsh,' Charlie corrected.

'That's an unusual nationality to find in Bute Street.' He extended a hand the size of a meat plate. 'Any friend of Feodor is a friend of mine,' he shouted, pumping William's hand up and down enthusiastically then turned to Eddie. He bowed elaborately before Diana and Alma and kissed their hands. 'Especially young ladies as beautiful as you. But then, Feodor, you always have had good taste in women.' He lifted an enormous shaggy eyebrow in Charlie's direction.

'And as they're my friends,' Charlie smiled pleasantly, 'I expect you to treat them like princesses.'

'Why wouldn't I?'

'Because you're drunk, Nicky.'

'And what else would I be on my name day? Come. Come?' he beckoned them through the front door of his house and into the kitchen where the table was groaning from the weight of punch bowls, bottles and an array of odd glasses. Charlie extracted two bottles of beer from the bag he'd brought, and handed them to the boys, depositing the remainder beneath the table.

'Punch for the ladies.' Nicky slopped out the fruit-covered contents of a punch bowl into two large glasses. 'And for the men, a man's drink, eh Feo,' he said, producing a flask of clear liquid. Swigging it directly from the bottle, he downed a third before handing it over to Charlie, who did the same. 'You want some in your beer?' he asked the boys.

'Go easy,' Charlie warned William and Eddie, somewhat incongruously considering the face he was making after swallowing Nicky's vodka. 'And especially you,' he whispered to Diana and Alma. 'I know what this man puts in his drink.'

'You know nothing, Feo,' Nicky shouted at the top of his voice. 'You never have. Come on, it is time for dancing,' he cried as the sound of music drifted in from the street.

'Feodor, you have come to see us.'

'Mama Davydova!' Feodor swept a fat old lady off her feet, and kissed her soundly on the mouth.

'I have a feeling this is going to prove an interesting party,' William muttered as he sipped sparingly from his beer bottle.

'And I have the feeling that I never knew Charlie at all,' Diana echoed in bewilderment as an assortment of women dragged him away from them, out into the street.

'Come, come, you dance.' Nicky put one arm the size of a tree trunk around Alma's shoulders, the other around Diana's, then, afraid after Charlie's warning that he might have offended them, he straightened up to his full height, removed his arms and offered them a hand each.

'Princesses,' he said with a twinkle in his eye.

Alma burst out laughing. 'Princesses it is.'

'I won't give up, Bethan. I want you to know that. I won't ever give up.' The sky had darkened to a rich, dark gold in the west. Over in the woods on their left a skylark was singing its last plaintive evensong.

'I can't argue with you any more, I can't even think straight.' Bethan was sitting with her back against an enormous chestnut tree whose branches spread over a quarter of the lawn. She was annoyed with herself for breaking down and crying when Andrew had offered to drive her home an hour ago. He had tried to comfort her, but his apologetic words and gentle caresses had only served to upset her all the more. She had been unable to regain control of her emotions, crying bitter, salt tears that had left her throat burning, her eyes heavy and an after-taste of exhaustion that made her feel weak and totally unable to cope, either with Andrew's constant pleading, or with the thought of going home to face Evan and Phyllis's caring concern. 'I only know that I can't risk my own, or your, happiness again. It hurts too much when it all goes wrong.'

'And the baby?' he pressed, attempting to come to terms with the idea of becoming a father for the second time.

'I'll look after him,' she said trying not to think of Edmund, and how she had failed him.

'And me?'

'You can see him. You can . . .'

'Say hello to both of you when I pass you in the street? Think about what you're doing, Bethan. We could be a family . . .' he wanted but couldn't bring himself to say 'again'. He moved closer, sitting opposite her on the stone steps of a wooden summerhouse that had fallen into dereliction.

'A family!' She had a sudden very real image of herself and Andrew sitting out on cane chairs in this garden with babies playing on a rug at their feet. Then she thought of her life in Graig Avenue, surrounded by people yet always alone, because she missed the close, loving relationship that she and Andrew had once shared – and could share again until – until when? Until something else went wrong? She rose abruptly, dusting off the skirt of her dress with her hands.

'Look, as we're here and I have the key—' he played for time, wanting to keep her with him and prepared to go to almost any lengths to do so – 'won't you at least look around the house with me? It may save me making another trip.'

'Andrew, I'm not going to change my mind about living with you because of a house.'

'I know that.' He smiled at her, the old boyish smile that had once made her heart turn somersaults. 'But I have to live somewhere, and I rather like the look of this place.'

She reluctantly followed as he led the way through a tiled porch that was about the same size as the room Charlie lived in. The hall would have swallowed the back kitchen in Graig Avenue three times over and still had room to spare. Doors opened from it on to vast imposing room, after room . . . so many rooms.

'You're thinking of living here by yourself?' she asked in stunned amazement, taken aback by the sheer size of the place.

'I need a house.'

'But Andrew, this is ridiculous.'

'I'll grant you it needs some money spent on it, and it has to be decorated, but when it's finished it could be quite lovely.'

'It's too big for any sense.'

'That's only because it has no furniture in it at the moment.' He consulted the estate agent's sheet. 'Look at this.' He opened a door on to a huge kitchen that ran the full width of the back of the house.

'More doors?'

'Butler's pantry, ordinary pantry, dairy . . . stores . . .'

'A butler's pantry?'

'It would make a marvellous storage cupboard.'

'For what? I don't know of any housewife who makes enough jam to fill those shelves.' She left him and walked back into the hall where she sat on the bottom step of the magnificent sweeping staircase.

'I know it doesn't look too good now, but believe me it's solid, all it needs is decorating.'

'It's so isolated.'

'That's one of its attractions.' He sat beside her, careful to leave a few inches of space between them. 'I had hoped we could get to know one another again without too many distractions.'

'Junior doctors are always on call in Pontypridd. It's not like London.'

'We'll have a live-in maid so you won't be alone when I have to go out.' He sensed a yielding, but was wary of pushing too hard, too fast.

'How many bedrooms are there?'

'Four main ones, and eight smaller ones.'

'And you want one live-in maid?'

'We'll get as much help as we need.'

'On a junior doctor's salary?'

'I have money set aside.'

'You won't have it for long if you take this place on.'

'Bethan . . .'

'No.' She left the hall and walked outside into the garden.

'Bethan, I know I've behaved badly. I know I don't deserve another chance, but I love you. I need you. The flat, London, it was all so empty without you. I'm sorry I made such a lousy father. I'm sorry I didn't understand about Edmund. Please . . .'

'If we were going to live together again, I would want a say in where we live and how it's furnished, and that,' she pointed to the huge house behind them, 'isn't it.'

'Then you'll look at something else with me?'

She hesitated, caught in a trap of his making. 'I didn't intend to say that.'

'You still love me.'

'I loved Edmund as much.'

'I know.'

'Andrew, we could go on this way for ever, fighting all the time, hurting one another . . .'

'I promise I'll never, never hurt you again.'

'No one can make a promise like that.' She smiled despite the pain gnawing inside her. Two steps and she could be at his side. In his arms. It was that easy. Two steps . . .

'All we need is a beginning, something to build on. Beth, can you honestly say that you haven't woken up lonely in the night?'

'I've been lonely,' she admitted.

'Then give me one more chance.'

She looked up at him, her dark eyes frightened, enormous in her pale face. 'You don't know what you're asking, or what you'll be getting. I feel . . . I feel cold, Andrew. Cold and dead.'

'I want you however you are.'

'I won't be easy to live with.'

'I don't want easy, just you,' he persisted urgently, hope rising within him.

368

'I want a smaller house than this one.'

'You can have whatever house you like. I'll even live on the Graig if it will make you happy.'

'That would be too great a sacrifice to ask for.' He detected the glimmer of a smile. 'And if you were hoping that by offering me the Graig I'd reciprocate by agreeing to live on the Common, you're mistaken.'

'There's some nice houses in Graigwen.'

'So they say.'

'Bethan, can we try again?'

'I'll never forget Edmund.'

'I wouldn't want you to.'

'And if this one isn't perfect?'

'You'll have to teach me to love him. I don't seem to be very good at it.'

Two steps. She clung to him, her hands around his neck. 'I'm sorry, Beth,' he murmured, brushing the top of her head with his chin.

'Both of us are going to have to get into the habit of talking, of trying harder.'

'I know. Here, I have something for you.' He pulled a jeweller's box out of his pocket and opened it.

'My locket! You redeemed it.'

'I wanted to give it back to you months ago, but there never seemed to be a right time until now. Here,' he fastened it around her neck.

'What do you think of old furniture?' she asked, fingering the locket as they walked towards his car.

'What kind of old furniture?' he enquired suspiciously, wondering if she was testing him.

'Late Victorian.'

'You know I hate it.'

'I like it,' she said determinedly, thinking of Rhiannon Pugh's furniture stored in Mavis's house. She had always liked it, and if she could persuade Andrew to buy it for her, Phyllis would have some money of her own for once. 'Tell you what. How about we compromise? You can have a modern dining room and I'll have an old-fashioned parlour.'

'Fine, as long as you share your parlour with the children's toys, and we have a modern sitting room for company. There's room for both in this house, and it's going cheap too.'

'No.'

'I'll let you furnish the kitchen and bedrooms as well.'

'I'll hold you to that.'

'Does that mean you'll reconsider the house?'

'I've reconsidered enough for one day.'

'Do you want to drive around Pontypridd and look at more houses, or do you want to come back to the New Inn and have dinner with me?' He halted in front of the car and pulled her gently towards him.

'You want to show me your room?'

'It's a nice one.'

'I'm sure it is.'

As he opened the car door, he bent to kiss her. They had a long way to go, but they'd made a beginning. And he was determined that in this beginning would be the right end, for both of them.

Mama Davydova was playing an instrument that Charlie, during one of his more lucid moments had gravely informed Alma was a balalaika. The soft, haunting melody filled the street with a romantic atmosphere eminently suited to the twilight and the shadowy silhouettes of the women as they moved swiftly and silently, clearing the tables of empty plates and replacing them with full ones.

Nicky was slumped in an easy chair he'd carried outside his front door, his head resting low on his chest, his long hair falling across his face, concealing his eyes. Alma was sure he was asleep, but when the playing stopped he was the first on his feet, clapping and cheering, making more noise than half a dozen ordinary mortals. A guitar strummed somewhere behind them, another picked up the tune, and another, until a rousing Cossack dance-beat echoed through the air. Nicky looked round, saw Charlie and slapped his arm across Charlie's shoulders. Both men shed their jackets and began to dance, side by side, twisting and turning on their heels, their slow movements gradually, almost imperceptibly, growing faster and faster with the throb of the music until they whirled like dervishes, jumping higher into the air than Alma would have thought possible, to the accompaniment of resounding whoops from the crowd.

'Is that a Cossack dance?' Alma asked Mama Davydova, who'd taken Nicky's chair.

'Yes. We are all Cossacks,' she smiled. 'Nicky especially. Even here he behaves like a Cossack,' she replied a little sadly.

'And Charlie?' William asked. He'd always been curious about Charlie. After three years of living with the man, once in the same room, he knew virtually nothing about him other than that he was Russian.

'Charlie?' Mama Davydova looked puzzled.

'Feodor,' Alma, who'd made a note of the name Nicky had called him, corrected.

'No, he was a . . . how do you say it . . . he worked the land.'

'A farmer?' Alma hazarded.

'His father and grandfather were *boyars* – landowners. Their kind didn't fare too well after the Revolution.'

'Is that why he came to Wales?' Alma asked shyly.

'No.' The old woman realised that she'd said more than she'd intended. 'No that isn't why he came. You want some *blinys?* Pancakes,' she explained in answer to Alma's puzzled look. 'Come, get them with me.'

Alma followed her into the kitchen, and helped lay the ready-cooked pancakes on plates covered with hand-crocheted lace clothes.

'You love Feodor,' Mama Davydova informed her gravely.

'No.' Alma reddened in embarrassment. 'I work for him.'

'No, you love him,' the old woman repeated. 'I have seen the way you look at him, and the way he looks at you. He loves you. But it will be very difficult for him to admit that he can love again. And that will be very hard, for both of you,' she finished enigmatically, as she picked up a plate and walked down the passage.

The dance had finished and Charlie, his unbuttoned waistcoat hanging loose over his shirt, was standing with Nicky sharing the inevitable vodka bottle.

'*Blinys*, you're an angel Mama.' He planted a vodka-flavoured kiss on the old woman's cheek as he helped himself from her plate.

'You need food, otherwise you will get as drunk as my Nicky.' She pinched his cheek before sinking into the chair that stood outside the front door. 'Come you,' the old woman called to Alma, 'come and sit next to me. I will tell your fortune.'

'And mine?' Diana asked, walking over with Alma.

'It is only the truly young who want their fortune told,' the old woman said to Charlie.

'Those who have lived through more than they bargained for already know their fate,' he replied in Russian. He looked away from the girls towards the end of the street. Alma followed his line of vision. Just beyond a group of Russians, Negroes, and a stolid German shepherding his family of solemn-faced young men and pigtailed daughters, she saw a crowd of sailors.

'Russian ship's come in.' Nicky exchanged a look with Charlie and both of them moved swiftly towards the sailors, pushing their way through a noisy, dancing crowd that had gathered around a Negro jazz band.

'I had no idea Charlie knew so many people.' William looked on amazed as his red-faced boss was greeted by the sailors.

'When they speak it sounds as though they're all choking on their tongues,' Eddie commented.

'You have hard decisions facing you,' Mama Davydova said as she gripped Alma's palm tightly. 'You have the chance of happiness, but it will only come once, and like all good things it will not last. Recognise your destiny when it comes, take it and make the most of it while you can, my child.'

Alma scarcely followed what the old woman was saying. Her attention was still fixed on Charlie. Even across the length of the street she could see that he had become grave, serious, as though he had heard bad news.

'Now mine,' Diana pleaded, laughing at a joke of Eddie's as she gave the old woman her palm.

Alma left them and walked past a woman who was passing around plates of little meat and fish pies.

'Dance!'

'Come on Nicky, Feo!'

The sailors took up the cry. Someone handed Alma a cup of stew, so hot and spicy it burnt the roof of her mouth. The Negroes blasted on their brass instruments, the music grew deafening, the atmosphere more and more raucous. She gazed at Charlie, unable to reach him, only watch as he moved in a world she could never hope to understand, let alone enter. Why had it taken Mama Davydova to tell her what she should have known? Charlie loved her. Why else would he have helped her when she had most needed it? Lending her money, offering her a job, a place to live, saving her from Bobby. And she loved him. But it had taken a party that emphasised their very different worlds to make her realise just how much.

'Alma?'

The music had finished and Charlie was swaying alarmingly on his feet before her. As he staggered she caught him.

'Take him into the house,' Nicky suggested, as she almost collapsed beneath Charlie's weight. 'Splash his head with cold water.'

'I warned you, Nicky. Feodor isn't used to vodka, not the way you drink it, not any more.'

'He'll be all right Mama. You always fuss.' Nicky flipped the cork from a bottle of vodka that one of the sailors had handed him and drank deeply. 'Here.' Putting his shoulder beneath Charlie's he helped Alma to half carry, half drag him into the house. 'In the front room,' he said, his voice slurring thickly. 'There on the bed.'

'You'll stay with him?' the old woman asked Alma as she walked in behind them.

'I will.' There was a flannel next to a huge ewer of cold water on the washstand. Alma wrung it out and laid it on Charlie's forehead.

'You won't be disturbed.' The door closed, and Alma sat beside Charlie who was struggling to sit up.

'Do you want water?' She poured some from a jug into a glass on the stand.

'No!' Charlie lashed out and knocked the glass from her hand. It shattered against the wall, water spraying into both their faces. She picked up the jagged pieces and heaped them in the corner. When she turned to face him again she saw pure anguish in his face.

'Charlie!' She knelt on the floor before him. 'What's the matter?' He put his hands either side of her face and ran his fingers slowly down her cheeks. She placed her hands over his and he helped her to her feet. Then he rose. Lifting her off her feet, he turned and laid her on the bed.

He was beside her, kissing her, his hands stroking her breasts beneath the flimsy fabric of her dress. He muttered a few Russian words, and she found herself hoping against hope that it wasn't another woman's name. His lip brushed lightly over her earlobes, her throat, her mouth. His weight pressed her down into the mattress as he lifted his arms and pulled off his waistcoat. His shirt was next, wrenched over his head. Then his vest.

'Alma.' This time he whispered her name clearly as he ran his fingers through her curls. 'Alma . . .'

A passion she had thought she would never experience again stirred within her. Her skin flamed where Charlie touched her. A need, a hunger, all-enveloping, all-consuming burned within her. She only knew that she

374

wanted him, here and now, as she had never wanted anything in her life before.

She had no recollection of removing her clothes, only an acute awareness of his naked body as it stretched out alongside hers. His bare thighs moved tantalisingly over her legs, his hands fondled her breasts, teasing, stroking the sensitive skin of her nipples. His tongue was in her mouth. She could taste the cool, clean flavour of vodka on his breath, as he caressed and aroused her to the point where pain and ecstasy seemed to be one and the same, before finally piercing her body with his own.

She cried out, and he thrust into her again, and again, mercilessly driving harder and harder, evoking shameless, intuitive responses. All inhibition fell away as she allowed herself to be transported into a world of sensuality where nothing mattered except the satisfaction of the urgent cravings he had kindled within her. She clawed the smooth skin on his back, trying to pin him closer to her, so close that their bodies would merge.

Lost in passion, neither Alma nor Charlie heard the door opening nor saw the look on William's face as he hastily closed it.

'I think Charlie's a little the worse for wear,' he said to Eddie and Diana. 'If we're going to take that last bus we should make a move.'

'But what about Alma?' Diana protested. 'We can't just leave her here.'

'Alma wants to stay with Charlie.'

'But her mother will worry—'

'We will get them home,' the old woman reassured Diana as she shooed them out of her passage. 'Feodor and his young lady are safe with us. My Nicky will see to it that they get home before morning.'

'His young lady?' Diana looked blankly at William. 'I didn't know Alma was Charlie's young lady?'

'She is now,' William murmured darkly.

Chapter Twenty-Three

'I'M PREGNANT, WILL.'

Vera had waited until after they'd made love to tell him. She was sitting on the floor of the shed behind the shop, stark naked except for a thick gold chain around her neck and a pair of gypsy hoop earrings. The earrings had cost William every penny of his savings, but the wild, ecstatic thank-you he had received had more than justified the expense.

'Are you sure?' His heart began to pound erratically against his ribs. This was one eventuality that hadn't crossed his mind.

'It's not George's.' She turned a miserable face to his. She hated the idea of bearing a child. For her it loomed as a watershed, the dividing line between youth and old age. She'd soon be fat and old like her mother. Vera's mother had been pregnant at sixteen and had a dozen by the time she was thirty. Vera knew all about morning sickness, varicose veins, stretch marks; bloated, swollen, heavily veined breasts, and smelly whining babies who demanded constant feeding and nappy changes.

'I know it's not George's.' William pulled on his trousers and reached for his cigarettes.

'How . . .'

'You told me when we first met that you never do it with him, not properly anyway.'

'I did?'

'Don't you remember?'

'Yes,' she lied quickly, resolving to keep a tighter rein on her mouth in future. 'What am I going to do, Will?' She rose to her feet and clung to him, genuinely frightened.

'We could go away,' he suggested in desperation.

'Where?'

'I don't know.' He drew impatiently on his cigarette. 'I'll have to think about it.'

'I know what would be easiest, Will.' Her eyes reminded him of a cornered cat's.

'What?'

'If we got rid of it. There must be ways . . .'

'If there are I don't know of any.'

'I've heard women say all you need is money. There's this man and all he wants is twenty pounds . . .'

'Twenty pounds! I can't get hold of that kind of money, Vera.'

'Oh Will!' She began to sob.

'Ssh, you don't want anyone to hear you, do you?'

'No.' She took the handkerchief he handed her and dried her tears.

'You ought to dress.' He bundled her clothes together and pushed them towards her. Her nakedness suddenly disturbed him, for a new and entirely different reason. Normally at this stage of the afternoon she would have dragged him down on top of her for second helpings, but her news had sapped all his desire. He stared at her flat stomach, imagining a baby growing in its depths – a smaller version of himself. He was beset by the oddest feeling: a peculiar mixture of tenderness and protectiveness. He didn't love Vera, at least not like he loved Tina, but she was carrying his child and that entitled her to some consideration. And then again, she was good in bed – very good. He could live with a wife who doled out what Vera did, every night of his life.

'We'll have to go away together,' he said finally. 'There's no other way out. I'll try and get hold of some money.'

'Where?'

'I don't know yet. I have to think. I don't suppose you have any ideas?'

'No.'

'Wherever we go it's bound to be hard at first, at least until I get a job, but we'll make it. Rent a room somewhere . . .'

'Oh Will,' she ran her fingers inside the waistband of his trousers and kissed him on the mouth. 'You are good to me. How soon can we go?'

'Just as soon as I can arrange it.'

'We could go to London. See all the sights. I've always wanted to, and George would never think of looking for us there.'

'My cousin Bethan says that things there are just as bad as down here. There's thousands out of work. People are even sleeping in the streets . . .'

'We wouldn't end up there, would we?' There was genuine alarm in her voice.

'Not if I can help it,' he said grimly. 'Don't worry. I'll find something. Now you'd better go, before Charlie starts looking for me.'

'All right, Will.' She clipped on her suspender belt and rolled on a stocking. Usually he liked to watch her dress. It was always suspender belt and stockings first, followed by wispy bits of lace that revealed more than they concealed. She never wore knickers, and dressed only in her underclothes as she was, to all intents and purposes, as good as naked. Then she'd slip a dress on top and look neat and demure. Every time William caught sight of her walking around the market his senses were inflamed by the thought of how she'd look if she suddenly lost her dress.

'Vera?'

'Yes, Will?' She smiled at him over her shoulder as she began rolling the second stocking on to her leg.

'You won't sleep with George any more, will you? This is my baby and if we're going away together soon . . .'

'Will, he's my husband. I live with him.'

'Couldn't you move in with your mother for a while?'

Vera thought of her mother's cramped house. She wouldn't have a bed to herself, or wardrobe space for her clothes. And she'd have to go back to eating bread and dripping instead of the best cuts of meat and cream cakes she bought with George's money. 'I can't go home Will,' she protested.

'Why?'

'Just think about it, sweetheart.' She turned to face him, her breasts and thighs still bare. 'If I moved out of George's house into my mother's he'd realise something was wrong.'

'You've been unhappy with him for a long time. Tell him you've had enough of his perverted ways.'

'Don't you see, he might suspect us if I moved out. He'd come after me and then heaven only knows what he'd do.'

'But I can't let you carry on living with him. Look if I get some money together you could go up to Ynysybwl . . .'

'Ynysybwl?' She stared at him in stunned amazement. Ynysybwl was a small, quiet village. Even more of a backwater than Pontypridd, and only a few miles up the road.

'Mate of mine lives there. If I explain to his missus he'd put you up until I arrange something. You could share a room with his kids.'

'No, Will,' she said firmly.

'I can't bear the thought of you and him . . .'

'Then I'll move into the spare room.'

'Promise?'

'I promise,' she murmured, suddenly realising just how much she'd lose if she left George. The trips to Cardiff, the clothes. The van at her disposal – and the car as soon as he got round to buying it . . .

'Vera?'

'You're right, Will. I must go.' She tweaked a clump of black curling hair on his chest.

'And George?'

'How many times do I have to tell you that I never do the things I do with you, with George.'

'You sleep in the same bed with him, that's enough.'

'For what he does he may as well be my sister.'

'He looks at you.'

'He's my husband.'

'Not for much longer.'

'Will, don't tell me you're going to get jealous like him?'

'When you're living with me,' he patted her naked buttocks, 'you bet, Vera.' He looked away quickly, as a sick feeling rose in his stomach and an image of Tina flooded into his mind.

Alma dropped the heavy tray on to the table. Thursday afternoon baking sessions had become a real chore. Charlie was already looking around for someone to help out part time with the cooking, or so he'd made a point of telling William within her earshot. He'd avoided speaking to her directly since that Sunday in Cardiff. Nicky had asked one of his friends, a taxi driver, to take them home to Pontypridd, and they had reached the shop at four in the morning. Just in time to start the baking. They had set to work, and at the end of the day he had apologised to her for his behaviour, hurrying out before she had a chance to reply. Since then he'd kept communication between them to a bare minimum, and she noticed that he went to great lengths to avoid being left alone with her, even for a moment.

She wondered just how much – if anything – he remembered of that night. She thought of it often, without any feeling of shame or embarrassment, simply a sense of loss that she would never again experience the wonder of that passionate abandon with Charlie again. The old Russian woman had been right: happiness *was* fragile, and tenuous. Every time she reached out to grasp it, it crumbled to dust in her hands.

Alma went back to the oven to bring out the second tray. Superficially her life was running smoothly for the first time since her father's death. She'd managed to put the traumatic events of last Christmas behind her. Charlie had been right: as time went on and there was no sign of her producing the bastard that half the town's population had expected, people had not only stopped talking about her but had started to give her sympathetic looks. Most went out of their way to be pleasant when they called into the shop, and even her mother had finally settled into the flat, arranging things so she could find her way around, sending for one of Betty Lane's children every day after school so she could walk in the park. Laura had been paid back, so the only money they owed was to Charlie, and although they had money enough – just – to pay him back he wouldn't take it. So she had left their small nest egg in the Post Office savings bank, and looked on the extra two shillings a week she would get in nine months' time almost as a pay rise. Both she and her mother had a warm place to live in, enough to eat, and an indoor bathroom. Outwardly life was good, so good, that occasionally she had nightmares that it was all a dream and she'd wake up back in Morgan Street, her security, her calm quiet days, her restored reputation, all taken from her.

'Hello Alma. Sorry to trouble you. Is your Mam in?'

'Upstairs.' She smiled at the minister who'd baptised Betty Lane's children. Primed by Betty's stories of Lena and Alma's misfortunes he'd welcomed both of them into his flock with open arms. 'You wouldn't like to take a couple of pasties up with you?' she asked.

'Not this time, not unless your mam wants them.' He returned her smile rather sheepishly. He was young, and unmarried, and he called in on Mrs Moore far more often than he needed to. But with a warm welcome and food guaranteed every time, it was hard to pass by. 'I've come to take your mam to the Mothers' Union lunch. The ladies have been hard at it all morning in the parish hall.'

'That is kind of you. She looks forward to chapel events.'

'We enjoy having her. I'll bring her back this afternoon, safe and sound.'

'I know you will.'

'Whisking Mrs Moore off again to the high life, Mr Jones?' William walked in with a ham on each shoulder.

'Something like that.' Will's joking always made the minister feel a little uneasy. 'Well I must be off.'

Charlie followed in behind William with a side of beef and a leg of pork.

'Thank you for your donation to the fund for the poor, Charlie,' the minister called out loudly. 'Due to the generosity of the town's traders everyone on our books will have an Easter dinner.'

'If you preach to your parishioners to shop here, trade will go up and I'll be able to donate more at Christmas,' Charlie replied drily.

'I don't think advertisements would go down very well from the pulpit, Charlie, but I'll see what I can do. Goodbye everybody.' He backed out of the door.

'Doesn't that man understand a joke?' Eddie asked as he came in with a tray full of pigs' heads and trotters.

'His heart's in the right place,' Alma said, grateful because he'd steered her mother out of the depression that had marred their early days in the flat. 'Do you want this beef spiced, pressed or roast, Charlie?'

'Roast, but as soon as the shop's closed we'll take a break, and start cooking early this afternoon.'

She nodded, served the last customer and clanged the door shut, locking it firmly and leaving the keys in the lock. William walked in through the Penuel Lane entrance with a dozen and a half baps that he'd bought from the baker.

'Make mine ham, Alma,' he called as he dumped the rolls on the shop counter.

'Eddie? Charlie?' she asked as she began cutting the bread rolls open.

'Pork,' Eddie called back.

'Beef,' Charlie replied quietly.

A picnic-style lunch had become a ritual every Thursday, the one day when all four of them could eat

382

together. Not that William joined them often; he usually took his rolls outside to eat in the park. With Tina, Charlie presumed. Alma knew better. She lifted down three of the smallest serving plates and set out the rolls: five each for William, Eddie and Charlie, two for herself. The kettle was already boiling for tea.

'See you in half an hour, Charlie,' William murmured as he grabbed his plate of rolls. 'Mind if I listen to your radio upstairs, Alma?'

Charlie had bought two radios to pacify Frank Clayton next door. He'd put one in the back kitchen in Graig Avenue, and the other in Alma's living room, using the excuse that it would be a distraction in the shop, and Alma's mother could come down and tell them if anything important was on. It was the first time William had asked if he could use the flat. Alma suspected he wouldn't have asked at all if her mother had been in, which meant that Vera Collins would be coming through the door.

'Don't go moving anything up there, Will,' she warned sternly, 'or my mother will be falling over when she gets back.'

'I'll sit on the floor in front of the set and won't move.'

'There are chairs up there.'

He left just as Charlie and Eddie came in to wash their hands in the back.

'Want company, Will?' Eddie shouted after him.

'No thanks. I know you're bored rigid by cricket, and I want to listen to the scores, not you gabbling.'

'Since when has Will taken to listening to cricket?' Eddie asked innocently. Alma shrugged her shoulders. She heard the front door that led to the upstairs flat open and close quietly. She knew Vera only by sight, but her middle-aged husband, coupled with her flashy dress sense and thick layers of make-up, was enough to make Alma suspicious of Vera's motives for carrying on with William. And she couldn't help feeling sorry for Will; he bore all the hallmarks of a man besotted. Just like her, she thought resentfully as she sat across the table from Charlie to eat her own rolls.

They'd barely had time to take their first bite when there was an almighty hammering on the side door. George Collins's voice thundered through the letterbox.

'I know you're in there, you little slut! Open up or I'll smash the door down.'

'Quick!' Alma grabbed Charlie's hand.

'What—' he reluctantly abandoned his roll.

'Quick, don't argue!' she whispered urgently. 'Eddie, give us a couple of minutes then open the door.' She raced up the stairs pulling a bewildered Charlie in her wake. Throwing open the living-room door they saw Vera clutching her dress to her naked body, and William hopping about ineffectually trying to extract one of the two legs he'd thrust into a single trouser leg.

'Both of you, shut yourselves in the bathroom. Quick!' she commanded. 'And don't forget to lock the door. Vera, leave your coat and hat, I'll need them.'

William needed no second bidding. He grabbed his clothes, pulled Vera's wrist and dragged her behind him. Alma tossed Vera's hat and coat on to the chair. The door burst open downstairs just as she threw her arms around Charlie's neck. She kissed him soundly on the lips, expecting a hard dry response after the strained silence that had fallen between them since the weekend, but to her amazement he pressed her close, kissing her back. Locked together in one another's arms in the centre of the room they were barely conscious of the thunder of boots thumping up the stairs, accompanied by Eddie's shouted protests.

'There she is! Damned slut!' George grabbed Alma's shoulder and tore her away from Charlie, who retaliated by hitting him soundly on the jaw. George reeled backwards, looking in amazement from the coat on the settee to Alma's red hair, and to Charlie and back.

'It was her, Mr Collins. I swear it. I saw her come in here,' a small weasel-faced man protested as he hid behind Eddie's broad shoulders.

'What's going on here?' Charlie demanded sternly.

'My wife. She came in here.'

'The shop's closed.'

'I know, but she's . . . she . . . she's carrying on with that good-looking boy who works for you.'

'She isn't, Mr Collins,' Eddie protested, the picture of absolute innocence, as he realised what Alma had done.

'Not you . . . the other one, what's his name?'

'If you mean William, he's out on the meat van delivering to my boss's shops in Cardiff. Has this man done any damage, Eddie?'

'I think the lock's broken on the door downstairs, sir,' Eddie invented a humble subservience in honour of the occasion.

'I'll see it's fixed, I'll . . .' George's eyes lit up as he spotted the hat and coat on the settee. 'This is my wife's coat,' he crowed triumphantly.

'It's mine,' Alma snatched it.

'A likely story. Where did you buy it?'

'In Cardiff, in Howell's, not that it's any of your business,' she said haughtily, carrying it over to the window-seat.

'Didn't know shop-girls could afford to go to Howell's,' he commented snidely.

'I bought it for her,' Charlie said belligerently. 'Now if you don't mind, you'd better apologise and leave, before I call the police.'

'I'm sorry, the lock—'

'I'll fix the lock and send you the bill. Eddie, see them out.'

Charlie and Alma sat side by side on the settee, listening as George Collins and the detective he'd hired went down the stairs. Eddie closed the door behind them and crept back up.

'They walked off in the direction of the Fairfield.'

'Go downstairs, stay in the shop and keep an eye

open in case they come back. You've bolted both doors?'

Eddie nodded.

'Alma and her mother will just have to use the shop door until I get a chance to fix the other one. Go on boy, take a look outside, then finish your rolls.'

A very sheepish William crept out of the bathroom in response to Charlie's call. Charlie said nothing, simply sat and stared at him.

'Charlie . . .' William began hesitantly.

'Just get the young lady out of here while you still have a head on your shoulders, and you'd better get Eddie to help you, in case they're still lurking around.'

'I'll go up the lane to the library, Mr Raschenko,' Vera waved at him shyly from the landing. 'George will never think of looking for me there.'

'If I were you I'd think of sticking to the library from now on.'

Alma handed her the hat and coat. 'You'll need these.'

'It's not what you think,' William explained, red-faced. 'Vera and I are going away together . . .'

'We are not, William Powell,' she countered indignantly.

'Yes we are.' He turned to her. 'The baby—'

'Is my husband's,' she said quickly. 'Look William it was nice while it lasted, but I'm married to George.'

'You said you loved me.'

'I never did.'

'Seems to me that young lady wants to eat her cake, have it and own the baker's,' Alma said as William followed her downstairs.

'I'd better take you to Howell's some time and buy you a hat and coat,' Charlie said as the connecting door to the shop slammed shut.

'I didn't like the cloth or the style.'

'How long has that been going on?'

'I noticed it as soon as the shop opened. Probably it started some time before.'

He sat forward and rested his head in his hands. It would be so easy to reach out and touch her face as he'd done in Cardiff . . . He stretched out his hands. She looked down at his fingers, heavily scared by thick, white, heat-puckered skin.

'Alma I . . .' he left the seat and paced uneasily towards the window. 'I'm sorry,' he looked down into the street away from her.

'It seems it's my lot in life to fall in love with men who don't love me,' she said sadly. 'First Ronnie, now you.'

'Alma?' he looked round. She'd already gone. He stared out of the window until he saw Vera teetering on high heels along the pavement on the other side of the road. Then he turned and followed Alma slowly down the stairs.

'You should see the house. I never thought a daughter of mine would be living in a place like that. Phyllis was a bit upset of course, seeing all Rhiannon's bits and pieces again, but it's not as if we have anywhere for them, and our Bethan has really done them proud. Putting them in pride of place. It's so big, and it has so much land besides the garden. Two huge fields, heaven only knows what they're going to do with them. And although both of them seem a bit quiet, Andrew as well as Bethan, I think it might work out this time.'

'I hope so,' Charlie muttered mechanically.

Evan picked up his and Charlie's glasses from the table in the back room of the Graig Hotel. 'Same again?'

'Yes, thanks.' It was Charlie's round, and the fact that Evan was buying the drinks spoke volumes about Charlie's state of mind.

'All right, mate, I've said nothing up until now. But I can't stand it any more. What's up with you?'

Charlie took his fresh pint and sipped it. 'Nothing.'

'For once in my life things are working out the way I want them to. Bethan and Andrew are back together. I'm happy as a pig in muck living in sin with Phyllis and the boy. William's had his wild streak curbed for a while, but you're walking around as though the end of the world is in sight. What is it?'

Charlie looked around the rom. Fortunately they were the only ones in it.

'It's that pretty redhead you've got working for you in the shop, isn't it?'

Charlie looked at him, but didn't answer.

'Well it makes sense, doesn't it?' Evan continued. 'You make a stand against the gossips, you take her in, decorate a flat for her, give her a job, pay her debts . . . No one keeps any secrets in this town,' Evan said, in reply to the look of surprise on Charlie's face. 'You love her, don't you?'

'I'm in no position to love anyone.'

'You're a man, aren't you?'

Charlie pushed his pint glass away from him. 'Not much of one.'

'My advice, whatever it's worth, is to go and see her. Tell her what's worrying you, it can't be that bad. You only have one short life. No one knows how short. Perhaps it was the spell in prison that gave me the courage to live the way I want to – where are you going?'

'I'm taking your advice.'

'You're going to see her now? At this hour?'

'Yes.'

'Well I hope you sort it out,' Evan said. He left his chair.

'You leaving early too?'

'I've got a lot to go home to these days,' Evan smiled. 'There's nothing like a cosy kitchen, the love of a good woman and a warm bed. Why don't you try it, Charlie? Believe you me, it's everything it's cracked up to be.'

Evenings were lonely for Alma. Her mother, loath to break the habit of half a lifetime, when the cold and hunger of Morgan Street had driven her early to bed, still retired to her room before eight every evening, leaving Alma to her own devices. Alma had taken to spending most of her free time sitting alone in the living room above the shop, looking out of the window at the deserted street and listening to the radio.

The room was far more comfortable than the back kitchen of Morgan Street had ever been, even during her father's day. Light, airy, it was neatly, and thanks to some of the things Charlie had bought from Phyllis, better furnished than it would have been if they'd had to rely on their own poor sticks.

Earlier in the evening she had gone for a solitary walk in the park, where the sight of the courting couples had depressed her even more. A library book was lying open on her lap, but even that irritated her. She didn't want to read about Lucy Manet's happiness with her husband in *A Tale of Two Cities*. Besides, the book conjured up images of the film, and now she had the time and money enough to go to the cinema she resented having to sit there listening to the muffled giggles of the couples in the back row.

The whole world seemed to be pairing off, with the sole exception of her. She heard a key turn in the lock of the shop door below her. Craning her neck, she saw the crown of Charlie's blond head disappearing inside. He must have forgotten something. She glanced up at the chiming clock he had hung on the wall for her mother. Ten-thirty: she had to be up again in a few hours. She should have gone to bed hours ago instead of listening to the concert of Noel Coward songs. As she left her seat she heard Charlie's footsteps on the landing outside the room.

'Charlie, have you forgotten something?' she asked as she opened the door.

'No. I saw you sitting at the window, so I thought I'd call in.'

'Would you like a cup of tea, or cocoa?' she enquired remembering her manners.

'No.' He twisted the brim of his hat in his hand. 'I just want to talk to you.'

'About the shop?'

'No, about what you said today.'

'I spoke out of turn. I'm sorry, it was just the excitement of seeing George Collins come charging after William.'

'You weren't talking out of turn. Not after what happened in Cardiff.'

'I wondered if you remembered.'

'I was drunk, but not that drunk.' He thrust his hands into his trouser pockets as though he couldn't trust himself to keep them off her.

'I know you don't love me. Do you want me to leave here, not work for you any more? Is that it?' she sat down abruptly, hoping with all her heart that he wouldn't give her notice. She was afraid of losing her job, but not as afraid of losing all contact with him. Of walking out of the shop and never, ever seeing him again.

'It's nothing to do with work,' he said impatiently. He went to the window and looked down at the fountain. 'I like you very much Alma, you must realise that.'

'Like,' she echoed dismally.

'If it were possible, I'd say love. I wish I could marry you – but I already have a wife.'

The silence in the room was deafening. Alma felt as if the air was whirling around her, closing in, crushing.

He turned to face her. Leaning against the wall, he crossed his arms. 'I'm here because I want to explain, but now I'm not sure where to start. In the beginning, when I first saw you, I tried to tell myself that I felt sorry for you. That I wanted to help you because you reminded me so much of Masha . . .'

'Your wife?' She asked him in a small voice.

'Yes.' He resumed his study of the fountain. 'She looked a lot like you, tall, slender with pale skin, red hair and green eyes. But that's not why I wanted you to work for me. I know you're a special woman, Alma, a woman who deserves better than a man who looks at you and sees another.'

'Is that what you do, Charlie?'

'My name isn't Charlie,' he said harshly. 'It's Feodor, Feodor Raschenko.'

'If you love your Masha so much, why aren't you with her?' she was trembling, almost too afraid to listen to his answer, but she had to ask the question.

'I'm not with her because I have no idea where she is.'

'She left you?'

'Not willingly.'

Now he'd begun, he wanted to talk, to unburden himself of the events that had irrevocably changed his life, making every day a marathon in which the twin hurdles of loneliness and painful memories had to be overcome. 'I grew up in a small village near Moscow. Just distance enough to make it the country, but near enough to travel there in a day. That was the problem. It was a beautiful place. People used to say so all the time, but when you live somewhere you take it for granted. Forget its beauty as well as its faults.'

'I suppose you do,' Alma interposed, thinking of her house in Morgan Street. How she had looked on it as home for years, not realising just how uncomfortable a place it was until she'd been able to contrast it with this flat.

He hesitated for a moment, and when he spoke again his voice was harsh, rasping. 'The party leaders found out about it, saw it and wanted it. They moved everyone out.'

'Moved?' she looked at him uncomprehendingly.

'They wanted dachas, summer houses. The peasants were in the way. I lived in a house that had been my father's and his father's before him. It had been built by a Rashchenko four hundred years ago. But none of that mattered. Not to them. And they had the power and the control.' He clenched his jaw and she noticed a small pulse on his temple throbbing.

'But if it was your house and your land . . .'

'You don't understand Russia.' He shook his head at her naivety. 'We didn't know what was coming, and if we

391

had, there would have been nothing that any of us could have done to change it.'

'But surely you have laws . . . police . . .'

'The party's laws, and the party's police. It was the police who moved everyone out. I wasn't even there. Masha was having a baby, I had walked to the next village to get a cot from her brother. When I came back there was nothing.'

'Nothing?'

'Nothing,' he repeated flatly. 'Most of the old houses had been flattened to the ground. Builders were already at work. Fires burned, fed by our furniture, clothes, things we had valued for years. I asked them where the people had gone and they told me, the East. I went to the station. It was deserted: no trains, no people. I asked questions, so many questions I was arrested, but that was what I wanted. I thought if I was sent East I would find her.'

'But you didn't?' There was the same look of pain and anguish on his face that she had seen in Cardiff.

'I was put in a prison. I escaped into the woods one day when I was sent out in a work party. It was spring, the snow had melted, there were no tracks for them to follow. I hid in the forest, lived with the nomads and looked for Masha and our child. For four years I looked for them. When the nomads were rounded up by the state militia I volunteered to be a seaman. They didn't think to check my identity, they simply assumed I was a member of the tribe I had been living with. They sent me to St Petersburg. I got a berth on a steamer to Cardiff.'

'And there you left the ship?'

'Jumped ship,' he corrected. 'So you see I am wanted for more than one crime in Russia. For escaping from prison, for jumping ship, for asking too many questions. People have been shot for less.'

'But you never found your wife?'

'I have never found anyone who knew what happened to her or the people in my village. Russia is not like here. People disappear all the time. Every time a Russian ship docks in Cardiff I try to meet it. I ask every sailor who comes in if he has any news. I have sent letters back with them to my wife's brother, but there has been no word. And now, even if I should find her, I am here and she would not be allowed to leave.' He turned his back on her and stared blindly out of the window. 'Sometimes, just sometimes I think it would have been easier if I had returned to the village and found her dead. I would have known then that I had to mourn. I almost envied Bethan when her son died. I never knew whether Masha had my son or my daughter.'

'How many years is it since you left your village to get that cot?' she asked after a long silence.

'Nine years next month.' He closed his eyes, and her heart went out to him.

'You could live out the rest of your life waiting for a reunion that may never happen.'

'I have no choice. I have nothing to give anyone I . . .'

She recalled the old woman's words: 'Recognise your destiny when it comes. Take it, and make the most of it while you can.'

'You have something to give me,' she whispered.

'You don't understand. I think of Masha all the time. I see her . . .'

'Since you met me?'

'More often since I met you,' he acknowledged honestly.

'You said yourself that you can't go back.'

'I can't,' he admitted wretchedly.

'All my life I've lived for the here and now, because I've been too afraid to look further than the present. For the first time I want to look forward. I want to live with you. Wake up beside you every morning, go to bed with you every night.'

'You'd live with me after what I've just told you?'

'I'd live with you.'

'I could marry you. No one here knows about Masha except you, but it would not be legal, and if it was discovered it would be one more crime to lay on my head.'

'It might be worth risking, especially if we had a child.'

'I love you, Alma. But you'd have to understand about Masha. She will always be the first one, and my wife.'

'You're not my first man, Charlie. There was Ronnie. You know that.'

'It doesn't matter.'

He kissed her and she kissed him back. Locking her fingers into his she led him quietly towards the door so as not to disturb her mother. They had one another. Tonight he would sleep in her bed, and tomorrow . . . tomorrow they would talk about a marriage – of sorts. Masha was as much a part of Charlie's past as Ronnie was of hers. There was no going back for either of them. When his emotions were less raw he would see that, and understand. They were going to live out the rest of their lives in Pontypridd where nothing ever happened. Masha was in Russia. Ronnie was in Italy. There was no chance of them ever meeting again. No going back . . .

The pips that preceded the news beeped on the radio. He bent his head to hers and kissed her again. She loved him; that was all that mattered. Not that he had a wife and child somewhere he would never see again. She loved him, and he loved her. There was no going back . . .

'I love you, Charlie.'

'Can you say Feodor?'

'I love you, Feodor.'

'*The Czech crisis deepens as German troops continue to mass on the Czechoslovakian border. Herr Hitler has announced that he has no aggressive intentions . . .*'

No going back . . .